Highwaypersons

Debts and Duties

By Geoffrey Monmouth

WOO /H)

Cast of Characters

In alphabetical order

Note: real historical characters are marked *

John Aris, an elderly highwayman, formerly a gentleman, Gwyneth Evans' lover.

Francis Atterbury*, a bishop with Jacobite sympathies.

Alan Ball, a Lancashire farmer and fisherman.

Major Boyle, an administrator at the Horse Guards and a Jacobite.

Charles Butler, the Duke of Ormonde's nephew, a Jacobite.

Colonel Iain Campbell, a fanatical anti-Jacobite.

John Campbell*, Duke of Argyll, commander of the British Army in Scotland.

Private William Campbell, a cousin and devotee of Iain.

Olwen Davies, Rhodri Jones's housekeeper and mistress.

Perseus de Clare, an aristocrat and officer.

Lord Derwentwater*, one of the leaders of the Jacobite forces at Preston.

Colonel Eddy Edwards, Royal Welch Artillery, Billy's commanding officer.

Robert Erskine*, Earl of Mar, leader of the Scottish Jacobites.

Gareth Evans, Billy's uncle, chief ostler at The Coach and Horses. The name is also Billy's alias.

Gwyneth Evans, Billy's aunt, Gareth's wife, a servant at The Coach and Horses.

General Forster*, commander of the Jacobites at Preston.

Captain George Graham, conspirator with Lt-Col. Campbell.

Howell Hopkins, a wealthy merchant in Cardiff, one of Billy's father's principal creditors.

Mari Hughes, camp follower of the Glamorgan Fusiliers.

Richard Jenkins, a merchant, son of one of Rhys Rhys's creditors.

Anne Jones, wife of Arthur.

Arthur Jones, landlord of The Coach and Horses.

Henrietta Jones, wife of Rhodri.

Rhodri Jones, Member of Parliament for Cardiff.

General Sir William Jones, commander of Billy's division.

Emlyn Lloyd, farmer in the Little Rhondda, Owain Rhys's employer.

Donald MacDonald, Laird of Glencoe.

Duncan MacDonald, a crofter in the Highlands.

Moira MacDonald, Duncan's wife.

Alex MacGregor, a fanatical Highlander at Preston.

Gordon MacGregor, a crofter, brother of Moira MacDonald's late husband.

Flora MacGregor, Gordon's wife.

Jimmy MacGregor, a Highlander assisting Charles Butler,a friend of Rob Roy.

Rob Roy MacGregor*, a Highland outlaw and Jacobite leader.

Helen MacKenzie, daughter of Lewis Pryce,widow of Kenny MacKenzie.

Kenny MacKenzie, deceased, an aristocrat and officer.

Catherine MacNichol, wife of Iain, aristocrat, duellist.

Captain Iain MacNichol, son of the Major.

Major MacNichol, Warden of Chepstow Castle.

Rev. David (Dai) Morgan, Presbyterian minister, Megan's brother, Billy and Bethan's cousin.

Rev. Huw Morgan, Presbyterian minister, Billy's uncle, David and Megan's father.

Madoc Morgan, a ship's master, employed by Richard Jenkins.

Mair Morgan, wife of David, daughter of a farmer/fisherman from Ogmore.

Megan Morgan, a whore at The Mermaid, David's sister, Billy and Bethan's cousin.

Bombardier Allan Morris, a soldier in Billy's gun-crew.

Alistair Murray, a gentleman in Crief, in the Highlands.

Colonel John Murray, commander of the Royal Scots Borderers.

Rev. Abraham Phillips, a wealthy Presbyterian minister, one of Billy's father's creditors.

James Pryce, son of Lewis, brother of Helen MacKenzie.

Jane Pryce, wife of James.

Lewis Pryce*, Member of Parliament for Cardiganshire.

Idris Pugh, a farmer in the Little Rhondda.

Billy Rhys, a farmer's son, ostler, artilleryman and highwayman.

Owain Rhys, Billy's younger brother, a shepherd.

Rhys Rhys, Billy's father, formerly a farmer, now in debtors' prison.

Rhona Rhys, Billy's older sister, a housekeeper for the Pughs.

Peter Rigby, a Lancashire farmer.

Captain Rimmer, a Jacobite in the Lancashire Irregulars at Preston.

Sandy Sanderson, an officer on General Wills' staff.

Lord Seaforth*, head of the MacKenzies, one of the Jacobite leaders at Preston.

Angus Stewart, a crofter in the Highlands.

James Edward Francis Stewart*, the Pretender, known as King James III by his followers, the Jacobites.

Morag Stewart, wife of Angus.

Robert Stewart, a Highland Laird.
Hatty Sutton, a fishwife in Preston.
Thomas Thomas, a petty criminal, former artilleryman.
Bethan (Elizabeth) Tudor, Billy's sister, wife of Henry.
Henry Tudor, a minor aristocrat, Bethan's missing husband.
Llewellyn Tudor, son of Henry and Bethan.
Captain Heinrich von Herrenhausen, a German cavalry officer.
General Wills*, commander of the British Army at Preston.
Greta, a Flemish camp follower with the Artillery.
Meredith, servant of Major MacNichol at Chepstow.

Sian, a maid in Rhodri Jones's household. **Tegwyn**, a whore at The Mermaid Inn.

Chapter 1

September 1713

They waited. They watched. They all had strong feelings, certainly, but also certainly uncertain ones. Anyway they were contradictory. The three of them were standing among some trees at the side of the main road from Cardiff to Bridgend, waiting for the coach they planned to rob.

Billy was nervous, exhilarated, hopeful, afraid and guilty, all at once. He was nervous, because he did not know how things would go; exhilarated because it was a chance to get his revenge on the man who had contributed most to his family's ruin; hopeful, because he hoped to gain enough money to get his father out of debtors prison; and guilty, because he could not get away from the knowledge that what they were about to do was wrong. His mother had always said that two wrongs did not make a right and God Himself had said, "Thou shalt not steal." However much he told himself that he was only stealing back what had belonged to his family in the first place, his conscience was not satisfied. Then there was fear. He did not know which he was more afraid of: being killed or killing someone else. He had killed before, but that was for Queen and country in the War of the Spanish Succession. This was different. He was also worried for the others. He had got them into this. One was an old highwayman who was their mentor, but the other was as new to this as he was. She was his sister.

Bethan was tense and exhilarated. She was anxious about what was to happen, but there was more. She was aware of her mixed motives. Of course, she wanted to help her brother, as she always had. Of course, she wanted to rescue her father from prison and regain the farm. Of course, she wanted to make Lewis Pryce and his family pay, so that he, and hopefully all their other creditors, would be repaid with their own money. The word 'irony' came to mind. She had learned it as a child, yet had never before known a situation it fitted so well. However, she felt vaguely aware that there was something else. Excitement. For some time, she had found life rather dull. She had gone back to working as a maid at an inn. Years ago, she had found it interesting. Not the work, but the variety of people she saw passing through. Now it was not enough. Was this what she wanted? A life of crime? Would nothing else satisfy her? She would find out in time.

John was nervous too, although he had done this many times before. He was never relaxed until a robbery was over. He knew the many ways things could go wrong. He was especially concerned for his two protégés. He had known them both since they were in their early teens and had always been fond of them. He had taught them some of his skills: riding, fencing, loading and firing a pistol, as well as some of his less obvious tricks. He had worried about them when they had gone off to war. That was ten years ago. Bethan had gone first, with her new husband. John had wondered how she would fare, as Henry could not afford to have her live in the comparative safety and luxury that some of the officers' wives enjoyed. She

7

would have to make do, but she was a survivor. He had been more surprised when he heard that Billy had joined, a year or so later. He was not the type, John had thought. Too sensitive. At least he was clever, but being clever was not always enough. Now they were both safely back, albeit without Henry, but John had never thought they would soon be with him waiting to rob a coach. He had been shocked when Billy had suggested the robbery, and had been incredulous when Bethan had insisted on joining them just because he had said the job required more than two people. John felt responsible. Would they be doing this if he had not turned up at the inn just as they were watching the Pryces displaying their wealth with such complacency? He hoped they would do everything just as he had instructed.

All their musings were interrupted by the sound of an approaching coach. They soon saw it was the one they were waiting for. It was an unusually big expensive one drawn by six heavy horses of the kind commonly seen in many of the English shires, but rarely in Wales where the smaller cobs were of more use, especially on hill farms. There were two servants riding ahead of the coach. They called out to the coachman to warn him that the road was blocked by a collapsed retaining wall on one side, whilst the verge on the other side was largely under water, where a nearby drainage ditch had overflowed. After a brief discussion, one of the riders dismounted and waded through a series of puddles, trying to assess the depth and to determine a safe route.

The three robbers prepared to move out into the open when the coach would be at its slowest and most vulnerable. In fact, the conditions helped them more than they could have hoped. The coachman drove his team skilfully, turning the lead horses right to miss the broken wall, then left towards the road, while preventing the others from trying to cut the corner. That would have made the coach bump over some of the large stones, which the three robbers had pushed across the road to ensure the coach would have to take a slow and winding route. The coach looked to be navigating the obstacles well, and John was just about to signal to the others to make their move when it lurched and came to a halt, tilting noticeably towards them, the front wheels turning at almost a right angle to the main body of the coach, as it had just been making a tight turn when the nearside front wheel had sunk into a pothole. It had been impossible to gauge the depth because it was filled with water, and the luckless outriders had not managed to check every inch of the ground in front of them. John and Billy began walking towards the coach. Bethan followed at a distance, just visible, coming out of the shadows. They were all well armed, but each held only one pistol, pointed forwards but not cocked. Then the nearside door of the coach opened and a head emerged, followed by a significant proportion of a somewhat corpulent body. Its owner held onto the frame and conversed with the coachman, who was confident enough to speak plainly, whilst respectfully, to his master, who then called out to the outriders and to two other servants sitting on the dickie seat at the back. The man then appeared to speak into the coach as he stepped inside. The two servants jumped down and ran to the door, pulling out a set of steps, before standing ready to help the passengers to alight.

The first passenger out was a young man who motioned to them to stand aside while he jumped down. That was a mistake. His feet stuck in mud whilst the rest of him continued forwards propelled by the energy of the jump. He fell flat on his face. The servants managed to refrain from laughing, doubtless the result of years of practice. Next came the older man, who not only used the steps, but also allowed the servants to hold him and ensure a safe passage from the doorway to the ground.

Four women came out next with a great deal of fuss, aided with a lot of show by all the men. The robbers waited until the entire group was assembled on the ground before making their presence known. As agreed, Billy acted as the principal spokesman. He called out, "Throw all your weapons to the ground!" The young man, who was still trying to wipe mud off his clothes, hesitated as he drew a pistol, as if contemplating how best to employ it. Billy helped him come to a decision, saying, "On the ground with it, now! Or you'll be on the ground again yourself." You could say that their relationship got off to a bad start. On the other hand, the man did as he was told, thus avoiding the necessity for violence. The disarming achieved, Billy called out, "Put all your money, jewellery and other valuables in these saddlebags. This doesn't apply to you servants."

As Billy went along the line the travellers had automatically formed, he pushed his pistol into his belt inside his coat, whilst John and Bethan made a show of cocking their weapons. The men looked as if the point was not lost on them, as they emptied their pockets into the saddlebags. Billy then went over to the women, who were all wearing an impressive selection of rings, necklaces, brooches and other items that looked highly saleable. Each of them in turn tried to persuade him to let her keep some particular item because it had such sentimental value. He thought how little anyone had cared about the sentimental value the farm had had for his family as he resisted all their pleas. When he had completed the task of removing these adornments from their persons, Billy called to his audience, "Bring out any valuable objects from your luggage." Seeing their astonishment he added, "All right! I don't mean to take everything in your trunks and bags, only money, gold, silver, jewellery and that sort of stuff."

The older man turned to the servants and said, "Go on! Bring down that trunk." He pointed to one strapped to the back of the coach. Once down, he unlocked it and stood aside so Billy could go through it. It contained mainly clothes but there were also a few mirrors and brushes with silver handles, which he took. Billy then said, "Right! Now fetch out the luggage from inside the coach." He knew that good quality vehicles usually had spaces under the seats for boxes and bags. The servants climbed up into the coach and, with a great deal of moaning and groaning, lifted out a number of interesting pieces of luggage. Again, the older man opened them so that the contents could be seen. Nothing struck Billy as worth adding to the weight the horses were going to have to carry, but he noticed one small chest that looked as if it would contain something interesting. His suspicions were aroused when, for the first time, the older man seemed reluctant to open it, saying, "It contains important papers, but they will be of little value to you. You will not readily sell them."

Billy demanded, "Let me see!" Its owner hesitated but did as he had been asked. He was right. It was full of papers, including some that showed he was a shareholder in the East India Company. They were probably worth a lot of money, but only if you knew about such things. Billy guessed they would get caught if they tried ineptly to sell them. The gentleman looked relieved when Billy shut the chest without removing anything.

One of the women surprised everyone by saying, "Oh! I have left something in the coach. I must go back and fetch it." Billy wondered if she was afraid that he and his companions would do a lot of damage if they searched it. He was wrong. A heavy bag flew out of the door, nearly knocking Billy off his feet and there followed the sound of the other door opening. Billy ran round the back of the coach, while John called out, "All right! Just stay where you are, the rest of you." The woman landed remarkably lightly from the big drop and took off at a run, lifting her skirt for speed. Nobody could see where she hoped to go, but she was certainly going. Billy began to run after her, but slowly, appreciating how treacherous the ground was. She soon found out too. One of her feet went down into soft mud, causing her to fall flat on her face. Billy caught up with her by the time she got to her hands and knees.

"Allow me!"

"I wouldn't allow you to do anything for me!" Ignoring that rebuff, he reached a hand out to her.

"Don't touch me, you vile creature!" Ignoring her again, he grabbed an arm and pulled her to her feet. She began to struggle. He tightened his grip and half dragged and half pushed her back around the coach to be greeted with a chorus of contradictory expressions.

"Well done!"

"Good try!"

"Bad luck!"

"Stupid girl!"

"What were you trying to do?"

Billy had been about to announce that all their business was concluded and the family could resume their journey, when he noticed something. He could feel through the girl's glove that she must have been wearing rings that she had not handed over. He said, "I must ask you to remove your gloves."

"No!"

The young man who had fallen in the mud called out, "Here! You want a glove? Have mine." With that, he threw one of his gloves at Billy, obviously intending it as a challenge. Billy knew better than to take it up.

"What use is one glove to me? Keep it."

The young man began to insult Billy, but the older man told him to be quiet. The girl took her gloves off but clenched her fists. Billy could see a couple of rings and said, "You'd better let me see those."

"No!"

He stepped forwards and grabbed her arm again. She brought her knee up between his legs but succeeded only in hitting his thigh. She got her right hand free and tried to grab the pistol from his belt. He pushed forwards to trap her hand between their bodies, whilst twisting her left arm behind her back. As they struggled, she moved backwards until she was against the coach.

Billy said, "Under different circumstances I could enjoy this."

"I know what I'd enjoy." she replied. "Watching you hang!"

"I fear you may have to prepare for disappointment, as I have no intention of letting that happen." Their faces had come very close, so he tried to kiss her. Bethan wondered whether this was because he found her attractive or because he thought it would annoy her. It did. She bit him on the jaw. He winced and pulled back. She laughed and spat. He put his right hand to her chin, pushed her face upwards, forcing the mouth closed and kissed her, saying, "That will do for now. Perhaps we can resume some other time. Now give me your rings while you still have your fingers." With that, he drew his pistol, without cocking it, and pressed the end of the barrel against her ribs.

She handed over her rings, saying, "You are the most despicable creature I have ever had the misfortune to encounter."

Bethan nearly called out to say that this woman must have led a very sheltered existence, but remembered having promised to stay silent, in case her voice betrayed her sex. The other women handed over a few remaining

14

rings and other jewellery without further protest, but the youngest and smallest said, "How naughty do I have to be to get a kiss?" Billy obliged her. She did not struggle or bite. Some of the others looked shocked. The young man called out, "Let go of her, you monster!" at which she laughed as they separated. As Billy began to turn away, she grabbed him and kissed him in return. He was too surprised to react in any way.

She laughed again as she let go. Stepping back and turning to the whole group, Billy then said in a loud voice, "That is all we came for. Please resume your journey and we shall resume ours. God speed!" John stepped forward and conspicuously removed the charges from the pistols the travellers had dropped.

The older man said, "Let us get the coach free of this hole before we replace our luggage." The coachman resumed his seat and urged the horses forward. They had been almost asleep so they moved off rather jerkily. The coach shook, the harness strained and suddenly with a lurch, it came free of the pothole. It went forwards rather too quickly, as the ground went slightly downhill for the next few yards. At that moment one of the wheel horses, that is one of those nearest the coach, lost its footing, slithered and fell onto its side. The coachman tried to pull the rest to a halt, and several voices called out, "Whoa!" Billy surprised everyone by rushing forwards, grabbing the nearer lead horse and urging him on. He kept him, and thus the team, moving until they had pulled the coach onto level ground, having dragged the fallen animal through the mud. There were gasps and shouts of outrage from most of those present, even John, but the coachman spoke in

Billy's defence, saying, "He did the right thing. I was a fool to try to pull up. A coach this size would not have stopped while going downhill. It would have rolled forwards and crushed the beast under the wheel. Being dragged a few yards won't have done too much harm." Turning to Billy he said, "Well done! That was quick thinking."

The little band of thieves left the travellers in the process of putting their luggage back on board.

Chapter 2

As they rode back towards Cardiff, they were silent at first. After a while, Billy said, "I'm sorry I got a bit rough with that girl. I got a bit carried away."

John laughed and said, "We all get carried away sometimes, but it was a good thing you had us two to watch your back. Some of the others might have taken advantage."

Bethan said, "Don't worry, bach, she was asking for it. Besides, I think she rather liked you. Not as much as her friend, perhaps." "I doubt that. You should have heard some of the things she said to me."

"What people say and what they mean are often two different things. I think you're too sensitive. You always were."

They rode on in silence again, thoughts going round in their minds. They began to wonder how it had come to this, realising that they had just become criminals. It seemed so out of character for both of them, yet in a way, Billy could see his whole life up to then had been an ideal preparation for it. He kept hearing in his mind a verse from the Bible, in the Book of Esther Chapter 4 verse 14, where Esther was facing a crisis and her uncle Mordecai said, "Who knows but for this cause came you to this hour?" The difference was that Esther was about to save her countrymen from being massacred. Billy felt a lot less worthy. He could not see the hand of God being involved in preparing him for a life of crime. Yet he knew he had been well prepared in certain ways. He tried to explain these thoughts and John said, "I don't know about that. I hope you are not thinking of all the things I taught you. I had not intended to lead you astray. But they say your character is established by the time you are seven anyway."

Billy and Bethan could not imagine anyone who knew them when they were seven guessing that they would rob a coach when they grew up. Was it the inn or the War that had changed them? They were born on a farm in the Rhondda Valley. Or to be precise, between the two Rhonddas, for the Rhondda Valley splits just north of the village of Porth into the Big Rhondda and Little Rhondda, or "Rhondda Fawr" and "Rhondda Fach" as they say in Welsh. Penrhys Farm is on top of the ridge between the two. The name is appropriate, as "pen" means head or top and Penrhys is the top of the hill belonging to the Rhys family: Billy's family. His father and his father, and nobody knows how many Rhys's before him, had farmed that place until it had been taken by their creditors.

Their father, Rhys Rhys, was every inch a farmer: thickset ruddy-complexioned, easygoing, hardworking and uncomplicated. On the other hand, their mother came from a long line of nonconformist ministers. She had been tall, slim, elegant and intelligent. She was more educated than most women in Wales in those days. It was she who managed the money as well as the home, whilst Father got on with the farming. The two older brothers and the youngest all took after their father in every way. Their elder sister, Rhona, was a female version of them and was excellent at helping in the house and at lots of jobs on the farm. On the other hand, Billy took after their mother in both looks and temperament, whilst Bethan was somewhere in between regarding both.

They turned off the road and up a lane, where they changed their clothes, so they would not look suspicious. As they resumed their journey, Billy and Bethan thought of that coach approaching its destination at Ogmore, somewhat later than expected. They talked about their memories of Ogmore, especially the Manse. Billy said, "I remember when we first went to live with our cousins at Ogmore. I was six, so you must have been seven. I never understood why we went."

His sister replied, "Mam had a difficult pregnancy and a very difficult time in labour. The baby only lived for a couple of days. After that, she took months to recover her strength. Rhona was twelve then and nursed Mam. She even managed to do most of the cooking and cleaning. Our older brothers helped with some of her chores as well as helping work the farm, but you and I were just extra burdens for everyone else, so they sent us to live with Uncle Huw and Aunt Efa."

Bethan was referring to the Reverend Huw Morgan, the Presbyterian Minister of Ogmore, their mother's cousin. That was when they had become close to their second cousins, Megan and David, Dai as he was usually known, who were six and seven respectively. He was average-sized and solid-built, whilst she was tall and slim. In fact, some said she looked like a feminine version of Billy, apart from being red-haired, like her brother, whilst Billy, Bethan and all their siblings were dark like their parents.

Huw Morgan was a learned man himself, and a great believer in education for girls as well as boys, to the surprise and disapproval of many people. He held classes most days, attended by several local children as well as his own and, of course, his visiting nephew and niece. He taught them to read and write in English, Welsh, Latin and French. As well as the Bible, he encouraged them to read a lot of English and Welsh poetry and history. He also taught mathematics.

Bethan said, "You always enjoyed the lessons, didn't you? Took to it well."

"So did you. Perhaps it runs in the family, or perhaps it was Uncle Huw's enthusiasm that got to us. I enjoyed his sermons too. I can still remember a lot of them, unfortunately! He was a good preacher. Of course, going to chapel every week, it's no wonder we both know the Psalms and a lot of prayers."

As they reminisced, John just listened. He had not known much about their early childhood and found it all very interesting. It explained a lot, such as their education and their sense of morality.

After a while, they drew near to Cowbridge. Bethan said, "I expect you'll remember this place too. They moved here while we were still with them, because Uncle Huw became the Minister here."

"Yes, I remember being impressed even as a child at how much bigger and more prosperous the village was, probably because it was surrounded by bigger and more prosperous farms. At Ogmore it seemed as if half the people were fishermen who did a bit of farming to bring in a bit more money, and the other half were farmers who did a bit of fishing."

Bethan added, "At Ogmore, a lot of the children were rough, and we had to learn to take care of ourselves."

"It was a good thing Megan was stronger than she looked, but I noticed she used cunning rather than strength to win fights, as well as arguments, but you did both enjoy a good fight."

"I can't think what you mean! But I remember you always tried to avoid fighting, using words instead whenever you could. Funny you going for a soldier, wasn't it?"

John thought it strange too, but Billy did not want to go into that. Instead he said, "When we were at Cowbridge, Uncle Huw got a big carthorse of the kind they say you often find in many parts of England. They used them on a lot of the farms around Cowbridge too, but I never saw one in the Rhondda. I'm glad I had a chance to learn how to handle a horse like him: not to be afraid just because he was so big, but not to try to master him by force. I know any horse is stronger than a man, so it's always best to use skill rather than strength to control one, but that is even more true when you've got one as big as him. That was a lesson I've often found useful. What was he called?"

"Samson, after the strongest man in the Bible."

As they rode through Cowbridge, Billy said, "I hope Uncle Huw and the others won't notice us. I'm ashamed to have got into crime, but it's too late to change our minds."

John thought the conversation was getting rather depressing, so he asked, "How did you keep up your studies after you left there? You have always seemed far more educated than most farmers' children."

Billy answered, "Well, after our time with Uncle Huw and Aunt Efa, we went back to living on the farm. Mam encouraged us to keep up our studies, trying to make time for us to practice reading and writing whenever possible, even if the others couldn't see the sense in it and thought we were just trying to get out of our chores."

Bethan added, "Which you probably were!"

Billy continued, "Do you remember when we first came to live at the inn? There was a professor from Oxford, David Davies, who used to stay there on his way to and from his family home in Pembrokeshire. He used to talk about Greeks and Romans. He even lent us books. We enjoyed his visits. You remember him, don't you, John?"

"Oh, yes. I have always visited the inn when I've been in Cardiff and have been friends with your uncle and aunt for years. What made you two leave the farm and come to the inn?"

Bethan answered, "Mam had been ill again when I was twelve and Billy was about ten. By then the rest of the family had despaired of either of us earning our keep at the farm. Not that we wanted to. We would've happily gone to live and work in a town somewhere. And that was just what happened."

John was puzzled. He asked, "So how did you come to be at the inn?"

Billy said, "Well, our Uncle Gareth got me a job as a stableboy and Aunt Gwyneth got Beth one as a maid-of-all-work. She was glad that 'all' didn't include kitchen work. So would a lot of others have been if they'd known how bad a cook Beth was."

Bethan opened her mouth to protest but changed her mind, recognising the truth of the remark.

John did not need much more explanation as he knew that their mother's younger sister, Gwyneth, was married to Gareth Evans, the head ostler at the inn, which was named, unimaginatively but appropriately, The Coach and Horses. She worked as an assistant to the innkeeper's wife in almost everything except cooking. The kitchen was the cook's highly protected domain. Gwyneth had two sons who had both left home and gone to sea. John also knew that Gareth had been impressed by Billy's ability at handling big carthorses, as it was increasingly common for coaches and wagons coming from England to be drawn by such animals.

Billy continued, "Life at the inn was educational in other ways too. So many different kinds of people visited it: gentlemen, merchants, servants, travellers, farmers, clergymen, soldiers and labourers. They came from all over Wales and from the South and Midlands of England. We used to enjoy mimicking different accents and mannerisms. Bethan could have passed herself off just as easily as a noblewoman or as a fishwife."

John said it was time for him to leave them, as they had agreed, to take most of the newly acquired property to a secret place, while Billy and Bethan carried on towards Cardiff. Their Aunt Gwyneth had invited them to eat with her and their Uncle Gareth that evening, which they were glad to do, although they agreed they would have to be careful to avoid the subject of their activities during the day.

Bethan asked Billy, "Do you think Aunt Gwyneth and Uncle Gary know what John does for a living?"

"I expect they've got a good idea, but I don't think they'll have asked him, and I don't suppose he'll have told them. It's probably best, so they can honestly say they didn't know. By the way, do you think Uncle Gary knows Aunt Gwyneth and John are lovers?"

"I think the answer is the same. He probably pretends not to notice." "So we'd better be careful what we say tonight.

Especially if they ask what we've been doing today."

Bethan said, "What about my little Llewellyn? What are we going to tell him?"

"We can't keep it from him forever. He's nearly ten years old and a bright lad."

"I don't suppose he'll want to hear that I've become a highwayman. Or would you call me a highwaywoman?"

"I don't know. I feel awkward about it too, but I felt awkward before about letting Dada stay in jail while we did nothing about it."

Bethan worried about what sort of life her son would have. A criminal? Yet she doubted if she would prefer him to spend his life working as a stableboy or menial servant. They rode on in silence.

Soon they could see the familiar landmark of the great grey shape of Cardiff Castle and knew that once past its broken South Wall it would be only another hundred yards to the inn. However, the castle did not seem to be getting any closer as time went by, so the last four or five miles of the journey seemed longer than the previous fifteen.

Gwyneth, Billy and Bethan's aunt was a beauty and much younger than her sister, their mother. She was not exactly a whore, but she had several lovers. One was the Professor at Jesus College, Oxford, about whom they had been telling John. He had been fascinated to discover that Billy and Bethan were keen on reading. He also used to tell them, and anyone else who would listen, stories from Greek and Roman mythology. Another of her lovers was a carter who talked about the places he had been when he had driven his cart all over the country. He also enjoyed talking to Gareth about horses. Then there was John, the highwayman, of course. Apart from teaching them about guns and swords, he introduced them to the art of riding: not just to get around, but to handle a horse at speed with safety. His horses were usually failed racehorses, very different from either cobs or carthorses. They were always black or dark brown. Billy and Bethan realised why.

It was nearly dark when they finally rode into the inn's stableyard. They put the horses to bed before going into the cottage where their aunt and uncle lived, which formed the end of the coachhouse. Billy had a room above the stables.

As soon as Billy and Bethan arrived, their aunt said, "Your Uncle Gary will be with us in a minute. So will Llewellyn. They're just getting washed and making themselves presentable. I'm hoping our friend John will be joining us soon. He said not to wait as he had some business to attend to but hopes to be able to come for supper." They had not thought he could hide the loot and get back at a civilized hour, but he was a man of many surprises. He certainly surprised them by arriving in another change of clothes, with gifts of wine and brandy, before the meal was ready, just as Gareth and Llewellyn came into the room. Although the boy was pleased to see his mother, he was more interested in pestering Uncle Billy. He had somehow got the idea that his uncle led an interesting life. Billy was getting nervous in case the conversation drifted to where it should not, when John rescued it by asking, "How long have you two been back from the War? I have been away a lot and haven't seen you for years until today."

Bethan said, "I've only been here a few weeks. Billy was here a bit ahead of me."

Gareth was a man of few words, especially when his wife was around, but he did manage to say, "Well, you only came here a couple of months ago, Billy, but I know you got back from the War about a year ago or more. Didn't you go living up at Penrhys again?"

Billy explained, "Well, I have only been back at the inn for a few weeks more than Beth, but I came home over a year ago, to find our Dada had lost the farm. The creditors had taken it. After they sold it, the new owners decided to rent it out in parts. Well, rather than give up,

Dada rented the top part and tried to grow crops on the higher slopes, where they didn't want to grow. When I was young, we never even kept our sheep at the very top in winter. We moved everything down to the sheltered fields on the north-east side, nearer the big house. So last winter we were really struggling. It was cold enough in summer! It was so exposed up there.

The wind seemed to go right through the walls of the cottage and right through us. We kept losing money until the creditors moved against us again, and Dada went to gaol. I was powerless to do anything, although I tried everything I could think of. In the end, we just didn't have enough money."

Gareth opened a bottle of hock and poured a measure into each of their glasses. However careful he was he could not help seeming clumsy, being a big strong man with big hands that almost engulfed the glasses. Billy gratefully took a sip.

Gwyneth said, "Pity your mother died while you were both away. But perhaps that's as well. She didn't live to see what's become of Dada and the farm, like."

Billy replied, "It might not have happened if she had lived. She was the clever one, especially with money. Dada was hopeless. A good farmer but no idea about making money. Or keeping it. He kept borrowing. He even tried gambling during that last year. He had never been a gambler, but he was so desperate. Of course, he was not good at that either. That was why our eldest brother, Rhys, left home. He went away to work on a farm down by Swansea and refused to help, because he blamed Dada so much. Later he got the chance to make a new life

27

in the New World. He came to see us just before he left. Our youngest brother, Owain, stayed until Dada went to gaol. Then he got a job as a shepherd on our neighbour's farm. He says he wants to rent that hilltop again and see if he can make a go of it. I don't think he will. Our older sister, Rhona stayed to the end. Then she went to work as a servant to the people who bought the farm. It was one way to hang on to it, I suppose, but I don't think Beth or I could stand being there as servants like that."

He stopped talking as Gwyneth served a thick soup, called "cawl" in Welsh, with some fresh bread. One thing she liked about the inn was its food, and she got her ingredients from the kitchen when the cook was in a good mood.

John said, "Didn't you say you had three brothers? What about the third one?"

Billy answered, "Poor Dewi died after a stupid accident, just before Beth got married. Fell into a stream and drowned in about six inches of water. We could hardly believe it." He sat pensively for a minute.

Gwyneth decided to change the subject. "I wondered why you stayed out there so long, Beth, when I thought your Henry disappeared years ago? Couldn't you get back?"

Bethan said, "Well, it's a bit complicated, see? You know that big battle, Malplaquet? That was four years ago in 1709. There were thousands on both sides and lots were killed. My Henry didn't come back to camp afterwards, so I went to look for him. I mean, there were lots of men lying wounded out there, and plenty more wandering around lost. It was chaos. I'd never seen anything like it, and I'd seen battles before." Billy added, "She's right about that. I was there too. It was worse than anything I'd seen before or since. The sheer size of it for a start. I never knew what was going on. It was just as bad afterwards."

Bethan resumed the story, "When I couldn't find him, I went round asking everyone: the men, the officers, the camp followers, even the prisoners. General Jones asked the French if they had him among their prisoners, but they weren't sure. They had so many, see? Some of the women said he might have deserted. Had enough, like. But he wouldn't. He was no coward, and even if he wanted to desert the Army he would never have deserted me, or our little Llew." She paused and fought back her tears.

They all concentrated on their cawl until she resumed. "So I stayed with the Army hoping he'd turn up. General Jones said he was officially ''missing'' and couldn't say anything more definite than that. So I only came back to Wales when the regiment came back after the Peace was signed about a month ago."

John wondered how she had survived in Army camps for such a long time without a husband, but decided not to ask as it might have been indelicate.

Gwyneth asked, "What about your husband's parents? Have you been to see them?"

"When I first got back, I did, but things didn't go too well. For a start, they believed it was my fault that he had joined the Army in the first place. He'd been going to be a minster. It wasn't my idea to go. He wanted to go and be a hero, like half the young men we knew. Apart from that they just couldn't see why I hadn't come home as soon as Henry went missing. But if he'd come back, he'd have come back to his regiment more likely than coming back to Wales. Or, if there had been any news, it's the Army that would have heard first, isn't it?"

She looked around and there were nods and grunts of agreement.

"I decided to come here and see if there was any work for me, and I was lucky, finding work and finding Billy was here. That's the first bit of luck I've had for years, and the innkeeper and his wife, Arthur and Anne, have been so good to little Llew, I couldn't have brought him to a better place."

By this time they had finished the cawl and were ready for the next course, which was a meat pie. Llewellyn asked, "Will Dada come home here? He never lived here. We all lived with the Army ever since I can remember."

Bethan said, "The Army will send him here. He'll want to come to you and me, wherever we are." The boy said, "A lot of people say he's dead!"

John said, "A lot of people think I'm dead and here I am. I'm alive, aren't I?" The boy nodded.

Billy said, "Did you know, there was a time when lots of people said the Duke of Marlborough was dead? You know, John Churchill, the general at the top. The one who kept leading us to victory. The French wanted to believe it, of course, but then when he turned up again, the French were terrified. Some thought it was a ghost, but others said he couldn't be killed. Me? I say, don't believe a rumour unless you can find out for sure if it's true." Llewellyn looked pensive.

John said, "Do you think Henry would want to be a vicar now? Did the War change him?"

Bethan answered, "I don't know. He really took to army life. He liked the excitement. He loved fencing. I used to practice with him. I'm glad you taught me and Billy to fence before the War. I don't know if he was really meant to be a vicar, but he thought he was."

John said, "Of course, life in the Army will be different now the War's over. A lot of soldiers will probably find it hard to adapt. There again, there'll be some who'll be relieved the danger's over and they can enjoy a different sort of army life."

Gareth said, "So, what about you, Billy? How did you come to be home so early from the War? Well, no! What I was really wondering was why you didn't come home a lot sooner. Well, really, what I mean is why did you join in the first place? I mean, I've known you a long time. I know you're good at lots of things, but, well, I just could never see you as a soldier."

John added, "You were always hopeless at fighting or fencing. Bethan was better than you. You never struck me as the type. I was different. Came from a long line of officers. I did my fair share of soldiering when I was your age. I was more the type. I fitted in all right. Loved the excitement. Sounds like Henry was the same."

Billy tried to drain a last drop of wine from his empty glass. Gareth took the hint and topped up all their glasses. Just then it started to rain. It sounded quite loud against the windows and on the roof. Billy thought he would get very little sleep if it carried on after he went to bed. The wind and rain always seemed to sound very loud on the roof of the hayloft and on the tiny window of his room.

John wondered how Billy had coped with army life and how on earth he had managed to become a sergeant. He had a feeling it could be a long story. Before he could ask, Gareth reminded them of the question he had asked. "Why did you come back early?" He had to repeat the question and raise his voice because of the noise of the rain.

Billy said, "The Glamorgans and the Welch Artillery took part in the capture of Bouchain, at the end of 1711. It was the last major action of the War. Well, what happened next is hard to believe. General Churchill, the Duke of Marlborough, the man who had led us to victory so many times, was dismissed. They say it was all about politics, not his ability as a general. So early the next year they sent James Butler, the Duke of Ormonde, to replace him. He did nothing. So we didn't follow up our victories. We could have defeated the French totally, according to most of the experienced officers, but we didn't try. Then there were the peace talks that seemed to go on for ever."

Bethan swallowed the last of her pie and said, "I remember everyone getting fed up with those talks."

Billy continued, "Anyway, I'd had enough of the whole thing by then and I wasn't really doing anything worthwhile, as far as I could see. Also, I'd had a letter from Uncle Huw, saying Father had been having money troubles and things were generally not going well for him.

To be fair, Huw did try to help him, but he didn't have the kind of money he needed by then. So I asked Eddy, that's my Colonel, Edward Edwards, for a discharge and after some arguing we compromised. He gave me a period of extended leave without pay, so I could be called back if things hotted up. It also meant that as I was still a soldier, my commission might still come through. When I got home, I joined Dada and Owain working on the part of Penrhys that he was renting. All in vain, as you know."

John drained the last of his wine and said, "Well, I've learned a lot this evening. Thank you everyone, and of course, thank you, Gwyneth, for an excellent meal. Now I think we all need to get to bed." Then he went to his room and waited. As he expected, about an hour later Gwyneth came to him. She said, "My Gareth's sleeping soundly now. He usually does if he's had a bit to drink, like tonight. I hope you enjoyed this evening."

"Oh, yes, I certainly did, but not as much as I'm going to enjoy the rest of tonight."
She giggled as she began to make sure they both did enjoy the rest of the night. She got up just before dawn and crept back in time to be lying beside Gareth when he woke up.

Meanwhile, John lay half awake, still savouring what had gone before. He began to think of all the things Billy and Bethan had avoided telling him and the others. He deduced that they had reasons to keep certain things to themselves. He guessed that these things would be particularly interesting. He knew that there was a right and a wrong time to ask about such things. He would wait. However, he acknowledged to himself that there were many things they did not know about him. Many things.

Chapter 3

The next morning Arthur Jones, the innkeeper, sent for Billy and Bethan. They went to his family's private rooms with some anxiety. Had he become suspicious of their activity the previous day? He had given them permission to take the day off. Without pay, of course. Or had they offended him in some way? They were surprised to find that he greeted them in a pleasant manner, but seemed uncharacteristically nervous.

Arthur said, "You know I was happy to have you both back after all these years you've been away, and I've been glad of your help when we've been so busy over this summer. I mean, you've both worked hard and done whatever I've asked, and Billy, you're at least as good as your uncle with the horses, especially these big ones that we seem to be seeing more of. Well you see, the thing is, there's not been that much trade lately, on account of all the bad weather we've been having, I dare say. Well, anyway, the point is, I can't go on employing you, at least not until things pick up a bit. There's more money going out of here than what's coming in these days. I can't just let it go on, like, now can I? See what I mean?"

What they saw was that they were going to lose not only their paltry wages, but the roof over their heads and the free meals they were getting. They stood there, trying to think what to say. It was Arthur who filled the awkward silence, saying, "Well, of course we don't want to see you go. Like I was saying, we like you and you're good workers, see? You can keep your rooms. After all nobody else wants them at the moment. That's the trouble! If you're around at mealtimes you can always eat here. Of course, if things pick up – and they'd better, see, or we're in real trouble – we'll be wanting you back again, if you're still around, like, all right?"

They were relieved. In fact, they had been discussing how to get enough time off to carry out some more robberies without giving up their jobs. It was useful to stay at an inn, as that was the best place to pick up useful information about such things as people's travel plans and houses that were empty. This was an ideal solution.

For the rest of that day they contemplated the future and filled each other in on a few things. Billy told Bethan who their father's creditors had been and who had bought the farm at such a low price. They planned how to find out about the movements of their intended victims and how to exploit such knowledge. They took it in turns to point out the likely hazards and then tried to invent ways of dealing with them, recalling some of the things John had taught them. Bethan reminded Billy that people used to talk about a mysterious highwayman they nicknamed Merlin because he seemed like a magician: apparently able to disappear into thin air and equally able to make other people's property disappear. They knew that this man was John and they knew how he and other "magicians" used deception, including disguise and distraction, to mislead people.

They carried out a series of robberies. Sometimes they held up coaches, other times they broke into people's houses. Usually the three of them worked together.

Sometimes only two. Billy did work alone occasionally, but he found a helper was always useful if only as a lookout or a distraction. The victims were all either their father's creditors or others who had benefitted from the family's misfortunes. They did not know how far they were from being able to pay off all their father's debts, as they had to wait for the valuables to be sold, but they knew they had a long way to go.

At the inn, they heard people talking about the sudden increase in the number of robberies and the failure of the authorities to find the culprit. Some said they thought Merlin had returned, whilst others said Merlin would be too old, if he was still alive. All three had a good laugh about that.

Billy and Bethan sometimes visited the other members of their family. They always took them presents and a little money. They did not say how they had acquired it.

The first one they visited was their father. They spoke in Welsh, as his English was minimal. He said, "It's really good of you to come. I'm glad you're both all right, and little Llewellyn. I wish I could see him, but not in here. I don't want him to think of his grandfather like this."

Bethan said, "Perhaps you won't be in here too much longer. Then we can all get together again. Billy and I are working on ways of making money so we can pay off your debts."

"I can't see how you can do that, but it's good of you to try. Don't worry about me. I'm not too badly off. Prisoners are allowed to buy food and drink or anything else we want. Sometimes the turnkeys, that's the gaolers, buy things for us, for a fee of course. There's also some trusted prisoners who are allowed out to get things for themselves and others. They also need paying, but it's all right." Billy and Bethan could, however, use their eyes, ears and especially noses, to tell that things were not quite as pleasant as he wanted them to think.

Their father continued, "I've had visits from Uncle Huw. He prayed with me and read a few bits from the Bible. That was a comfort. Then young Owain's been to see me at times and so's your sister, Rhona, but neither of them get much time off from their work. Anyhow, they can't get here that easily, can they?"

Billy said, "We'll be visiting them soon. We miss them as well as you, you know. It's a pity we can't be together."

"I know. Do give them my love. Your Uncle Gareth and Aunt Gwyneth have been quite a few times. I had to laugh once, when Gwyneth came by herself and some of the other prisoners thought she was a whore. Of course, we do get some whores visiting here. They must have arrangements with the turnkeys. It's a good thing our Gwyneth knows how to deal with that sort of thing. She says she gets enough of it at the inn."

Bethan said, "We're both grateful to them too. They helped us get our jobs back at the inn and they've been kind to us ever since we've been back."

Her father said, "I'm glad. You know, I can't believe your Henry went missing like that. I don't know what to say. It must be terrible for you. I always liked him and I thought you two were so right for each other, but war is a terrible thing. I'm glad I never went for a soldier. A farmer's what I always was and always wanted to be. Oh! Don't look so upset, you two. I didn't mean to make you miserable. We can't always have everything we want in life. I'm more sorry for you than for myself. I've gone and lost your inheritance by my own stupidity."

Billy said, "We don't blame you. We just want to help. And we will. Give us time. We're working on it."

They did not mention buying the farm back, neither did they give any indication of how they were going about raising the money. Apart from the fact that their father would not have approved, there were lots of ears in the prison and plenty of tongues too.

Their next visit was to their sister Rhona at the house that had once been theirs. The new tenants, Idris and Rhianna Pugh, clearly thought they were doing the brother and sister a big favour in allowing them to visit and spoke most condescendingly. Billy and Bethan were sorry to see how subservient Rhona had become, and how she seemed to have aged. She said, "It's hard work. I suppose they are demanding, but I want to keep the place nice and make sure everything's done properly. I want to feel I earn my keep and I'm not just being kept out of charity." Billy and Bethan found it hard to imagine the Pughs doing anything out of charity. They did not say so, nor mention their criminal activities, as there was always someone within earshot.

Bethan said, "We know how you've always worked and we can see you do keep this place as well as you used to, but I wish these people valued you as much as we did, and we do."

Billy said, "Wouldn't you do better somewhere else? I'm sure you could get more money and be treated better at lots of other farms."

"I don't know. While I'm here, I feel as if we haven't lost the place completely. Do you understand?"

Billy and Bethan looked thoughtful. He said, "I can see what you mean, but I don't think I would feel the same." Bethan agreed.

On the way back to the inn, Bethan said to Billy that she wanted to find Rhona somewhere better, but they could not see how it could be done. It was all very different from the way the Joneses treated everyone at the inn. Later they enjoyed mimicking these people and managed to have a laugh, but remained somewhat bitter towards them.

Their visit to their brother Owain was very different. He was working on a farm near the village of Maerdy, which is in the valley of the Little Rhondda. It was more sheltered than Penrhys and the land more fertile. When they arrived at the farm, they were welcomed most hospitably by the farmer, Emlyn Lloyd, who had been a friend of their father. In fact, although he had lent him money, which remained owing, he said he was prepared to contribute to any collection they might organise to try to get him out of gaol. His ability to contribute was somewhat limited, but they were touched at his desire to help.

Emlyn Lloyd explained that Owain was living in a shepherd's hut near the ridge, as the flock was still grazing the higher slopes at that time of year, despite the wet weather. It was a steep climb, and they were glad of a breather when they reached the hut near the top of the ridge. They were not surprised to find that Owain was not there, but they soon found him repairing a dry stone wall. He was accompanied by the two sheepdogs they had had for years and the dogs were pleased when they recognised Billy and Bethan, wagging their tails and trying to jump up. Since they had last seen him he had matured, and now, at eighteen, he was a younger version of their father and no longer the child they had left behind when they went off to war.

They had lunch in the hut. Fortunately they had brought some from the inn, as Owain was no better cook than Bethan. He said, "I'm happy working here. I love the quiet and the work. I don't think I'd like to live in a town like Cardiff, but I like being with the Lloyd family when I can."

Bethan asked, "Do you like being in company?"

"Well, they're nice people."

"Is there any one of them that you like most?"

He looked embarrassed and took a long time to say, "Well, I don't know."

"Is it one of the girls? I think one or two of them will be about your age."

"Well, I suppose I do like the youngest one, Morganna."

"How serious is it? What does she think of you?"

"I think she likes me, but I daren't say anything because I can't ask her to marry me."

"Why not? What's wrong with you? Don't her parents like you?"

"I think they do, but they know I've no money and not good prospects, have I?"

Billy said, "We might be able to help, so don't give up."

Owain said, "I can't see how. You've no money, have you?"

Since there was nobody to overhear, they decided to tell him how they were improving the family's finances. He was by turns incredulous, scandalised and amused.

He finally said, "I want to join you. Let's all be highwaymen together. Or is it highwaypeople?"

Billy said, "I'd love to be working with you, but I don't want to risk getting you into trouble. It's bad enough with Beth, but all right, I'll think about it, but not just yet. You concentrate on doing what you're good at: farming, and don't be afraid to get to know Morganna."

"All right. But if you want to come here to hide or to hide some of the stuff you've stolen, I'll be glad to help. Nobody ever comes up here and I know all the places to hide things."

"We'll remember that. But keep out of trouble for now."

Chapter 4

A couple of months after their first robbery, Llewellyn came to Billy to say there was a gentleman to see him. He had asked for the ostler. The boy had assumed this must have meant Gareth, but the gentleman was adamant that he wanted to see the younger man. Billy went inside with a mixture of curiosity and anxiety. The gentleman was in one of the small private rooms and was eating and drinking alone. As Billy went into that room, Bethan went through a hidden door that led into a passage coming out behind a false panel in the wall of that room. She had heard that it had been created during the Civil War to allow royalists to hide when the New Model Army came calling. It still had its uses. Bethan used the passage to listen to the conversation.

The stranger was dressed well but unpretentiously. He invited Billy to sit down and offered him a glass of port wine and a slice of game pie. He took up the offer. Bethan envied him.

The man said, "I know who you are. You are the leader of that band of scoundrels who robbed me and my family on the road to Bridgend in September. Please don't waste your time denying it. I am not a fool."

Billy replied, "If you were really so sure, you would not be sitting there discussing it. You would be accompanied by soldiers or sheriff's officers to arrest me. Anyway, I assure you that you are mistaken."

The man said, "I see that you are no fool either. Very well, I shall be frank with you. I have puzzled long and hard over the question of your identity, as have all who were with me that day. I have no proof such as would satisfy a Justice of the Peace. I know, for I am one. Yet in my heart I know. It was my coachman who pointed you out to me. That incident with the horses, when you acted swiftly to avert a tragedy. He knew you must have been used to working with horses, and specifically coachhorses. Then we realised that one of the ostlers at this inn looked rather like one of the robbers, and would have been able to discover where we were going and so be waiting for us. You must be that man."

Billy was enjoying the pie and the port, but was unclear as to the man's purpose.

He said, "If you are so sure, but know you have no proof, I fail to see the point of your coming here."

"I have to ask you a favour. It grieves me very much, as you can probably imagine, but my situation leaves me no other option."

"I cannot imagine any favour I could do you, nor any reason why I should. Surely you can see that to return any of your property', if I had it, or knew how to obtain it, would be an admission of guilt."

"Please listen! Allow me to clarify the position. There is something you have taken that is of great importance to me. Yet I suspect it will be of little value to you. So I am willing to buy it back. Nobody need know."

If this was his idea of clarifying things, he was failing. Billy was more confused than before. So was Bethan. "What you have that I want is a series of letters. They concern matters of a political nature, of the sort you will hardly find interesting. There are, however, others who would find them only too interesting, and I am prepared to pay you – yes even you – to keep them out of their hands." "You amaze me, but I really cannot help you. Believe me, I would if I could. Not because I owe you any favours, but because I do need the money. The fact is that whatever else I may or may not have done, I have not taken any letters from you."

"Do you not recall making me open a box which contained nothing but papers? I thought at the time that you examined several items but replaced them all. However, when I looked for certain letters, once I had returned to Cardiganshire, they were missing. I know they were there when we left London, and I know that the box was not opened in between, save on that one occasion. Nobody else has access to it, nor needs any. I can but conclude that you exercised some sleight of hand such as is common among men of your occupation, thus temporarily deceiving me."

"You do me too much honour!" Billy lied. He did know how to do tricks such as that. He went on, "Besides, I would have had no use for your letters, as you say. You must look elsewhere for your thief."

"If that is so, there is no more to be said. Now I can but bid you 'Good Day', and to say that I do sincerely thank you for saving the horse and for your restraint when my son and my daughter spoke and acted foolishly."

Bethan had to suppress laughter as she recalled those antics. Billy could think of no response other than to bid the gentleman a good day in return and leave.

Over the next few weeks, John introduced Billy and Bethan to some of his contacts who could buy the stolen property, some in Cardiff, others in Pontypridd, Bridgend and Monmouth. He explained that he used so many because each had his or her own speciality, and also because it was not good to let any one of them know how much he had stolen at any one time. He warned them to be careful not to try to sell too much at once, or to be seen to be spending too much money, although Billy did treat himself to some new clothes including a pale buff coat and a big hat with a white plume. John thought he was going to look too conspicuous. He always wore black or dark brown clothes, as Billy had until then.

Billy explained, "You know you told me, years ago, that most highwaymen wear black or dark clothes and ride black or dark brown horses? Well, I thought that everyone probably knows that. So if I wear bright clothes and ride a grey horse, nobody will think I am up to anything. Of course I'll change at some point before actually holding up a coach or breaking into a house, but I'll change back again as soon as I get away. I know I always ride a dark bay horse, but I'm hoping to buy a grey to ride as well."

John said, "I like it but be careful spending money. People might get suspicious."

"Oh, it's all right! I'll tell people, quite truthfully, that the Army owed me several months' arrears of pay. I won't mention that I still haven't got it." He showed him a dark coat he usually tied to his saddle and put on over his bright clothes at the right time. Then he showed how he could remove the plume from his hat and hide it in a bag or one of his pockets. He would then put a black band over the buff one around the hat. Lastly, he showed John a fair wig he had bought. Since Billy was naturally dark, the wig was the final touch that changed his look quite dramatically.

John said, "I always thought you were good. You learn quickly and must have a natural talent for this sort of thing. But now I think you're better than I imagined."

Bethan agreed and began to think how she could add to her wardrobe for the same effect.

Chapter 5

Billy and Bethan wondered how to rob one of their father's richest creditors, Howell Hopkins, a merchant and shipowner, who seldom travelled far out of Cardiff, and never left his house unguarded. Bethan wondered if it would be worth visiting one of the inns near the docks where such men often met. They discussed this over lunch with John, who they guessed had contacts in hostelries in many parts of town.

The old highwayman said, "If he's involved in shipping you'll probably find him at the Mermaid. They all meet there to discuss business. Be careful. These merchants are different from most of the people we know. They seem to speak a different language, and you have to understand at least a bit about trade or you'll seem like a fool. They're also likely to take money from you if they think you're naïve. If you go there, look for a whore called Tegwyn. She's a big lump. Loud and cheerful. She knows everyone. Tell her I said she should help you. She'll want paying for her information, but it'll be worth it."

After that they said very little but tried to concentrate on their lunch, which they regretted as it was well below the cook's usual standard. John said as much. Billy replied, "Don't be too hard on Cook. She can only work with what she's got and all the good food's been eaten by that big party who were in here. You can't make a silk purse out of a sow's ear."

"I think they made this stew out of a sow's ear!" said Bethan.

"Well, at least it's better than anything you ever cooked." commented her brother.

John, said, "Don't involve me in your family quarrels. Oh, tell Tegwyn I know an artist who'd like to paint her. He painted our stables quite well. She'll know you really are a friend of mine." They hoped Tegwyn had a sense of humour.

When John had gone, Billy said he was nervous about getting to know the merchants at the Mermaid.

Bethan was quite optimistic. "It should be easy for you to seem like a naïve young gentleman with more money than sense. They'll probably try to involve you in some scheme. If so, just go along with it except for parting with any money. They'll probably tell you a lot more than they realise." He thought she was right.

Billy put on his best clothes and his best English accent, like some of the better guests at the inn and many of the officers that he had known. He went to the Mermaid, where he listened to a lot of talk he scarcely understood.

A man dressed rather shabbily was sitting drinking alone. He suddenly looked at Billy as if he recognised him and approached him. He had rather been counting on not being recognised. The man greeted Billy with a heavy Welsh accent. "Hello, Sarge, remember me?"

He did. Regrettably. Thomas Thomas. A liar, thief and cheat from Billy's regiment. He could have done without his company.

Thomas continued, "You looks as if you done all right. Better'n me any'ow. You got out early, is it?

Didn't miss a lot. We 'ardly 'ad anything to do after you'd gone."

Billy suspected he had found plenty to do. Unofficially. He wondered about trying to hold the conversation in Welsh, but remembered that Thomas's Welsh was not much better than his English.

Thomas said, "Good to see you. As always."

Billy knew he was lying. They had not always got on well. He remembered Thomas had taken money from a lot of his comrades by various artifices. Billy guessed that he must want something.

"Well, 'ow 'bout lending an 'and to an ole mate?"

"It depends what sort of hand you want." "I got in bother after you went. Weren't fair. I got blamed for a lotta stuff I 'adn't done, see?"

Billy thought that even if it were true, it would scarcely offset the things he had done but had got away with. He said, "It's too late for me to do anything about that, now."

"Right. But you could tell your rich pals as I'm all right, like. I'm looking for work but I got no whatdoyoucallems? Them papers you get at the end?"

"Do you mean 'discharge papers' perhaps?"

"That's it!"

"I thought every soldier was entitled to his discharge papers when he was discharged. Was there a mistake?" "Yes! No! I mean, like, I got 'em but they're no good, like."

"Do you mean they say you were dishonourably discharged?"

49

"Think so. Can't read, like, but showed 'em to a boss taking on men, and 'e laughed. Said I'd no chance with them, like. So I 'aven't kept 'em, like. Any'ow, can you say I was a good'un? They'd believe you, dressed like that."

"What sort of work are you looking for?" Billy hoped he was not looking for a job handling money.

"Gunner. What I'm good at, isn't it, see? I 'eard there's more trade than ever now. At sea like. Only there's more pirates too. So a lot o' merchants are putting extra guns on their ships. So they wants gunners now. They say the money's not bad an'all."

Billy smiled. He was relieved. Sending the man off to sea appealed to him.

"Yes. I think I can help you, but I'll want you to help me too. You'll have to say I was an officer but not in any Welsh regiment. They might know people who would know me. Say I was in the Irish Artillery. I could know you from when we were stationed together."

"Right!"

"Oh, yes! Say that my family's got money. Call me Captain Gareth Evans." Billy had decided to use his uncle's name. There were plenty of Evanses in Wales and plenty of Gareths.

"Always a pleasure 'elping old pals, isn't it?"

Billy was uncomfortable at the thought of asking a favour from him, but he had hardly any choice.

Two women had come in while Billy was talking to Thomas. They sat together chatting. After a minute or two, the big blonde said, "What's the matter with you,

Megan, cariad? You've not been listening to me. You seem to be staring at those two men. That scruffy one looks as if he can hardly afford a drink, let alone a woman. Is it the smart one you're looking at?"

"Well, now you mention it, that gentleman does look sort of familiar, but I can't think why," replied the tall redhead. "But it's the other one I'm watching. Not for the reason you think."

The blonde got up to get a drink. Megan thought about the men. She was grateful to her companion, Tegwyn, for taking her under her wing. She was generous and good-natured, but she was bossy. She kept the other women in order. Most of them liked her, but they did not like to cross her. Her thoughts were interrupted as the big woman returned with a jug of wine and two glasses.

"All right. Tell me about him, then. What's interesting about him?"

"Well, he says his name's Thomas Thomas. It might be, I suppose. He's been coming in here quite a bit. Looking for work, he says. As if he'd find any in here! Always seems to have money for drink. Don't know where he gets it from. Made a fool of me once. Didn't think I'd see him in here again. Just remember not to trust him. Some of the girls call him a loveable rogue. I reckon they're half right." They laughed and sipped their wine.

"How did he make a fool of you? You're not innocent."

"He took a fancy to me one day and talked me into going upstairs with him. Got away without paying."

"Didn't you get his money off him first?"

"Of course. I'm not that stupid! It was when I was checking my money afterwards that I noticed a coin with a clipped edge. You know. Some tricksters clip off little bits of silver and melt them down. Do it enough and you've quite a profit." "Were you sure it was him?"

"No! The thing is that someone else had given me a clipped coin and I'd kept it, because I didn't want to get caught using it, in case someone accused me of being in on the trick. Well, when I noticed this one, just after Thomas had gone, I went to compare it with the first one and it wasn't there. He'd taken it out of my purse and paid me with my own money!" Tegwyn laughed. A lot.

Megan continued, "All right! I was caught. I'm trying to warn you. Don't make me feel any worse than I do."

"Well, let's go and talk to those two men. You can deal with your old pal, while I get to know this new fellow."

Billy had been looking at all the women in the inn. There were a couple of big ones, so he asked, "Do you know Tegwyn?"

They laughed. The big blonde said, "I'm Tegwyn. Who wants me?"

Billy said "I am Captain Gareth Evans, late of the Irish Artillery. I have come on the recommendation of a former acquaintance of yours, called John Aris."

"Doing me favours now, is it? Well, as you're here, let's have a drink together."

Megan took Thomas to another table. She said,

"You've got a cheek, coming in here again! I hope you're not going to try to rob or cheat any of our clients.
What do you want with that gentleman you were just with?"

"All right, cariad. Calm down, isn't it? He's an old friend. We was in the Army together. He's a real gentleman. I told 'im I come looking for work. I 'ope Billy, I mean Captain Evans, can talk to some o' them rich men as comes in, so they'll give me a job."

"I hope it's honest work you're looking for. We don't want trouble. And you can pay me with real money, not clipped or forged. Not my own, if you please!"

"I'll see you right as soon as I gets a bit of money. It won't be long, I'm sure."

"All right. Just remember, I know you and I'm keeping an eye on you. Two eyes. Well, now we're both here, you can help me finish Tegwyn's wine, since she's having a drink with your old captain."

They sat and chatted in a more friendly way as they finished the wine. She remembered why so many women called him a loveable rogue. Perhaps they were more than half right.

Billy ordered some Burgundy wine, but Tegwyn interrupted, saying the Burgundy was very poor and he would prefer the Hock. He took her advice.

He said, "The gentleman who now calls himself John, says he knows an artist who could paint you. He says he did a good job painting his stables."

"Cheeky devil! He'd better keep away from me. Well, you obviously know him. See that painting?

Guess who it is?"

He looked at a painting on the wall. It was a picture of a mermaid. She looked very similar to the one on the sign outside. He had noticed that mermaids were always depicted as fair-haired and big-breasted. As he had never seen a real one, he had no idea how typical that was. As he studied the painting he realised the top half of the creature looked very similar to Tegwyn. She was a big woman, but not unattractive. Voluptuous was the word.

She said, "The artist who painted me was going to use one of the other girls as his model, but changed his mind, saying I was the type he wanted. She was right jealous. We had words about it. I'll bet she told John."

While she was talking, the wine arrived. Billy had drunk plenty of Hock in the Netherlands, as it came from the nearby Rhineland, and he had acquired a taste for it. This one was quite acceptable. They chatted about various things, until Billy pulled a golden guinea out of his pocket. Her eyes became larger, her smile wider. He said, "John said I should give you this if we shared a bed. I am to expect a sovereign in change."

She hit him playfully saying, "He must think I'm as cheap as his other doxies! Wait 'til the next time we meet."

"He said you'd say that. However, there's something else. I want some information. Now that will be worth a guinea at least." "What do you want to know?"

"Do you know someone called Howell Hopkins?"

"He's a very rich and successful merchant. He's involved in lots of things but mainly shipping. He comes in here when he wants to meet people and talk business or when he fancies a game of cards."

"Thanks. What's he like?"

"Honest. Dead straight. He can't stand cheats and liars. In business, in cards or anything. He's no fool. If you want to do business with him, be careful. He won't cheat you, but he's not soft, and he usually comes out best in any dealings he has."

Billy realised he was planning to rob an honest man, feeling uneasy.

"All right. What if I asked his advice about business? I might ask him what he thinks would be a good investment."

"He'll know. Whatever he tells you will be his true opinion. And he's usually right."

"Well, that's all worth knowing. You can keep the guinea. I'll tell John that you were worth every penny!" They laughed.

Then she took Billy upstairs. When he came down again, he was greeted by three merchants. He introduced himself as Captain Evans.

"Glad to meet you," said an elderly, distinguished-looking one. "I am Howell Hopkins." Then, pointing to a young man apparently in his twenties added, "This is my friend James Pryce. His family are from Cardiganshire, but he often visits my other friend here." He indicated the little man of about James's age on his right, "This is our friend Richard Jenkins of St Fagans."

Billy was horrified. He realised that James Pryce was the young man who had unsuccessfully challenged him to a duel when he was robbing his first coach. He hoped he looked and sounded sufficiently different to avoid detection. He knew that St Fagans was a village only a few miles west of Cardiff. There was a castle there. If James Pryce was friends with the inhabitants, he might visit Cardiff quite often. Too often. He also knew that the Jenkins family of St Fagans were among those he planned to rob. They had bought Penrhys at a bargain price and leased it out in sections.

Billy told them he wanted to meet someone who could advise him about investments, as he had recently received a legacy. They said they would be happy to chat later, but had some business to discuss together first.

Billy left them while he had some lunch. He saw Thomas approach the three merchants. After a short while he came and joined him, saying, "Them's the sort what can 'elp me. They all got money in ships and can get me work if I'm lucky. I told 'em what a fine officer you are, and I know you'll speak up for me too." As Billy finished his meal, the three merchants seemed to have finished their discussions and were relaxing around a large carafe of wine. Howell Hopkins beckoned him to join them and said, "Your friend over there says you'll confirm that he's a good man with a gun. Is that so?"

"Yes. If you want a gunner, he should be all right. Of course, I saw him in the Army. I don't know how he'd cope at sea."

The merchant said, "He's from Swansea. We can tell from his accent. They've got webbed feet there." Billy remembered why he spoke so strangely.

Richard Jenkins then said, "All right. I'll talk to one of my captains, Madoc Morgan, who I'll be seeing soon. He's still looking for another gunner. Tell Mr. Thomas to come and see me in two or three days."

"Never mind him. How do you fancy a game of cards?" asked James Pryce.

Billy hesitated, but the other two pressed him. So he agreed. He knew he would have to be honest, even if it meant losing, as he dared not get a bad reputation if he was to get into Howell Hopkins's good books. Billy won a few hands and lost a few, but overall was showing a small profit and was thinking of calling it a day. However, Richard Jenkins became rather agitated. He had been losing to all the others. He said he was determined to win some of his money back. He was certain his luck would change soon. Billy had heard that before. He remembered his father had often thought like that. He reluctantly let him borrow some of his winnings to allow him to keep playing.

After another hour, Jenkins had lost even more. They all tried to persuade him to give up, but he would not. Richard said, "Most of my money's tied up at sea at present and the cargoes aren't strictly mine to sell, because I've got partners I'd need to consult, but I've got a coach and pair outside. Will any of you accept that as security?" They all agreed. Richard started to win some money back, but kept on too long, losing it all and more, mostly to Billy. They all went outside to look at the coach. It was a good one, but the horses interested Billy more: one chestnut and one pale grey. They were smaller than typical English carthorses but bigger than Welsh cobs. Billy walked up to them and had a look. He said he would take the grey to clear all Richard's debts to him, and he would pay off the other two, as the horse was worth more than the debt. Jenkins was relieved and thanked Billy for his generosity. He said the horse was called Caledin, after Sir Lancelot's horse. Billy thought it would go well with Merlin. He was pleased to have acquired such a good horse and to have got off to a good start with the three merchants. He had also got on well with Tegwyn. He was, however, anxious about how to proceed in his dealings with Howell Hopkins.

Chapter 6

One evening, not long after Billy's visit to the Mermaid, he and Bethan had just finished their meal when Llewellyn came in and announced, "There's a lady asking for you Billy. I mean a *real* lady too!"

Billy said, "Well you'd better send her in, I suppose." and, looking at his sister, added, "I think you'd better not go far." The lady who walked in was indeed every inch a real lady. A big strong-looking manservant accompanied her as far as the door and then took a seat outside the room. She had dark hair and as dark a complexion as Billy and Bethan. She was a real beauty and looked smart in her quality riding clothes. She also looked rather familiar, but Billy could not think why. She glared at Bethan as she passed her in the doorway.

Bethan again went into the secret passage. Billy offered his visitor a seat. She threw her hat, coat and gloves onto an empty chair and began to address him in an accusing tone, saying, "I know who you are."

He replied, "It is no secret. I am William Rhys. What of it? And may I know who you are?"

"I am Mrs Kenneth MacKenzie. Helen or Elen to my friends, but you need not concern yourself about that. I do not count you as one. I am the woman you robbed and humiliated on the road to Bridgend. In case you are thinking of taking advantage of me again, let me warn you that I am armed and that my man, Evans, is only outside the door."

"I do not know what you are talking about or why I should want to ill use a lady. Could it be another William Rhys that you seek?"

"I did not know the name of the man who attacked me, but I know it was you. You are the ostler here are you not?"

"I was until recently, but I never attacked or robbed anyone here, nor anywhere else. You are mistaken."

She got up and moved round the table to stand right in front of him. She put a hand to his face and said, "I can still see my teeth marks! Don't pretend you don't remember."

Billy had not been able to detect the teeth marks for some time, but his reaction must have given him away. She laughed and said, "I knew it. I thought I had remembered you, even though I didn't get a very good look at your face. You are despicable! A disgrace to Mankind!"

"Did you come here just to tell me that or did you wish to continue where we left off?"

She slapped his face. He winced and then put his left arm around her, pulling her to him, taking the precaution of putting his right hand to her chin to prevent her biting him again. They struggled. He bent her backwards over a table. He held her there for a moment and kissed her before releasing her.

Billy said, "I notice that you failed to make use of whatever weapons you claim to be carrying and you omitted to scream."

"I am restraining myself, albeit with difficulty, because I have come to ask something of you."

"If you are about to ask a favour, you are going the wrong way about it."

"I can't help that. You are so… infuriating! I cannot help thinking of my hurt and humiliation. If only my husband were here."

"So he could challenge me to a duel? Or fall in the mud? You are quite a pair."

"That wasn't him you fool! That was my brother. He *is* a fool. My husband is serving his country with the Royal Scots Borderers and has not yet returned from the Spanish Netherlands."

Billy thought the regiment would have been home by then, but was aware that you never could be sure with the Army.

"Are you ready to tell me the nature of the request you have for me, or must I listen to some more insults first?"

"I would like to ask for my rings back, and my necklace. They were gifts from my husband, and they are precious to me, but I expect you will have disposed of them by now. You probably gave them to one of your doxies like the one I saw with you just now. But I will accept my losses philosophically, as I have accepted my humiliation and ill-treatment at your hands."

He wondered how she behaved when she experienced misfortune that she did not accept philosophically.

"So what do you actually want from me?" "I want you to return the letters you stole from my father."

Billy was amazed. Did she not know of her father's visit?

"Why has he sent you?" he asked, "Did he think I would give in to your charms? If so he has badly misjudged us both."

"You are despicable!"

"You have already told me that."

"Of course he would not send a woman on such an errand. He does not know I am here, nor must he. He is in London and thinks I am joining my brother who is visiting a friend at St Fagans on my way to join him. He would not stoop so low as to ask a favour of the likes of you, even if his life depended on it! I am asking because I care for him. Ever since we arrived back at our home in Cardiganshire, after our interrupted journey, he has not been himself. He has been fretting over some letters he is certain were in that box you looked through. It has been terrible. Only you could have taken them, apart from members of the family and some of our most trusted servants. We've all been suspecting each other. The atmosphere has been awful. Father thinks it must have been you, but he has no idea who you are. But I do. And I was right. I only wish I had proof. I'd like to watch you hang, you blackguard!"

"You really know how to get round a man, don't you? But it doesn't matter. I don't have any of your father's letters and I don't know who might have them. Now perhaps you will leave me to pay attention to my doxies unless you would like to take their place for a while."

She marched out of the room without another word. Bethan emerged, laughing, from behind the false panel. "I told you she likes you. She'll be back for more. Just wait!"

Billy said, "You can laugh, but I don't know what it is about that woman that makes me so angry. I nearly lost my temper completely. I was afraid I was going to really hurt her."

"She didn't seem as afraid as you were. She's made of strong stuff, but be careful of that woman. She's dangerous. I just know it."

Chapter 7

Two days later Billy and Bethan decided to visit the Mermaid together. As soon as they went inside, Thomas greeted them. Although Billy found him something of an embarrassment, he was secretly glad that Thomas had helped confirm his new identity to the merchants. Thomas and Bethan remembered each other from their days in the Netherlands. Turning to Billy, he said, "You done me a right good turn you 'ave, Sarge, I mean *Captain Evans*. One of them rich men you was with, it was 'im as lost a lot to you when you played cards, got a lot of money in ships, so 'alf the ships' masters round 'ere likes to keep 'im 'appy. There's one of 'em coming in 'ere today that'll be looking for a gunner, and I should 'ave a good chance. So I told 'im what a good man you was, like. A real gentleman and a good soldier, like. So we looks after each other." Billy smiled and appeared to agree.

Just then Tegwyn appeared, scowled at Bethan and said, "Are you trying to steal my customers?"

Billy said, "This is my sister. I wanted her to meet some of my new friends here, including you. No need to be jealous."

Tegwyn, Billy and Bethan moved to a table by themselves. After a little chat Billy asked, "How would you like to earn another guinea?"

"Are you after more information or do you want to make love to me all day and half the night? I warn you that not many men are up to it, although lots think they are."

"I do want some more information, but I hope I'll get a bit more than that for my guinea. What do you know about those two merchants I met last time with Howell Hopkins?"

"Well that fellow who lost at cards is all right, just a fool when he gets started at gambling. He's quite clever with money apart from that. He's got a house in town, but his family live at St Fagans. They own most of the land for miles around there. They say his father's a hard man. Hard on everyone from what I've heard, including Richard. Very critical of his gambling and doesn't seem to realise how well his son is doing in business. I think that's why they keep apart most of the time." Tegwyn then took Billy upstairs. Thomas came and sat next to Bethan. She said she wanted to try the food. While they were waiting, a group of merchants came in. Thomas told Bethan they were the ones Billy had been playing cards with. He introduced her. They chatted a little and Richard Jenkins reassured Thomas that the ship's master, Madoc Morgan, would be coming later.

A tall smartly dressed gentleman came in. He was probably in his fifties, but the equally well-dressed woman with him looked about twenty years younger. Bethan had to suppress her shock as she recognised John and Gwyneth, although their wigs and make-up would have deceived anyone less familiar with them. Gwyneth drew admiring glances from the men and spiteful glares from the women. John greeted several of the merchants with easy familiarity. He looked surprised when he saw

Bethan but kept his poise and said, "I feel we have met before, but forgive me, Madam, that your name has for the moment escaped me."

"Oh, that's quite understandable. It's been so long. I am Mrs Tudor. My husband is Henry Tudor. His family claim to be descended from the Tudors who became Kings and Queens of England. I expect you will remember my brother, Captain Gareth Evans, late of the Irish Artillery. And this is Mr Thomas Thomas, an old acquaintance of my brother."

John said, "Pleased to meet you Mr Thomas. I am John Aris and this is my friend, Mrs Evans."

By then Gwyneth had composed herself enough to avoid saying anything foolish. She said, "My husband is also a Gareth Evans. There seem to be many of them around. In fact the one you know is my nephew, and this, of course, is my niece." Bethan was impressed with her aunt's English. She and her brother had apparently not been the only ones studying some of the inn's visitors.

John said, "We are here because there is a gentleman I wish to meet in order to discuss some business, and Mrs Evans also wishes to make his acquaintance, a Mr Richard Jenkins."

Jenkins had been admiring Gwyneth's beauty and responded enthusiastically, "I am he. In what way might I be of service?"

"My sons are both at sea and have been learning the trade for some three years now, since they were twelve and thirteen. I was hoping to help them advance their careers. They seem somewhat becalmed, as I believe they would say. I hope you might be the man to remedy that."

"Of course, Madam. Do bring them to see me when they are next ashore and I will be sure to help them. Have my card."

Then the food arrived, so Bethan and Thomas left the group and ate their lunch. John and Gwyneth continued to talk to the merchants.

Thomas said, "Thanks again. Thank Billy too. Oh! I mean, Gareth Evans. I knew you'd both look after me. He's a good'un, and you knows, you and me allus got on ever so well, isn't it?"

"Yes. I always know where I am with you. You never pretend you want something apart from the obvious and you don't treat me as if I'm stupid either."

"Well, that's all right then. After I've seen this ship's master, do you fancy seeing if they'll let us use one of their private rooms?" While they were talking, he had begun fondling her. She had not discouraged him.

"That could be asking for trouble. The women here think this is their territory."

She thought for a moment, noticing his disappointment and remembering some of the fun they had had together in the past. There were times when she missed those days. She made her mind up and said, "Why don't you come to the Coach and Horses tonight? I've got my own room there. Just mind you don't take any notice of any of the other women there." She felt a sudden wave of guilt come over her, at the thought of returning to something she had believed she had left behind in the Spanish Netherlands, but she managed to ignore it.

He said, "I 'aven't seen them women at that other place, but I'll bet they can't outdo you!"

Some other women approached them. One said, "Have you got another woman, Thomas?"

"Don't be cross! She's an old friend."

"I can see you're friends and I can see she's old, but she doesn't belong here."

"I don't suppose I'm any older than you, and we were only talking," snapped Bethan.

"Yes! Talking about going off somewhere else for a bit of you-know-what."

A voice from behind said, "Is this another of your brothers? How many have you got? You didn't come in with this one." It was Tegwyn. Billy was not with her. "I think you're trying to take over our business."

One of the others said, "I saw her chatting to them other three. Are they next?"

Tegwyn said, "Are you sure that Gareth's your brother? Doesn't look like it. What about those three?"

One of the other girls said, "Perhaps she's their mother." They all laughed.

Bethan looked really angry. She said, "Are you calling me a liar?"

Tegwyn said, "In here, I'll call you anything I like. What'll you do about it?"

Bethan picked up a glass of wine and threw it in her face. She looked stunned for a moment. The others all gasped. Thomas laughed. Chairs scraped as people turned to see what was happening. Tegwyn picked up a pint of ale from a nearby table and, ignoring its owner's protests, tipped it over Bethan's head. There was a moment of awed silence while she made a visible effort to control herself. She decided that there are times when self-control is overrated. She took a handful of Tegwyn's hair in one hand and tried to punch her with the other. Tegwyn grabbed both her wrists and they began to grapple. Tegwyn bent her backwards over a table while several men narrowly managed to rescue their drinks. Bethan struggled ineffectively. Tegwyn made the mistake of pressing hard on her opponent's face, bending her head backwards over the far edge of the table. This caused the table to topple. They found themselves rolling about on the floor. The other girls called encouragement to Tegwyn while Gwyneth, John and Thomas shouted for Bethan. Lots of others added to the din. Billy arrived and asked what the fight was about. Nobody answered.

Tegwyn rolled on top for a moment and whispered, as their faces touched, "You're stealing my men, you bloody whore. Admit it!"

"Make me, you fat lump!"

After more inconclusive rolling about, the stalemate was broken when Bethan rolled onto her back and immediately sat up, clutching Tegwyn's legs and bending them up over her back. The bigger woman struggled and almost broke free but Bethan just hung on. Both were struggling for breath, but Bethan managed to say, "Give up?"

"Yes, you bitch!" Bethan let go and they rolled apart, lying there for a few moments to get their breath before getting up.

Tegwyn said, "I'll believe whatever you say, today. So he's your brother. He's an old pal. You're not a whore."

"Don't worry. He really is her brother and she's not a whore," called Megan. "Don't you recognise your cousin, Megan Morgan?"

John and the others were staring in amazement. While Bethan was the centre of attention, Billy told Megan about the need to maintain his Captain Evans persona.

When things quietened down, Bethan asked, "When did you first recognise us?"

"I wondered from the moment I saw you. Your voices seemed more familiar than your looks, especially when you got angry."

"So why didn't you step in before we started fighting? I seem to remember that you were egging us on." "I thought it would be a good fight. I was right. You always were good. I did cheer for you once it started."

"Thanks. You're too kind."

Thomas said, "Well, I'm glad Meg didn't stop you. I alus knew you was a fighter. Glad you still are." With that, he went to speak to the ship's master who had arrived during the fight.

Tegwyn said, "I'm sorry I thought you were a whore, but it did look like it, you know."

Bethan said, "I hate to admit it but in a way I am a whore. Well, not quite. It's not as simple as that. There's a lot of things none of you know. Not even my brother. I think I owe you the truth."

Billy looked as astonished as he was. He said, "Yes, please, let's have the truth, but not in front of everyone." The crowd that had gathered around them had started to disperse, but a few people were still listening.

Tegwyn said, "All right, you'd better come into the big back room." She led the way, followed by Billy, Bethan, Megan, John, and Gwyneth. Nerys, one of the other whores, joined them. She was smaller than most of them and one of the oldest, probably over forty, which fact her wig and make-up did not completely hide.

Thomas was still deep in conversation with Madoc Morgan, the ship's master. He knew all he needed to know about Bethan already.

Chapter 8

The big back room turned out to be not as big as Billy and Bethan had expected. They all had to squash in as best they could. Tegwyn installed herself confidently in a big armchair. Billy, Bethan and Megan shared a chaise longue with Nerys perched uncomfortably on one end. John sat in the other armchair with Gwyneth on his lap. Tegwyn said, "I don't know about you lot, but I think I'm going to need something to drink, if we're in for as long a session as it looks like. I've had enough wine for a bit. Anybody else fancy a cup of tea?" There were several nods and grunts. Nerys got up and went out showing no expression on her face. Bethan wondered if that was because of all the make-up.

Tegwyn said, "Well, Bethan. You're the one that's got us all confused. So come on now, cariad: are you a whore or not?"

Bethan replied, "Well, you see, it's a bit complicated. I mean, it depends how you look at it, you know? Anyway, do you mean now or some time in the past?"

There were several groans and grimaces. Billy did not believe what he was hearing. John threw his eyes up at the ceiling. Gwyneth sighed and shook her head.

Megan said, "Please! Please! Are you going to tell us or aren't you? Teg, if you want to hit her I'll help you, just to make her come clean."

Tegwyn said, "Thanks for the offer. So, Bethan, how about it?"

Nerys came back in and said, "Ivor's bringing the tea in a minute. Now, where have we got to?"

Tegwyn said, "Thanks. You haven't missed anything. This woman's trying our patience."

Bethan began again, "Well, what it is, see, is that I got married when I was fifteen, and within a year, in 1703, when the War started, my husband went off in the Army to fight the French, like a lot of young men. I went with him and shared his tent and his food. I did as much marching as the soldiers. We had seven happy years. Our son, Llewellyn, was born right at the start. Things went all right until the Battle of Malplaquet in 1709. My Henry went missing. I tried ever so hard to find him, but I still don't know what happened to him or even whether he's dead or alive. So I stayed with the Army for a long time hoping he'd turn up, but he didn't. Well, while I was waiting, I had lots of offers from men. A few wanted to marry me, but most had something less permanent in mind." At that there were several chuckles and knowing looks. Gwyneth and Billy looked serious. Bethan went on, "Then a fever went all through the camp and there were plenty that needed nursing, and I did my best for a lot of them. Saved some anyway."

There was a knock at the door and an old man came in with a tray of tea things. He hesitated, but a look from Nerys sent him out of the room. She took over the role of serving the tea. When everyone had a cup, Bethan resumed her story. "After that everyone seemed to think I was one of the camp followers. By then I didn't much care, see? I'd lost the only man I really wanted and had no money or anything, so I sort of gave in. Sometimes I thought about what my parents would have said, or Uncle Huw, the minister, but, well, they weren't there, like, were they? At least it meant I was going to be all right for money, so I could take care of my little boy as well as myself, see? I only came back to Wales when the Fusiliers came back after the Peace was signed. I haven't been with a man since then, but Thomas Thomas was one of the men who shared my bed a few times back then. I liked him. So when I saw him again today I remembered, and I didn't mind when he started getting, you know, when he…" "We know!" said Tegwyn and Nerys.

"What!" said Megan.

"You poor thing." said Gwyneth.

"Well, that explains a bit." said John.

"I had never thought…" said Billy.

"Now I see what you meant about not knowing whether or not you're a whore." said Tegwyn.

John said, "It's time we were off or people will think I've taken you away."

John was thinking that he now knew about Bethan but still had a lot of questions about Billy. How had he coped with the Army well enough to become a sergeant? How had he taken to being a highwayman so well? How had he developed such a devious mind?

On their way back to the Coach and Horses, Gwyneth said, "That poor girl! What she's been through. No wonder she was prepared to help you and Billy with some of your robberies."

"How did you know about that? Come to that, how did you know about me?"

"I'm not stupid! I know you're a gentleman but you've no home and no family. I know you never seem to work but always have money. You keep disappearing and never talk about where you go or what you do. I can put two and two together. And when Billy and Bethan go off all day or all night with you, what should I think you're up to?"

"Why have you never said anything before?"

"For what purpose? You would probably have denied it. In a way, I'd rather you didn't tell me in as many words. Just as my Gareth knows about us, but we never talk about it. I try not to be too obvious. I love him. He's a good man, and he loves our two boys, although he probably realises they're not his. Never you mind whose they are either. Sometimes it's best to not know. You probably realise that I've got other lovers just as I know you've got other women. Don't lie! I know. But let's not talk about them. We enjoy being together when we can, and I'm glad you're looking after Billy and Bethan. Well, in your own way. If they're going to be criminals, I'd rather they were good ones."

"You are an amazing woman."

"Yes!"

A little later, Billy and Bethan managed to see Megan in private to tell her about their illegal activities and the reason for them. She was fascinated and said she would love to join them on their escapades. She wanted to help them get their father out of gaol, but she admitted she would like the adventure. As they left, she thought it a shame Billy did not have a woman. She had had worse men.

Highwaypersons: Debts and Duties *by Geoffrey Monmouth*

Chapter 9

July 1714

It was almost a whole year since the siblings had taken to crime, when Gareth came into the inn and said to Billy, "There's a lady asking for you. She's got a manservant with her. She says she wants to talk to you alone." While Billy was wondering what to do, Gareth said, "Oh, here she is now." as a lady dressed in smart clothes entered. It was Lewis Pryce's daughter. The servant was Evans who had accompanied her on her last visit. Billy and Bethan had hoped it was her last visit.

Billy said, "There is nowhere available for a private conversation at present, but anyway, I find it hard to imagine anything we could have to say to each other, apart from that which we said when last we met. I am sure you will recall that conversation."

"I am not surprised to discover that your imagination is somewhat limited. What I have to say is for your ears only, and I assure you that you will not have heard it before."

Immediately, a small party came out of one of the back rooms. Billy had no excuse. He and Helen went in. "To what do I owe this… visit?" Billy asked. "I do not want to presume that it is going to be a pleasure."

"I need your help."

"Can you please repeat that? I thought for a moment you said you needed my help." He chuckled.

77

"That is what I said. Circumstances have arisen which make it necessary for me to seek the services of someone like you."

"An ostler?"

"A disgusting, crafty, dishonest, despicable, immoral scoundrel! And you are the only one it has so far been my lot to encounter!"

"I am sure there must be others if you gave it some thought."

"None to equal you in the qualities I have mentioned."

"Perhaps you should tell me what kind of work you have in mind. Robbing a coach?"

"I leave the details to you. What I want is to recover my father's letters."

"Please stop wasting your time, and mine. I really do not have them, nor do I have any idea who has."

"But I do!"

"Ah! Now I am beginning to see. You want me to steal them from this other person?"

"Exactly! You see, you can be quite clever when you try."

"Who is it and how do you know?"

"Rhodri Jones, the MP for Cardiff."

"You'd better have proof before you start making allegations about a man like him."

"That's just it. I don't have proof, but I'm pretty sure it's him. That's why I need you."

"To do what? Hold up his coach and ask him to hand over all the letters he's got, especially any addressed to your father?"

"How you go about it is up to you. I suppose you know lots of ways of robbing people. I just want you to get them back."

"Why are you so sure it's him?"

"Well, he used to be a friend of my father's. In fact, Father introduced us many years ago when I first visited London. Some people thought we would have been a good match, but a woman whom I considered a rival, Henrietta Russell, became his wife. I believe they have been very happy. In those days, Rhodri was friends with my Kenny too, but he seems to have changed over the years. He seems more devious."

"What's that got to do with these letters?"

"Well, my father and Rhodri are in the same group or 'connection' in Parliament. The Tories. They see a lot of each other. Father has him to dinner quite often, but Rhodri seems to be in some smaller clique within the Tories, and he's been trying to get my father to join them. At first it was just gentle persuasion, but lately it's become more serious. He's started telling my father which way to vote in divisions in the House. I've started to think there's something sinister going on. He may be trying to make Father do something wrong. Illegal I mean. I don't know. Ordinarily Father doesn't let anyone tell him what to do or say. This man must have some kind of power over him. All I can think of is those letters."

Billy had taken the precaution of taking a bottle of brandy and a couple of glasses to the room. He poured.

He had no desire to get involved in politics and could see no easy way of stealing the letters even if he wanted to. He did not know what he would be looking for or where to start. He asked, "What does your husband think of all this? I take it he has returned from the Netherlands by now."

"He is dead. Killed about the time you were robbing us. In fact, those pieces of jewellery you took were the last things he gave me. Our children and I are left with little but his memory."

"You have not mentioned your children until now. How old are they?"

"Kenneth is twelve, Lewis six and David two. They are living in my parents' home in Cardiganshire. I see you look surprised. I did make several visits to Kenny during quieter phases of the War, I am glad to say."

"Did your husband not leave you all his wealth?" "He managed to spend it before he died. He borrowed a substantial amount from my father last year. I haven't yet worked out where it all went. For years he was trying to rebuild his family home, Castell Coch. It was abandoned in the Civil War and fell into disrepair. He spent money on some architect, an Englishman called Horace Gray, who told him it needed partially demolishing, as it wasn't safe. Then they drew up plans together. This architect was supposed to be in charge of the rebuilding works, but Kenny said that, every time he went to see it after the demolition, nothing much had been done. Gray did manage to dig out a few places where he said new foundations were needed, but he never seemed to get anything rebuilt above ground level. They had hoped to re-use a lot of the original stone after the demolition, but Kenny found that people kept stealing stone and other materials from the site. Gray seemed to do nothing about it. When Kenny went away to the War, he left me in charge, but every time I visited it, I could see hardly any progress had been made. The one thing Gray was good at was producing bills. I agreed to pay them otherwise he would probably have walked away. Once people hear you don't pay your bills they don't want to work for you."

"Wouldn't people understand if you said that his work did not justify the cost?"

"It would be hard to prove that he wasn't entitled to the money. The last thing we would have wanted was to have to pay a lot of lawyers on top of everything else." She paused and concentrated on drinking her brandy. Billy thought she had finished her story, but then she began again.

"After several years I went out to the Netherlands to see Kenny. It was a happy time." Billy wondered what this had to do with anything. He wanted to get the conversation onto a more relevant topic. Or to end it.

"We discussed money and the building project. We agreed we had to pay what we apparently owed Gray and then stop the whole scheme before it cost us any more. Kenny said he had had a lot of expense over there. I never quite knew what. When I was there, he didn't seem to be living extravagantly. Perhaps he was gambling, but he never used to. I had to borrow from my father to pay the last of Gray's bills, as our bank said we had no money left. The rents we get from our lands are nearly all going to repay my father, as well as meeting the taxes and other costs we have to pay as landowners."

Billy thought it strange that a man of his class could lose all his wealth so easily, but he had heard of rich men losing their fortunes, usually through gambling. Otherwise, he was as surprised as she was. Not that it was his problem. He did, however, worry about his chances of getting paid, if he did recover the letters, but it hardly mattered, as he could see no way of doing so. He topped up the brandy again. Then he thought of another question.

"Did the fighting break out again? Last I heard, nothing much was going on over there. Of course, you can get killed in the most minor of skirmishes."

"No! That's what I find so annoying. He was killed in a duel. It was actually after the Peace was signed. I can't even find out what it was about. He must have picked the wrong man to challenge, or perhaps he accepted someone else's challenge. I don't even know that. But he was a very good swordsman. I suppose there's always someone better."

"Or luckier, perhaps." said Billy, beginning to feel some compassion for this annoying woman. Then he added, "Of course, in the end, whether you're killed by the enemy or in some personal quarrel, it makes little difference."

She coughed, and asked for more brandy, before saying, "You're wrong there, in this case, anyway. Because he wasn't killed in action, I can't have an Army Widow's Pension. Apparently, if he had survived the duel, he wouldn't have had an honourable discharge, as it's such a serious crime."

82

Billy knew that duelling was against Army Regulations even though it was not illegal in English Law. It was often overlooked, but if your case was being dealt with by a pedant, there was nothing to be done. He said, "I think you have been treated a little harshly. Has your father no influence in the Army?"

"I thought he had. One of Rhodri Jones's friends is a Major Boyle. He's one of his 'connections' I think. He was one of the people who ran the Army from London. I think he still does. He said he would sort it all out for us, but then said there was nothing he could do."

She said, "As if it wasn't bad enough, I couldn't even hold a funeral. They buried him over there somewhere. I don't know where. For a long time I couldn't find out anything, and eventually the letter Father got in response to his enquiries was most vague and unhelpful."

Billy knew about vague, unhelpful replies from the Army. He found himself warming towards this woman now she seemed vulnerable rather than arrogant. Feeling a little more compassion for this woman did not mean he wanted to get involved in her problems. He was however weakening. He said, "Well, all right. I don't know how I can help, but I'll do my best. Let me think about it. If I can think of a way to get your letters back, I'll try. Do you know where this Rhodri Jones lives?" She handed him a piece of paper on which was written the address. She had come prepared.

"How shall I find you if I have any news?"

"I thought you were good at that sort of thing. Try St Fagans Castle. Mr and Mrs Jenkins will probably know

83

where I am if I'm not with them. But they won't be at home after tomorrow: for the next few weeks they'll be in London."

"Could I leave a message with their servants?"

"No. They'll close the house. Those servants that aren't going with them will be back on their farms on the estate. If I don't hear from you, I'll find you."

She got up. She was definitely unsteady on her feet. She fell against Billy and giggled. It was too late for her to be riding to St Fagans in her inebriated condition. Billy found Bethan who asked Anne, the innkeeper's wife, if there were any vacant rooms. She laughed and said, "You want a whole room? Most people have to share. Let me see if there's anything suitable." There was not. Helen said she could manage to ride, but Bethan came to the rescue, saying, "There's room in my bed if you like." Her offer was accepted with some reluctance. Evans had to share with a group of travellers.

That night Bethan and Helen had a strange sort of conversation, partly no doubt due to the brandy. Helen was soft, tearful and grateful a lot of the time, but every now and then her belligerence would come through. They giggled as they undressed, comparing their figures. Helen was a real beauty, Bethan had to admit. Only to herself, of course. Helen assumed Bethan was Billy's mistress. She did not enlighten her. As they lay in bed, Bethan did answer some of her questions about him, but left her in the dark about many things. Helen talked a lot about her late husband whom she obviously loved and revered, and a little about her brothers and their wives about whom she was far less complimentary. Finally, they fell asleep.

84

Bethan dreamt about her Henry. She awoke with tears in her eyes. Then she heard Helen sobbing. She could guess who had been in her dreams.

She managed to get back to sleep until dawn.

In the morning Evans and his mistress rode out early towards St Fagans.

Bethan said to Billy, "Well that was interesting. She's a funny one. One minute she's calling you all sorts of things. 'Scoundrel' and 'blackguard' were about the most polite. Then she goes and says what a good man you are. I won't tell you all she said about that, or it might go to your head. Of course, I had to act dumb, so she wouldn't guess that I'd helped you to rob that coach. I think she must have really loved her husband. I do feel sorry for her, to be honest. But she's not half worried about those letters, I couldn't find out what she thinks is in them. Do you know?"

"I wish I did. It would help me to find them."

"Are you really going to try?"

"This morning I woke up with a bit of a headache and some regrets about making rash promises, but I do intend to do what I can."

"I think it's going to be a big waste of time, but I'll give you a hand if you like."

"Thanks. I could do with any help I can get. You can start by thinking up some ideas as to how we might begin."

"We could break into this man's house and look around. What if he keeps the letters with all his other ones?" Billy had no better idea.

85

They visited the house openly in daylight, pretending to be looking for another Rhodri Jones. They soon saw that it was going to be a challenge. It was big compared with a poor man's house, but nothing like as big as a castle or mansion. That meant that any noise would probably be heard by someone, unless the house was completely empty, whereas in some big house you could be all alone in one wing whilst the family and the servants were all in another. There also seemed to be enough servants coming and going for it to be unlikely that the house would ever be left totally empty. It was in good repair, meaning all the doors and windows probably shut properly.

Back at the inn, they saw John. They talked over the problem of the letters with him. He had instantly guessed that they were planning something. Perhaps that is an optimistic way of putting it. They had not progressed to the stage where they could actually plan anything, but his suspicions were entirely justified.

John said, "If I wanted to do something such as you are proposing, which I most certainly would not, I would try asking about this MP in the Mermaid or any other places where he might be known. You'd have to be careful not to arouse suspicion, but I've often got information out of people without them realising."

They agreed it would not hurt to try. John said he would visit one or two inns in the few days before he was to leave Cardiff again for a while. The other two would ask at the Mermaid. First, however, the three of them were to pay a visit to St Fagans.

Chapter 10

July 1714

A few weeks after the visit to St Fagans, while Billy was working in the stables at the Coach and Horses, a coach arrived. As it came to a halt, a servant jumped down and opened the door. A young man jumped out, nearly knocking him over. Billy remembered a young man falling in the mud when they had robbed their first coach. This was that man. James Pryce. A young lady appeared at the door and he lifted her down, swinging her round as people often do with a child. She was in fact quite small. She was the one who had flirted with Billy as he had robbed her. While Billy helped the coachman unharness the horses, he hoped neither of them recognised him. They never looked at Billy as they went into the inn.

While they were waiting for their food, John came in. He ordered some wine. Then he turned to the young couple asking if they had had a pleasant journey. He went on to recommend the Hock as a particularly good specimen. The lady smiled at him and thanked him for his advice. Her husband glared at John, saying he did not care for Hock. He preferred French wines. John replied diplomatically, but it seemed to have the effect of further antagonising the younger man, whilst amusing the lady. The husband ordered some Bordeaux wine. He then scolded his wife for flirting. She was unrepentant, saying he was imagining it. As soon as the wine arrived, they both began consuming it enthusiastically. They became

87

louder and more aggressive. He accused her of being over friendly towards every man she saw. She said it was his own fault for ignoring her whenever she was not making him jealous.

When they had finished their meal, he said he was hoping for a game of cards and found a few gentlemen who were interested. They included John, the earlier unpleasantness seemingly forgotten. The lady found herself abandoned. She sat and read a book for a while. When she reminded her husband it was time to be going, if they wanted to reach St Fagans before dark, he said they were staying at the inn for the night. He had already secured a room. At that she flew into a rage, saying he could stay if he liked but she was going. He said he would not permit it, and sent for the coachman, whom he loudly instructed that they were all staying the night. He was on no account to take the lady anywhere until he, her husband, was ready. She went out of the inn in a huff and asked Billy if she could hire a horse and carriage to drive home. He said he would talk to the innkeeper. She sat on a step and started to cry.

Meanwhile, her husband, James, was drinking. The card game was over. His companions had disappeared except for John, who was always good at keeping sober enough even when he had had a lot to drink. The younger man did not seem to share that characteristic. He was moving towards unconsciousness. After a few more drinks, he was incapable of standing. John got some of the servants to put him to bed. Bethan went to inform his wife. She could not find her. Nor could she find Billy. A worrying thought occurred to her. She climbed a ladder leading to the hayloft and crept along until there was only a thin wooden partition between her and Billy's room. She could hear things. Everything she heard worried her. She wanted to burst into the room and shout, "Stop, you fool! You're asking for trouble." but she did not. She kept listening and worrying.

"I hate my husband. He's such a fool. Yet he tries to treat me like a child. He tries to be a tyrant. He hasn't got the strength to be one. He's so weak. He's always antagonising other men, but never stands up to them. He's pathetic." Billy made some soothing sounds. She went on again, "We've been visiting my sister and her husband My husband accused me of flirting with my brother-in-law. Then, when I was upset, my father-in-law tried to comfort me and the fool even accused me of trying to seduce the old man. I wish I had. At least he's got something about him. So have you!" Things went quiet for a minute or two. Then for another. And another. Bethan gave up and went to bed and worried.

In the morning, the couple came down to breakfast together. He looked the worse for wear. She looked radiant. They seemed quite friendly towards each other as they went to their coach. He helped her up the step in a pleasant, if somewhat showy, manner.

Bethan said, "You fool, Billy! That girl was using you to get back at her husband. You should've seen her flirting with John earlier. And the way she antagonised her husband. She's not as sweet and helpless as you seem to think. If he'd caught you there'd have been trouble. Would she have been worth it? Don't answer that. Just think about what I said."

"I just felt sorry for her."

"Why? Can't you see that she's trouble? There are better women to spend your sympathy on."

They were rather frosty towards each other for the rest of the day, but gradually things went back to normal. Neither of them had any idea how much trouble that couple would cause.

Over the next few weeks, Billy and Bethan paid several visits to the Mermaid. They discovered that Rhodri Jones was not a frequent visitor to that establishment, so most of what they heard about him was gossip, and none of it of much use. They enjoyed playing cards with most of the merchants. They managed to win and lose roughly equal amounts most times. They were careful not to lose too much. Billy said it was frustrating to have to refrain from cheating, but they needed a reputation for honesty if they were to gain people's confidence to enable them to succeed in a worthwhile fraud.

They convinced everyone they were truly sorry to hear that St Fagans Castle had been robbed. They had to listen sympathetically while several people talked about robberies they had suffered. They had to appear to agree when some made suggestions as to how such crimes should be punished, and even when they expressed ludicrous opinions as to how the authorities should go about catching the culprits. The names they used seldom included "culprits", but everyone knew what they meant. Billy and Bethan often had difficulty in refraining from laughter, or else had to pretend to be laughing with the others at the thought of bringing the criminals to justice.

Early August 1714

One day, Richard Jenkins came in looking very excited. "Have you heard?" he shouted. "What?" called out several others.

"The Town Crier's been announcing that the Queen has died!"

Reactions varied, but everyone knew she was old and there had been reports that her health was not good.

Richard continued, "The Crier also said that they have made George of Hanover our new King." The main response was a chorus of questions.

"Who have?" "Can they do that?"

"I thought they said some other woman was to be Queen."

"Yes. Empress Dorothea or something?"

"Who on earth is George of Hanover?"

"What or where is Hanover?"

However, there were several know-alls in the inn.

"I knew she hadn't long to go."

"Years ago Parliament made the Electress Dorothea – not Empress you fool! – Anne's heir. When she died a couple of months ago, her son George stepped into her shoes. It's no surprise."

"What's an electress?"

"It's the female of an elector! The old girl was an electress, but George is an elector."

"I'm an elector. Does that mean I'm his equal?"

"No. You only elect your Member of Parliament. George is one of a handful of German nobility who elect the Holy Roman Emperor."

"Is Hanover in Germany?"

"Is it part of the Holy Roman Empire?"

"Yes, of course it is or they wouldn't have its ruler as one of the electors, would they? Do keep up!"

"Does that mean Britain's going to be in the Empire?"

"No! It means Hanover's going to be part of Britain."

"No, it doesn't! They'll still be two countries, but George will be head of both."

"If Hanover's just a city, is this George just the Lord Mayor or something and now he's jumped right up to being King?"

"It's more than one city. Hanover is the capital of a small country containing several towns and cities. It's quite important in Germany, in a way."

"Hanover was part of the Alliance against France during the War. They say George got on all right with Marlborough and most of the other generals. He seems all right."

"I've never heard of him."

"Do you fancy having a German for King?" "Well we've had a Dutchman and a Scotchman. Why not a German?"

"He can't be worse than old James the Second."

Billy and Bethan sat quietly sipping their glasses of Hock...from Germany. They tried to remember what they had heard about George and about Hanover.

Bethan said, "My Henry served alongside certain Hanoverian regiments at one time. The soldiers we met seemed to think highly of the Elector."

Billy said, "I remember General Jones speaking well of him on one occasion. Of course, he was thinking of him as a soldier, not as a king."

They wondered what difference the new monarch would make. After some pointless speculation, they decided that they could only wait and see.

Chapter 11

September 1714

A few weeks later, a small coach arrived drawn by two Welsh cobs. The coachman asked if there were any horses they could hire. He explained that he was driving his master, a Presbyterian minister, to a big conference of nonconformist clergy in London, and his pair were already tired, having come the dozen or so miles from Pontypridd that morning, which was the longest journey they had undertaken for a long time. Gareth agreed that such a long journey as was before them really required at least four fit horses. He spoke to Arthur Jones, who agreed he would hire out his own team of four, provided he could make use of the minister's pair until those were returned. Billy helped his uncle complete the changeover while the minister, his family and their servants were having lunch. Billy then asked Bethan to come to him in the coach house as soon as she had finished clearing away after lunch. When they were alone, he said, "Do you know who that was? It was Abraham Phillips, the minister from Pontypridd."

"You mean the rich one who lent Father a lot of money and insisted on its being repaid when it was due, despite our being about to lose the farm?"

"Yes! That's the one. His idea of Christian charity was a bit different from Uncle Huw's. He tried to help as far as he could and has never been repaid."

"Are you thinking of doing something wicked?"

"I don't think it's wicked to try to help Father. And I think Abraham Phillips deserves to lose some of his wealth."

"Are you thinking of holding up his coach or visiting his home while he's away?"

"I think the empty manse should be easier to rob than a coach full of people. Especially now John has gone away again. I wish we had another pair of hands even to rob an empty house."

"I know who else would like to be involved: Megan!"

Billy rode to the Mermaid and conferred with his cousin. She was thrilled. He promised to collect her around noon the next day, which was market day in Pontypridd.

Billy drove both women and Llewellyn in the dog-cart drawn by Caladin, with Merlin tethered to the back. They wore their loudest clothes and made a point of being seen. So unlike typical criminals. They waited until dark. They had picked a night when there was no moon, so it really was dark. Then Billy and Megan went into a back street and changed into plainer, darker clothes. With a pile of clothing and a couple of bags on the seat, they hoped it would seem that Bethan was not alone, if glimpsed by the light of a lantern as she drove back to the inn. Billy and Megan both rode Merlin to the manse, which was the last house in the road at the far end of town on the way to Treforest. It stood in large enough grounds to make it most unlikely that they would be noticed. They rode around to the back of the house where there were some empty stables and other outbuildings. They dismounted and tied Merlin to a metal ring in the wall of a stable, put there for that purpose. Billy turned towards the house, began to take a step forwards and fell over some solid object, landing with his face and chest on the ground and his legs above him, supported by what felt like a stone block. With Megan's help, he got to his feet. His shins hurt where they had encountered the block, especially his right one. His chest hurt where a pistol had dug into him. He examined this inconvenient object and came to the conclusion that it was a mounting block. That is a set of stone steps which enable riders to mount their horses more easily than from on the ground. A most desirable feature for any stable yard. Yet he wished this one did not have one. They found their way to the back of the house with no more incidents. They then tried two doors which were both locked. Billy tried to pick the lock on one. It took a long time. When he succeeded, he found that the door would still not open. It was apparently bolted on the inside. The other door did not seem to have a keyhole. He supposed that it too was bolted on the inside. They made their way cautiously round the house to the front door. It had an impressive lock, but Billy managed to pick it fairly quickly, and it was not bolted. Once inside he found a candlestick on a small table. He took out a tinderbox from his coat pocket and lit the candle. He did not want to fall over anything else in the dark. He found another candlestick in the first room they entered, so he lit that and gave it to Megan, saying, "I'll take the downstairs rooms while you go upstairs."

He searched the minister's study for valuables. He found only books and papers. He tried the dining room.

The plates were mostly pewter. He could not believe there were no silver ones, but if there were, they must have been hidden. He put the best ones in his saddlebags and went upstairs to see how Megan was faring in the master bedroom. Not much better. Mrs Lloyd must have taken most of her jewels with her. The vanity of some women! They found some in another bedroom. From the clothes in the drawers and the toys in the cupboards, it was obviously the children's room. The jewels were almost certainly cheap.

They were just discussing what to do next, when they heard the sound of a coach drawing up outside the front of the house. Shock, disbelief and fear ran through them. They rushed downstairs as fast as they could. They went into the kitchen and tried to open the back door. It was the one Billy had failed to open before, but he had unlocked it. He had now only to pull back the bolt. He did so, with some difficulty, and found the door would still not open.

There was no time to keep trying. He could hear the front door opening and voices. First, that of a man. Clear and confident, with good diction, typical of a preacher. "Why is this door unlocked? Is someone here? Where's a light? Bryn! Bring me a lantern from the coach. And a gun."

Then a woman's voice. Loud and common, like a servant or a farm girl. "There's no candle in the hall. What's going on? Stay there with the children Bronwen. Keep back!"

Megan tugged at Billy's arm and pointed to another door. They went through it, putting out both

97

candles as they shut it behind them. They tried to feel the walls. They were in a small room with no windows.

Billy whispered, "Any other time, I'd enjoy being shut in a small space with you." "So would I."

Something touched the back of Billy's neck. He nearly jumped out of his skin. He felt behind him. It was hanging by a string. A bird. Probably a pheasant. They were in the larder. They tried to keep still and silent.

Megan could hear Billy's breathing. Or was it her own? The man's voice again. "Come on Charlie, find 'im. Good boy!" Then the sound of paws running about in the hall. A dog. Just what they needed. The paws ran up the stairs. "Good boy! Find 'im. Stay here, Mair. I'll go up. Hold this." Then the sound of heavy feet stamping up the stairs and in and out of all the bedrooms. "Where is he? Go on boy. Find him!" More pattering of paws, then man and dog came back downstairs. "Perhaps they've gone. We'd better look around down here too though." Feet tramped into the study, and the dining room. Then somewhere else. Finally into the kitchen. The two fugitives heard a dog sniffing and scratching at the door to their hiding place. They could see light under the door. Someone had probably brought a lantern into the room. Billy drew a pistol and pointed it at the door. It was still uncocked. He hoped he was not going to need to use it.

The woman's voice. "No! Stupid dog! He's sniffing at the larder. I'll bet he can smell the pheasant. Come away!" They heard the dog go away and come back again. This was not their lucky day.

The man spoke again, "I think he may be telling us something. Is someone in there?" Then in a loud voice that would have served a sergeant on the parade ground, "COME OUT. NOW! OR I'LL SHOOT." Billy did not know if the man had a gun, or if he was willing to use it. Most clergymen dislike violence, but you could not be sure. Billy whispered very, very quietly, "Keep back, Meg. They don't know there's two of us." He knew that he would find the light in the room dazzling after the dark of the larder. He prayed he would not have to shoot a minister.

Billy took a deep breath and opened the door, cocking the pistol as he did so. Megan kept back in the dark of the larder. Billy saw a solidly built man still wearing his hat and coat. He was holding a heavy walking stick as if ready to use it as a club. Beside him was a Welsh Springer Spaniel. Hearing the name Charlie, Billy had rather expected to see a King Charles Spaniel, but he was not one to criticise anyone else for their choice of names for their animals. He said, "Drop the club and get out of my way! Let me go and nobody will get hurt."

The man replied, "Don't be a fool! Drop that gun." Then the woman, over to the right, beyond the table called out, "If you hurt my husband I'll shoot." She was holding a lantern and a small musket of the kind used for shooting birds. How deadly it was depended on what kind of shot you put in it, and how good a shot you were. At that range, anything could be pretty serious and you could hardly miss, even if encumbered with a lantern. Billy could see two children aged about six or seven, in the doorway. Was he going to shoot their father in front of them?

He placed the pistol on the table, saying, "All right! You win. Here. Everything I've taken is in these saddlebags. With that he stepped forwards, slipped the saddlebags off his shoulder and held them out at arm's length, ensuring they were between him and the woman. Then he swung them hard at the man, knocking him off his feet, making him crash into the table, and making his wife jump back. This gave Billy a clear run for the door into the hall. He just hoped the children would not get in the way. He bellowed at them, "Get out of my way!" and charged past them, turning left towards the front door, which he hoped would still be unlocked. He tripped over something. It was softer than a mounting block, But only just. He found himself on his face with his shins on top of the obstacle. Another of his pistols was digging into his hip. He tried to wriggle forwards to free his feet. Then he felt a heavy kick to the thigh. Then another. Now one to the ribs.

The woman's voice. "You disgusting creature, You blackguard! Rob a minister. How low can you get? Have you no thought for God or Man?"

The children joined in, shouting, "Go on, Mamma, give it to him! More! More!"

He thought she sounded like a less sophisticated version of Helen. He pushed himself up onto his hands and knees. She jumped on him and sat astride him, punching the back of his head and his shoulders, all the time keeping up the stream of insults, to the approval of her children. That was when Megan stepped in. She had come out of hiding and crept after them. She tried to pull the other woman away from Billy. With one hand she held her hair, with the other an arm. Billy got to his feet and tried to pull Megan towards him, calling out,

"Come on! Leave her. Let's go!"

At that moment, a hand grabbed Billy's shoulder and a fist connected with his face. He fell, over the obstacle over which he had fallen before. He was to learn later that it was a travelling bag. He could not think why a minister would take bricks with him on his travels, but it felt hard enough to be full of them both times. That was when he lost consciousness.

Chapter 12

Megan was fully conscious as two men and a woman roughly dragged her back into the kitchen, pushed her into a chair and tied her to it, hand and foot, in a sitting position. She watched them drag Billy into the room and leave him lying at full stretch on his back on the floor. She could see and hear that he was breathing. She did not know how hard they had hit him each time, but it mostly looked pretty hard.

After a time, Billy began to come to, at least to some extent. Every part of him hurt. Whenever he tried to move, he winced. He was aware that his shins hurt from the fall over the mounting block. So did his chest and his right elbow. The spaniel sniffed at each of the strangers gently. There was a man sitting in another chair, holding a cudgel and watching suspiciously. He was older than the other man, and even sitting down he looked to be smaller. From his clothes, Megan guessed he was the coachman. Next to him sat a girl of about fourteen, with an infant on her lap. She must have been Bronwen, presumably the maid.

The first man was standing in the middle of the room. He had removed his hat and coat. He held both Billy's best French pistols in his hands. They were not cocked. He twirled them absentmindedly. The boy and girl were sitting on stools at the table. They both saw Billy try to move and said, more or less together, "Look! He's waking up!"

Megan called out to Billy "Are you all right?" He made a feeble attempt at a laugh. He wondered why anyone might have thought he was in any way "all right". What Megan had really meant by "all right" was "not likely to die in the next hour or so".

He heard the other woman's voice from somewhere on the other side of him, raucous as ever, "Don't worry about him. He's got a lot less than he deserves. So 'ave you." The children laughed.

Megan said, "Are you only a Christian on Sundays?"

The other woman stepped past Billy quickly and slapped Megan's face, saying, "Don't you dare throw that at me, you slut! How low can you get? I heard you'd become a whore, but it seems you've become even worse. Robbing honest folk. Even a minister!"

Megan struggled against the ropes, managing to stand up, still tied to the chair, and lunged at her antagonist, butting her in the face. The children called out encouragement to their mother, who butted her in return, pushing her backwards forcing her into a sitting position. The maid looked terrified, clutching the youngest to her. The man pushed himself between them and said,

"All right. That's enough. Stop it and sit down, both of you. Mair, you should set a better example to the children." The coachman never appeared to take his eyes off Billy. He probably thought he was likely to take advantage of the distraction to get up to something. He would have, if it had lasted a bit longer. He still had a trick up his sleeve. Well, not literally, but they would soon see.

He said, "My leg hurts. I think I must have really damaged it. Can I just take a look at it?" There were various grunts and murmurs, which he took to mean assent, so he struggled into a sitting position and reached a right hand into the top of his right boot. He winced. Megan did not know whether it was genuine or if he was just trying to convince everyone that he was in pain. Either was a real possibility. Then he pulled his last pistol out of his boot, cocking it as he did so. He pointed it first at the man, then at the woman, then back to the man. "Now, I've had enough. I'm going, and I'm taking my friend with me. Don't try to stop me. I'm not in a good mood. Untie her. Keep away from the door." He struggled to his feet, keeping his eyes and his pistol on everyone in rapid succession. Nobody moved.

The man said, "Are you really going to shoot me, Gwilym Rhys?"

He was stunned. He and Megan stared at the speaker. "Have you forgotten me? Dai Morgan, your cousin? I'd heard you'd fallen into sin, but I didn't know how far. Megan too! I never thought my own sister would end up like this. Will you now sink even lower and become murderers?"

Billy uncocked and dropped the gun. Then he sank onto the one vacant chair in sight. Not only had he played his last ace and lost, but all the fight had gone out of him. It had not, however, all gone out of Megan. She snapped, "It's all right for you, isn't it? You haven't lost everything. You can afford to be honest. You and her. I thought you could have done better. Why did you let her hook you?"

Mair said, "Dai married me because we love each other. We was all friends once, back when we was kids, down at Ogmore. Remember?"

She was not ready to give up. "Mair Jones! We were never friends. You were always trouble when you were little. I thought we were all well rid of you and your family when we moved to Cowbridge. I knew Dai was making a big mistake when he married you. You were looking for a husband. How did you manage it?"

Mair got up and stepped towards her, saying, "I don't like hitting you while you're tied up, but just you keep going and I will. As if you haven't done enough to deserve it. Now you're insulting my family."

Megan again tried to stand up while tied to the chair and spat out, "Your family! How could I insult them? It's a fact that they were all poor, idle and useless, apart from being liars, cheats and drunks. What could anyone add to that to make it an insult?"

The children called out, "Go on Mam, give her another slap!"

Dai pushed between the two again, saying, "Quiet both of you! Sit down! Mind, you, I've a good mind to untie Meg and let you two get on with it. You had plenty of practice when you were little. I thought you'd both grown up by now, but I must be wrong. Let me tell you, Meg, that Mair did nothing to hook or catch me. I just liked her. No! Loved her. I still do. She's a bit rough, but she's had to be. She's become a real Christian, but seeing you seems to have brought out the worst in her, I'm sorry to say, though it's not surprising, is it? "

As the argument seemed to have slightly abated, Billy took advantage of the opportunity to ask some of the questions that were bothering him. He was trying not to think about other things that should have been bothering him more, such as how long he had before he was to go to the gallows.

He asked, "Meg, did you and Dai not recognise each other?"

"Well, you may remember we were in that dark room and I only came out when I heard the sound of a fight from the hall and went to help you. I ran past Dai who was on the floor, without a look."

Dai interrupted, "I think you did look a bit. You managed to hit me with your saddlebags. They were heavy too. So I was unconscious for a minute, I think."

"Well, yes. Anyway, I didn't see him again until I was tied up in here. It took me a few minutes to recognise him then. Well, I wasn't expecting him to be here, was I?"

One of the next questions ought to have been about the reason for his being there, but Mair, scarcely subdued by her husband's words, joined in again, saying,
"Oh! So it was all right to rob a manse if it wasn't your own brother's?"

"Believe me, if I'd known you were living here I'd have been all the more determined. And I wouldn't have been caught."

Dai spoke again, saying, "Well, no, this isn't our home. What it is, see, the minister here's Abraham Phillips, but he's gone to London with all his family. So he's asked me to look after things while he's away.

106

They've got someone else at Ogmore now, and I'm going to Pembrokeshire soon, where I've been invited to take up a permanent ministry. Well, I hope it'll be permanent. It's a good thing we got here when we did, or it could have looked as if we'd stolen all these things.
That would have been terrible."

Billy found himself in disagreement with him, as to what was a good thing, and what was terrible, but did not take it up. Instead, he said, "If you were laid out on the floor, you must have recovered pretty quickly. You gave me quite a punch. You haven't lost any of your old skill at fighting."

"No! That wasn't me. It was Bryn who hit you."

Bryn, who had been listening but saying nothing, now opened his mouth for the first time that evening, "That's right! After I passed the gun and the lantern to Mrs Morgan, I took the coach round the back. I was looking out in case anyone was trying to get away through there." Billy remembered struggling with the back door. Bryn went on, "I saw just the one horse in the yard, thanks to the lamp on the coach, so I thought it couldn't be a big gang of thieves. I went to go in by the back door but it was still locked, so I went back round to the front and as I came through the door I saw you and the two women fighting, so I gave you my best. Lucky for you, I forgot I had my cudgel in my hand." So, Billy thought, it was his lucky day after all. He had not realised. Bryn then looked as if a thought had just struck him. Billy wished it had been something more tangible than a thought, but there you are. He said, "Oh, dear! I haven't attended to the horses yet. I'd best be getting on with it. Oh yes, Master, should I put this fellow's horse in one of our stables for tonight?"

Dai said, "Yes. Thanks." He waved a hand to dismiss the man. He then turned to the maid, saying, "I think it's time you put the children to bed. There's no need for you all to stay here." This produced a chorus of protests, which he tried to overrule by words and gestures, until Mair joined in on the side of the children, arguing that they would not get to sleep with so much excitement.

Megan said, "Yes! They wouldn't want to miss the fight, if I get out of these bonds."

This caused a renewed burst of protest from the children, to which Mair added, "Mind what you wish for: you might get it."

It took Dai some considerable time and effort to restore calm and to assure the children that they would not be missing anything. He even promised that he would ensure any renewed violence would be postponed until morning.

After Bronwen had taken the children upstairs, Dai asked Billy, "How did it ever come to this? You were a good man once."

Billy and Megan told him. They hardly left out anything. They had nothing better to do and there was no point in lying, or in secrecy. The game definitely seemed to be up. Dai and Mair listened in silence through most of it. When they came towards the end of the tale, Billy explained the reason for choosing this house to rob.

That was when Dai interrupted. He said, "Abraham Phillips is a good man. He is honest and conscientious. He is well thought of by most of his congregation and almost everyone else. He would not have treated Uncle Rhys unfairly or dishonourably. He would not, on the other hand, have let him off a debt . I am sure he would say that if you enter into an agreement of any sort, voluntarily, you must stick to it. He would probably regard letting someone off a debt as being just as bad as claiming money from them that they did not owe him. Do you not see? I dare say that is the way most of the creditors thought, and why they let your father go to gaol. Surely, it is right for Christians to obey the Law? Even if some of Uncle Rhys's creditors have been a little harsh, it does not justify stealing from them. I am appalled at you."

Billy sat in silence. Megan did not. "It's easy for you. You haven't lost your farm or your liberty."

"I don't know whoever said doing right was always easy. It's certainly not in the Bible. We are called to do good to one another, not harm, whatever it costs us."

"Could you be so generous as to let me have a drink of water?" He could. He even fetched a cup for Billy. They considered the situation while they drank. Slowly.

Eventually Billy asked, "What would you have done in my place?"

"I would have prayed and trusted in God to do what was right."

Megan let out a sort of laugh. Or perhaps you should call it a sneer. She was unimpressed.

Billy seemed unsure what to say or think. He thought about it for a minute before responding. He said, "What should I have prayed for? Lots of money to fall from the sky? A change in the law? Or for all the creditors to change their minds and write off the debts?"

"I don't know. Try praying something. Invite God into the situation. Ask Him to help you. Perhaps He will help you to see a better way. I don't know. I'm not God. But I will pray for you."

Billy was touched at his obviously genuine faith and at his love. He could see he really did not want him, Megan, or Father, to suffer, but he believed in the Law: the Law of God and the Law of Man, which in this case amounted to the same thing. Billy knew he was right.

He just did not have his faith.

They all sat in silence for a minute or so. Then Megan said, "Well, all right Dai. What are you going to do now? Send for the Sheriff?"

"I don't know. I think we all need some sleep. I'll pray for God's guidance. I hope I'll know what to do in the morning."

Mair and Megan exchanged hostile glances, but kept quiet. Both were too impressed by Dai's piety and sincerity to argue or exchange any more insults.

Billy and Megan spent an uncomfortable night tied up on the floor in a spare bedroom. They did not get much sleep. They talked at times. They kept going over what went wrong and what might have been. Billy could not help wondering if all that had happened might have been part of God's plan. What was the rest of the plan? He prayed.

Chapter 13

In the morning they were allowed to join the family for breakfast. When Dai said grace, he added a few extra prayers. All highly appropriate.

After they had eaten he said he would let them go. They would, of course, have to hand over everything they had stolen that night. That was easy. It was all in the saddlebags and their pockets.

When they were about to go, Dai put all their pistols on the table. He said, "I suppose I ought to give these back to you. They are yours. But how did you come by them? These two look particularly fine quality. I doubt you could afford such weapons. Did you steal them?"

Billy said, "Strangely enough, I acquired them from a French officer I captured. He was a spy. He realised he would not be allowed to keep them, so he presented them to me. He congratulated me on outwitting him. He was amazed that a mere sergeant could be so clever. I thought I had been lucky, but I accepted the pistols. My colonel was pleased too. To be fair, I had not done anything that remarkable and I'd had a lot of luck."

"As a Christian, I do not believe in luck. It is the Will of God. So His Hand must have been upon you then. It still is, even if you don't know it."

He said he prayed they would give up their sinful ways. He said he would also pray that Billy's father would regain his freedom legitimately. Billy could not see how those prayers would be answered. But then, there were a lot of things he could not see.

Dai gave them back all their pistols and the two sets of saddlebags. Empty. They went out into the stable yard and found that Bryn had taken good care of Merlin. Billy said he was feeling stiff and sore and felt quite glad of the mounting block. He was at once aware of the irony of that remark.

The children came out to watch them leave. They had been silent all through breakfast apart from saying "Amen" at the conclusion of their father's prayers. Now they seemed quite animated again. They called out, "Are you going? Aren't you and Mam going to have a fight first? Dada kept stopping you last night. It's not fair."

Their mother laughed raucously and said, "She's getting off light this time. Sorry to disappoint you. I'd have enjoyed it too. Never mind. I expect we'll all meet again soon. Then we'll see!" Megan climbed up behind Billy and pulled a face at Mair. Then they rode off towards Cardiff.

The road was undulating and in a poor condition for most of the way, and as they were riding double, albeit with empty saddlebags, Billy kept Merlin to a slow pace, varying between his usual sluggish walk and the occasional steady trot until they came to a particularly inviting section. There was a long straight stretch, dipping towards the end, followed by a sharp turn, after which the road began to climb. Billy reminded Megan that it was usually fun to take it at a fast pace. Merlin seemed to agree. He showed his enthusiasm by apparently waking up and starting to pull at the bit. Billy steadied him for a moment and said to Megan, "How would you like a bit of a gallop?"

"Well, if you think Merlin's up to it, I don't mind."

"Then hang on tightly."

She took a firm hold round Billy's waist and pressed her chest against his back. They both rather enjoyed that. Billy managed to keep the horse from going straight into a wild gallop, but let him enjoy a brisk canter. They all enjoyed the run down the hill. Billy knew it was best to avoid trying to slow down on the corner, so he steadied Merlin a bit before it and then pushed him on to a faster pace, leaning slightly into the bend to help him, as did Megan. The ground was quite muddy at the corner, but a Welsh cob could cope with a bit of mud. Somehow there must have been something different this time, a pothole, a stone, or just deeper mud than it looked. Anyway, Merlin stumbled right on the corner, pushed on harder, regained his balance, despite the shifting weight of his two passengers, and came safely onto the uphill stretch. Or so it seemed at first. Then Billy noticed an unevenness in his gait. He allowed him to pull up, which he did as soon as he could.

They both dismounted. As soon as Billy picked up the near front foot he could see what was wrong. A shoe had been almost sucked off in the mud. It was hanging on by one nail. It would have been better if it had come right off. This way it would be a constant impediment to the horse and there was a danger of his cutting himself, if either a nail or the edge of the loose shoe were to catch the other leg as he moved.

113

They had various items in their pockets, including Billy's lock-picking apparatus and their pistols, but neither was carrying a farrier's tools. Billy tried to improvise. Eventually, he managed to break off the one nail, doing only minimal further damage to the hoof. He found it exhausting, due to having to work in a bent over position. He put the shoe in one of the saddlebags. Megan asked why. He explained that when they found a farrier, it would be easy for him to put the shoe back on, using new nails. Otherwise, he would have to make a new shoe. Also, a new one would be thicker than the other three, due to the wear they had had, making the horse slightly uneven, which could lead to discomfort or even lameness. Until he was re-shod, they would have to lead him.

They approached Cardiff from the north, along the appropriately named North Road. Somewhere near the edge of the town there was a forge. It was next door to an inn called The Forge. Billy hoped the farrier would be prepared to replace Merlin's shoe, even though he was not one of his regular clients, and farriers, like men of various trades, can be fussy about that sort of thing. He also hoped he was not going to be too busy. He did not want to have a long wait, when it was not a long job. On the other hand, he thought he would not mind a long wait if there was somewhere to sit down. Something to eat would be welcome, too.

When they got there, the forge was busy. Three horses were tethered, waiting to be shod, and they could hear the farrier working on one inside. Billy left Megan outside, holding Merlin, while he went in to speak to the farrier. He said they could leave Merlin tied up and he would look at him when he had finished all his regulars.

They tethered Merlin and went into the inn. They had no wine, only ale and cider. They chose ale. It was probably the wrong choice. They asked for something to eat. The maid said she would find out if there was anything, as they were a bit early. Billy thought travellers arrived at inns at all times and could always be hungry.

Billy said, "Now we're alone, there's something that's been puzzling me. How did you come to be working as a, well, you know, at the Mermaid? It seems such a big step from the manse at Cowbridge."

Megan said, "I was engaged to Rhion Despenser, the third son of the Squire, Walter Despenser. They are supposed to be descended from the former Lords of Glamorgan. They certainly own more land than anyone else for miles around Cowbridge. It was long after Beth and Henry and you went off to the War. That's when things went wrong. I must have been about nineteen. It was market day in Bridgend and our family went there, like half the population of Cowbridge and folk from a lot of other places. Well, I saw Rhion. We chatted happily for a while. After a bit he asked me to go with him somewhere and led me up a back alley. Then he kissed me. I enjoyed that, but he wanted more. One thing seemed to be leading to another. I began to panic and told him to stop. I was afraid we'd go too far. He was most offended. Said most women would be only too pleased. Said I didn't know how lucky I was. I said some insulting things to him, and ended with saying he should go and find

115

some of those unlucky women and make them grateful. Then I stormed off. I didn't know what to do, but my brother Dai found me. I told him and he agreed I shouldn't have let Rhion have his way, but thought I should be more forgiving. He said I needed to talk things over with him calmly. We'd probably both said things we didn't mean. He always was the diplomat, that one."

The maid came back and said there were some meat pies that should soon be ready soon. They thanked her and said they would have one each.

Megan continued, "When I had calmed down, I went looking for Rhion. I found him up the same alley with another girl. He had taken my advice. She was Mair Jones from Ogmore. Yes! The one who's now my sister-in-law. Always trouble. Fisherman's daughter. We'd had a few rows and fights back when we lived in Ogmore and never got on well whenever we met afterwards. Well, so much for calmness and diplomacy. I went mad. Laid into her good and proper. We never finished the fight. Several people heard the din and came and separated us. After that she ran off. I wanted to get back at him. Well, and her, to be honest. Make him see two can play at his game. Or four I suppose. As I wandered around the market, I saw the Carters. Do you remember them? They were carters. Father and son. Both called John. We used to call the son Little John but he grew into a big lad. Just like Robin Hood's pal. The name stuck and became what Father would call ironic. He was younger than me but looked older. I'd seen how he looked at me. And at a few other girls. That day he was hanging around rather bored. They had a cartload of stuff that wasn't selling. His father had gone off for a drink with some farmers and left him to mind the cart. Well, he called out to me and I stopped, and we chatted. I saw a few other girls looking at him and I felt so jealous. So I started being nice to him. I always was, but that day I was even nicer. We ended up on the cart, behind piles of boxes of stuff they couldn't sell. We did what I'd refused to do with Rhion. I know it sounds stupid, but there you are. I'm not as clear thinking as you or Dai or Bethan. I got carried away." She took a sip of her ale. Then another. She decided she had had better ale. Billy agreed.

Megan resumed her tale, "A couple of days later, Rhion came to see me at home. All apologies and everything. I felt guilty by then and forgave him. So we made it up. Next day he took me out for a walk. He tried his luck again. This time he was lucky. We were both happy and soon all set again to get married. Next thing, I found I was pregnant. I told Mama and she said we'd better get a move on with the wedding. Father was very angry but agreed to pressing the Despensers to agree to an early date for the wedding. He came back from the Big House looking terrible. He said Walter had heard the baby wasn't his son's. Couldn't be. Rhion had denied doing what he had and to make it worse, somebody had told him they'd seen me and Little John on the cart. I don't know how they could. I think they'd seen us talking, and then seen us not there and put two and two together. I said it was Rhion's and denied having gone on the cart with Little John. We never told him about it. There was no point. To be honest, I don't know which one was the father. Anyway, whatever the truth was, it didn't matter. The wedding was off. Mother insisted I had to part with the baby when it was born. Luckily she knew a couple who'd been married for a few years and couldn't have children. They were delighted to bring this one up as theirs. Father made the arrangements. I was in disgrace."

The pies arrived. The crusts were so hard Billy thought they should use them to fill holes in the road. When he did manage to break through his, it broke so suddenly that half of it landed on the floor. He let it stay there. The floor did not look clean.

Megan again resumed her story. "One day, a few months after the baby was born, I saw Rhion again. He was all apologies again and said he dare not admit to his father that he might have been my child's father. We argued. I slapped his face. He slapped mine. Then he apologised again. Then we kissed and made up. One thing led to another. I enjoyed it. He said he could have me as a mistress, but not as a wife. I was not pleased. I told him he was never going to have me again. I went away angry and hoping I was not pregnant again. When I got home I found a young man visiting us. He was Jacob Rogers, a farmer's son and a regular member of our church. Father explained that they had been discussing marriage. I was slow to catch on. He meant he wanted me to marry this man. He was a lot older than me and very boring. I couldn't stand the thought of marrying him. We argued. Father said I should be grateful that any decent man would consider marrying me. I thought we had kept my pregnancy a secret, but it seems there were rumours. Rumours can be powerful things."

By then they had both realised that what was inside the pies was a disappointment. The meat was tough and stringy and the gravy was watery. Billy agreed with Megan that they had had better days.

Then she began again, "It must have been a few months after that, when Dai came to my rescue again. The minister who had replaced Father at Ogmore, William Vaughan, had become ill. It looked like he was not going to recover soon, so Father sent Dai to more or less take over the running of the church. He lived in the manse, with the minister and his wife, so they could advise him if they needed to. I knew that he was quite capable of doing the job. He'd been studying for it all his life." She paused to take another big sip of her ale. Billy had given up on his.

He asked, "How did David's move help you?"

"Well, Dai asked if I could go with him. He said Mrs Vaughan would be too busy looking after her husband and their children to have time for any other duties, like visiting other sick folk or organising social events. I could be very useful. Father was glad to get me out of the house for a bit, I think. Anyway, I went. I enjoyed it most of the time. One thing I hated was seeing Mair Jones again. It was bad enough when she was just around in the village, but after a time, she started getting religious. Well that's what it looked like to most people. She was always at the church or the manse. Or anywhere Dai was. We had a few rows and even the odd fight. Dai was the peacemaker as ever. In the end he married her. I couldn't believe it. The Despensers all came to the wedding. That's when Rhion and I met again. We chatted a bit. He said he'd like to see me again and I agreed. We met several times in secret. By then I knew what to expect. In effect I was his mistress, but not the sort that gets kept in luxury like some I've heard of. Soon I was back in Cowbridge, since Dai didn't need me any more, once he was married, and Mair certainly didn't want me. I still managed to see Rhion at times. This time he did get me pregnant, but we both knew he'd have to deny it. The same couple took the baby. Father was so angry he said I wasn't allowed out of the house unless someone was with me to keep me out of trouble. After a few weeks of that, I was going out of my mind. I decided to run away. When we were all at Bridgend market again, I hid on a farmer's cart until we were out of Bridgend. Then I had a rather long and roundabout journey until I came to Cardiff and after a while found work at the Mermaid. I remembered Father speaking of it in the most disparaging terms, so I was sure he wouldn't go there. Nor any of his friends. By then I had lost hope of being respectable and it was my own fault. At first I was working as a servant, but I got plenty of offers of a different kind of work. After about a year, I could see no prospect of things getting any better, and I saw that the whores made more money than me. The work seemed more interesting too, to be honest. I was soon fond of the place and the girls, mostly. I think I fit in pretty well there, isn't it?"

"Do you ever see Rhion? Or John Carter?" "Yes. They both come to the Mermaid at times. They were both amazed when they first saw me there and said it wasn't fair and I deserved better, but neither had any sensible suggestions. Now we all accept the situation. I charge

Rhion extra when he has my services, but John gets them for nothing. Call me unfair if you like, but that's life."

They had both finished their "refreshments" and they looked forward to getting back to the Coach and Horses. At least the food was usually good and they were treated with some consideration.

Chapter 14

Eventually, Merlin was ready, and they rode him the rest of the way. Billy said he was not sure whether his aches and pains were more noticeable when riding or when walking. As they neared the inn, he said, "I'm looking forward to some decent food and a comfortable bed."

Megan said, "I'm not ready for bed yet. At least not to sleep. I'm ready for a fight or a man!"

"I suppose you could have both. There are some ruffians in the inn most nights. I'm sure one would knock you about a bit, if that's what you want."

"I know. I can think of one or two at the Mermaid who are very rough. Right now I might enjoy it. I'm so mad at some of the things Mair said, and at not having the chance to have a good go at her."

At the inn, they put Merlin in his stall and made sure he was all right. Billy noticed that Caledin was in his stall, so he guessed that Bethan had got back safely, but he wanted to check as soon as he could. Megan went with him, hoping not to be seen before she could change out of men's clothes. Then they went into the inn and found Llewellyn helping Anne clear some tables in one of the private rooms. He said his mother was upstairs, preparing a bath for one of the guests and would not be back for half an hour. They had been a bit worried about Billy and Megan, but Bethan had said you could never be sure how long one of those escapades would take. Billy said he and Megan were hoping to get something to eat as he had not found the fare at the Forge very pleasant or sustaining. They went into the main room.

There were two women sitting talking over a drink. Billy was surprised and concerned as he drew closer and saw that one was Gwyneth and the other was Helen MacKenzie. He was also surprised to see that they seemed surprisingly happy as they chatted. As soon as they saw him they got up and waved to him to come closer. Gwyneth looked relieved, whilst Helen reverted to her usual angry look. Billy could have done without another encounter with her that night. Or any other time, if he was to be honest.

Before anyone else could say anything, Helen snapped, "You are absolutely disgusting! How could you?"

He was wondering what in particular had aroused her fury this time, when Gwyneth pointed at the door to one of the small rooms and said, "You should go into that private room to talk."

He nodded, resignedly. As soon as they got into the little room, Helen snapped at Megan, "What have you come for?"

"Oh! I suppose you want Billy all to yourself, as usual. You can't get enough of him, can you?"

"How dare you! I'm not like you. I thought his doxy was the pretty one. Aren't you too thin for him?"

Megan had had a bad day and was in no mood for bending over backwards to be friendly. She responded sarcastically, "Well, you know what men are like, don't you? They all want a bit of variety at times. You must have found that out by now. You're not a child. Don't be jealous. You can have him for a bit if you want!"

"I don't want him! I wouldn't have this man if you gave him to me as a present. If you gave him to me for Christmas I'd give him back on Boxing Day."

"Yes, perhaps, but I'll bet you'd have worn him out in between."

"How dare you make such an insinuation!"

"Grow up! Neither of us is a virgin, or anything close. We understand each other."

Helen slapped her face, quite hard. She slapped hers. She hoped it was harder. Billy left the room, Megan laughed. Helen tried to run after him but found herself being swung round by one arm. She struggled unsuccessfully to free herself and punched Megan on the chest. She hung on to Helen's arm with one hand and punched her on the shoulder with the other. She kicked Megan on the shin. Megan butted Helen in the face and was surprised when she retaliated immediately in the same way. She punched her in the stomach got another kick on the shin. To save her shin from any more kicks, she grappled with Helen until they fell over and began rolling on the floor. Billy returned with a bottle of brandy and three glasses. He made himself comfortable in the best chair in the room, first placing it in a corner away from the fighting. Helen saw and muttered something insulting about men. Megan laughed. Helen spat in her face. They pulled each other's hair. Their legs became entangled. Megan thought Helen's were remarkably strong for a woman who probably did very little hard work. She tried hugging her with both arms. She winced and gasped. So did Megan. She had forgotten about a bruise on her chest where Mair had punched her particularly hard. Helen twisted Megan's right leg between both of hers. She managed to put pressure on the bruise that was developing where she had been kicked. It hurt a lot. Megan gasped and winced. Helen laughed. Megan tried to roll over on top of her. She rolled back. After a few more rolls, Megan managed to get on top but realised that being on top or underneath made very little difference to the pain in her leg or her chest. Helen sensed victory. She smiled wickedly and increased the pressure on her opponent's leg. She dug her fingers into her side. Megan wriggled. For a moment, Helen eased the pressure on Megan's leg. Megan tried to take advantage of the opportunity to free it, but Helen was too quick. The pressure and the pain returned. Worse than ever. Helen was smiling. Although it went very much against the grain, Megan admitted to herself that she was not going to win. Finally, she admitted to Helen that she had won. Helen got up clearly revelling in her triumph.

Billy came over and helped Megan to her feet. He said, "Bad luck! Now I think you'd better leave us. I suppose I do have to hear what this *lady* has come to say."

Megan was annoyed at having to do what Helen obviously wanted, but on the other hand she did not want to have to stay there with them either. Helen's smugness was unbearable. Megan congratulated her with all the insincerity she could muster and left the room. She saw Llewellyn and begged him to show her the secret passage so she could listen to Billy's conversation with Helen. In the passage she found Bethan. They had to suppress their giggles. Bethan whispered, "Pity you let her beat you. I was really hoping you'd win." Then they were silent so as to concentrate on listening.

Billy was experiencing mixed emotions. He had had a bad day, especially if you included the previous night. Not only did several parts of him still hurt, but he was also still thinking about the things his cousin Dai had said. Yet he could not quite bring himself to give up his new life of crime and trust God to rescue his father from gaol. This conflict had been put into abeyance when Helen had reappeared.

Billy had enjoyed the fight. He was aware that Helen was strong and had a violent side to her. He found her so annoying that he would have been quite happy to see her lose. He knew he would not feel as bad about watching a woman hit her as he had felt when he had got violent with her himself. At the same time, he had been anxious as he wondered about the reason for her visit. Her visits were always unpleasant experiences for him, yet there was something about her that attracted him, although he tried to deny that thought.

Once Megan left, he had no choice but to listen to whatever Helen had to say. The fact that she was so obviously triumphant from winning the fight made her all the more annoying. Billy decided it was time to face her. He said, "Now you have got me all to yourself, perhaps you will tell me what you came here for. Did you just want a little exercise?"

"No, but I do feel better for it. I hope your doxy will show more respect next time we meet." Billy doubted that but said nothing. Helen began repeating her insults, "You are the lowest of the low! I feel soiled by having had any dealings with you. You used me."

"What are you talking about? How have I used you?"

"Just because I told you St Fagans Castle was going to be unoccupied for a while, you took the opportunity to rob it. I feel as if I'm to blame. I suppose I am. For not expecting you to take advantage of me. And, since I have heard nothing from you, I take it that you have not found out anything useful about Rhodri Jones? I ask you to help me against my family's enemies and you do nothing but rob our friends. You really are despicable!"

"Is that why you came here, to make wild accusations? Apart from starting fights, of course. Is there anything else?" He avoided talking about his fruitless efforts at learning about Rhodri Jones. She looked as if she was ready to explode with anger, but just then, Llewellyn came in with the food Billy had ordered when he had gone out during the fight. It consisted of a meat pie each, a plate of bread and cheese and a jug of Burgundy Wine.

Helen waited until they were alone again before going back onto the attack. "Don't try to tell me it was not you who robbed St Fagans Castle. It's too much of a coincidence. And I didn't start the fight, it was that whore."

He interrupted, asking, "Well, are you going to get to the point?"

"Unlike you, it seems, I have found out something about Rhodri Jones. When he last came to see Father, he was complaining that he needed another secretary. He has a lot of correspondence to reply to, like any Member of Parliament, but made the mistake of recruiting a secretary in London. Well, he deals competently enough with most of it, but not when it's in Welsh. In fact, being an MP for Cardiff, Rhodri gets a lot of letters in Welsh. In fact more than you might think. Of course, most people in Wales, if they can read and write, can do so in English as well as, if not better than, in Welsh, but there are a surprising number who seem to insist on corresponding in Welsh to make a point. So Rhodri has to read them and reply to them himself, no matter how trivial their content."

Billy could not see what that had that got to do with him, but she explained, "All you have to do is get one of your more erudite friends to apply for the position. Once there, he will be able to see if he's got Father's letters and find out what's going on. I expect you know a few reprehensible characters who can read and write in Welsh who might be prepared to help us if you offered them money. Am I right?"

"I can think of one straight away."

"There's something else I wanted to tell you. I don't know what to make of it. Perhaps your devious mind will understand. My father has tried again to find out what happened to my Kenneth. He wrote another letter to the Horse Guards. Another friend of his, Sir William Wyndham, somehow found out and told him he would be well advised to give up. It makes me suspicious that there's something someone doesn't want us to find out."

"I agree it seems peculiar. I'll try to think how I can find out more. But I can't promise."

"I suppose that's the best I can hope for. I also would like to hope you won't rob any more of my friends, but that could be too much to hope, when dealing with your sort."

As soon as she left, Bethan and Megan came in through the hidden door. The three of them spent some time going over what Helen had said, as well as the events of the previous two days. Both women asked why Billy was even thinking of trying to do what Helen had asked.

He said, "I don't really know. Perhaps I want to do something for her or her father, to make up for robbing them. Obviously, I hope I can get him to release Father from his debts. Perhaps it's something to do with what Dai said yesterday. Also there's something Helen said that's been bothering me. I can't see why there's such great secrecy over her husband's death. The Army seems to be hiding something."

Bethan said, "I think I understand. Annoying as she is, I do sympathise with her a bit about losing her husband more than about being robbed. But you need to be careful. She's the dangerous sort."

It was very late. Megan said, "I don't see any point in going to the Mermaid now. Can I stay here tonight?"

Billy said, "I'll ask if there are any rooms free." Megan looked surprised and disappointed.

Bethan said, "You fool! Can't you take a hint?" Billy looked at his cousin as if a curtain had just been pulled back in his mind. "Oh! Sorry. Well, I'd love to share my bed with you if that's what you mean. I didn't know... I mean... are you sure? Don't you get enough of that at the Mermaid? I thought you'd ...never mind."
The last remark was a response to a kick from his sister.

In spite of what she had said, Megan was experiencing mixed emotions. Ever since her unexpected reunion with her brother, she had thought about what he had said. She also thought of his generosity in letting her and Billy go. She wondered if they really were right to keep on robbing people. Was it ever right? Then she thought about the sin of fornication. The sin she committed every day to earn her living. Such thoughts had come and gone during the journey back to Cardiff and since arriving at the inn. She had kept brushing them aside. Now she thought about fornication with Billy. She wondered whether the fact that she did not intend to take money from him made it better or worse. It hardly mattered unless she was going to change her life entirely. Dai had said she should pray and leave the rest up to God. Whatever he said, that was easier said than done. At least it was, when you were as deeply committed to sinning as she was. She made a conscious effort to push all these thoughts out of her mind and enjoy the rest of the night.

In the morning the three of them had another meeting in a small room leading from the kitchen, where they had breakfast with some of the other servants at the inn. Bethan said, "Are you still determined to do what that woman wants?"

"I think I'm going to try. Remember that Lewis Pryce has offered to pay generously for those letters. Apart from that, I don't see why it would hurt to try to find out about Kenny MacKenzie's death if we can. I'm just asking if you've any ideas as to how to do it. If he'd been in the Artillery or the Glamorgans, I'd know where to start. I could ask a few of my old comrades. The thing is, I don't know any of the Scots Borderers. Anyway they're all in Scotland!"

Bethan said, "Well, you must know some. And I know they don't all live in Scotland."

"All right. Let me think. I did meet a few of their officers, but I don't know where they are now, though."

They paused and thought for a moment. Billy noticed a half-empty bottle of gin under a table. He got up and brought it to their table. On the way he collected three glasses from a cupboard. They were different sizes but he managed to share out the drink into approximately equal amounts. After taking a sip, Bethan asked, "Did you ever meet Captain MacNichol? He seemed to know everyone and all their business. He was quite friendly with my Henry at one time. I think he was liaising with the Borderers, officially, on behalf of his colonel."

Billy said, "All right. So this fellow knew everyone's business and would probably know something about MacKenzie's death, but where is he now?"

"Chepstow."

"How do you know that? And do you know where in Chepstow?"

"He said his father was warden of Chepstow Castle. It kept changing hands during the Civil War and then was abandoned. Bits of it belong to the tenants, but the MacNichols were put in charge of the main building and they collect the rents and so on."

"I expect I met him sometime, but I don't think I knew him well enough to just turn up and ask a lot of questions."

"You must remember him. We were both at Malplaquet, weren't we? Well, after that our side took the town of Mons. This Captain MacNichol was in charge of setting up the garrison and trying to bring a bit of order to the chaos. You must have had some dealings with him. I went to see him to ask for his help in finding my Henry."

"That was not a job for a company commander. More like a senior staff officer."

"I think he was by then. I think he was a major on General Jones's staff. A little man, but not one you would forget. Well not one anyone else would forget."

"Oh! Now I remember, but I thought that was Colonel Campbell?"

"No! Major Campbell was another of General Jones's staff officers. The quiet one."

"I think I'm beginning to remember, now. I could pay him a visit. He might remember me. No harm in trying."

Megan said, "Well, what about this Rhodri Jones? Are you really going to just go there and ask to be his secretary?"

They were at a loss for a while, but eventually Bethan thought of a solution. She was not sure if she wanted him to do this, but she had to try to help. She said, "Why not go there looking for work of a different kind and see if anyone says anything about needing a secretary? Then you can send someone else for the job, but it would really be yourself in disguise. Of course, you could disguise yourself in the first place and go as you are the second time."

Billy drove Megan to the Mermaid. As she was about to step down from the dog-cart, she turned and kissed him. Passionately. Even after the previous night, it took him by surprise. She said, "Any time you want me to help with a robbery or anything, please say so. I enjoyed the excitement. And any time I can do anything else for you. Unless you prefer Tegwyn?"

"I like her. But you're special. You always were, when we were tiny. And I will be glad of your help again." They kissed again until she finally descended from the vehicle.

As the next day was Sunday, Billy and Bethan went to church for the first time in years. Before, during and after the service they prayed. They prayed for their father and the rest of the family. They prayed for a way out of a life of crime and sin. Billy prayed he would find the truth about Kenny MacKenzie's death. The sermon was embarrassingly appropriate. It was about the slippery slope of sin. It was based on the story of King Saul, a good man who disobeyed God in what seemed like minor things and ended up trying to kill David out of misplaced fear and jealousy. Apparently, one thing tends to lead to another. They thought a lot about Saul and the slippery slope.

Afterwards, Billy said he was feeling guilty about the life of crime he had got himself, Bethan and Megan into. Bethan asked, "Are you thinking of giving it up? What about Dada?"

"Well, I think we might have got nearly enough now to pay off his debts. Perhaps if I can earn some honest money working for this Rhodri Jones, we might not need to do any more robberies. Let's wait and see." Bethan said, "I don't mind waiting and seeing, but while we're waiting, we could try to work out how to rob Howell Hopkins. He's one of Dada's biggest creditors and one of the richest men in Cardiff, but so far we haven't anything like a plan."

"That makes sense. Let's talk to Megan and to John when we can. They might have some ideas. But let's look for those letters and try to find out what happened to Kenny MacKenzie too."

On Monday morning, Billy walked up to Rhodri Jones's back door, knowing his place, dressed as a poor man. A smart middle-aged woman came to the door.

Billy said, "I'm looking for work. Someone said there might be something here. I've worked on a farm, I've been a soldier, and I've been a servant. I don't mind what I do. I need to do something. Please give me a chance."

She looked unsympathetic. She said, "We have all the servants we need here, apart from a housemaid. Do you have a sister?"

"Yes, I do. She'll be pleased when I tell her. We both need work. I'll send her here this afternoon."

Just then Billy heard footsteps and a man's voice called out, "What is it, Olwen?"

"Nothing, Master, just a man looking for work. I've told him we have nothing to offer, but he's going to send his sister later. I'll see if she's suitable for the maid's job."

"Very good. Unless he can read and write in English and Welsh!" He chuckled at the apparent humour of this thought, then he added, with a hint of another laugh, "Ask if he knows much Latin too!"

Billy replied, before the woman had a chance to relay the message, "I'm afraid I'm just a poor farm lad, but I do know a gentleman who is seeking employment. He's fallen out with his family and needs to support himself. Is there really any work here for someone like that?"

The woman turned round and began to speak, but her master appeared immediately behind her and addressed Billy directly, saying, "I do indeed have need of a secretary. If this gentleman is available, please send him here as soon as he can come, but not too soon, as I have some important meetings this week. Tell him to come on Friday."

"Thank you, Sir. I'm certain the gentleman I'm thinking of will be here Friday. So will my sister. You're very kind."

Chapter 15

To make the most of the next few days, they decided to visit Major MacNichol. Billy set out on Merlin with his sister on Caledin. They had no need of any disguise or subterfuge. They dressed slightly smarter than their everyday clothes for working in the inn. Chepstow is about twenty miles along the coast to the east of Cardiff on the English border. The road was only slightly undulating and generally in better condition than the ones west of Cardiff, so they reached the castle by midday.

They remembered hearing it was in disrepair, but the sight of it still came as a shock. Some of the walls were broken in places and one of the main buildings seemed to have lost its roof. Thinking of what he had heard about Castell Coch, Billy wondered how many other castles in Wales were falling down.

They rode through the gatehouse unchallenged and saw that there were no gates. They guessed they had been sold or stolen for their wood. They rode on and found a side door to the keep that looked inviting. Billy dismounted and went up some steps to knock on the door. There was a big iron knocker, which made enough noise to ensure it would be heard if there was anyone in any of the rooms in that wing, but it took some continuous loud knocking before anyone came.

The servant who at last opened the door asked Billy his business and listened with undisguised scepticism, as he told him his name and said he was a former soldier acquainted with Major MacNichol, and that he had matters of importance to discuss with him.

He asked him to be more specific, but Billy declined. He had no intention of divulging the details to anyone but the Major. The man instructed him to wait while he enquired if his master was available, shutting the door in Billy's face as if he thought he was a thief. How could he? A few minutes later, a voice called from the door. It was the same servant. They began to approach. He called out, "The master will receive you. Please come with me."

Billy pointed out that the horses needed attending to. The man disappeared again. Several more minutes went by and a lad came to take the horses to the stables. Billy knocked again at the door. This time it was not long before it opened. The servant said, "This way, Sir, Madam." He then led them through a long passage to a door near the far end. It was then his turn to knock. He did so with the practiced skill of a good servant: neither too insistent nor too diffident. A man's voice sounded from in the room. The servant opened the door, preceded the visitors into the room and announced as if to a crowded hall, "Mr William Rhys, and Mrs Henry Tudor!"

It was in fact a small, pleasant room, furnished with a mixture of old and new items. Seated at one side of a stained glass window was Major MacNichol. He stood up and took a pace forwards, extending his hand in welcome. Billy shook the hand and Bethan curtsied. The Major did look familiar to them both. He said, "I must apologise, Sir. I do not recall making your acquaintance previously. What regiment were you in?" Billy told him.

137

Then Bethan reminded him about his trying, unsuccessfully, to help find her husband.

"I regret that I was unsuccessful in reuniting many a woman with her loved one at that time. Sorry! Do sit down. Would you care for some wine?" They would. He turned to the servant who had remained politely in the background and said, "A glass of Beaujolais for us all, please, Meredith." Billy hoped he meant one for each of them. He hated passing a glass around. They took their seats, as Meredith poured the wine and held out the tray for each in turn to take a glass. He then silently left the room.

Major MacNichol said, "Now, will you enlighten me as to what has prompted this visit? You did not give Meredith much detail, as I understand it."

Billy replied, "I am trying to discover what happened to an officer in the Royal Scots Borderers, Lieutenant-Colonel Kenneth MacKenzie. His wife's family, the Pryces, are second and third cousins of ours. You may have heard of her father, Mr Lewis Pryce, the Member of Parliament for Cardiganshire. None of us can find out the circumstances of his death, other than that he was killed in the Spanish Netherlands in a duel just after the end of the War."

"Oh, yes! We were good friends at the beginning of the War: both captains in the First Battalion. He soon went on to become a major and the regiment's adjutant. As the War continued, and they wanted to expand the Army, they created an extra battalion, the Fifth, and he was made its Commanding Officer. Did a jolly good job from all I heard. By then, I had become a staff officer under Major-General Jones. That was why I was put in charge of sorting out the mess after Malplaquet and creating some sort of order in Mons. In my new capacity, I had cause to have many dealings with the Borderers, and so used to see quite a bit of some of my old pals, including Kenny."

"Thank you for making all that a bit clearer, but do you know how he got into a duel?" asked Bethan.

"Not exactly. I can tell you that you are quite wrong about one thing, though. He was not killed in the Spanish Netherlands. He went to London to see some fellow at the Horse Guards to sort out an administrative muddle that had been going on for years. Old Jonesie gave him permission to go, so he could get to the bottom of it. The first time, Kenny's commanding officer, Colonel Murray went too, and I went with them. However, that last time Kenny went by himself. Somehow, he must have got into a row about something while he was there. Odd that. It wasn't like him. He was so good-natured. One reason Jonesie let him go was that he could trust him not to get too worked up with the pen-pushers at the Horse Guards, however frustrating things might get, and I know they can."

They finished the wine. Billy decided they had better stuff at the inn and declined a second glass. He noticed that it had started to rain, so he hoped they could keep the conversation going until it stopped. He asked, "Well, if it was just some administrative mess he had gone to sort out, I can't see how that could have got him into a duel. Did he mention any other business he had to do in London? Did he have any personal enemies at all?" "If he had, I certainly knew nothing about them. Now his wife! That was another story. She was a fiery one. You had to watch your step around her. It was just after Oudenarde that she first appeared. When he first got his own battalion. Surely you'll remember her getting into a duel? The other lady is now my daughterin-law. It was the talk of the camp for weeks. Where were you?"

It suddenly came to Bethan. She did remember the duel. Billy said, "The reason I missed it is quite simple. Just after Oudenarde, I was sent off with a detachment of artillery to help out our German allies. By the time I got back, the Army was on the move again."

"Oh, yes! By Jove, I've just placed you. You're a modest fellow, aren't you? I know about your little foray into the Ardennes. The Germans said you were a real hero. And you never got beyond sergeant? You were doing the work of a staff officer even before that, and if a German general's commendation didn't get you a commission, I don't know what would! Mind you, even having been on the staff of a general, I've never really understood how the minds of the top ranks work, if at all!"

Bethan was fascinated. Billy certainly was a modest fellow. He had never told her about being a hero to the Germans or anyone else. By this time the rain had become much worse and looked to be setting in for the day. They were dreading the ride back to Cardiff and were quite relieved when their host said, "I say, you've a long ride back and I don't know when you last ate. I expect lunch will be ready soon. Would you like to join us?"

"We certainly would be most grateful. Thank you very much."

Meredith reappeared as if by magic. Bethan suspected he had been listening outside the door. She knew about such things. The Major said to him, "Ah, there you are. Good. Please tell Cook we are to be joined by two more for lunch. You might tell my son and Mrs MacNichol too. I think she will be pleased to meet Mr Rhys and his charming sister. He's an interesting fellow."

He turned to them and said, "I wonder whether either of you ever met my son, Iain, or his wife, Catherine. They met out there in the Low Countries. He was a Lieutenant in the Borderers at first, as was her first husband. After he was killed she and my Iain became close and, well, in the end they married."

Meredith returned to say that lunch was ready. They followed him into the next room, which was the dining room. There they met the younger MacNichol and his wife. They both appeared to be aged about thirty. He looked like a younger version of his father but with less character. She was an attractive woman. She was quite slim with a pretty face. Her hair, or possibly a wig, was fair and arranged in the fashionable style. They all sat around the end of a long table.

Lunch was a pleasant, if unimaginative, mutton stew. The Major introduced Billy and Bethan in somewhat flattering terms and briefly outlined the substance of their conversation. His daughter-in-law said she had been fond of Kenny MacKenzie and hoped someone soon discovered the facts behind his demise. They then explained that due to the disrepair of the castle, they were living in only a few of the rooms, but found them more than adequate. The Major's father had gone to

141

live in London, leaving them to take care of his duties in Chepstow.   The   rain   intensified.   Bethan   looked despairingly out of the window. Mrs MacNicol asked, "Are you planning on returning to Cardiff this afternoon?"

"I fear so."

"Is   that   because   you   have   a pressing engagement? Forgive my inquisitiveness, but I do not envy you the journey."

"I suppose everything we planned to do tonight and tomorrow could be done another time."

"Then why not be our guests tonight? We are expecting visitors this evening, and I am sure they would enjoy your company as much as we would, and of course, there are plenty of empty bedrooms." Her husband nodded. She paused and looked out of the window again before adding, "Our friends live less than a mile from here and will be coming in a coach. The weather need not trouble them."

Billy felt sorry for the coachman, but did not expect the poor man's employers to share such feelings. He said, "If we are not causing too much inconvenience, I should be delighted to accept your hospitality." Bethan agreed.

The Major said, "Excellent. I think you will be surprised when you see who our other guests are. I regret, however, that my son and I have some accounts to check this afternoon. You must therefore excuse us if we leave you.   I am sure my daughter-in-law will be able to entertain you for much of the time, but I trust you will excuse her when she has to go to oversee the arrangements for tonight. You are, of course, welcome to use our library. There should be something there that will interest you."

As soon as they had finished lunch, Catherine went off, presumably to give the servants their instructions in preparation for the evening's activities, while her husband led the short distance to the library, where Billy and Bethan soon began investigating the volumes on its shelves and selecting one or two to read. Unfortunately, the light was very poor due to the bad weather. They felt there was a limit to the number of candles they could ask to be lit so early in the afternoon. Therefore, they found reading less pleasurable than they might have. They also found the gloom rather depressing. All that changed after about an hour when Catherine MacNichol came in and sat beside them on a curved window-seat. She could brighten up any room. It helped that she brought a bottle of wine and three glasses. It was the same unpleasant stuff her father-in-law had given them, but they were getting used to it.

After some reminiscing about life in Army camps, they returned to the subject of the duel. Bethan asked whether Catherine had been there long when she first met Helen MacKenzie. She told the whole story.

"I had gone over there at the start. I have relatives in The Hague and I stayed with them when it seemed too dangerous to be with my husband. Oh, yes, I mean, my first husband, another captain in the Borderers, John Robertson. He was killed at Oudenarde. Major MacKenzie was very kind to me, and always a perfect gentleman, although everyone knew he often enjoyed the company of the camp followers. Not only their company, of course. I am sorry to blacken his memory, as he was a good man, but it will help you to understand what happened."

She took another sip of her wine, which she appeared to be enjoying, before recommencing her tale.

"Well, one day I went to visit him in his tent. As I arrived, his orderly said he would see if the Major was available. While I waited, a scantily clad woman with dishevelled hair came out of the tent and told me to go away. She said he had no need for my sort. Well, I was furious. I assumed she was one of the camp followers. So I answered her somewhat impolitely, and the conversation rapidly descended from there. When she announced that she was his wife, I laughed and said I must look naïve if she expected me to believe that. She borrowed a glove and struck me across the face with it, to challenge me to a duel. I accepted. It might sound stupid but I was very angry. It might not seem quite so stupid when I tell you that I come from a long line of swordsmen and swordswomen, and I am rather accomplished at that art. When we arrived at the field we had chosen, I saw we had quite a crowd of spectators, including most of the officers of the regiment who were not on duty."

Catherine stood up to illustrate her story with dramatic gestures.

"We both began cautiously, testing each other, and realised we were evenly matched. She was slightly taller than me and no less agile. I got a cut on the shoulder, which I ignored. After some cautious exchanges, and ineffective ploys, my sword slid along hers until the hilts were pressing against each other. Our faces were only inches apart. We pushed against each other. I felt her leg hook around mine as she tried to trip me. I resisted and twisted slightly to one side to upset her balance. The referee asked, 'Is this a duel or a wrestling match?' and Helen muttered to me, 'Whichever you prefer,' before stepping backwards one pace. The referee held his stick between us and called for us to take our positions, *en garde*, and resume the fight."

Billy had never understood people's obsession with rules in what could often be a fight to the death.

Catherine continued, "After a while I lost my footing dodging one of her strokes and found myself on my back with her sword tickling my throat. I was obliged to lie still. The referee insisted that Helen be acknowledged the winner. At that point Kenny identified himself as her husband. I could hardly believe it. She had only just arrived unexpectedly the evening before our first encounter."

Billy asked, "Did you keep out of her way afterwards?"

"No! We treated each other with civility, as well as respect, from then on. Once one has fought a duel, whatever the outcome, all that went before is forgotten. There is no room for grudges or revenge. I think it is an excellent tradition. When we realised that neither of us was a camp follower, as we had assumed, we both saw a certain humour in the situation." She suddenly noticed how the light was fading, and walked around the room lighting additional candles. The effect was quite pleasant, but it added little to the overall visibility in the room.

Memories of the duel began to come back to Bethan. This helped her to identify Kenny MacKenzie among all the names and faces she had known at that time. She also began to remember Catherine. She had not known her well, but had seen her. She said, "Do forgive me! I was there, but I had no idea that you were one of the duellists, or that Helen MacKenzie was the other. Of course, I had never met her before. Our branch of the family and hers do not see each other often. We come from Glamorgan, not Cardiganshire. That duel was the talk of the Army for ages. Did Helen return to Britain soon afterwards? I don't remember seeing her again. However, the Glamorgans, my husband's regiment, were sent away just after that as part of the big push to Lille. She must have left by the time the Borderers moved up to join them."

"Well, she stayed with her husband only about six weeks. She visited him again a few times over the years, but I don't think those visits were as memorable as the first."

The rain hammered on the windows. Billy and Bethan were glad they had been offered a night's lodging.

Catherine added, "So you see, she was the aggressive one. He was far milder. I could believe she got into another duel rather than him, but you never know. Now, I think we might have met. Didn't you get into a series of fights with one of the camp followers?"

"Yes. Most of them kept away from men whose wives were living in camp with them, but one or two were quite brazen. There was a big Flemish girl who kept trying to seduce Henry. I lost my temper with her once. She said she'd flatten me. I dared her to try. She tried. And she succeeded. That was the first time. She was so smug afterwards. I couldn't let her get away with that. We had a few more fights. I won some and lost some."

Catherine said, "Now I remember. Yes. I saw one. That was you? You had some nerve, going back for more after that first thrashing. You say you didn't know Helen back then. Do you know her well now?"

"We have met!"

"I should think that would have been fun. I could well imagine you two getting into a fight, if not a duel." Bethan said, "I do fence but I've never been in a duel."

"Good. Perhaps we can test each other's skill sometime. I so rarely have anyone to fence with apart from Iain." Then she went off to check on the progress of the arrangements for dinner.

Billy and Bethan shared their recollections of Kenny MacKenzie, now that they had managed to place him. He was quite a character, but not one to look for trouble. He probably left that up to Helen.

Iain MacNichol came in and said, "Sorry I couldn't be with you earlier. Hope Cathy looked after you well. I've just finished going through some accounts with Father. We've got some of the tenants coming for a meeting tomorrow, and we want everything to be in order by then. Bit of a nuisance, but can't be helped."

They sympathised.

He said, "I think I do remember you both. I heard about your husband. I wish I could say something helpful. Always feel lost when I try to talk to families of fellows who got killed or whatever. There's nothing you can say that'll make it any better. I was a lieutenant in Father's regiment at first. Became a captain after Bouchain. Then it all got a bit dull. Ormonde never seemed to get things going, did he?"

They agreed. Bethan was hoping he would not remember her as a camp follower.

Billy said, "Yes. It's funny really. I used to hate all the slaughter and the fear, but I got bored with army life when nothing was happening."

"Hope it turned out all right. You know, my Cathy used to enjoy the excitement. She got bored when it was too quiet. I wouldn't have been surprised if she'd got into another duel."

Billy said, "Do you know the Pryces well?"

"Yes. Father used to see a lot of Lewis Pryce in London. I know James quite well. He helps his father with his administrative stuff. The older brother, also Lewis, spends most of his time in Cardiganshire. I believe he loves it. James and I both prefer London. So do Catherine and James's wife, Jane. He'd like to go into Parliament himself, but he's hardly any money. It can be an expensive business, and his Jane is good at spending money. She's as bad as Cathy. Of course, she thinks I'm mean, but I think 'careful' would be a better word." He laughed.

Bethan was not sure Catherine would have found it funny.

Chapter 16

Before long the other guests arrived and Billy and Bethan went to meet them for a glass of wine before going into dinner. First to arrive were Major-General Sir William Jones and his wife Lady Margaret. The MacNichols were amused at the astonishment all round. The General soon recovered his composure and said, "Shame you're still waiting for your commission. I had hoped even the Horse Guards would see sense by now. I didn't know you two were friends with the MacNichols."

Billy said, "We don't know them very well. We came here to ask them something, and were delighted that they were so hospitable as to invite us to stay for dinner." When the Joneses were admiring some of the tapestries on the wall, Billy whispered to Bethan, "I don't know whether to tell Jonesie why we're here. I'm inclined to wait until we know a bit more before involving him." Bethan agreed.

Before any of them could say much more, the other guests arrived: Mr Perseus de Clare of about Billy's age, and his mother, Lady Caroline de Clare. Major MacNichol introduced everyone fully, presumably to avoid any misunderstandings or social gaffes. "Mr de Clare is from Pembrokeshire, and is descended from some of the first Normans to come to Wales. The family have lands in Pembrokeshire, as well as somewhat nearer to here. He is engaged to be married to the daughter of another nobleman in that region."

Bethan asked Lady de Clare, "Do you come from Pembrokeshire too?"

The Major answered for her, "Lady de Clare is related to the Cavendish family, who have lands and titles in many parts of England."

Billy wondered where Perseus de Clare's father was. On his estates in Pembrokeshire? Why was his wife not with him? He did not understand the ways of the aristocracy.

Sir William said, "I was going to say that this gentleman was intending to join the Army, in fact the Borderers, as is customary in his family, but I believe you have been having second thoughts. Is that correct?"

"Yes. I believe God is calling me into His service. I hope to be ordained into the Church, sometime next year, although many of my friends and family disapprove."

Billy said, "I don't. My uncle and my cousin are both Presbyterian ministers in Wales. My sister and I were fortunate enough to live with them for a few years in our childhood. A most happy time. It is to our uncle that we owe our education."

Sir William said, "By George, I didn't know that. Often wondered. Mr de Clare must be guided by his own conscience, as we all must, but I know plenty of fine officers who hold their faith very dear. So if you have second, no third thoughts, do come to me and I'll sort something out for you."

Billy assumed this meant he would arrange a commission for the young man. Much as he had always liked the General, he noticed that he had not managed to sort anything out for a poor Welsh sergeant, despite a German general's commendation. He decided not to dwell on that thought and spoil his evening.

After the introductions they all joined in conversation ranging over many subjects. As they chatted, Lady de Clare said to Billy, "Do you fence?"

"Not really. Bethan's the one who can use a sword in our family!"

"Very true," commented the General. This fetched a few laughs.

Catherine said, "What's so funny? I'm as good with a sword as most men."

Lady Jones said, "That's true. Yet you're an exception. I would be surprised if Bethan was in the same class."

Bethan was rather annoyed at that, despite being aware that it was probably true. She said, "If I'd known, I'd have brought my sword. Then we could have found out."

Catherine said, "Don't worry about that. We've plenty you can borrow if you like." She led them into another room. It was sparsely furnished, but all around the walls there were weapons of all kinds, as well as shields and banners. A few suits of armour stood in the corners.

Iain said, "If you think you're up to it, pick one and have a go. I'm sure we'd all enjoy watching."

There were murmurs of agreement, but Lady Jones said, "Just a minute! I didn't mean to start anything. I was just remarking."

Bethan said, "Don't worry. Nobody's making me do anything I don't want to. I'd like to find out how good Mrs MacNichol is."

The Major said, "I don't mind letting you two have a little friendly fencing practice before dinner, but do be careful. I don't want any bloodshed or injury."

Iain said, "Just go to the first blood, will you?"

Catherine agreed. Bethan selected a light sword that looked easily handled. Catherine went straight to what was presumably her favourite. The Major stepped into the role of referee.

They began cautiously. Catherine was obviously confident and a more graceful mover than her opponent. Bethan thought that could be her downfall. She tried to appear clumsier than she was. Because she was rather broad in the beam, a lot of people assumed she was a slow mover in every respect. She had surprised a lot of people over the years in many situations. She was cautious and defensive at first. Once, they found their swords sliding down each other's blades until their knuckle guards met. They pushed against each other. Bethan was stronger. Catherine went back a pace. Bethan kept up the pressure without making the mistake of overbalancing. She felt a leg trying to trip her. She resisted. Catherine smiled. Bethan gave a little and immediately pushed back again, making her retreat another pace. She pushed a shoulder into Catherine's chest, making her go back, trying to trip Bethan as she moved forwards. She failed. Then Catherine jumped back and whipped her sword round to take a jab at her opponent. She parried it. They began fencing properly again. Catherine tended to dominate, but their close encounter had shaken her. Bethan kept giving ground and Catherine began to look confident again until her opponent went on the offensive. They again found themselves face to face and knuckle to knuckle. Bethan pushed forwards until their shoulders touched. Catherine twisted her body round. Bethan was pitched over to land on the floor on her side, still holding her sword. Catherine could have cut her almost anywhere on the body before she could get to her feet, and so she did not hurry to make her thrust, but took careful aim. That was her mistake. Bethan flicked her sword backwards from the wrist and caught her on the leg. She did not notice but stroked the tip of her sword across Bethan's left shoulder, drawing a fine line of blood. The Major called out for both to stop. Catherine turned to him looking victorious while Bethan struggled to her feet. Catherine bowed first to him then to her, saying smugly, "First blood! As we agreed."

Bethan surprised her by smiling and nodding while she tried to get her breath back.

The Major said, "Yes, first blood!" and pointed to the scratch on Catherine's leg. She looked down. She looked furious. For a moment it looked as if she was going to continue the fight. Then she smiled at her opponent. They saluted each other with their swords. They curtsied. The others insisted they had their cuts treated before going into dinner.

Everyone agreed the fight had been a close thing and congratulated both swordswomen.

The meal was edible but not a great credit to the cook. However, they served a good wine.

The de Clares wanted to know something of Billy's wartime exploits, and were highly entertained by his accounts, ending with his showing them a gold medal he had been awarded by a German general when on attachment to the Imperial Army, that is the Army of the Holy Roman Empire. Bethan had never heard most of the stories before and knew Billy was prone to understating his own achievements, so was particularly impressed.

Eventually everyone had had enough of the subject and the Major said, "How are you getting on with that artist fellow, Sir William? Has he started yet?"

"Oh, yes. Peter Monamy. I like him although he's from London and from a family of Roundheads. He's been staying with us. Painting Lady Margaret for a couple of hours every day. He's away now seeing another gentleman about a possible commission to paint one of his children. They say he's very good with children. My Margaret hardly counts as a child, but she can be difficult at times, can't you?"

His wife replied, "Yes. I'm amazed myself at how well I've behaved for him. Sitting quietly for all that time every day. I did find it a bit irritating that he spent a lot of time making me sit in different poses, different clothes and in different places, before he made his mind up which version of me he wanted to paint."

Her husband said, "He must be clever to get you to be so obedient!"

"He is good with people, but I think I'm being so cooperative because I really want to have my portrait painted. I've seen one or two paintings of other young ladies. Well, some not-so-young as well. Now I want one too, only better, of course. This fellow's only just beginning to make a name for himself, but I think he'll be famous some day."

Her husband said, "He's had a struggle so far. Had to take some poorer jobs just to keep his hand in. To pay his creditors too. Says he's even had to paint a couple of inn signs, would you believe. Could have been worse. Could have had to paint the inns."

Everyone laughed. Billy thought of the sign at the Mermaid.

Lady de Clare said, "At least you'll end up with something worth having. Portraits are always nice to have. I've heard that some of these new artist fellows have got funny ideas. They say some have started painting buildings. I don't mean painting the woodwork. I mean painting pictures of buildings and even of the countryside round about. Some lord or something's agreed to having his castle painted. I suppose he wants to be able to look at it without having to bother going outside. Lazy devil!" They laughed again.

Iain MacNichol said, "I'm not surprised. These arty types are always looking for something new. Either a new style, new colours or new subjects. There's an old friend of mine, who used to be quite good, I thought. Now he's started painting horses. I even heard he'd painted a cow. Of course, someone could have been joking, but he really does do horses. What next? Trees?"

Sir William said, "I hadn't realised how lucky I was to find this fellow. I think most people would rather look at my Margaret than at a tree or a horse." All the others murmured their agreement. However, Bethan thought she would like to see paintings of trees, horses and buildings, just for a change.

Sir William finished by saying, "Funnily enough, this Monamy fellow says he's branching out into some of those things too. I told him to stick to portraits."

When they went up to their room, Bethan asked Billy if there were a lot more escapades he had not told her about. He said he could hardly give an account of every mission or every military action he had been involved in. Then she said, "That Cathy's a funny one. She's been so friendly, but when we got into that swordfight, she seemed to be taking it seriously. I like her, but I'm a bit wary of her."

Billy replied, "Yes. I can't understand her. Her and Helen are alike. I'm not surprised they got into a duel."

By morning the rain had stopped. As Billy and Bethan left, Catherine came to bid them farewell. She said, "Do call again. We all enjoyed meeting you." Then she whispered, "Any time you fancy another swordfight, or perhaps a wrestling match. We're both fighters."

Chapter 17

October 1714

Billy and Bethan agreed that they were not much further forward in finding out what happened to Kenny MacKenzie. If anything, they were all the more confused. Why had the Army said he was killed abroad if it had happened in London? Why would a man so good natured get into a duel? Anger at an administrative muddle hardly seemed a likely explanation. They agreed that their next move was to find a way into Rhodri Jones's house to look for the mysterious letters. Before doing so they were to visit their father again, as it might be their last chance for a while.

On the Friday, they went to Rhodri Jones's house again. Bethan dressed as a typical maid, as she did every day at the inn. She was to claim to be the widow of a soldier. She would not say he was an officer, as they did not want Rhodri Jones or his other servants to suspect that she was literate. She pretended that her husband and her brother had both served under Billy. He dressed in his best clothes and took on the persona of Captain Gareth Evans, the young gentleman known to the regulars at the Mermaid. He merely had to say that he had made some bad investments and was no longer a man of property. The housekeeper, Olwen Williams, questioned Bethan and agreed to take her on for a trial period, whilst Rhodri himself invited Billy for a chat in his study, resulting in his also becoming an employee in that house.

They both enjoyed working there. Bethan got on well with Mrs Williams, unlike previous maids who had been either incompetent, insubordinate or both. She actually found the work less demanding than at the inn. That was because there were no constant interruptions and unexpected demands, so it was easier to get on with whatever task was before her. They both found themselves living in better accommodation than they had been used to, although Bethan would rather not have had to share a room with Sian, the fifteen-year-old kitchen maid, whose conversation seemed particularly tedious.

Billy and Bethan noticed that the housekeeper shared Rhodri's bed. They later learned that Mr Williams had deserted her, probably for another woman. The cook, on the other hand, seemed happy in her marriage to Rhodri's manservant, Robert Roberts.

Billy found Rhodri a good man to work for. He was clear in his instructions and explanations. He was patient with Billy's questions. He demanded high standards in both the grammar and the content of letters. He also required Billy to make copies of all the letters he wrote, in case any queries arose for which accurate recollection was essential, as was so often the case. Billy would have expected as much from a Member of Parliament. Rhodri's manner towards them and to most other people was pleasant. It was only because of what Helen had said, that they were sceptical and assumed it was an artificial cover to conceal his real character.

He told Billy he was married, but his wife preferred to live in London with their children, as he admitted was also true of himself, but he often had duties in Cardiff. He mentioned that he would soon be going to join her as they were to attend the Coronation of King George, and Parliament would be assembling shortly after that, probably until Christmas, as he was aware that there was a lot of business for Members to enact. He would require Billy's presence in London but Bethan was to stay behind to help look after the Cardiff house.

Billy found it easy to search through Rhodri's office, without arousing suspicion, as a lot of the letters he received referred to previous correspondence, and even where they did not, it was always worth checking. Rhodri complimented him on his thoroughness. For the first two weeks, he found nothing of any relevance to the real purpose for his being there, but then, quite unexpectedly, he came across a letter from a Reverend Joseph Hartley, vicar of Saint Martin-n-the-Fields Church, London. It was addressed to Rhodri Jones at his London address in The Strand. Billy had no idea where either place was.

The letter assured Mr Jones that the late Colonel MacKenzie's remains had been given a Christian burial according to the proper rites of the Church of England, and he was now buried in St Martin's Churchyard. The vicar awaited instructions regarding a headstone, promising Mr Jones that he would ensure the stonemason followed his instructions. He also confirmed that the few personal effects which the deceased had had with him were stored in a safe place in the vestry, also pending further instructions. The writer regretted that the deceased had become so estranged from his family that none of them had attended the burial, but, should any of them feel differently with the passage of time, he, Reverend Hartley, would be happy to receive them and show them the grave. So much for Kenny being buried in the Spanish Netherlands. Billy wondered what his personal effects included. He was determined to find out.

The next day Rhodri received a letter from his wife. He announced to Bethan, "My wife says she is concerned that one of her maids has left and another is somewhat inexperienced. She asks if I could bring a maid with me in addition to my manservant. Mrs Williams has been most satisfied with your services since you have been with us. I would, therefore, be most grateful if you could, even at such short notice, consent to accompanying me and others of this household on our imminent visit to my London residence. Are you able to agree that you will come?"

She could not believe her luck. She wanted to see if Rhodri would take the missing letters to London where she might have a chance to purloin them. She wanted to see if she could learn anything about Kenny MacKenzie's death which might escape Billy. Above all, she wanted to see London. She agreed enthusiastically. She then decided to be bold and take advantage of the good mood Rhodri was in. She said, "I have a son, who is in service as a stableboy in this town. I am a little uneasy at leaving him for so long. Would you by any chance have use for his services too?"

Rhodri agreed as well as suggesting taking Caledin and his own hunter, so they could share some of the burden with his four coachhorses on the long drive. That also meant that both men would have suitable mounts when in London.

Chapter 18

Billy's first impression of London was of size and activity. He tried to remember if it had been like that when he had passed through on his way to and from the Continent. Perhaps it had grown or at least had become busier. Or perhaps he had just not taken it all in before.
It made Cardiff seem like a sleepy little village.

As they drove through the streets, he noticed the contrast between the different buildings. Rhodri explained that a lot of the city had been rebuilt after the Great Fire of 1666. Most of the new buildings were in the new style, which reminded Billy of places he had seen on the Continent. The style was based on logic and symmetry in keeping with the new "enlightened" and "scientific" thinking of the educated classes. The buildings tended to be made of straight lines with doors and windows in proportion. Rhodri said the older ones were in his opinion more typically English. They had often been built in phases and had lots of irregular features. The new ones also tended to be mainly in brick, whereas many older buildings were half-timbered or even made fully of wood.

The newer roads were wider to make room for larger coaches and wagons to pass through them. This reflected the growth of trade and the fact that more people could afford big coaches, unlike the many people who still experienced severe poverty. London was certainly going through a time of change.

The London house was no bigger than the one in Cardiff, but it was more luxurious, due to the more expensive furniture, carpets and other contents. Billy did not spend all his time in the house. He enjoyed going out and seeing some of the sights of London when he accompanied Rhodri on visits, mainly to other Members of Parliament. Bethan, on the other hand, was obliged to be in the house about her duties most of the time. One day, however Billy had a surprise. Rhodri said, "I must ask a favour of you, one which I hope you will not find too burdensome."

"Of course." he replied, "You are always generous to me. You need only ask."

"I have to go away for a week or so. I have to visit a friend in Surrey. I find however that my wife and I have been invited to dinner with some other friends in London during that time. The former requires my presence, as there will be political discussions, whereas the latter is purely social. Mrs Jones has expressed a strong desire to attend the dinner party. The answer would seem to be obvious: that I should go to the country and leave my wife in Town. However, you will doubtless appreciate that an uneven number at dinner is not liked. Some actually consider it to be bad luck. So what I am asking of you is that you stay here while I am away and accompany Mrs Jones to the dinner, and any other functions she wishes to attend. I know you to be capable of conducting yourself appropriately in all circumstances. Additionally, your learning should make you a most acceptable guest in erudite society."

"I am sure it will be no inconvenience. I shall be delighted."

"I am grateful to you. Unfortunately, I am unable to allow my gratitude to relieve you of your other duties. Not only will you need to look after my usual correspondence, but I will doubtless return with some new instructions for you, resulting from matters that will have been discussed in Surrey."

"I am sure I will cope."

"Thank you. Now, when I go away, I shall take the coach. The journey should require only four horses, so you will still have your own grey. You may use the chaise if you wish, as of course will Mrs Jones. I will instruct the servants to regard you as the master in my absence."

"I trust you will enjoy your visit to the countryside and that your political business will be successful." said Billy.

Bethan was pleased for Billy, but also somewhat jealous. However, it was good opportunity to look through Rhodri's correspondence.

The next day Mrs Jones said to Billy, "If you are to accompany me anywhere, I think you should get yourself some new clothes. Yours are probably acceptable in Cardiff, but they do look so provincial, not to mention old-fashioned. I must insist on taking you to my husband's tailor to get something more suitable. In fact, I will say the same to Bethan. I would like her to accompany us to the dinner, as I have no other suitable maid to take, and I like my servants to reflect well upon this household in their appearance as well as their behaviour. I am so pleased with Bethan in every respect that I want to treat her to some new clothes too. She can

163

come with us. I can advise both of you. Please do not object. It will be a pleasure."

Billy had no intention of objecting and knew Bethan would not. So, after they had left Rhodri's tailors, they spent the rest of the day visiting some of the establishments where Mrs Jones bought her clothes. She tactfully directed Bethan to the cheaper dresses, but after seeing her suitably attired as a servant, Billy paid for her to buy some more expensive clothes for other occasions, Mrs Jones also helped her to choose these too. Bethan took care not to appear to be trying to eclipse her employer. She knew she was kind, but rightly guessed that she was as vain as most ladies of her class.

When Billy was next alone with her, Mrs Jones said, "I am beginning to think that you are somewhat attracted to Bethan. I cannot say that I blame you. I am sure many young men are. I am also pretty sure that she is attracted to you. Just be discreet. I promise not to get in your way." He had a good laugh with his sister when he told her. They agreed it would be convenient to encourage the misconception.

Soon it was time for the dinner party. Billy had been afraid he would show his relative ignorance and arouse suspicion, but was rescued by the host, Francis Atterbury, a man who liked the sound of his own voice. All Billy had to do was listen and give voice to agreement with whatever he said, occasionally asking a question, which tended to set him off on another discourse. Billy did not mind, because he found him genuinely interesting. He was the former Dean of Christchurch, Oxford, who had just been appointed Dean of Westminster and Bishop of Rochester. He said those two ecclesiastical posts were always one appointment.

He introduced Billy to his other guests. One of them was Helen MacKenzie. She was being escorted by Charles Butler, a nephew of the Duke of Ormonde, who had replaced Marlborough as commander of the Army in 1712. In fact, it had just been announced that the new King had reinstated Marlborough. That was to prove to be one of the King's best decisions. It probably saved his crown.

Charles was not only well connected socially: he was charming, tall and handsome. Many of the women envied Helen. Her mother was also there. She informed everyone that her husband was unable to be there because he too was at a gathering of his political connection at a country house in Surrey. Mrs Pryce was escorted by an elderly widower who was noted for his knowledge of art. She did not recognise Billy, but her daughter gave him some rather worrying looks and made certain ambiguous remarks, which let Billy and Bethan know they had been recognised, whilst leaving everyone else in ignorance. This clearly amused Helen, who was in any case enjoying the evening, due largely to the attention she was receiving from Charles Butler.

Before dinner, Billy remained in close attendance on Mrs Jones, as expected, letting her do most of the talking. They were served glasses of the wine he had always known as sack, but people in London were beginning to call it sherry after the port of Jerez in southern Spain through which it was imported.

Helen mentioned that Rhodri had been most insistent that her father joined him at the Surrey house party. Billy wondered if there was any way he could speak to her in private without arousing suspicion, as he wanted her to know about the things he had learned concerning her husband's death. He could not think of anything. Billy was sitting between Mrs Pryce and an old lady, who entertained everyone with her witty remarks and amusing recollections of her early life. However, it was Mrs Pryce who gave Billy the shock of the evening. Towards the end of dinner, before the ladies and the gentlemen left the table and gathered in two separate rooms, she said to Billy, in a loud, carrying voice, "I notice that you appear to enjoy my daughter's company." He felt on dangerous ground, so he tried to be tactful.

He replied, "Of course, Madam, what gentleman would not. She is a most attractive and interesting lady."

"I was wondering if you would care to see her on another occasion. I have been worried about her since her dear husband's death. She so lacks male companions."

"But surely, Mr Butler is a most suitable companion, is he not?"

"Indeed Sir. You are quite right. However, Mr Butler tells us that he is soon to travel to France on some errand on behalf of his uncle. He may be gone for some time."

"How unfortunate! Well, if you think my company would be acceptable, I would be delighted to escort your daughter to some other social functions. Do you know what sort of thing she enjoys?" He was tempted to suggest a hanging, but refrained.

"I am aware that she enjoys the theatre. There is a revival of *The Way of the World,* a Restoration comedy by William Congreve, that I always enjoy, at the new Haymarket Theatre. Perhaps you are familiar with it?" "Alas no!" replied Billy, "But if you enjoy it, I'm sure I would. Especially if I had such a lovely companion to share the experience."

"Well, that's settled then. I shall mention it to her as soon as I am able and suggest you send her a note inviting her. Please choose whatever day you wish. Sadly, she has few engagements." She handed him a card with her name and London address printed on it.

The rest of the evening passed pleasantly enough. After dinner, Billy enjoyed cards and more wine with the other men, and had to endure some bad jokes and the smoke of their clay pipes. He wondered what business Ormonde had in France, but heard several people comment that now we were at peace, we were developing trading and other friendly ties with the French. Some said that trend would increase once the old King Louis XIV died, as was considered to be imminent. Since his successor was to be a boy in his teens, his uncle, the Duke of Orleans, would probably become Regent. He was likely to favour peace and cooperation with Britain. That was something to be hoped for anyway.

On the way back to Rhodri's house, Mrs Jones was pleased when Billy told her he was to take Helen MacKenzie to the theatre. She teased him about it in a good-humoured way. She said that she and Helen had known each other from before they were married and that Charles Butler had been a friend of both their husbands in those days. She went on to say that she hoped Rhodri would take her to the play in question when he returned, as she liked Congreave's work.

On the evening in question, Billy drove the chaise, drawn by Caledin, to collect Helen. As soon as they had got away from the house Helen began. "What are you doing in London?" Billy found it difficult to talk as he was having to concentrate on driving, being on unfamiliar roads which were a lot busier than anything Caledin or he had encountered before.

"Bethan and I are both working for Rhodri Jones to please you. He's made us come with him. Anyway, it's a chance to see if the letters are in his London house."

"Have you made any progress?"

Billy merely said, "Steady now! Good boy!"

"Well?" said Helen.

"What?"

"Have you found them?"

He appeared to be ignoring her. She repeated her question.

"No!"

"You are useless! I thought you were a cunning, devious criminal. So far, you've achieved nothing. You just seem to be enjoying yourself. You seem to be very friendly with Mrs Jones while Rhodri's away."

"Go on! Forward! Good boy! Steady now! What? Did you say something?"

At the Haymarket, Billy gave one of a local gang of awaiting boys a few coins to look after the horse and the vehicle until he returned. After the play, they went to a tavern near the theatre, which Mrs. Jones had recommended. They were pleased to find the food as good as she had said. The wine was not. Helen paused in devouring a piece of roast duck to say, "Well, what have you got to tell me? Anything you could possibly call success, apart from your worming your way into favour with Mrs Jones? Poor woman." Billy continued eating for a minute, enjoying his meal and gaining a moment to think.

"Are you jealous of every woman I befriend? Do you know that you're the only one that does not like me? Even your mother seemed to take to me."

"If only she knew! Is that all you have achieved since coming to London? Deceiving innocent women? Have you done anything more useful?"

He told her about the letter from the vicar who had buried her husband. That brought about a sharp change in her manner. She was subdued. She had to make an effort to hold back her tears.

Eventually she composed herself enough to say to Billy, "Could you take me to the church? I would like to see his grave, if nothing else."

"Of course. Can you get away again?"

"Yes. I shall say you are taking me out for a drive in the chaise, so I can show you some of London's many interesting sights, as you are here for the first time."

"Good. Tomorrow I will be busy with several errands for Rhodri. So I will come for you the day after."

"Let us not delay. Come at nine."

Billy asked Henrietta Jones if he could go out in the chaise on the day in question. Of course, she agreed all the more enthusiastically when he asked if he could take Bethan as well.

When the day came, they drove to St Martin's-in-the-Fields. Conveniently, the vicar was there. Billy introduced himself as a second cousin of the late Kenny MacKenzie and Helen as his widow. He described Bethan as a good friend of Helen. Both women succeeded in making it look as if that might have been true. The vicar was happy to show them the grave. The inscription on the headstone read: *Kenneth Alexander MacKenzie 1675–1713.*

After a few minutes at the graveside, they went back into the church. Billy asked if the vicar still had Kenny's personal effects. He said he would gladly hand over the few items he had, but he assumed everything else must have been kept by his regiment at their headquarters in Edinburgh. They followed him into the vestry where he showed them the box in which he had put everything. He then said, "I should warn you that, given the circumstances of the gentleman's death, it might be upsetting for the lady to see the bloodstained coat."

Billy said, "But was he not buried in it?"

"No. He was not buried in his uniform. I understand his friends brought some of his other clothes from his lodgings. It was apparently considered inappropriate for him to be buried in uniform under the circumstances."

Helen burst out, "What was inappropriate about burying an officer in the uniform in which he had served his country for so many years?"

The vicar took a deep breath and said, "Please understand that it was not my decision. I was informed that it was an Army tradition to deny that privilege to anyone killed in a private quarrel. I was not informed of the exact circumstances of the quarrel, nor of the details of how he met his death." That pre-empted Billy's next two questions. The vicar then said, "Oh! Please forgive me. There is something else I should give you." He fumbled in a corner of the room and produced a sword, adding, "This was his also."

Helen said, "I see it has been cleaned."

"Oh, no! This is how it was."

"You mean he fought a duel without getting a drop of blood on his sword?"

"I understood it was a duel with pistols."

"How odd," commented Helen, before sitting in silence.

They examined the sword and its scabbard. A fine specimen, typically Scottish, with a basket handle and a lot of decoration, including a lion's head as its pommel. The blade had been repaired and re-sharpened many times. Billy opened the box and took out a black bicorn hat with a cockade in the regimental colours. Then out came the coat. A typical officer's red coat. It had once been of good quality, but was not new. There were signs of repairs and worn areas. Not the coat of a man given to extravagance. Helen insisted on seeing it. She gasped and said, "He was shot in the back! Look at the bloodstain and the hole."

Billy corrected her. "Please do not be misled. The shot went into him here, at the front, by this little hole. The bigger hole and the greater amount of blood will always be found where the shot comes out. Believe me, I do know."

"Oh, yes. I am aware of your experience in such matters."

The vicar said, "Did you serve with him?"

"Not in the same regiment, but I was in the War."

Helen gasped and looked daggers at Billy. Of course, he could not explain at that moment.

They sat there studying the coat for a long time until the vicar tactfully asked, "Can I be of any further service?"

"No. We are most grateful. We must be going now," replied Billy.

"I am glad at least some of his family have come here. I was sorry to hear he was estranged from you all. We must be grateful to his friend Mr Jones who arranged a Christian funeral and a headstone."

"Yes, indeed. He is a good man." said Helen.

They took their leave and Billy carried the box and the sword to the chaise.

Bethan said, "I think we had better take at least some of the tour of London we had told people about, so I can answer if anyone asks where we have been." Helen agreed and pointed out some of the buildings and other sights as they drove through the City. They stopped for lunch at an inn. Billy put the box in a lockable compartment under the seat of the chaise, but could see no way of making the sword secure, so he wore it, hanging from its sash. They sat in a quiet corner and ordered a fish pie each, as Helen said the place was renowned for them.

Helen said, "I can't believe Kenny would get himself into a duel with pistols. He was a great swordsman, but a hopeless shot."

Billy said, "He was not killed in a duel. He was murdered."

"Surely, if he was shot in the chest, not in the back, his opponent must simply have been a better shot."

"There are other marks around the entry hole in the front. Scorch marks, made by the flames or sparks coming out of the barrel of the gun that killed him."

"That must happen all the time."

"You have to shoot from very close range for that. It could not happen if you were twenty paces apart. Not even twenty very short paces." "Oh my God! Are you sure?"

"Yes."

"I suppose you have killed a lot of men at close and long distances."

"Not as you think. I was in the War, as I said. I saw men killed in lots of ways. I won't forget. Try as I may. As I do. Never again, I hope!."

"Don't you have to do that all the time in your present... er... occupation?"

"No. I rely on skill rather than violence."

They sat in silence, looking down. As they left, Helen said, "Whoever told me those fish pies were good was a liar." The other two agreed. They drove around a few more of London's historic streets before they returned Helen to the house her father rented. On the way she said, "What we now need to know is who killed Kenny."

Billy added, "And why? And I've still got to find those letters."

As they approached the house, she said she knew where she could hide the box, but not the sword. So Billy took the sword. He could pretend he had met someone he knew who had borrowed it and had now returned it.

With the encouragement of Mrs Jones and Mrs Pryce, Billy and Helen saw each other a few more times. They went to another play, *the Country Wife*, by William Wycherly. She showed him a few more interesting parts of London. Bethan usually had to stay and work in Rhodri's house, which was frustrating. They were all frustrated at the lack of progress in their investigations. They had made none since the visit to the church. Billy was usually busy with work for Rhodri. Then Charles Butler returned from France and began paying attention to Helen again. Billy was relieved, because he was finding it awkward to be with her when he had nothing to report. Bethan was also relieved, because she was concerned he would get too involved with the troublesome Helen.

Chapter 19

Christmas 1714

November passed and it was December. People began talking about their plans for Christmas. One day, at breakfast, Rhodri explained that all his household would be returning with him to Cardiff as soon as Parliament rose for the Recess. Henrietta shocked them by casually announcing that the Pryces would be spending Christmas in London but would be visiting them in Cardiff on New Year's Day on their way back to Cardiganshire. Billy just hoped they would not recognise him.

Despite this alarming news, Billy and Bethan enjoyed the journey back to Cardiff due to the company of both Rhodri and his wife. Once back in Cardiff, life was not quite back to normal. Since Rhodri had brought his wife and children with him, Bethan and the other servants had more work, but she found it pleasant to have them all there. Of course, that was not how Olwen regarded it. Billy was kept busy too, as was Rhodri, dealing with all the correspondence which had accumulated. Olwen had ceased forwarding it as Christmas approached, for she knew they would be returning.

As Rhodri and his family would be visiting other relatives in and around Cardiff on Christmas Day and Boxing Day, both siblings took time off to go and visit their families. They visited their father on Christmas Day, making it a fairly festive time in spite of the circumstances. On Boxing Day, they managed to visit both their brother, Owain, and their sister, Rhona, but had all too little time to spend with each of them. Bethan enjoyed riding Caledin on those visits, but she loved the way Billy and Merlin acted like two old friends.

The next day they went back to Rhodri's house and were soon back at their usual duties. During the day Rhodri went out to visit someone, leaving Billy alone in the study. Bethan joined him, saying she needed to polish the furniture. Mrs Jones came in and teased them again about their being more than just good friends.

When Billy left the room, she said, "I hope you won't mind my saying, but I think he's attracted to you, and you seem to be his type. I mean, he seems to be attracted to big, buxom girls." She smiled and took a deep breath, causing Bethan to notice that Henrietta was not slender herself. "There was Helen MacKenzie, the daughter of our friends, the Pryces, whom he seemed to like. She's got her eyes on Charles Butler. You can't blame her. He's a charming man and a duke's nephew. I'm afraid poor Gareth can't compete with his sort, but I think he should have a woman. A big one! I hope things go all right for you two."

Before she could reply, they heard Rhodri returning. His wife went to greet him and Bethan got on with more polishing. Later, she went into the study and Billy told her that Mrs Jones had had a similar conversation with him. "Who would have thought that we would have seemed so well suited?" he said. They giggled. As Bethan turned to leave, he slapped her on the posterior, saying, "I suppose you're not bad to look at, come to think of it. In a way!" Bethan replied with an offensive gesture.

That night Bethan went to Billy in his room. Both Olwen and Henrietta Jones noticed and drew the same erroneous conclusion. Bethan said, "I found a few letters. I don't know if they're the ones, but it's odd that they weren't in the study. They were in a book in his bedroom. Henrietta came in while I was reading them, but she didn't realise that's what I was doing, because she doesn't know I can read. I said I was cleaning and tidying the room and, when I knocked the book off the table and they fell out. She thought I was just putting them back."

"All right. What did they say?"

"It's a funny thing. They didn't say much. I don't know what the fuss is about. One of them was thanking someone for his advice and good wishes but was not going to follow it. The other one said something about seeing how the obstacle could be removed and hoped whoever it was would help."

"Were they addressed to Lewis Pryce? And who were they from?"

"It wasn't clear. They began with 'My Dear Friend' and were signed 'J' whoever that is."

"There must be something in them that means more than we realise. Otherwise, why keep them in the bedroom and not in the study? Is there any way I can get to seeing them?"

"I doubt it. I can't be seen looking at them again, without arousing suspicion. And you can't go poking around in Rhodri's bedroom, can you?"

The next few days passed peacefully. It was late afternoon on New Year's Day, 1715, when Lewis Pryce arrived, accompanied by his wife, their younger son and daughter-in-law. Billy was relieved to see that Helen was not with them. His relief was, however, only limited, as he knew he had to try hard to avoid being recognised, not only by the father, but also by the son. Despite what Helen had said, he detected no awkwardness between the two parliamentarians. Indeed, they seemed like the old friends that they were. He was glad, because it meant Lewis was occupied in conversation with Rhodri most of the time. When he mentioned, at the end of dinner, that they would be departing early the next morning, Billy was again relieved, only to be horrified, when Mrs Jones said, "Oh, no! I was so hoping to be able to spend time with Mrs Pryce. I know some of my friends here would love to meet her."

Both Rhodri and Lewis paused, trying to find the right words to say, as Rhodri helped himself to another glass of porter, when Mrs Pryce said, "Oh! How delightful. We often pass through Cardiff, but never seem to have time to see the city. I am told it is worth seeing. The castle, the cathedral and many beautiful buildings. This would be a good time, too. The weather is quite pleasant for the time of year. Everywhere looks better with a little sunshine."

Billy managed to hide his feelings, clinging to the hope that either Rhodri or Lewis would rescue him. However, the two husbands acquiesced, like men who know when they are beaten. Rhodri said, "Of course, you are most welcome. However, I must warn you that I have promised to visit a few people tomorrow and may have to leave you alone, save for the servants and, of course, my secretary Captain Evans." Of course, Captain Evans had no option but to smile and say what a pleasure that would be. He had seldom told so big a lie.

Billy had a sleepless night, followed by a morning spent trying to control his nerves and to make polite conversation over breakfast, and afterwards, until the ladies went out for their tour of Cardiff, while Rhodri went off to pay the visits to which he had committed himself, leaving Billy to entertain Lewis Pryce. Bethan took them some tea and heard some innocuous remarks about impressions of London. Just as she was leaving the room Lewis said, "What are you doing here?" It was fortunate that she was not carrying anything or she would have dropped it. As she closed the door behind her, she heard Billy say, "I am Mr Jones's secretary, as he has said."

Lewis Pryce replied, "Do not treat me like a fool, Mr Rhys. I know who you are. I ask merely why you are carrying out this ridiculous pretence. To what end?"

"What gave me away?"

"You really do think I am stupid. I knew from when I saw you in London. I once saw you in the street accompanying Rhodri somewhere. I suspected it was you. I could not imagine what you were doing there, so I thought I must have been mistaken. Then I saw you taking my daughter somewhere in a chaise. By then I was sure, although she says she does not believe you are both Gareth Evans and Billy Rhys, not to mention Merlin or whatever they call him. What are you doing?"

"I am trying to find those letters you are so worried about."

"What has that got to do with Rhodri Jones?" "Your daughter told me she suspected him. I could think of no better way of getting into this house and seeing his correspondence than working for him as I am."

"I do not understand you. You are a complete mystery to me. Why do you try to help me, or my daughter? Rhodri speaks well of you. You have gone beyond what was necessary for your purpose. You do your job very well. You have treated my daughter better than she deserves. Even your violence is always restrained."

"How do you know? Your daughter has only ever come to me in secret?"

"I had my suspicions, but her servant, Evans, has kept me informed. He has worked for me since before Helen was born and has always protected her. He would not have let you or anyone harm her. I mean really harm. But he has held himself back because you have held yourself back. Helen always was headstrong. I've had to chastise her often enough myself when she was little, but it never did much good. On reflection, I now think I let her have her own way too often when she was young. Well, it's too late now."

Billy struggled to take all this in. Before he could respond, Lewis began again, saying, "You are obviously more educated than an ostler. Who are you?"

He was trying to gather his wits when Bethan came in and asked if they would like some tea and Welshcakes that Mrs Roberts had just made. They both said they would. Billy began to tell the whole story. He had reached the part where he explained why he had chosen Lewis in particular as a target for his criminal activities, when Bethan came back in carrying a large tray with the tea and Welshcakes. She hesitated, hoping to hear some of the conversation, but soon realised that she had no choice but to leave the room.

When she had gone, Lewis said, "Well, now a lot of things are beginning to make sense. I have to tell you that you and your father are sadly mistaken about me. I did lend him money on several occasions, and he has repaid only a small portion of it. I eventually told him I would lend him no more. I said to him, as I have said to my younger son and to my late son-in-law that every man must at some point in his life take responsibility for his financial affairs. Nobody can go on borrowing and wasting money forever. I don't care whether it is on personal extravagance or unwise business expenditure. All three of them were borrowing my money and wasting it, one way or another. Where you are wrong is that I did not foreclose on your father. Others presumably did, hence the loss of your farm. I am truly sorry for that, but it was not of my doing. Indeed, it could not have been, for I never took it or anything else as surety. I lent to your father on the basis of trust. Of course, there is documentation, but it does not give me the right to claim the farm or anything else. It remains an unpaid debt. I do not intend to relieve him of it, but it must stay unsatisfied until such time as he is in a position to repay it."

Billy sat drinking the last of the tea. He felt really guilty about having so misjudged this man. He wondered

181

why his father had misinformed him. It occurred to him that his father might have been wrong in his recollection of who had lent him money and on what terms. What a mess!

Billy said, "I fear I have done you a greater wrong than I knew. I had blamed you unfairly for our misfortunes. It may seem ridiculous at this stage, but, for what it's worth, I offer you my apologies. I cannot return all your property, but I shall, in due course, at least repay you something of its worth. Much of it has been sold."

"For what it's worth, just between us, your apology is accepted. However, I will not accept payment from you if it comes from the proceeds of crime, unless you merely return what is mine. If you manage to save money from what Rhodri pays you, or any other honest source, I will accept it."

"How can you know where it comes from?"

"Strangely enough, I am prepared to take your word for it. You are, I believe, in your soul, an honest man. If I am wrong, well, that is my problem. As to my daughter, I believe she is sadly mistaken about many things. She thinks Rhodri Jones is an evil man. I cannot see it. He keeps trying to draw me into his parliamentary connection. Unfortunately, he and some of his friends have plans which could have tragic consequences for this country if they were put into effect. I doubt that they will be. I think he and his friends all have more sense. He has hinted at dire consequences for myself if I should betray them, and certainly, possession of those letters would give him a hold over me, but that is all conjecture. I cannot see how he could have acquired them, nor that he would do anything to ruin me or the nation."

Billy had eaten several of the Welshcakes and was thinking he had better let Lewis catch up. He also decided it was time to enlighten him a little further. He said, "I agree with you that Mr Jones seems to be a man of extremely good character, and it is hard to believe your daughter could be right about him. However, I think he does have the letters."

"Where are they?"

"I know where Bethan said they were, but as you are in this house and he is not, I doubt that Rhodri would have left them there now. I suppose we could ask her to have another look. But she said they seemed to contain nothing worth your getting so distressed."

"I would really like to have them. Please ask the woman to try again." When she came in again they did ask her and she agreed to try.

Billy said, "I think it is time to tell me what this is all about. Who is 'J'?"

"He is the man they call the Pretender. Prince James Edward Francis Stewart, the son of the late King James the Second who was deposed in 1688. His supporters are known as Jacobites. They would make young James king."

"I have heard such talk, but surely that is it: just talk? I know the French said they'd make James king if they won the War, but they did not, so surely all that is over."

"Did you not notice at the dinner party that when they drank the toast to the King, they all held their glasses over the finger-bowls?"

"Yes, I thought it a bit odd, but so what?"

"It is a sign of a Jacobite. They mean 'the King over the water' – that is James the Third as he likes to be called. It's just a dream, but some of them think it could become reality. My fear is that the Government may take them seriously and start arresting people they suspect of what they would call treason. Those letters could be interpreted to mean that I am involved."

While Billy was trying to take all this in, Bethan came back to tell them she had pretended to tidy Rhodri's bedroom and had had a look in the book where the letters had been, only to find them gone, as she had expected. She had even checked a few other books to no avail. They thanked her, and she went out to get on with her other duties. Lewis said, "I knew old King James at one time. I was at the Court when he was Duke of York and his brother Charles was King, in the last few years of his reign. I liked James. Yet I feared he would be too much like his father, Charles the First, and I was right. When he was King, he would take no notice of anyone: the Lords, the Commons, the Church or the judges. He made enemies all round. I was not alone in regretting the way things turned out. A lot of us didn't mind his Catholicism. It was when he tried to impose it on the rest of us that we knew we had to stand up against him."

"Then how do you come to be mixed up with the Jacobites if you were in agreement with the people who rebelled against James?"

"I still thought of James as a good man and indeed as a friend. I went to visit him once at his new home in St Germain in Paris, during one of those periods when Britain and France were at peace, when sanity reigned. I met the young James. He too was very likeable, and I think the whole family enjoyed my visit. Well, many years later, when Queen Anne's last child had died, she told her ministers that she would like her half-brother James to succeed her. They arranged for some unofficial contacts with him to see if it could be arranged, and I was one of those who were sent."

"What happened? What went wrong?" asked Billy looking dazed.

"We tried to explain that if he was to be acceptable to Parliament and to the British people, he would have to become a Protestant and to agree to ruling with and through Parliament. He was, sadly, as stubborn as his father and grandfather. He would not change his religion and was not prepared to negotiate at all. He said he was the rightful King and that right did not depend on Parliament or anyone else. He would claim the throne when it became vacant."

Billy asked, "If Prince James was not prepared to meet the Government's conditions for becoming King, surely you would have severed your connections with him, wouldn't you?"

"No! Neither I nor most of those who had been in contact with him. Some actually plotted to help him gain the throne by force. Others probably just wanted to keep on good terms with him in case he did ever become our king. I believe even the Duke of Marlborough was among

185

them. As for me, I continued to try to persuade him to see reason. He could have had the Crown on a plate if he had been prepared to bend a little, rather than risk everything trying to take it by force. I wanted him to succeed, but not at the cost of all our religious and other freedoms that we have won at great cost over many years. I know I am not alone in thinking that way."

Billy began to understand. "So do you mean that the obstacle he was referring to was his religion?"

"Yes. Or arguably Parliament's opposition to it. Yet anyone reading those letters on their own could suppose that the obstacle was King George and that we were discussing ways of removing him. Even my good wishes could be interpreted as wishing him success in seizing the Crown by force."

Bethan made them another pot of tea and took it in to them with another plate of Welshcakes. At least there was something to be pleased about that morning. Bethan noticed that Billy still looked worried and thoughtful, but so too did Lewis.

Billy said, "Surely, all this is being blown out of proportion. King George is not going to be afraid of a few people drinking their wine over the fingerbowl, and nobody would be mad enough to try to seize power by force without the backing of the French or some other powerful nation. The opportunity is past. Everyone says the French, and all Europe, have had enough of war to last them for years."

"I hope you're right! How I hope so. Not only for my own sake, but for the country. Yet I fear some may be mad enough to try something even now. I can't imagine

Rhodri would be one, but his possessing the letters worries me."

He had hardly got the words out of his mouth, and another Welshcake into it, when they heard Rhodri returning. He came into the room and told them something of his visit. He was glad to say that an elderly friend of his was recovering well from a recent illness. Rhodri seemed in every way a kind, diligent and honourable man. He drank some tea and ate a couple of Welshcakes before saying it was time for his next visit. He was meeting the local vicar who wanted his money as well as his advice for a scheme to help the poor. Billy thought Helen would have said the man was a hypocrite, using his outward goodness to conceal his inner wickedness, but he could not really accept that. Everything about him seemed genuine.

These thoughts made it all the harder for Billy to say what he knew he had to say next to Lewis, as soon as Rhodri had left. He said, "So your daughter was right in suspecting that Rhodri had the letters. I have to tell you something else too. Your son-in-law was not killed in a duel in the Netherlands. He was murdered in London."

After a long pause, Lewis asked, "How can you possibly know that?"

Billy told what he had discovered, as Lewis listened, shaking his head in astonishment. Finally he said, "Are you saying that you think Rhodri killed him or was complicit in the act?"

"I honestly do not know. I think he must have helped cover it up, but whether he knew before the event, I don't know. I find it hard to believe he would even help cover it up. It is so out of character. The longer I have been here the more I have come to like and respect him. Yet what I have discovered suggests there are things I do not know about him."

They ended their conversation as they heard the sound of people arriving. The tour of Cardiff was over.

Chapter 20

A few months later, Rhodri received a letter which he did not show anyone, but suddenly announced that it was time for him to go to London again. This time he would not require Billy's services. On the contrary, he would prefer it if he would stay in Cardiff and deal with most of his correspondence on his behalf, forwarding to him only those items which needed his personal attention. Billy was slightly embarrassed by this sign of the confidence Rhodri placed in him by then. Henrietta dithered but finally decided to leave Bethan in Cardiff and engage a new maid in London.

Billy and Bethan enjoyed the next few months, as they had greater freedom than ever to pursue matters of our own, whilst ensuring Rhodri's affairs were always dealt with properly. They managed to pay more visits to their father, their brother Owain, their elder sister Rhona, the Coach and Horses and the Mermaid. They also carried out more robberies.

At last Bethan found the letters. She was cleaning Rhodri's room when she knocked a book off a shelf and the letters fell out of it. Billy read them and sent them by post to Lewis Pryce.

The next morning, Billy and Bethan were greeted by a very anxious Olwen. She said to Billy, "Here's a letter for you from Mr Jones. I think I know what's in it, for I've had one too."

He opened the letter and, remembering just in time that the housekeeper and the servants had no idea Bethan could read, he read it to her. Rhodri said he was taking Mrs Jones and the children on a visit to France. They would probably be away for a month, possibly two. He had enclosed a letter to his bankers in London authorising Billy to draw his salary and reasonable expenses from his account. He said he had written a similar letter to them concerning Olwen so that she could keep the house while he was away. He apologised for the inconvenience but pointed out that he could hardly send a lot of gold coins in the post. They all wasted a lot of time that day speculating as to what had caused Rhodri's sudden departure.

The next day Billy was catching up on Rhodri's usual correspondence, and Bethan was polishing the furniture, when Helen arrived. Evans, as usual, accompanied her. Billy received her in the study, where Bethan remained, pretending to be polishing. He greeted his visitor with the words, "Are you mad? What if Rhodri had been here?"

"Well, he knows we know each other from London. He shouldn't find a visit suspicious. Anyway, have you found those letters yet? We are running out of time."

"Yes. Bethan found them. I have sent them in the post to your father."

"You are useless! Father doesn't know I've asked you. He'll be most upset at the thought of owing anything to a scoundrel like you."

"I sent them to your father because they are rightfully his."

"I suppose you also asked Father for money." "No. I am sure he will do whatever he considers to be right in the circumstances. Of course, some would think you might show some gratitude, but I am not counting on it."

"You are impossible!"

"Well, what's so urgent now? What's changed?"

Sian came in and offered them some tea. Billy accepted, and she went out before Helen could insult him again.

Helen said, "I don't know what's going on, but Father and a lot of his friends seem very worried about something. He won't tell me anything. I'm sure it's something to do with those letters. Oh! Why couldn't you have given them to me? I'll probably see him before the post reaches him. I came back from London with him in the coach. I asked him to leave me in Cardiff so I can visit some friends. He's on his way back to Cardigan."

Sian came in with the tea. As Helen and Billy sat drinking the tea, Bethan tried to reason with her, saying, "I can't see what else Billy could have done, or more importantly, what we can do now. Anyway, you can't be sure that whatever's the matter with your father and his friends is anything to do with those letters."

Billy went on to tell her about Rhodri's letter to him, and suggested he was worried too, in spite of the fact that he thought he possessed the letters. Helen began to insult them again when there was the sound of a visitor being admitted at the front door. Megan came in followed by Gwyneth who addressed Billy, saying, "I didn't know where you were, so I went to the Mermaid and Megan said

191

you'd be here. We've brought Merlin, in case you want to make a run for it."

Llewellyn said, "Shall I get Caledin ready, so you can take him too?"

Megan answered before Billy could think, "Yes, please. Good idea." "What's the matter?" asked Billy.

"There's trouble! I don't know whether you should go to the inn and face it or make a run for it now while you've got the chance."

"What sort of trouble?"

Gwyneth said, "A lot of soldiers have come to the inn. There's an officer with them. Says he's looking for you. Gareth and I told him you're not there, but you'll be back in a day or two. I hoped he'd either go away or wait long enough for us to work something out, but he seems ready to start searching the town."

"Did you get his name?"

"I think it was Edwards. Or was it Edward something? He asked for Sergeant William Rhys, by the way, so he must know you used to be a soldier." Helen said, "Were you a sergeant once?"

He ignored her. He said to Gwyneth, "My commanding officer was Eddy Edwards. I'll go and see what he wants. I don't think he's come to arrest me."

Then he turned to Helen and said, "I regret, Madam, that I must leave you. I am just going to get into my riding clothes. Then I'll ride to the inn."

They all left Helen. Billy rushed upstairs and changed into the clothes he wore for robbing coaches: breeches, boots and his long brown coat. Outside he found Llewellyn holding Caledin and Merlin. As he mounted

Merlin, Bethan and Llewellyn mounted Caledin, and they all rode off towards the inn. Megan ran after Billy and scrambled up behind him to ride pillion.

At the inn Billy was relieved to see it was indeed his old commanding officer, Eddie Edwards, surrounded by artillerymen. They greeted each other with affection. Then Eddy said, "Can't beat about the bush. Too urgent. You're wanted! Called back to the Regiment. Get your old uniform if you still have it. If not, never mind, you can get a new one from Maindy Barracks. "

"Wait a minute! What's all this about? Anyone would think there was a war on. I'm not in the Army any more, so I don't have to re-join, you know."

"You've never been properly discharged and now's the time for technicalities like that to matter. I'll tell you what it's about, but not here, in front of everyone."

"All right. Let's go in here." He led him into one of the private rooms. Llewellyn and his mother went round via the secret passage and listened behind the hidden door that was a false panel. Billy said, "What's going on? Have we started another war already?"

"No, not exactly. It's the Jacobites. They've started a rebellion to put the Pretender on the throne. We've got to move fast."

"Who's backing them? France or Spain?" "Don't know! Funny thing. All our intelligence says they're not involved. I know it sounds ridiculous for them to try on their own, but there you are. As far as we know, there's risings in Scotland, Wales, the Westcountry, the North and Oxford. I don't know how much support they've got in each area, but we think the worst rising's in Scotland. Don't worry, you won't be asked to fight Welshmen. We're off up north as soon as we can. General Wills is commanding up there but he needs reinforcements, especially artillery. So that's us. Someone else'll be dealing with whatever's going on in

Wales. Are you ready?"

Billy agreed. Then he ran to his room above the stables and got into his old uniform. He put the clothes he had been wearing into a bag, in case he needed to do any secret intelligence work. He also took several pistols and some of the money he had hidden. He had decided against donating either of his horses to the Army, so he said he would ride Merlin to Maindy and Bethan and Megan agreed to following on Caledin, so they could take both horses back to the inn. He said his farewells to Llewellyn, Gwyneth and Gareth briefly.

At Maindy, Billy saw that the Glamorgan Fusiliers were also mustering. He dismounted. So did Bethan and Megan. They tried to say goodbye. He hugged the women and kissed them.

Megan said, "I expect you'll enjoy getting to know some of the camp followers on this campaign."

"I don't think so. It's all too rushed for anyone to arrange for them to join us."

Bethan said, "I'll miss you! Please come back. I don't want to lose another man."

"Don't worry about me. I always survive."

Some of the men made comments about his having two good-looking women to leave behind. While they were laughing at this, Helen arrived, followed by Evans. She came up and handed Billy a sword. It was her husband's.

He said, "I was keeping that safe for you. How did you find it?"

"You're not the only one who can be devious. I bribed the boy. Bring it back safely!" She sounded as if she cared.

Billy tried to say something. She kissed him. With feeling. They held each other for a long time. There were lots of laughs and bawdy comments from the onlookers. One said, "You'd best be careful! Those other two could be jealous."

"I wouldn't mind a fight with either of them!" said Helen. Bethan and Megan were tempted but decided it would keep for another time.

Billy walked away, carrying the sword. Helen rode off followed by Evans. Bethan and Megan stood for a minute gazing after Billy. Then they too remounted and rode off.

Chapter 21

Billy found his unit. He was amazed when he saw who was nominally in charge of the gun and its crew: Lieutenant Perseus de Clare, who had been a civilian when they had met at Chepstow. He was clearly new to the Army and to the Artillery in particular. Billy could see that he had not much idea of what he was supposed to be doing. Fortunately, he had enough sense to let Billy get on with the job rather than interfering and so displaying his ignorance. The bombardier, Allan Morris, on the other hand, was obviously experienced and a big help in getting the crew organised. As soon as enough men of the Royal Welsh Artillery were assembled, they were ordered to take charge of the heavy guns that were stored there and harness up. This gave Billy little opportunity for getting to know his crew, or to exchange more than the briefest of greetings with Allan. The social niceties would have to wait.

Someone was getting a baggage train organised. It would be starting to get dark by the time every unit was ready for inspection and Billy expected to be told to set out at first light. However, Eddy gave the order to mount and someone issued lanterns. They were going to be travelling into the night. Eddy led out along the road. Billy had been given a black carthorse to ride. Someone said he was a bit of a handful in harness, prone to upsetting the others. Billy reflected that the drawback of being known as a good horseman was that you always got the most difficult mounts. He rode alongside the gun, falling in either ahead or behind whenever the road became too narrow.

They set out at a brisk trot, but Billy had difficulty keeping his horse in place. He kept trying to overtake, as the train was obviously not going fast enough for him. Billy could not explain to him that he had a long ride ahead and he needed to save his energy. After a couple of hours they reached Caerleon-on-Usk, a town associated with the Romans and also with King Arthur. It was that thought that prompted Billy to name the horse after one of Arthur's knights, Cae, or Kay as the English call him. Just after Caerleon, they stopped in a field beside the road for about a half-hour's rest.

Billy had a chance to talk to the lieutenant for the first time, asking what he wanted him to call him. He said, he was happy to be known as Perse informally, but Lieutenant de Clare in front of the men. Billy asked whether he was still intending to be a vicar. He said he still felt called to the Church, but recently his older brother had died. He had been upholding the family's military tradition, so now it fell on Perseus to step in. He feared he would have to give up his priestly aspirations permanently, as he would be inheriting a viscountcy some day, and it would obviously not do to be a viscount and a reverend at once. Billy could not see what was obvious about it. By then it was dark, and they wondered how much longer they would be travelling that night. Billy remembered one or two occasions when the Duke of Marlborough had kept the whole Army marching all night so as to surprise the Enemy. When Eddy approached, checking on the condition of the men and the horses,

Perseus asked him what was the plan. He said he had been ordered to get up to Lancashire as soon as possible and there link up with General Wills.

It was apparent that they had neither infantry nor cavalry to protect them in the event of encountering the Enemy sooner than expected. Eddy said they had been promised a cavalry escort, but it had not materialised. That did not change the fact that his orders were to proceed northwards with all haste.

Once Eddy was satisfied they were all fit to carry on, he ordered them to remount. However, as it was dark by then, he ordered them to proceed at a brisk walk with lighted lanterns. Billy had no idea where they were or if they were going in the right direction. He just hoped the officers leading the column knew. He could not think how they could read maps, signposts or milestones in the dark, even with the aid of lanterns, yet somehow they succeeded remarkably well. They did not get lost once that night. They did, however, find it very difficult to control the guns on the hilly roads. Going uphill was difficult enough, but downhill there was a constant danger that a gun would build up too much speed or overshoot a bend. They even tied ropes to the gun-carriages and some of the men hauled back on them to steady the vehicles downhill. They considered it a great achievement that only once did a gun leave the road and go down into a ditch. That, of course, led to their having to spend a lot of time waiting while its crew, with a few others, pulled it back up onto the road. Fortunately, no real damage was done to it, or to any of the men or horses.

It was a long time before they were able to stop and rest, as they could not stop on a hill. That phase of the journey went very slowly and was both tiring and trying. The journey and the night seemed to be neverending, so Billy was reassured when they turned off the road for another rest, by the sight of a castle which loomed over them and showed its dark form even against the night sky. He tried to recognise it. One of the men said it was Raglan Castle. He knew it, because he came from Raglan. They let the horses graze and they finished off the small amounts of food and drink they had. Billy wondered how far behind the baggage train was. And the cavalry escort.

Bethan and Megan rode back to the Coach and Horses. After about an hour, some soldiers came in. They were from the Glamorgan Militia. A well-dressed civilian was with them. He announced that he was a magistrate and had a warrant for the arrest of William Rhys, otherwise known as the notorious highwayman "Merlin". The cousins were appalled. When nobody claimed to know where Billy was, the men began to search the premises. Bethan wondered how they knew. Above all, she wondered how to help him. She told the others she was going to try to warn him to keep away from the inn and anywhere else where he was well known.

Bethan waited until the searchers had left. Then she rode Merlin to Maindy. She could see things were even busier than before. Men were still arriving, others were being drilled and inspected. She had to ask several people before she discovered that the Artillery had left for the north some hours previously. She was horrified. She rode back to the inn and told the others that she was going to try to catch up with Billy. She was sure Merlin could travel faster than an artillery train, especially in the dark. She rushed to her room and changed into breeches and boots. She took a supply of money, a pistol and some ammunition. As she went back downstairs, she bumped into Gwyneth who handed her a bag containing some food and wine for the journey. Bethan kissed her and Llewellyn and went out. In the stableyard, she almost collided with Megan who was holding both Merlin and Caledin. She insisted on going with her cousin. Bethan said there was no need, but she had no time to argue and secretly was glad of her company.

Bethan had managed to ascertain that the Artillery was going via Monmouth and Hereford. She had some idea where Monmouth was but was unsure of her ability to find it in the dark. She hoped for the best. It was almost dark by the time they left. As they rode through Caerleon they saw a few women. They asked them the way to Monmouth. The local women wasted a lot of time asking the strangers who they were, why they were dressed like men, why they were going to Monmouth and why they did not wait until morning as it was dangerous in the dark. Eventually the inquisitors were satisfied enough to set the riders on the right road and to assure them the main road went all the way to Monmouth.

As they rode, they could not believe the Army had managed to stay ahead for so long. They kept discussing whether they were on the wrong road, or if the Army could be. They also found that, in the dark, any noise can be a source of anxiety and any movement in the shadows can seem sinister. They found it nervewracking. They were grateful that Merlin and Caledin were well behaved. Merlin was almost imperturbable, whilst Caledin merely threw up his head or twitched his ears at every potential alarm. It would not have done for all of them to be nervous.

One of the best-known facts about Wales is that it is full of hills. The area they were passing through was somewhere in Monmouthshire, they supposed. That is not like the Brecon Beacons or Snowdonia, but it is hilly. The hills varied in steepness and in length. The road sometimes went up for a short distance before starting to level out or descend, whereas at other times it seemed to go on climbing for ages. They had to take it slowly because of the darkness and the poor state of the road. They could not risk falling into a ditch.

Bethan thought the artillery must be having to take it even more slowly, as she knew how hard it was to drive a farm cart up and down hills on twisty roads. She could only imagine how much harder it would be in the dark. She could also guess that a heavy gun was harder to control than a farm cart. She felt sorry for Billy and his comrades. She thought the Artillery must be finding the journey even harder than they were. They were bound to catch up with them soon, surely?

She explained her thoughts to Megan to try to cheer them both up. It was about midnight when they saw the dark form of a castle standing out against the slightly less dark sky. Was it Monmouth? Bethan thought Monmouth was a big town. This castle seemed to be in a village. What other castles lay between Cardiff and

Monmouth? Raglan? Then they saw a crossroads with a signpost. With the aid of the tinderbox, they saw which was the way to Monmouth.

They rode on.

Billy felt as if he had hardly dismounted when the order came to start moving again. He was starting to feel a few aches and pains. He loved riding, but you can have too much of a good thing. A lot of the men were moaning, whilst others suffered in silence. At least his tiredness was offset by finding Cae less tiring to ride.

Even his enthusiasm had run low.

As they passed through Monmouth Billy heard a clock chime. Then the watchman cried, "Four o'clock and all's well!" Billy hoped he was right: that they were not about to be ambushed, or to find General Wills had been defeated. In war, all is seldom well.

They stopped for a rest somewhere just beyond the town. Unlike during their previous stops, there was hardly any sound of conversation coming from the men. Eddy rode along the column again, checking on its condition. He was much more economical with words than was his custom. All too soon he gave the order to move. After each rest they seemed to move off with renewed energy, but each time it lasted more briefly. This time it was barely noticeable. One of the men asked, "Hey, Sarge, how far are we going?"

"I don't know. How far is Lancashire?" Perse overheard and said, "From Cardiff to Lancashire is about a hundred and fifty miles, perhaps more."

"How far 'ave we come?"

"At least forty miles by now." A moan went along the train as everyone realised how much more lay ahead.

Billy moaned silently but called out, "It doesn't matter! We've just got to keep going until we get there." He refrained from mentioning that he was not expecting to get any rest when they got there. General Wills' plans were not likely to include much relaxation.

After a while, the dawn began to break and they managed to see where they were going, at least to some extent. The start of the new day seemed to brighten their spirits, especially as it looked like being a sunny day. Billy wondered what they were going to eat and what effect empty bellies would have on morale. He soon heard a few murmurs as the men began to think the same thing. He said, "Perhaps General Wills will buy us all lunch when we get there. He'll be so pleased to see us!"

One of the men said, "Hey, Sarge! I think we'll be in Hereford soon. I come from by there. Is it Tuesday?"

"It is. But what of it?"

"Tuesday's market day in Hereford. We'll 'ave trouble getting these guns through the town once it gets busy."

Billy thanked him and rode ahead with Perse to telll Eddy. He seemed irritated at first, but then said, "Good! That gives me an idea. We'll have breakfast in Hereford. Pass it on!" They passed it on. The news was greeted with cheers. Billy wondered what they were going to eat, but knew Eddy would not have made such an announcement if he had been unable to keep his promise.

By the time Hereford came into view it was daylight. The Adjutant rode on ahead, accompanied by a few soldiers. They came back with several cartloads of food for the men and the horses. They stopped for a couple of hours before going through the town. The Adjutant had promised various merchants in the town that they would be paid for everything they provided, but he did not say when or how.

Eddy sent for Billy and Perse, and said, "I need someone to ride ahead. Look for any sign of the rebels. Or the cavalry escort we were promised. No point sending anyone before. Too dark to see a thing. Of course, it'll be easier for the rebels to spot us too, so we'll have to be alert all the time. What do you say?"

Billy had a feeling that he knew what he was supposed to say and said it.

Eddy said, "Jolly good! Now, Perse, do you think you can manage without him for a bit?"

"Yes, Sir. I think Bombardier Morris will be able to look after me until Billy gets back."

So Billy rode off just before the others began to get ready to move again.

Chapter 22

Bethan and Megan arrived at Hereford about an hour after the Army had left. They saw the field where the horses and the guns had churned up the ground. They saw other signs that a lot of horses had been there. In the town they went through the market. They heard about the Army's visit. Bethan said, "I wonder if we could catch them at their next stop?"

Megan replied, "I think we need some food and rest. So do the horses."

They bought some food for themselves and a small sack of oats. Then they made their way through the crowds and found a field beyond the town where they could let the horses eat and where they could sit on a dry mound that was slightly less uncomfortable than what they had been sitting on for most of the night. After a couple of hours, they set off again. Travelling in daylight was far pleasanter than at night. They were sure they must be gaining on the Army at that stage, as they thought the guns would have to move slowly to travel through a lot of hilly country along the Welsh border for most of that day, although it was not as bad as that which they had experienced during the night.

At Ludlow, they discovered that the artillery train was resting in a field just beyond the town in the shadow of the castle. They pushed on with renewed enthusiasm. Merlin and Caledin soon covered the distance. All the women had to do now was find Billy among all these men. Before they could begin, they were challenged by a sentry.

The conversation did not go very well. The women were not in any mood for playing games. The soldier seemed to be ridiculously pedantic. Did he really think they were about to attack the soldiers or spearhead a Jacobite push? Of course, he was not in a good mood either. He was not pleased at being given sentry duty after such a long hard ride. Bethan told him who they were and that they wanted to see Sergeant William Rhys for whom they had an urgent message. They were not going to tell him what the message was. They had the feeling this would end badly. They might get arrested or have to give up and go away. Neither prospect appealed to them.

They were rescued by a knight in shining armour. Well, actually, he was in artillery uniform. His was made of finer stuff and was better tailored than most. He was tall and handsome. He spoke beautifully. He was every inch a gentleman. He reminded Bethan of her Henry, except that Henry was dark haired when he was fair. "What's the trouble, Davies? What do these ladies want?" He called them ladies. Most perceptive of him, they thought.

"She wants 'er brother, Sir. The redhead's their cousin, she says. I told 'em they can't come into camp without permission. Says 'er brother's Sergeant Gwilym Rhys. I said 'e's not 'ere. She won't believe me Sir."

"Dear me! Where have you come from, ladies? Do you live locally?"

"We've come from Cardiff, like you. You were a couple of hours ahead of us and it's taken a night and a day to catch up with you."

"You mean you've ridden all night?"

"Well, we had no choice. You lot kept going all night. So we had to."

"Absolutely remarkable! Were you not afraid to ride alone in the dark?"

"A bit, but we just had to carry on. I expect you know what that's like. I know the Army. My husband's Lieutenant Henry Tudor of the Glamorgan Fusiliers. I went with him to the Netherlands in the War."

"Is he with the Glamorgans now?"

"I don't know where he is. He went missing at Malplaquet and I haven't heard since."

"Dear me! I think we've met. As guests of Major MacNichol at Chepstow Castle. Well, well! I am Lieutenant Perseus de Clare. You poor woman. You'd better come with me now and have a chat. Well, and a rest, I think. Both of you." They walked through the temporary encampment. Men were sitting or lying on the grass, apart from the unlucky ones with sentry duty. They stopped by one of the guns. Having tethered the horses, the officer offered each of his guests a seat on an ammunition box and addressed them again, "Sergeant Rhys is in my gun-crew. You have unfortunately missed him. He has ridden on ahead of us to see if there's any sign of the Enemy on the way. We may see your brother soon, if he has anything to report. Otherwise, we may have to go as far as Shrewsbury or even Whitchurch before we catch up with him. The Adjutant has ridden back into Ludlow with a handful of men to see if he can buy us some food and drink. When he gets back I'll make sure you're taken care of. After that, I don't know what to say for the best. You could ride on trying to find Billy, but he might not be on the main road all the time. Or, you could find somewhere to stay round here and get some rest before you go back to Cardiff. Don't underestimate how dangerous the roads could be for a couple of ladies travelling alone. In a way, you might have been safer in the dark. Others couldn't see you. Of course, you'd be most welcome to come with us. I will ensure you are safe and well looked after."

Another officer approached. Perseus made the introductions, "Sir!, May I present Mrs Elizabeth Tudor, wife of Lieutenant Henry Tudor of the Glamorgans and sister of our very own Sergeant William Rhys, and their cousin, Miss Megan Morgan. Ladies, may I present Colonel Edwards, the commander of this regiment."

Colonel Edwards bowed and said, "Delighted to meet you, ladies. May I ask how you came to be with us this morning?"

After Bethan repeated the story, he said, "You seem like most determined and resourceful women. I am not surprised to learn that you are related to Billy Rhys. Welcome to our temporary encampment. I know I can rely on Mr de Clare to look after you."

Just then there was a stir in the camp as the Adjutant returned followed by four carts laden with various kinds of food and drink. He took charge of its distribution. Messrs De Clare and Edwards escorted the women to the front of the queue and ensured they had the pick of everything on offer. There were murmurs about favouritism and a number of comments to the effect that some of the men were hungry for things other than food, but nobody risked antagonising the Colonel.

They walked back to de Clare's gun and sat together on ammunition boxes while they ate and drank. Together they went over the options and the women decided their best plan was to stay with the artillery until Billy returned. As they sat there, another man joined them. De Clare introduced him, saying, "Ladies, may I present Bombardier Allan Morris. He is acting as my sergeant until Mr Rhys returns. Morris! These ladies are to be travelling with us for a while. They are Sergeant Rhys's sister and their cousin. They are to be treated with every respect and consideration."

"Yes, Sir! It'll be a pleasure." The bombardier looked pleased despite the extra responsibility. The women noticed that he was quite a good-looking young man and had a pleasant manner. It was all the pleasanter for the sight of two attractive women. Colonel Edwards went back to see the Adjutant.

Bethan smiled and said, "You're all being so kind. We must try not to make a nuisance of ourselves."

De Clare said, "I'm going to have to ask you to prepare to remount soon. We're about to get moving again." They had expected the Army to stay in the temporary camp overnight. However, it was not their decision, so they got up and began to walk to where they had left their horses. Perseus went with them and said he would re-saddle their horses and help the ladies to mount. They said there was no need but he insisted. He saddled both horses quickly and gently. Then he helped Bethan to mount. Some men merely hold the offside stirrup to prevent the saddle slipping when you try to mount. Others make a step by clasping their hands and lifting your foot.

209

Still others go down on all fours and let you step on their backs. This man put his arms around Bethan and lifted her right into the saddle. It was a shock but exciting. He was so strong and gentle. He then helped her to put her feet in the stirrups and put a hand on her thigh while helping settle her into the right place in the saddle. Bethan wanted to jump down and ask him to do it all again. Megan could hardly wait for her turn. As soon as he had put her safely onto Caledin, he said, "Best get moving now." Then he went off.

Megan said, "Did you know many men like him when you were with the Army before?"

"Only a few. This one is special isn't he?"

"Yes. He's nearly as strong as some of the prizefighters I know, and he makes most gentlemen seem common. I wonder if he's got a woman?"

"What's it to you? I'll bet half the men you've had were married and the rest probably had other women."

"True! Of course, we won't talk about your days as a camp follower. Anyway, this journey's been a nightmare until now. Meeting him's made it worthwhile. Come to that, the bombardier's quite nice too, isn't he?"

"I agree. I wonder which one of us they'll prefer?" They both laughed.

Horses were hitched to the guns and the men got into place ready for inspection. Bombardier Morris had got his crew into place as quickly and efficiently as the best of the rest. He looked satisfied. Then he saw the women and gave them each a smile, a wave and a salute. They returned all three. They trotted up and watched as the Colonel inspected each gun and crew. He found all to be in order with de Clare's crew, and the women felt a strange pride because they knew it was Billy's, even though he was not there. The Colonel gave the order to mount and the men mounted almost simultaneously.

Then he rode out onto the road followed by each gun in turn. Ammunition carts and men riding and leading reserve horses filled in the gaps between the guns. Then they moved off at a steady walk. The women rode next to Lieutenant de Clare.

They took the opportunity to chat and get to know each other. He told them what he had told Billy about his family and his abandoned hopes to be a clergyman. Megan pondered what he had said. She commented, "It's strange that a lot of nonconformists think all Church of England vicars are in the job for the wrong reason. I know because my father and brothers are Presbyterian ministers. Perhaps they just haven't met many like you."

"I think there are quite a few vicars around who have been called by God. Of course, I can't deny there are a few who shouldn't be in the job. But that's probably the same for soldiers, barristers, sailors and even farmers."

Bethan agreed. She knew Billy was not meant to be a farmer but could easily have been one.

They had to go very slowly down a hill on a bend to prevent the gun running away with itself and overturning.

Megan asked, "Is Perseus a common name in Pembrokeshire?"

"No, I was named after a hero from Greek mythology. My father's very fond of classical literature."

Bethan said, "I remember Perseus. Billy and I learned a few Greek and Roman legends from a Professor David Davies of Jesus College, Oxford, who sometimes used to come to the inn where we worked before the War."

"How extraordinary! I'm delighted to hear it. I met your Professor Davies at Oxford. By the way, my friends call me Perse. I wish you would. It sounds more normal, doesn't it? I feel a bit embarrassed. The men call me Sir, but Eddy, that's Colonel Edwards, calls me Perse when he's not being official."

"Thanks, you can call me Bethan or Beth. You probably know it's the Welsh version of Elizabeth, after the great Queen my parents used to tell me about. Billy was named after William of Orange. He was born in 1688, the year we got rid of King James and William became our king. Billy says the Jacobites are trying to put the clock back."

"I think he's right!"

Chapter 23

The Artillery had to go through a lot of hilly country for most of that day. Even though they carried on as long as there was any light, Eddy finally accepted they were not going to reach Shrewsbury until the next day, and so they made camp. One of the men said he thought they were on part of Wenlock Edge, but someone else said they had gone beyond it and were somewhere called the Long Mynd. Bethan and Megan could see little point in the argument, but resigned themselves to an uncomfortable night, as Eddy did not want the men to waste time making a proper camp.

Luckily, the weather had stayed mild and dry, so even without tents or other shelter everyone hoped to get some sleep. Bombardier Morris made sure the women got enough food and blankets. They lay between Perse and one of the wheels of the gun. Morris lay at their feet. During the night they were awakened by the sound of a sentry challenging someone. He was evidently a "friend", as he was allowed to proceed into the camp. They tried to get back to sleep, but were both just dozing off again when they heard a familiar voice. "Hello Bethan! Hello Megan!" It was Billy. They sat up. So did Perse. Billy sat on the ground beside them and said,

"I've just got back. Had to report to Eddy. He told me you were here. What on earth's going on?"

Bethan said, "I've got something important to tell you, and Meg's insisted on coming. It's been good to have her company. Of course, we didn't know how long it'd take to catch up. You lot can't half move fast! And we'd no idea you'd be off on one of your jaunts ahead of the rest. Luckily your Eddy, and especially Perse, have been very good to us." Seeing another figure moving, she added, "And so has Bombardier Morris."

A voice in the dark, called, "It's a pleasure, Madam!"

Billy said, "All right. So what's so urgent you've ridden all this way to tell me?"

"Not now. There are too many ears round here. It'll have to wait."

"Not for long. Eddy wants to see me in the morning. I think he'll be sending me out on another of my jolly jaunts."

Perse said, "When we move off in the morning, you two ladies could ride ahead with Mr Rhys for a while, so you can talk in private. Then wait for the rest of us to catch up with you." They agreed. Then they all tried to get some sleep.

In the morning, they found that Billy was right. Eddy sent for him, while he was trying to eat some breakfast. He crammed the last of it into his mouth, and hurried to where the Colonel was talking to Perse. Eddy turned and said, "Ah yes! Billy Rhys. I need to send you on another exploring mission, if you and your horse are up to it."

Billy had checked on Merlin and Caledin as well as Cae, and was relieved to see they had come to no harm. He answered his commanding officer, "Yes Sir! We can manage. What is it?"

"I expect we'll be in Cheshire by the end of today, and ready to cross the Mersey into Lancashire sometime tomorrow. The thing is, we don't know where General Wills is, or the Enemy. I believe the General was planning to make sure Manchester didn't fall into their hands before going after them. Of course, there might not be any rebels in Lancashire, only in Yorkshire or somewhere. You know how hard it is to get reliable information in war. The Enemy can be most inconsiderate. Not only that, I'm not sure where to cross the Mersey. I don't want to waste time wandering all over the countryside, nor do I want to encounter the Enemy unexpectedly. So the mission is, as usual, to find out what's what and report back. Don't get into trouble. Here, take this." He handed Billy a map of the North West of England. Billy had no confidence in its accuracy but it was better than nothing. Probably.

"Right, Sir. Thank you. But where will I find you? You'll be moving."

"We'll aim to cross the Mersey at Warrington, if we can. So you'll find us somewhere on the road between here and there, I expect."

"Yes Sir! don't worry. I'll find you." Billy was not worried about finding his regiment again. Finding General Wills was going to be the problem. And not finding the Enemy. Eddy wished him luck and he went to get Cae. Perse followed him. The women came too, and Billy was surprised that they both refused his offer to help them mount, but accepted that from Perse.

Once out of the camp, they told him that the Jacobites were not the only ones he needed to beware of.

215

They all speculated as to how anyone had guessed his identity. He was almost tearful, as he thought of the trouble the women had gone to in order to warn him, as well as the risks they had run. He asked, "What do you plan to do now? Go back home, if you can find some other travellers to protect you?"

Bethan answered, "We're better off with the Army. Your comrades, Perse and Allan, are both very kind."

Megan added, "And we'll all be together again as soon as you get back from your little one-man expedition." She refrained from adding, "If all goes well," but they all thought it.

Billy carried on at a steady trot. Cae seemed glad to be on the move again. The women waited until the column caught up.

They kept moving most of the day with only a few short breaks. Some time in the afternoon they passed through Whitchurch. One of the men in Billy's crew said he knew it, and they would soon be leaving Shropshire and entering Cheshire. A few hours later, they were told to pull off the road and rest. Eddy was talking to the Adjutant. They showed signs of irritation, which was unusual. Eddy led his horse back to the guns and asked Perse how well he knew Cheshire. He hardly knew it. Eddy was visibly disappointed. Then the order was given to remount and move off again.

By the time it was dark the women had no idea where they were. They had the feeling nobody else was too sure either. They camped again in a field. Everyone had to make the most of such rations as were left over, as they had not acquired any fresh food since Shrewsbury. Eddy said they could light small fires to heat their food, but to make sure they were only small. He did not want to advertise their position. The women sat with Perse and Allan. Bethan said, "Surely the Enemy must know where we are, whether we light fires or not?"

Allan replied, "Sorry, but I think you're wrong. We've been travelling faster than they expect. They might be able to guess we're somewhere in Cheshire, perhaps, but not exactly where, unless they've been spying on us more closely than any of us have thought. Of course, I've told our sentries to be fully alert. I'd hate to find I was wrong and the beggars take us by surprise."

Perse agreed and added, "At least we haven't yet come across the Enemy. We worry about what's going on, because we don't know anything, but I expect the Jacobites are just as worried. They can't know how many we are or how soon we'll join up with General Wills' force. We don't know what's happened to the cavalry escort we're supposed to have had, but so far we've done all right without them. So let's not be too worried. We should pray. If our cause is right, we should be confident God will grant us the victory." He led in a prayer. Bethan and Megan felt strange. They had not heard anyone pray aloud for a long time. They reminded each other they should pray more often.

After supper, the women borrowed a lantern and strolled along the horse lines to check on Merlin and Caledin. A voice hailed them from the darkness, "Hello girls! How are you?"

They nearly jumped out of their skins, but Bethan managed to reply fairly calmly, "I'm fine. Who's that?"

"Thomas Thomas! Sorry to scare you, cariad." He approached, pushing between a couple of horses. "I was sorry we couldn't talk, earlier. How's Billy?"

"He was all right this morning when he left. I just hope he still is."

"I was amazed to see you, but pleased. I've been waiting for a chance to see you ever since I saw you. Well, I know I've seen you in the distance quite a lot, but I mean, seeing you like this. Of course, I can't really see you now, but, you know what I mean, isn't it? Tonight I couldn't get away any earlier. I've been playing cards with a few of the lads, see? They was all very keen."

Megan thought she would not be keen on playing cards in darkness with nothing but a dim lantern and a small fire to shed a little light. Least of all with someone like Thomas. She supposed men learned from experience. How else?

He said, "Why did you come? There's no other women with us."

Bethan answered, "We've got some news for Billy and we wanted him to get it before he got back to Cardiff. I can't explain, but it is important."

By then Thomas was standing very close to her. She passed the lantern to Megan who moved away from them, displaying uncommon tact. He moved closer to Bethan. Then she stepped closer, so their bodies were touching. She said, "Thanks. Goodnight, then." She kissed him on the cheek. He put his arms around her waist and squeezed, while he kissed her on the lips. She put her arms around his neck and pressed herself against him, still kissing him.

When they paused for breath, he said, "I suppose I really had better go now. If I stay any longer I'll end up staying all night."

"Yes. I know. Some other time, I hope. Please!" She gave him one more quick kiss and turned away before she got carried away. She looked for Megan with the lantern and they went back to Perse and his crew. Bethan kept thinking of Thomas and Perse until she finally fell asleep, while Megan kept thinking of Allan and Perse. They both kept thinking of Billy.

The next day they were up early, as ever, and pushed on through the Cheshire countryside. During the afternoon, they could see some spires and tall buildings in the distance. Everyone wondered if they were nearing Warrington. They came to a village and Eddy asked a local man its name. He said "Rowton" or something like that. Eddy and the Adjutant had another look at the map. They both cursed loudly. They found another local man and asked for directions to Warrington. They cursed again. Eddy sent the column along a narrow lane leading in a north-easterly direction out of the village. Moans went up from all along the column. The women were not surprised. They had been heading in a northwesterly direction for most of the day. How far out of their way had they come? Every man in the train had his own opinion on that. Few would have reflected well on the Colonel. The women had no idea where they were. They hoped someone had.

When they made camp, Allan reported to Perse that he was satisfied all was as well as it could be, adding, "I've had a hard time getting the lads to stop moaning and settle down. To be honest I don't blame them. All this hard riding and then it's been a waste of time. Where do you think we went wrong?"

Perse said, "I've been trying to think. My best guess is that we took a wrong road out of Whitchurch, and nobody ever noticed until we were within sight of Chester. To be fair to Eddy, it was probably an easy mistake to make, and we've hardly seen any signposts all day. Well, that's life!"

Later Bethan met Thomas again. He was unexpectedly serious, saying, "You said you'd got some important news for Billy. What's up?"

"Sorry, but I can't tell you. Billy might. Some day. It doesn't affect you, though."

"If it's trouble, I don't mind 'elping, like, even if I don't know the 'ole story. Billy's been good to me, isn't it?"

"Thanks, I don't think there's anything you can do for us now, but I'll tell Billy when I see him, and we'll both remember you offered, whatever happens."

Bethan thought it was strange how she believed Thomas, considering that she knew he was a liar and a cheat. She had so often had men make and break promises. Supposedly better men too. She moved closer and said, "Thanks. I'm glad you're here." By then they were touching. He took hold of her and kissed her. She had to tear herself away. She said, "It's time to go to bed. Except there are no beds. And I do mean separately."

Bethan thought about some of the men she had kissed and wished the next one would be Perse. Then she knew she did not. The others were different. None expected her to regard him as her one true love.

Chapter 24

The next day they went in a series of zigzags along country lanes. The women were sure they could not have made much real progress. In the late afternoon, they could make out one church steeple. The Adjutant rode ahead and returned to say they were near a small town called Frodsham. He added that there would be a market there the next day, so Eddy saw an opportunity to replenish their provisions. Beyond Frodsham there was some open land where they made camp.

Although supper was even poorer than usual, they were all encouraged by the thought of getting something better the next day. They also would not have as early a start as usual, since they would have to wait for the stallholders to arrive and set up. Then the news came that the next morning they would stay in camp while the regiment's farrier checked the horses' feet and did any necessary shoeing. The men would give all the guns, gun carriages and various other things the cleaning and maintenance that had had to be kept to a minimum while the train had been on the move. That in turn meant staying a whole day, so it would be worthwhile pitching the tents they had brought among their few supplies. Everyone was happy about these developments, even those who were to be on sentry duty.

While Perse was having a meeting with Eddy and the other officers, Allan supervised the pitching of the tents for his crew and the cooking of the last of their rations.

The next day went according to plan. There was even an extra delight. Eddy bought several barrels of ale to be distributed among all the men. And the women. Spirits definitely rose. Megan found it frustrating that Allan Morris was so diligent in his duties that he had very little time for her. She had almost given up on Perse. He was sincere in his religion. He was not looking for the services of a camp follower. Allan was a good man, but not too good to indulge himself when the opportunity presented itself. Megan was going to make sure that it did. Bethan was welcome to Thomas. For now.

That night was the pleasantest they had spent since leaving Cardiff: a decent meal and a relatively comfortable bed. The following morning they enjoyed the best breakfast they had had for days before the men got everything ready for another day on the road. They had been going for about an hour when someone called out, "Cavalry ahead!" They all strained their eyes as they stared into the distance. They could see dust. Then, grey shapes of lots of horses and riders. Perse looked through his telescope. He said it did look like cavalry.

Eddy called out, "Halt! Make ready to defend yourselves!"

Perse said, "All right, let's get this gun unlimbered and facing forwards!"

Allan said, "Sir! I think the Colonel means for us to be ready with small arms. There's no time for getting the guns set up, and we've not much room either, with ditches on both sides of the road."

Perse noticed that the other crews were not unlimbering, but most were drawing swords or pistols.

223

Someone was issuing muskets from somewhere. Perse handed the telescope to Bethan. They looked like hussars. She hoped they were the escort they had been hearing about. She did not know whether the Jacobites had any hussars.

Eddy called, "It's all right! They're Germans!" They waited. He was right. A troop of hussars came into view. There was one man in a black coat. Bethan stared hard, until she had to give in to demands to pass the telescope to Megan. It was Billy. He was safe. He was riding a good-looking bay hunter and leading Cae. Some of the carthorse's friends neighed to him and he replied, while Billy and a cavalry officer rode up to Eddy. They saluted and Billy introduced Major Heinrich von Herrenhausen of the Osnabruck Hussars. Eddy remembered him from the escapade in the Ardennes, where Billy had become a hero to the Germans, and was delighted to meet him again. When they had finished talking, von Herrenhausen ordered his men to turn about. As soon as they moved off, Eddy ordered the Artillery to follow.

Billy fell in beside Perse, who said, "Welcome back Billy! Glad you're all right. As you can see, your sister, your cousin and our crew are safe." The women waved and he waved back. As Perse was in the way, it was difficult for them to talk to Billy. The women had to strain to hear his conversation with Perse over the clattering of hooves and the rumbling of wheels. Perse said, "Do you know where we're going?"

"Warrington! We'll cross the River Mersey there, then go due north for a bit towards Preston, where the

Jacobites have taken refuge. General Wills wants us to get a move on. The way he went on about it anyone would think I was to blame for delaying our progress.

Still, I can see why he's in a bad mood. He said, 'As if it's not bad enough having all these Lancastrian rebels to deal with, there's a load more come down from Northumberland to join in, and now we've got a lot of wild Scotchmen to contend with. We've managed to get them all into one place. The rest of Lancashire's pretty well clear of rebels by now. But we've been suffering losses. Probably more than they have. One thing I need is artillery. We've got the blackguards bottled up in the town, but they're holding out rather stubbornly. Can't even stop the devils coming and going as they please, bringing food and God knows what else. I'd like to block them in and besiege the place. Bring them to their knees that way. Trouble is we've not got enough men to completely encircle the town, so if any more of your Welsh lot could see fit to coming and joining us, I'd be really grateful. Anytime they please, of course!' I was glad to get away from him."

Perse agreed it was unfair to blame Billy when he seemed to have done a good job.

Billy asked, "Where have you been? I couldn't find you, nor could the Hussars, for a long time."

Perse explained and then asked, "Why have we got a German escort? Haven't we got any cavalry of our own?"

"Heinrich says there's been a bit of a row about that. The Duke of Marlborough ordered us to get up north as fast as possible, and said someone should send us an

225

escort. He was furious when he found all our cavalry had been sent off to deal with the rebels in Scotland, the Westcountry and I don't know where else. He had to ask the King to send us these Germans. They're some of the ones he brought over here when he first came to England. I met Heinrich and some of these fellows during the War. They're a good lot."

Bethan asked, "How do you come to have a new horse?"

"One of General Wills' staff officers, Sandy Sanderson, offered me the loan of him. He's a good horse. His owner was killed in a skirmish just outside Manchester and they haven't decided what to do with the horse. He hadn't been ridden since, so he was ready for some work, whilst poor old Cae had hardly had a rest since Cardiff."

"What's the new one called?"

"Jamie. His owner named him after the Pretender. Liked giving commands to 'King James the Third' I expect."

They rode on and reached Warrington about noon. Eddy announced that they were in Lancashire. They were surprised and delighted to find that it was flatter than Cheshire and much flatter than Wales. Therefore, they were able to keep up a steady trot most of the afternoon without tiring the horses. When it was dark, Eddy made them carry on at a walk, taking frequent breaks, so they could reach Preston by dawn.

Chapter 25

November 1715

At first light, they reached General Wills' camp. Lieutenant Sanderson greeted them and said, "The General's anxious to speak with Colonel Edwards and whoever commands the cavalry, so he would appreciate it if your adjutant could take charge of placing the guns and so on. There's a big area south-west of the town that's not covered, so the devils keep popping in and out as they please. He'd like you to go somewhere over there and discourage that sort of thing. They're cheeky blighters. Keep trying all sorts."

They went off to the General's tent while Major Davies, the Adjutant, started deploying the guns. The Germans were stationed behind and around the area indicated for the guns. Billy went off to try to obtain some more tents, as they had very few, hoping to find some food too. By the time they were properly set up, Eddy was back. He sent for his officers and sergeants.

He said, "Glad you've got everything set up all right. Well done! I see you've got quite a few tents for us, Rhys. Good! Any joy with the food?"

"Some should be coming our way shortly, Sir. And some for the Germans."

"Well now, I expect everyone wants some sleep before anything else. I know I do! Well, I hope we can all get some soon enough, but first I've promised the General we'll just let the Enemy know we've arrived.

Might help them see sense when they know there's heavy guns around. A few shots should do the trick. Let's not waste ammo, since the supply train's not here yet. Just blanks should do. Every other gun. Soon as you like. Smartly!"

Billy ensured his gun was fired with good synchronisation with the others. After ensuring the crew had reloaded the gun, he and Perse lay down in their tent and went to sleep. After about an hour, they were awakened by a commotion. Billy and Perse rushed out of the tent and saw Allan, who said, "These Germans are no fools! They just stopped a load of supplies for the Jacobites. They'll be ours now. With a bit of luck, the food shortage'll be getting worse now we're here, and it might make the Enemy give up and save a lot of bloodshed all round."

Perse said, "I hope so, but I feel sorry for the ordinary townspeople, who will be suffering just as much as the rebels, if not worse. I do hope this doesn't go on too long."

After a few more hours' sleep, Billy, Bethan and Megan began an exploration of the camp. Suddenly a voice called out, "Well! Fancy! Good to see you, Sir." It was Thomas. Billy and he had not seen each other until then, and the women had not mentioned him.

Billy said, "I thought you were at sea these days."

"I was, Sir, I mean Sarge, but I was ashore for a bit when a recruiting party comes into The Ship Inn. I says 'No' at first, but after a few drinks, well, a lot really, I sort of gave in. Pity I'm not in your crew, isn't it?" Billy was glad he was not in his crew.

There followed two days of intense inactivity, after which the Glamorgan Fusiliers arrived along with two other Welsh infantry regiments and the baggage train. Billy saw a few men he recognised and a few women he hoped Bethan would not recognise. He was pleased when they told him Major-General Jones was commanding the whole Welsh contingent. He and Eddy both respected Jones.

General Wills was pleased the reinforcements had arrived. He could now completely surround Preston, so as to tighten the screw of the food shortages and repel any sorties more effectively. The Glamorgans were placed on some low-lying ground just in front of the heavy guns, which could easily fire over their heads if the Jacobites attacked. Everyone was happy that they were better protected against anything the Enemy might try.

Later, Bethan and Megan were sitting with Billy in the opening to the tent, while he was cleaning his pistols, when they heard voices. One was of a young man, little more than a child. "Do as I ask! Either take me to Mr Rhys or get out of the way and let me look for myself."

The three of them got up and walked round the tent. There they saw Llewellyn.

"It's all right, Bombardier, this is my nephew."

As Allan went away, the others led Llewellyn into the tent.

"What are you doing here?" asked Bethan.

"When you went off, I knew I wanted to come, as I've lived in army camps when I was younger." "That was then, but you're too old now. Someone's likely to try to make you join."

The boy burst out angrily, saying, "I want to be a soldier, like Dada and Uncle Billy. If I can't be a real soldier, I can be a drummer boy. When I followed you to Maindy barracks, I saw a lot of boys getting onto a wagon. I knew some of them. So I joined them. Then I joined the Army."

"You've not joined until I agree. Can you help me, Billy?"

"Well, you're both here now. And Megan. I would have preferred you all to stay in Cardiff. You'll get into trouble if you just hang around here, Llew, unless you do join up." The boy looked pleased, but his mother looked shocked. Billy ignored her and continued, "I know you would be a terrible drummer. I've heard your attempts at making music. Anyway, they've probably got enough. What we need in the Artillery is powder-monkeys. Join us if you like." Bethan and Megan looked bewildered.

Llewellyn asked, "What's that?"

"A young fellow like you who fetches and carries for us. Mostly kegs of gunpowder. Some of them help with the horses too, and I know you'd be good at that. Uncle Gareth's taught you, as he once taught me. Now, go and find the bombardier again and tell him to fetch my horse, then we'll go and see the Adjutant." The lad went out, looking pleased.

Seeing Bethan's face, Billy said, "He'll be better off in the Artillery. I can keep an eye on him, and we don't usually go as close to harm as the infantry. We can hardly send him home, and he'll get into mischief if he's around here with nothing to do. Besides, he's old enough to have a mind of his own. Be proud of him!" He resumed cleaning and loading his pistols.

Bethan said, "I suppose you're right. After all, his father was a soldier. I wish I knew what would be best for him for the future, but for now I suppose being a 'powder something' will have to do."

"Powder-monkey. After we go to the Adjutant, I want to take Llew to meet Perse. Did you remember that he wanted to be a clergyman? We don't seem able to get away from them." He wondered if there was a reason for that.

Soon they heard Allan's voice calling. They all went out. Allan said, "This young fellow's been telling me about himself. He certainly knows how to tack up a horse, and he's checked Jamie's feet for you. I hope they do let him join us. It'd be a shame to waste him on one of those other regiments, now. But why did you want your horse? The lad says you're only going to see the Adjutant and you could've walked to his tent in the time it takes to get mounted."

"I wanted you two to get to know each other, and I think we'll be going to see the Adjutant of the Glamorgans afterwards. They might think they have a claim on him, so we'd best put them straight." He mounted, and Allan helped Llewellyn to get up behind him for the short ride. Both adjutants readily agreed to Lewellyn's being in Billy's crew. Perse came in and was charming to the boy. He told Billy he was impressed at the education of all his family, and especially at their religious knowledge. He said he looked forward to some intelligent conversations with them. He also encouraged Llewellyn to keep up his studies even while in the Army.

When they were alone, Megan said to Bethan, "It's not just intelligent conversations I want to have with Perse, and I expect you feel the same."

Bethan replied, "I don't know. I like him and I certainly am attracted to him, but I don't want to hurt him."

"How?"

"We obviously can't get married, and it would hurt him if I led him on, only to end it."

"I wasn't thinking of marrying him, just having fun."

"That's all right with men like Thomas and probably Allan, but with Perse, I'd want it to be different. He's different. Don't you see?"

"In a way, but I think you're making it too complicated. Men all want the same thing. Either give them what they want, or don't. There's no need to get so philosophical. You won't mind if I get into his bed if you don't want to?"

"No...but be kind to him, or I will mind!"

The next morning they were awakened by the sound of musket fire, and Billy guessed the Enemy had made a sortie. He pulled on his boots and his coat as fast as he could, armed himself with his sword and several pistols and ran out of the tent. Bethan followed, with Megan not far behind. Bethan knew to keep out of the way, but even from just outside the tent she could see and hear almost everything that went on.

Billy's guesses were apparently correct. Eddy was there, along with Perse, both only partly dressed. Eddy ordered the guns to fire over the infantry. Some of the Enemy had crept close, using undulations in the ground for cover, and were engaging the Glamorgans in hand-to-hand fighting. One of the infantry officers came and spoke briefly with Eddy, who ordered the guns to be reloaded with grapeshot. Some of the gunners struggled to unload the roundshot they had already loaded, while another fired wide, its crew presumably thinking that was the quickest way to empty it. Perse looked anxious, knowing his crew had just finished reloading, and asked

Billy, "What's the best way? To unload or fire wide?"

Allan asked, "Could we double-load?" Perse looked confused.

Billy said, "Yes! Do it!" then added, "Begging your pardon, Sir, but no time to explain." Perse nodded in approval.

The men simply rammed a bag of small lead shot, called grapeshot, into the barrel. Megan wondered whether the gun would fire with both the grapeshot and the usual round ball loaded, but it merely meant that its range and accuracy would be reduced. Billy did not consider range or accuracy to be an issue. He was right. A bugle called the infantry to fall back, just before the crew had finished loading with grapeshot. Infantrymen came running back past all the guns, hotly pursued by the Enemy. Billy was amazed at the sight. The rebels were wearing what appeared to be multi-coloured dresses and bonnets with long feathers sticking out. They were wielding heavy swords similar to the one Helen had given

Billy. He wondered if these were the Scotsmen he had heard were among the rebels.

Eddy called out to fire as they judged fit. As soon as he could see no redcoats in the line of fire, Perse gave the order. Some of the other guns fired at about the same time. The result was devastating. The ground was instantly littered with dead, dying and badly wounded men. Some had lost limbs or even heads. Others were simply peppered with lead shot. Many were screaming and writhing in agony. Despite this, those who were unharmed, or only slightly wounded, kept coming with perhaps greater ferocity. Before the men had finished reloading again, some of the Jacobites had reached the guns. Billy shot two of them with his pistols. Perse engaged another with his sword. The fine English blade snapped in two as soon as it met one of the heavier Highland weapons. Billy threw him his sword and drew his small pistol while calling to Allan to continue reloading, as he could see another wave of Jacobites approaching. Perse was a good swordsman, but he was treating the fight like a duel. The Highlanders were not. Soon several blades cut into him and he fell down wounded. Billy used a ramrod as a club to try to fend off some of Perse's attackers as well as his own. The women could see he was losing. Bethan thought about trying to help him. He was becoming surrounded and was running out of options, when the Enemy began retreating. Suddenly she saw why. The Glamorgans had regrouped and were counter attacking. Billy was thankful that they were using their bayonets. He was sure that, if they had fired their muskets, some of them would have hit some of the artillerymen, including him.

One of the Jacobites seemed particularly reluctant to give up attacking Billy and did so only when another, presumably an officer, shouted at him with words Billy was unable to decipher. Then Allan shouted "FIRE!" and another round of grapeshot was released with similar results to the first, except that it hit rebels in the back. Some of the other guns fired at about the same time. Then there came the sound of thundering hooves, and the Osnabruck Hussars came through a gap in the infantry and cut down many of those rebels who had survived up to then.

Bethan knelt to examine Perse. He was conscious but bleeding from several wounds. Billy ordered a stretcher-party to take him to the surgeons, accompanied by a few other men of his crew who had lesser wounds. Billy started looking round for his sword. Megan tried to help but could not find it. He guessed one of the Jacobites must have taken it as a trophy. He would doubtless be telling people in years to come how he had gained it by some great feat of valour.

The Adjutant appeared checking for casualties. Billy asked him, "What on Earth was all that about? Why did they attack us? Surely they knew they could not win, and were better off just defending their positions in the town?"

"Don't you know? Another supply train was trying to get through to them, and they hoped to divert us enough to stop us intercepting it. It didn't work. The

Hussars got it, before they went after the devils. At least we're all right for supplies now."

Billy went to see how Perse was. He had several sword slashes on his body and had a particularly bad wound on one leg. His wounds had been cleaned and bandaged. Now he needed rest. He apologised for putting Billy in danger, adding that he was annoyed with himself for forgetting he had a loaded pistol in his belt. Billy pointed out that shooting one of his attackers would have been a good idea, but would not have saved him from the rest of them. Bethan and Megan came and joined them.

Billy said, "I have seldom literally looked the Enemy in the eye, and I do not remember ever seeing such anger and hatred. Some of those I was fending off looked as if they had personal grudges against me. I never felt any such thing with the French, although they wanted to kill me."

Perse had never been in battle before, so it was all new to him, but he had noticed, as they had carried him along on the stretcher, all the dead and wounded Jacobites. He said, "I know that's what we're here for: to kill or be killed. I'm glad we did our duty. Thanks for doing mine as well as yours! Eddy said you were a good man. I'm glad we succeeded in stopping them. I wanted to defeat them, but I suppose I never thought what it would be like. I mean the broken bodies, severed limbs, torn flesh. I think the sight of the wounded was worse than the dead. You could see the pain. What's going to happen to the ones who've lost limbs or are too badly hurt to work again? I know they're the Enemy, but they're human beings. I just didn't expect it to be like this." There was little anyone could say to comfort him. Megan promised to fetch him anything he wanted. He said he would like his bible, and his pipe and tobacco. She fetched them straight away.

Several officers were checking on the condition of the wounded. Billy recognised Major MacNichol, who greeted him with some surprise, saying, "Glad to see you, Sergeant Rhys. I was going to stay at home this time, but Jonesie came to see me himself and offered me the command of the Third Battalion of the Glamorgans, which I just couldn't refuse. So, I'm a LieutenantColonel Now. My son's here too, on Jonesie's staff. He's brought Catherine, with him. She really wanted to come. Don't know why. Then, when you've seen as many battles as I have, the novelty wears off."

Billy said, "As you're a Scotsman, perhaps you can tell me if the fellows who attacked us so fiercely today were also Scots. Do they all dress like that?"

"Yes, they were Scots. Highlanders. Only Highlanders dress like that. Those garments are called 'plaid' and the pattern is called 'tartan'. Each clan is a sort of extended family. They all have the same surname and each clan has its own tartan, so they can always recognise each other. A bit like our uniforms and regimental colours."

General Wills appeared. He congratulated all the artillerymen on a fine display of their craft and said the arrival of the big guns and of the other reinforcements was turning things around.

It was late afternoon when a man left the camp carrying a white flag. Bethan asked Billy what was going

on. He said, "Now they can see we've got them surrounded, they might see sense. Eddy says the General hopes to arrange a parlay. By the way, until
Perse is with us again, Eddy's put me in charge of our lot. He's making me an acting lieutenant. General Wills says he'll do his best to get it made permanent. Perse told him I saved his life and assumed command of our crew most effectively, although I thought the counterattack by the infantry was more important in saving both our lives, but why argue with a superior officer?"

Later, the women went with Billy to visit Perse again. They attracted some interesting comments from both men and women along the way. Pure envy, they agreed. Perse was most grateful to have an experienced nurse and, as he knew Bethan was quite well educated, he said she would be a good companion for him as well as a nurse. She was flattered. Later, Megan teased her, saying she would have less competition for Allan while Bethan was busy nursing Perse. Bethan moved into the hospital tent with a few of the other camp followers.

Chapter 26

The next morning the General sent some of his staff officers into the town under a white flag. The parlay was obviously going to happen. Everyone else could only wait and hope. Billy had just finished inspecting his crew, and was walking through the camp towards the hospital tent, accompanied by Megan, when they heard a commotion coming from among the Glamorgan Fusiliers, as if a fight had broken out. A crowd had gathered around and were shouting unintelligibly. Two boys were fighting. One of them turned out to be Llewellyn. Billy helped another sergeant separate them. He asked what it was about. The boys were silent at first, then both tried to speak at once. Eventually he discovered that the other boy had said that Llewellyn's father was a deserter. He asked why he believed that. The lad said, "Everyone knows. He used to be in this regiment. My mum remembers him."

At that, a woman spoke up, saying, "That's right, I do! He was a god-botherer. They're all the same. No guts. Can't cope when things get rough. I wasn't surprised when he cleared off after a battle." Mari Williams had been a camp follower in the Netherlands. She had not got on with Bethan in those days. It looked as if a family tradition was being established.

The boy said, "See!" and Llewellyn took a swing at him again. Then they began a rapid exchange of punches. Llewellyn was bigger than the other boy and just as strong but not as good a fighter. The other boy seemed to land two punches on him for every one that went the other way. Luckily, before he came to too much harm, Billy and the other sergeant pulled them apart again.

Megan stood in front of the boy's mother. "How dare you say that about Llew's father! What do you know? I'm his wife's cousin and I know Henry was no deserter."

"His wife! I remember her. It didn't take her long to start throwing herself at other men, did it? She even tried my husband. I'll bet she was pleased when her man ran away, to give her a better chance at all the others, isn't it?"

Megan had had enough. She stepped towards the other woman. Mari was slightly smaller but wiry. She had a thin, mean face. It reminded Megan of an axe. Megan stepped closer and said, "Take that back or else!" The woman spat in her face. Billy and the other sergeant had to restrain the two boys again. Megan grabbed Mari by the hair. They butted each other. Megan made a very fast move, caught Mari unawares and tripped her. As soon as she hit the ground, Megan dropped on top of her and tried to pin her down. Mari wriggled and pulled ferocious faces at her. She did not have to try very hard: she looked fierce enough all the time. Megan sat on her, and punched her shoulders while kneeling astride her. After a few blows Megan asked if Mari wanted her to stop.

"Yeah! Stop breathing!" Megan pulled her head up and down. Twice. Then some more punches. She paused.

"Stop! Please stop!" She stopped.

Several other people were shouting at them and at each other. Suddenly everyone went quiet and looked behind Billy. All the men present saluted. There were two officers on horseback looking over the heads of the crowd. Billy recognised Colonel MacNichol and MajorGeneral Jones. The latter said, "That was a good fight. I can't order you women like the men, but let's not have too much of this. I don't want the camp descending into chaos." Then he turned to the two boys and said, "Glad to see you've both got the right spirit. We need fighters. But you need to learn to save it for the Enemy. We don't want to be injuring each other, do we? Sparing them the trouble." He looked around, then added, "Someone should talk to the boys about 'the fog of war' where so much is uncertain. We all need to be careful about jumping to conclusions. I don't think Lieutenant Henry Tudor was a deserter." Llew was moved to hear him say that in front of the crowd. He looked as if he was about to ride off, but then he paused and looked at Megan. He said, "I don't think we've met, Madam. My name is Jones. Major-General William Jones. May I know your name?"

"Megan Morgan, Sir. Sergeant Rhys's cousin."

"Is he here? Oh, yes, I see him. Good day, Sergeant. I remember your sister, Mrs Tudor. She was quite a fighter too. Runs in the family, does it? Pity she's not here. I liked her." There were some knowing looks and sniggers.

Billy replied, "Thank you, Sir. She is here. In the hospital tent, nursing Lieutenant de Clare, Sir."

"Good! Please tell her I'd like to see her. I've something to say to her. I'll be free after supper. In my tent." With that he rode off and a lot of people made suggestive comments. Mari looked furious.

When they got to the hospital tent, Billy and Megan told Bethan what had happened. Megan said she had been really furious at the woman for insulting Bethan and Henry, but at least she had enjoyed the fight. Perse was appalled that Megan and Llewellyn had both got into fights. He said, "So, one of the things your antagonist said to enrage you was to insult 'godbotherers' was it? No need to worry. God won't be bothered by insults of that sort. He's had to endure worse! Glad you and your cousins haven't lost your faith completely. Obviously, it has been sorely tried. But then, that's the case for all the saints, you know. It's never easy."

Bethan, by contrast, congratulated Megan on her victory over Mari and thanked her for sticking up for her and Henry, but she was worried about Llewellyn. They all agreed to try to think how to teach him to defend himself better.

Later, Eddy went to a meeting in the General's tent. Then he called the regiment to assemble and said the General had announced that a Colonel Oxburgh had agreed to the terms of surrender on behalf of General Thomas Forster, the leader of the Jacobites. Eddy said they could not yet strike camp or even reduce their vigilance, as, until the Jacobites had actually lain down their arms, there was the possibility of a last-minute attack, but everyone could expect to be going home soon.

A few hours later, they heard shouting from in the town, accompanied by drumbeats. It did not sound promising. Then a man came riding from the town carrying a white flag. Eddy said, "Looks like they want to talk again. Perhaps they want to improve the terms of the surrender. I think I'll go over to the General's tent and be ready when he summons all the colonels." Billy did not like the fact that the noise from the town continued unabated. It did not sound like preparations for surrendering.

When Eddy came back he said, "I am sorry to say that the surrender is not going ahead. It seems Mr Forster can speak only for the English rebels. He has failed to obtain agreement to our terms from the Scots. The noises we have been hearing are the Scots venting their anger at being ignored. They are threatening people with dire consequences if any should try to desert or make peace without their consent. We must be ready for any eventuality. Stay alert. You have all done well up to now. Don't let anything go wrong at this stage. I hope we may yet persuade them to surrender, but if not, I am sure you do not need me to tell you what the alternative is. Dismiss!"

For the rest of the day, everyone speculated as to how things were going. Would there be more negotiations? What should General Wills do to defeat the rebels? Would he do it? This was, of course, utterly unproductive and merely added to the anxiety and confusion. Billy, Allan and Llewellyn continued to participate in the discussion while Megan went to keep Perse company, enabling Bethan to go and get changed for

243

her meeting with the Major-General. She had been wearing breeches ever since leaving Cardiff. Now she changed into a dress she had bought for the occasion, from an officer's wife. She had thought of wearing a blouse under it, as it was so low-cut, but she decided against it. That evening she was going to give the man his money's worth.

She had to endure more offers and comments as she walked through the camp, especially when she passed the Glamorgan Fusiliers' section of the encampment. When Mari Williams saw her, they exchanged words and only just refrained from exchanging blows. Bethan then came to a tent next to General Wills' headquarters. It was only about the same size as most of the tents, but General Jones had this one to himself, whereas most had to accommodate six or more men.

As she entered, Bethan saw Jonesie sitting on a stool facing her across a trestle table. There was another stool for her. Behind him was a bed. A real bed. Almost everyone else had to sleep on the ground. Bethan was not sure how comfortable or stable the bed would be. It was on a thin wooden frame. She could not see what supported its occupant under the blankets. She had misgivings. At least the ground seldom gave way.

He invited her to sit on the stool. She did so. She would have preferred an ammunition box, but could hardly say so. He continued, "You look most attractive. That can't be easy in such primitive surroundings. However, I fear that you may have misunderstood me. I really do want to talk to you. Not just to ask you to share my bed. We can discuss that later, but first things first. I need to tell you that I have news of your husband." Bethan nearly fell off the stool. "I have received some letters he wrote to you from captivity in France. It seems they have been passed around for some time and came to me only recently. I did not have an address for you other than a farm in the Rhondda from which they had already been returned to the Army. Had I known you would be here, I would, of course, have brought them with me. I shall be sure to give them to you when we return to Cardiff."

"You mean he's alive?"

"I hope so, although I must warn you against being overoptimistic. If he were alive, why would he not have contacted you by now? All prisoners have been repatriated since the Peace was signed. I received a letter from Martial Vendome, passed to me from the Duke of Ormonde, about a year after the Peace. He apologised for the fact that a number of British and Dutch prisoners had been kept by the garrison at Amiens far longer than they should have been."

"Why?"

"The Martial had no idea they were there. He sent us a list of names and your husband's was on it. He also apologised for the fact that the garrison commander at Amiens had not released letters to or from the prisoners until the Peace was signed. So your Henry's letters were among a large number sent to the British Embassy in Paris from Amiens. From there they went to the Horse Guards from where they were dispatched to the addresses on them. In Henry's case, as I said, they were returned to the Horse Guards from a farm in the Rhondda. The Horse

Guards eventually sent them to me in the hope that I would know where to find you, which, regrettably, I did not."

Bethan wondered why her sister Rhona had not sent them to her. Then she thought that Rhona's employers might not have let her know. To be fair to them, they had no reason to know that Mrs Tudor was one of the Rhys family who used to live at Penrhys.

She responded, "So he was taken prisoner? Why was he sent to Amiens?"

"Monsieur Vendome did not say, but I have no reason to suppose the French Army is any more efficient or reliable than our own. I must warn you that I have heard that some of the prisoners at Amiens tried to escape, towards the end of the War. They had no way of knowing that their liberation was imminent. Several of them succeeded at first, but were intercepted by a French patrol and a skirmish ensued. Some were killed, others wounded. I have written to the French authorities asking for names and details. I believe Martial Vendome's list was compiled before the escape, so your husband could be among the dead or the wounded. Of course, he might have been one of the lucky ones who actually made it either to the Channel or to the Netherlands. Where he would have gone next, I cannot say." Bethan asked, "How can I find out?"

"I must ask you to wait until I receive more details from the French. The British Embassy are trying their best. Now, I think we both need a brandy!" He poured one for each of them. Quite large ones.

His gaze had strayed to Bethan's cleavage several times during their conversation. Meanwhile, she kept looking at the bed. He thought she was hinting, when in fact she was just thinking how flimsy it looked. He said, "After all that, I hope you don't feel obliged to get into my bed."

"Well, I came here expecting that. You really stunned me with the news, but now I don't want to think about Henry. Not when I still don't know for sure whether he's dead or alive. A night with you could be just what I need. I was just wondering how strong that bed is. It doesn't look as if it could take your weight, let alone mine on top of yours. Or, underneath it, even!" "It's stronger than it looks. I've had heavier women than you in it with me. You may recall I like big women. Do you remember a big Flemish whore who
joined us during the War? Greta?"

"I certainly do! We had a few scraps."

"Oh, yes. I remember. Well, she's with us now. Married a gunner at the end of the War. I've had her in this bed, and if it can stand her weight on top of mine, or beneath, it'll stand yours." He offered another brandy.

"No thanks. I'm ready for you while I'm sober."

He liked big women. She liked big men. Some people imagine generals as slim and soft. Weedy even. This one was over six feet tall and muscular. The bed was stronger than it looked. They tested it thoroughly.

Since leaving Cardiff, Bethan had had many uncomfortable nights. Some of the days had left a lot to be desired too. Now she was enjoying herself. Except when she thought of Henry.

Chapter 27

The next morning Billy was summoned to General Wills's tent. There with the General sat Jonesie, Eddy, Colonel MacNichol, Heinrich and several other officers.

The General began, "You know what's been going on. You know we all want to finish this as soon as we can. I'm going to try once more to talk to the scoundrels. This time I'm going to insist on talking to the Scots as well as the English. I'm sending Colonel MacNichol. He's a Scotchman, even though he lives in England. I hope that'll count for something."

Billy saw the look on the Colonel's face, and they both suppressed smiles, as they resisted the temptation to mention that Chepstow is in Wales. There were some who counted Monmouthshire as England, but Billy did not take any notice of them. General Wills was in full flow, so it would have been futile to try to interrupt. He said, "If they don't surrender this time, properly I mean, I'm going to order the big guns to start bombarding the town. Just to give them one last chance, I'll let you gunners find targets that won't matter too much at first. You know: empty buildings, tall spires, open spaces. Just to help them concentrate their minds, you see. After that, I'll give them a chance to change those minds. Surrender. If that doesn't do the trick, Eddy, I'll want your fellows to aim for the rebel positions. Let's try to avoid killing civilians if we can. Obviously, however good you are, you're bound to kill some innocent people, but that's war, I regret to say."

There was a long pause. Billy looked around.

Everyone looked puzzled. Eddy said, "Well, Sir, thank you for explaining all that. Would you like to say anything to Acting Lieutenant Rhys in particular?"

"What? Oh, yes! Thank you. Now, Mr Rhys, I've heard a lot about you. Sorry we got off to a bad start, but I was in a very bad mood when we first met. Anyway, Colonel Edwards and Major-General Jones have both told me good things about you. Not only about your handling of the situation yesterday, but also about your secret activities in the Netherlands. Excellent stuff! Well, I think that's just what we need now. If you carry this off, your promotion will be permanent. I give you my word. In the absence of the Duke of Marlborough, I'm in command here, and if I give a battlefield promotion, it's valid. You can count on me. Can I count on you?" Another pause. Most looked as puzzled as before.

Billy asked, "I'm sorry to be a bit slow on the uptake, Sir, but I don't see what it is that you want me to do?"

"Oh! Did I not make that clear? Well, we need to know where in Preston the different sorts of targets are. Unless anyone knows already, and they've certainly not told me, the only thing is for someone to go in and have a look. Obviously you can't make drawings or notes. You'll just have to commit everything to memory. They say you're good at that. Well that's it. Any questions?"

Billy was too stunned to put into words the numerous questions which were clamouring for attention in his mind. Fortunately, Jonesie was more lucid. He asked, "How do you intend Mr Rhys to get into the town? They'll be on the lookout for any strangers approaching from our direction, and since we've now got the place pretty well surrounded, that means just about any direction, surely?"

The General looked somewhat embarrassed. He had not thought of a specific plan. Even Merlin, the real one, would have found himself stretched to magic himself into Preston at that time, Billy thought. Eddy asked if he could see a map of the area. One of the staff officers passed him one and he studied it.

Another Colonel, George Campbell, said, "Why on earth are we bothering with this? It's just another delay. Whatever we do we can't avoid killing civilians. It's not our fault that the devils have chosen to hide in the town among the local people. Anyway, half these Lancastrians are Jacobites underneath."

Billy thought that that implied the other half were not, but he said nothing. Heinrich, however, spoke up, saying, "I don't think the Duke of Marlborough or the King himself will be pleased if there's a heavy death-toll among civilians. They don't really want too many dead even among the rebels. They don't want it to look as if they're tyrants. So anything we can do to save lives will be pleasing to them."

Campbell said, "I suppose those two gentlemen always take you into their confidence about such things, Major, do they?" Heinrich just smiled.

General Wills said, "Well, he's probably right. Anyway, *I* don't want a bloodbath, if I can help it!"

Before the argument got any more heated, Eddy looked up from perusing the map and said, "As I thought! The town is a port and is situated on an estuary. The River

Ribble runs through the town but opens up into the estuary just beyond it. Surely the town can be approached from the sea, can't it?"

Colonel MacNichol said, "I thought the Navy were doing something about that."

The General replied, "Well, only a bit. Their main concern is watching for any reinforcements arriving, not only here, but anywhere. One of our biggest fears is the French or the Spanish or anyone deciding to take advantage of the situation. All our intelligence chaps say it won't happen, but the Admiralty don't trust 'em, the French I mean, not the intelligence people!" Jonesie suppressed a laugh. General Wills continued, "Anyway they're probably stopping any big merchant ships coming into Preston, but I don't think they'd bother with a small craft. What do you say, Rhys? Does that give you the basis for a plan?"

"Yes Sir. Very helpful."

Billy was inwardly cursing Eddy for making the mission seem even remotely practicable. He had hoped for a moment that they would all agree it could not be done. On the other hand, he did agree with the General that it would be good to minimise civilian casualties whilst making any bombardment as effective as possible.

The General then tried to wrap up the meeting, saying, "Oh, yes! If there's anything you need, just say so. Gentlemen, you all heard that? I want everyone to give Lieutenant Rhys all the cooperation he needs, all right? Good. Oh, yes, this is all a big secret. No need to tell anyone else, at least no more than they have to know. Anything you want to ask for right now, Rhys?"

"Can I recruit someone else to manage the boat, when we find one? I'm not much of a sailor, Sir. To say the least."

"Have you anyone in mind?"

"Yes Sir, Gunner Thomas Thomas. He's a good sailor, and I think he'd be good at this sort of thing."

Eddy looked amused. The General asked, "Is he a decent, honest fellow? One we can trust?"

"No Sir! He's a natural liar and a cheat. I hope he can deceive the Jacobites the way he's deceived a lot of other people. His only loyalty is to himself. We can rely on that."

There were several gasps and a few chuckles. The General said, "I see what you mean, Edwards. This fellow really is a crafty one. Should make a fine officer. Yes. You have my authority to do as you have asked. Anything else?"

"Is it all right if Thomas makes money out of this?"

"How?"

"I was thinking of pretending to be traders, selling supplies to the townspeople. I'd like to be able to draw the stuff from our supplies and let Thomas keep the money we make."

"If you think that's necessary, I'll agree. Is that all?"

Billy decided to make the most of the opportunity and asked, "The only thing I was thinking was that I'd like Bombardier Morris to be promoted to Sergeant. Not just acting. I think he's good enough, Sir." Eddy and Jonesie agreed.

Billy went out with very mixed emotions. He could see what a great honour it was to have such confidence placed in him, and he expected the General would ensure he got a permanent commission, but it was probably the most dangerous operation he had ever undertaken.

He told Allan of his promotion and went to find Thomas. He sold the scheme to him as if the General had not realised that they were going to make money out of it. Thomas saw it as a heaven-sent opportunity. They went to select a cartload of assorted supplies and a cart to carry them in. The women became suspicious and pestered Billy and Thomas to tell what was going on. Eventually they took them into their confidence. They demanded to go with them. Thomas said taking a woman could make them look more like traders and less like soldiers. Billy had reservations but had to admit that the women had proved valuable on some of the illegal activities they had carried out. Megan reminded him that she was a better sailor than Billy or Bethan, who anyway was reluctant to leave Perse until he was more recovered.

So Billy gave in. He told Perse that he was going away with Thomas and Megan on an undercover mission. Perse said he wished he could come. Billy thought Perse was not someone he would choose for such an enterprise. He lacked the devious nature and the ability to lie convincingly, that Thomas had. Then Perse promised to pray for them until they were safely back. They were touched by his concern. Bethan and Megan also prayed. So did Billy.

Chapter 28

The three of them drove the cartload of supplies away from camp and went south before turning west, so as not to seem to be coming from the camp. They found a village called Longton, on the River Dane, which ran into the Ribble Estuary. They drove to a farm that had fields going down to the river and found the farmer. His name was Peter Rigby and he did have a boat, but it was hardly bigger than a Welsh Coracle and nowhere near suitable. When they explained what they needed, he said his brother-in-law, Alan Ball, might be able to help. He had a farm on the other side of the river in a village called Hesketh Bank. Peter Rigby rowed across the river and came back with his brother-in-law in the bigger boat.

Alan Ball said he did a bit of fishing as well as farming. It made Billy think of his time in Ogmore. When they asked to hire the boat, he was reluctant, explaining that the tides and currents around there were treacherous if you were unfamiliar with them, and there were a lot of mudflats where you could get stuck at low tide. When Billy offered enough money, he said he would come with them and skipper the boat until they were safe enough, but he did not want to go into the town, as he was afraid of getting caught up in any fighting. They could put him on dry land just before the town, where some friends lived.

Both men helped unload the cart into the boat, which had a single triangular sail and two sets of oars. None of them had much to do at first as the current took the boat down the river, but as soon as it reached the estuary they all had to work hard, using sail and oars at times, to navigate out into the main channel through the various currents, before they could relax and let the tide do most of the work. As they approached the town, they saw a small farmhouse on the south bank. They moored at a jetty next to another similar boat. Mr Ball told them the main entrance to the town from the river was called Fishergate, for obvious reasons, and was near the market. They thanked him and gave him part of the money they had agreed, withholding the rest to encourage him to wait for them.

Once they found a berth in Preston's docks, they had no trouble attracting the attention of plenty of citizens, anxious to see what goods they had for sale. Billy left Thomas and Megan to conduct the business while he went for a walk around the town. He noticed a few areas where the rebels were concentrated and a few apparently empty buildings. However, as not all the rebels wore any kind of uniform, and as many were sharing accommodation with local people, there were many places which he could not properly categorise as targets for either warning shots, or for serious bombardment.

Just as he got back to the boat, a group of armed men approached. One of them got straight to the point. "What are you doing here?"

Billy answered, "I'm a trader. William Rhys. My partners and I have brought a lot of supplies here by boat to sell to the local people."

"Let's look at what you've got. But first, tell us why you went wandering all the way into the town." "That's easy. I'm looking for the commanding officer of your force. I've brought some things he'll be interested in."

"What things?"

"I'll tell him. Who are you, by the way?"

"I'm Captain Rimmer of the Lancashire Irregulars and these are some of my men. Come on, let's stop wasting time – show me what you've brought us!"

"I'm not selling what I've got to a mere Captain."

He hit Billy across the face and shouted, "You'll do as I say, whoever you are, understand?" There followed a bit of a scuffle. None of the Welsh party drew a pistol, as they did not want to escalate things. Suddenly the irregulars all stood to attention. A man in a fancy uniform had appeared.

He asked, "What's going on?"

Captain Rimmer gave a somewhat biased account of the proceedings.

The gentleman said to Billy, "Well, Sir, perhaps you will talk to me. I am Lord Derwentwater. I am in charge of supplies here. I do not think we need trouble General Forster with such trivia. Let us look at what's in your boat."

Billy introduced Thomas and Megan. Captain Rimmer said, "I recognise this boat. It's a local fishing boat. You can smell it. What are you lot up to? You're not selling fish."

Thomas said, "Well, well! And there's me thinking the English was stupid. You're dead right. We're traders. We had a spot of bother with our boat and so we came to a sort of arrangement with this boat's owner. It's what we call 'doing business,' isn't it?"

The irregulars were still suspicious. One of them said, "Hang on! You lot aren't from 'ere. Where are you from?"

Megan said, "You're as observant as your captain. You must be due for a promotion. Yes, we're Welsh. King James does have supporters in Wales you know. Some of them have sent us with these supplies to help you out. We were hoping you'd be grateful."

Lord Derwentwater said, "So if these things are gifts, why are you taking money?"

Thomas answered, "Well you see, we've had a few difficulties on the way, isn't it? So there's been what you might call 'expenses'. But I'm sure you'll all agree you're getting your money's worth."

Billy said to Lord Derwentwater, "You and your men can buy whatever has not yet been sold, but there are some things we've kept back just for the General."

Captain Rimmer asked sceptically, "What's so special it's only for him?"

Billy paused to get everyone's attention and said, "Powder and shot." Thomas and Megan lifted a blanket covering a few kegs beneath the stern platform. The irregulars inspected first the kegs, lifting the tops off some, then the rest of the cargo.

Rimmer obviously had a suspicious mind. He said, "Some of these things look like British Army issue. What's going on?"

Thomas looked at Billy and said, "Well, well!

Whatever next? Do you think them fellers what sold 'em to us was soldiers? I've 'eard you can get into a lotta trouble in the Army for selling Army property, isn't it? It's not our problem, mind you, is it? I mean, we never got on with the English Army anyway."

Lord Derwentwater said. "We'll take this ammunition, but we're not paying for it. You're making enough money from the other stuff you're selling. You can give us a hand carrying it too. One of our lads can keep an eye on the boat."

Rimmer said, "Yes, Sir! Right. Blundell. You like boats. Take care of this'un until we get back. Any looters, you shoot. That's orders. Right! Come on you lot."

Rimmer's men picked up some of the kegs. Billy and Thomas picked up one each and followed them. Megan remained and continued trading. Lord Derwentwater led the way to a church that was being used as a store for various kinds of supplies and apparently as sleeping quarters for some of the rebels. They stacked the kegs alongside the existing stock. More irregulars came and went. Billy was glad he had now identified the location of the rebels' stores. He had also noticed that the houses immediately opposite the church were being used by the rebels. Their mission had been a success. Or at least it would be once they got back to camp.

They turned to go. As they approached the door of the church, a group of Highlanders came in. One of them looked straight at Billy, who tried to ignore him and carry on. The man stepped in front of him and burst into a stream of words, while pointing a finger at him. Although he did not understand one syllable, he guessed from the tone that he was not offering the hand of friendship. Several others joined in. He could only assume that this was some Scottish language. It was certainly nothing he had heard before. Lord Derwentwater demanded a translation. In case Billy and Thomas had been in any doubt that things were not going their way, the Scotsmen pointed their weapons at them. The biggest of the Highlanders silenced the others and addressed Lord Derwentwater, saying, "Wee Alex says he kens who these are. They're twa Sassenachs from the Army oot there!" He waved a hand in an extravagant gesture encompassing most of the rest of the world. He went on, "He says he came reet face-tae-face wi' this one. He's the swine who had them fire one o' their great guns at us that killed one o' his brothers an' tore lumps off another."

Lord Derwentwater turned to Billy and asked politely, "Well, now! What do you have to say for yourself?"

"I don't know what he's talking about. We're three Welsh traders come here with supplies to help you at great risk to ourselves. I think we should be entitled to your gratitude, not wild accusations."

Thomas said, "That's right! But I dunno what he's saying. Who is he anyway? And what's a Sassenach?"

His Lordship answered, "He's accusing you two of being English soldiers. He says his comrade recognised your partner from the skirmish we had yesterday. Oh, yes! A Sassenach is a derogatory term used in Scotland to refer to an Englishman."

Billy said, "We're Welsh! And if I know anything about a skirmish, I know it's pretty confusing. He must be mistaken."

The big fellow translated those words for the benefit of the others. The accuser seemed to take offence at what he heard and came back with more angry words. Billy thought he heard the word "MacKenzie".

The big man turned to him again and said, "Is your name 'MacKenzie' or hae you killed a MacKenzie?"

He was stunned. Was it a coincidence that he was trying to find the killer of Kenneth MacKenzie? He said, "My name is William Rhys, and I have never killed a MacKenzie. Is that your name?" Remembering what Colonel MacNichol had told him, he wondered if these men were of the clan MacKenzie.

The big man spoke to one of the other Highlanders, who went off in a hurry. "We're all MacGregors. This is oor tartan. My name's Robert Roy MacGregor. But there are MacKenzies here. William MacKenzie, the Earl of Seaforth, is their leader. Ye'll be meeting him soon."

Billy hoped the Earl would be more reasonable than these MacGregors, who all looked ready to kill him and Thomas at the least excuse. He also hoped he spoke better English than this Robert Roy character. He did not have long to wait. The Highlander returned followed by a gentleman wearing clothing of a more familiar kind than that of the MacGregors, but with tartan breeches and a tartan scarf. The others pointed Billy and Thomas out to him.

He bowed and said in clear English but with a Scottish accent, "I am Lord Seaforth. Is one of you a MacKenzie?"

"No, my Lord."

"Then how did you come by this sword?" He asked, holding out the sword Helen had lent Billy the day he left Cardiff. The sword he lost during the skirmish.

Billy knew that to acknowledge it was to admit to being a soldier and therefore a spy. He said, "Why do you suppose I have had anything to do with it?"

The others must have divined the meaning from Billy's tone and expression. They all started shouting at once. The Earl spoke to them in their own language, thus restoring quiet and order, before addressing Billy again, saying, "The MacGregors are certain they saw you give the sword to another English officer during the skirmish."

Before he could say anything else, the cacophony began again. Rob Roy shouted in English, of sorts, above the din, "Why waste time? Let's search the Sassenachs tae see what they're hiding!"

The Earl nodded and two of the MacGregors tore Billy's coat from him. Then some of them went through the coat while the others searched his waistcoat and breeches. Two more searched Thomas. Billy was hopeful that they would not find all the pockets in his coat. He was not surprised when they found his small pistol, which made some of them very excited. Lord MacKenzie clearly regarded it as of no consequence. Similarly, the few items discovered when they searched

Thomas revealed nothing of his identity. He doubtless had experience of being searched and knew how to hide things.

They were hopeful that they would soon be released, but Lord Derwentwater intervened, saying, "Well, do it thoroughly, as you're doing it. You have not searched their hats or their boots." He was sharper than Billy had realised. Unfortunately. The next search unearthed a letter folded into the lining of Billy's hat. It was from General Wills, requiring all officers and other soldiers to give Billy their full cooperation. The two lords read it with interest. The two Welshmen felt this was going to turn out unhappily for them. Lord Derwentwater passed the letter to Captain Rimmer, who showed it to his men. Lord Seaforth translated it aloud to the Highlanders. Its significance evidently did not elude any of them. For a minute it looked as if the two Welshmen were going to be torn apart on the spot.

Billy decided there was only one thing to do: go onto the offensive. He had nothing to lose. If he got the chance to say anything, above the clamour. The two lords managed to quieten the others again. He said, "All right! So now you know. I'll tell what my mission was. There's no longer any point in deception. But I want to speak to whoever is in command here. I won't waste my breath on lesser men!"

Rob Roy drew a dagger, took a step towards Billy, so their faces were only inches apart and said,

"You'll talk tae me or I'll slit yer lying throat!"

Billy laughed. Thomas cringed. Rob Roy looked even angrier than before, if that were possible.

Thomas called out, "Tell him, you fool! They'll kill us both."

Rob Roy asked, "Wha's sae funny?"

"If you slit my throat, how will I talk?"

"I think yer friend here'll do the talking!"

"He might, but he doesn't know much. His job's to obey orders. He doesn't know the whole mission."

Lord Derwentwater interrupted the discussion, saying, "I think the General will want to question them himself."

Lord Seaforth replied, "Aye. But they're all busy the noo with that Colonel the English have sent."

Lord Derwentwater said, "I think it will be worth interrupting their negotiations. This may have a bearing on them."

Chapter 29

They went across the road into a big house. The two lords went into what was apparently the dining room, while the rest of the group waited.

After a minute or two, the door opened and someone ushered Billy and Thomas in. The man beckoned Rob Roy to follow, but excluded the rest. A group of men variously attired sat around a long table. The only one Billy recognised, apart from the ones who had brought him there, was Colonel MacNichol, who saw in the arrival of Billy and Thomas a sign that his mission was over. As well as his life.

Billy and Thomas were invited to sit. Lord Derwentwater introduced them. There was silence. Billy broke it by asking, "Might I know to whom I have the honour of speaking? Perhaps you could tell me which one of you is in command."

The most soberly dressed man in the room replied, with an English accent, "I am General Forster. I command the English forces here. The Scots are led by their various clan chiefs or their representatives, but their overall commander is Lord Mackintosh of Borlum, leader of the Mackintoshes. Lord Seaforth commands the MacKenzies; Lord Kenmure, the Gordons; Lord Nairne, the Murrays; Lord Winton, the Setons; Lord Nithsdale, the Maxwells and, in the absence of his chief, Mr MacGregor, the MacGregors." As he spoke he waved a hand vaguely in the direction of each of the people he named.

Billy noted that there was apparently no real chain of command, at least among the Scots, which he thought was a recipe for failure. Even when the British had fought on the Continent with an alliance of several sovereign nations, there had been one overall commander, the Duke of Marlborough. No wonder it had been difficult to negotiate a surrender. He felt sorry for General Forster, who concluded the introductions by saying, "This is Colonel Oxburgh, my second-incommand. I take it that you already know Colonel MacNichol?" Billy nodded. The Colonel looked at his hands.

The General said, "Now perhaps you will be kind enough to inform us all about the purpose of your visit to this town. You might even care to explain why General Wills is trying to negotiate a peaceful end to this conflict while you are trying to do what one must assume to be the opposite. Oh. Forgive my bad manners. Please have some wine. I would not want you to be too dry to tell us everything."

Billy accepted a glass, as did Thomas, and began, "It is really quite simple. General Wills wants this whole business over as soon as possible with the least loss of life on both sides, and especially among the civilian population of this town. Colonel MacNichol is trying to achieve that by negotiation. If that fails, the General will order an artillery bombardment of the town. He wants to target those who are in armed rebellion against King George. My mission was to identify suitable targets. This I had done prior to being recognised by one of the Highlanders. If I fail to return with the information, the General will order an indiscriminate bombardment

265

followed by an infantry attack, which will probably also have to be indiscriminate. There are those who would be quite happy with that outcome. I thought they were only on our side, but now I can see that some of you seem to be of the same mind. Be clear that you have three options. You can negotiate a surrender, you can let me go and expect to be the targets of our heavy guns, or kill me and force the General to destroy the whole town."

To Billy's amazement, Thomas intervened at that point, saying, "Oh, no! Just 'ang on! There's another choice, if they're as brave as they say."

There were puzzled looks all round the table. Billy drank some more wine as he tried to think what his companion could mean. General Forster prompted him by asking, "Well? What have we not thought of?"

"You could come out and fight us in the open. Show you're not cowards, hiding behind these townsfolk."

There were gasps and murmurs. Billy nearly choked on his wine. Rob Roy stood up, banged his fist on the table and shouted, "Ye'll tak that back ye damned Sassenach or we'll see who's a cooward!"

Lord Derwentwater spoke quietly to him and managed to calm him down somewhat.

Lord Seaforth said, "How dare you impugn our honour!"

Thomas replied, "Honour! Is that what you call it? I dunno what 'impue' or whatever means, but 'ow can I impue summat as don't exist? I know what I am. Yeah! A thief an' a cheat. I done some bad things in my time an'

I've 'ad some friends what was worse. But none of us come close to you lot. We never let an 'ole town die for nothing. Call that honour? I'd like to insult you, but I can't, 'cos all the bad words I know don't get near to what I think of you lot. Leaders? Gentlemen? I'm glad I'm just a poor thief an' a scoundrel what's got no honour."

There was an awkward silence. Billy wanted to cheer, but thought it best to wait for a more opportune time. Colonel MacNichol was still looking down to avoid looking anyone in the eye. General Forster broke the silence, saying, "Well, I think these gentlemen have told us all we need to know about their mission. I see no need to detain them further." He looked around at the angry faces and added, "I also see no point in punishing them. Please escort them to their boat and let them go unmolested. That's an order! Lord Derwentwater, please ensure it is obeyed."

They were led from the room by Rob Roy to find the rest of his little band of MacGregors waiting in the hall along with Captain Rimmer and his men. They all fell in to form an escort with the prisoners somewhere in the middle. Lords Derwentwater and Seaforth brought up the rear. When they got to the quay, Billy was relieved to find the boat still there. Blundell was sitting in the stern pointing a musket at a group of men who were gathered. Megan was sitting close to him. Lord Seaforth went up to Billy and handed him his pistols and a few other items the Highlanders had found during their search. He then said, "Will you now tell me how you came by a MacKenzie sword?"

"It was lent to me by a third cousin of mine who is the widow of Lieutenant-Colonel Kenneth MacKenzie, late of the Royal Scots Borderers, whose home was in Wales."

"Ah! Now I see. Did he live in a red castle?"

"No, but he owned a ruin called Castell Coch, which means 'red castle'. Had you heard of him?"

"I've heard of a branch of the family that went to England with King James the Sixth and First. He rewarded them with various houses, lands and titles. I remember hearing about a red castle in Wales. Well, you might as well have the sword back. We're not thieves, whatever else you may think we are." He handed over the sword and they shook hands. Billy and Thomas were about to board the boat when a hand grabbed Billy's arm. He found himself face-to-face with Wee Alex who looked as bitter and angry as ever. He said something unintelligible but full of feeling. The other Scotsmen muttered what sounded like approval. Billy looked around for an interpreter. Lord Seaforth said, "He wants satisfaction for what you did to his brothers. He says it's time to see if you can use that sword."

He realised that it would do no good to try telling him he was a useless swordsman. Rob Roy said, "I wanted tae say the same, but he's got there first. I've got honour tae defend!" Thomas laughed. Rob Roy looked at him and said, "As for you! Me and you hae got a wee something tae settle too."

Lord Derwentwater said, "Remember what the General said: we're not to harm them." Various murmurs went around. Several faces looked disappointed, but even the Highlanders seemed to have some respect for His Lordship and for the General.

Just when Billy thought he and his companions were going to get away safely, Lord Seaforth said, "I ken fine what he said, but this is personal. A man's got a right to challenge whoever insults his honour or kills his kin. But let it be done fairly, one against one."

Billy resignedly took off his coat and hat, then his waistcoat. He drew the sword, handing the scabbard to Thomas. He walked away from the quayside to a patch of muddy grass between two buildings opposite. He could see no reason to add drowning to the risks he was facing. Wee Alex threw his bonnet and his plaid to one of his kinsmen and stood in his shirtsleeves. A musket fired. Billy nearly jumped out of his skin. Private Blundell of the Lancashire irregulars had fired from the boat towards the quay. The crowd froze, looking shocked. The soldier shouted, "That's a warning! The next one won't miss! Behave yourselves, you thieving beggars!"

Captain Rimmer called out, "What's that for, Blundell?"

"A few of 'em was trying to rob the boat, Sir."

Rimmer's voice became louder, "Well done! Glad you're alert. Make sure the next one doesn't miss! That's an order. It goes for all of you. These people came here at great risk to save these ungrateful creatures and anyway we've already got orders to shoot looters."

Lord Derwentwater said, "How do you know about their mission?"

"We were listening outside the door, Sir. We could hear nearly every word."

Wee Alex drew everyone's attention back to business by shouting something. He and Billy circled each other and crossed swords a few times. Billy was fighting very cautiously and defensively. To his surprise, so was the Highlander. Alex gradually became bolder. Billy kept backing away and parrying his blows. He noticed that he fought with a slashing rather than a stabbing action. Not that it made much difference. Billy's tutor in fencing, John Aris, the highwayman, had despaired of Billy's ever becoming proficient. So he realised his chances of survival were slim. Wee Alex was faster and more athletic than him as well as a more skilful swordsman. It was also an uneven fight as he was determined to kill Billy, whilst Billy merely wanted to survive. He never wanted to kill anyone.

Then Billy remembered something Eddy had told him many years before. He had said that the essence of winning a fight was the same whether it was a swordfight, a street brawl or a full-scale battle involving thousands. It was to bring your strengths to bear and to play on your opponent's weaknesses. All Billy had to do was to identify them. He had to think of at least one way in which he was better than his opponent. He did not have much time in which to reflect. He was too busy trying to avoid being cut to pieces. He saw the hatred in those eyes and felt renewed fear.

Suddenly it came to him. His opponent's very anger was his biggest weakness. How many times had he heard about the importance of keeping calm in battle?

Lots of people, including Eddy, had said that Marlborough's ability to keep calm and think clearly was one of his greatest strengths. Billy needed to antagonise Wee Alex even more so as to make him make a mistake. Ordinarily he would have said something to annoy the Highlander, but he was hampered by the latter's lack of knowledge of English. Then he remembered how much he had managed to discern from the tone of the Highlanders' voices, their faces and postures. He pulled faces and made insulting remarks in the most sarcastic tones.

It started to work. The Scotsman slashed more violently and with less skill than before. Their swords crossed and their hands slid towards each other until the cross-pieces of both handguards were pressing against each other. Their faces were inches apart. Billy sneered at him and taunted him. They pushed against each other, and it looked as if they were about equal in strength. Billy eased the pressure and immediately increased it again, causing the Scotsman to slip slightly. He butted him in the face and followed up with a punch from his left fist before stepping back a couple of paces. Alex came at him slashing wildly. Billy went back another couple of paces and then counterattacked, going forwards briefly and then swiping his sword across his opponent's chest before stepping back again. It was not close enough to do any real damage but he managed to slash Alex's shirt and touch his chest enough to draw blood. He was enraged. Billy parried the anticipated blow and they found themselves face-to-face and handto-hand again. Billy pushed his sword against him while twisting the hilt upwards, then hit him in the face with the pommel of the MacKenzie sword. That is the ball at the end of the hilt which acts as a grip and as a counterweight. It also acts as a club sometimes. Alex reeled. Billy followed up his advantage, pushing forwards while parrying a half-hearted attempt at a cut. His right shoulder pushed against Alex's chest making him stagger backwards. Billy tripped him with his right foot, while punching him in the face again with his left hand. Alex made the mistake of trying to attack when he should have gone back a bit more to recover. His face came forwards against Billy's left fist, doubling the impact. He tripped and fell. Billy stepped onto his sword with his left foot. He tried to kick his legs up at Billy who kicked him in the ribs. Then Billy held his sword against the Highlander's chest.

Billy called out, without taking his eyes off Alex, who roared defiance, "Will someone ask him if he wants to live?" Someone did. More defiant roars. Billy slid the point of his blade slowly up and down Alex's body. Up to his throat, back to his chest, down to his belly and lower, calling out again, "Ask him where he wants my next cut." He roared again. Someone called out to him in his own language. He lay still, breathing heavily, his eyes shut.

Lord Seaforth came and stood next to them. He spoke quietly to Alex who grunted in response. His Lordship said, "It's all right. It's over. Let him up." Then he bent down and took Alex's sword from him. Billy lifted his blade and stepped back. Alex got up looking angry still, but the fire had gone out of him. He spoke quietly but with feeling to Lord Seaforth who said, "He acknowledges you are the winner. You can go."

Billy was relieved he had neither been killed nor had to kill his opponent. He and Thomas began walking towards the boat. Rob Roy called out, "Will ye go wi'oot settling oor question of honour?"

Thomas turned and said, "If you really want to! But I've never used a sword in my life, so where's your honour if you beat me? Or do you want to use pistols?" "I'll fight ye wi' ma bare hands!" With that the Scotsman took off his sword-belt, his bonnet and his plaid, to stand defiantly where Billy had just been fighting with his kinsman. Thomas took off his coat, waistcoat and shirt, handing them to Billy, before going to stand in front of the Highlander. Billy thought they looked strangely comical: Thomas wearing only his breeches, and Rob Roy wearing only his shirt. Alex's shirt had come down almost to his knees although it had ridden up at times. Rob Roy, however, was taller and his shirt revealed rather more whenever he moved, to the entertainment of a group of women on the quayside.

The two fighters wasted little time on preliminaries. They began by exchanging punches. Neither of them made much use of footwork except that they exchanged kicks occasionally, as if giving their fists a rest.

They were evenly matched. The Scotsman was taller, but both were equally well-built and wellmuscled. They were also obviously both very tough, neither showing signs of taking much notice of the blows he received. The onlookers called out encouragement and advice to both combatants. Billy was surprised to notice that Captain Rimmer's men seemed to be supporting Thomas.

After a while, Rob Roy moved closer and was rewarded with a butt to the face and a punch to the stomach. None of this seemed to bother him much. He returned the butt and closed with Thomas in order to hug him as if trying to crush him. Thomas appeared to take no notice, so Rob lifted him off the ground. Billy was expecting him to throw him down, but suddenly Rob let out a cry of pain and lowered Thomas steadily. He had grabbed Rob by the testicles, forcing him to let go. They stepped apart before resuming an exchange of punches. Then Thomas moved closer and they grabbed each other by the arms and grappled. Rob pushed Thomas backwards until he was pressing him against a wall. Thomas pushed back hard then pulled his opponent towards him, twisting sideways at the same time. Rob crashed into the wall and gave a gasp of pain.

They grappled some more until they both lost their balance and fell, still gripping each other. Thomas managed to twist so as to land on top, lying chest to chest. He tried to pin Rob down by lying diagonally across him, his left hand pressing Rob's right arm down and his right hand pressing into Rob's face. Then Thomas let out a cry. He had failed to immobilise his opponent's left hand, which had found its way to his crotch and was clearly inflicting pain. Rob laughed, but not for long. Thomas's left hand let go of Rob's right and slid down his body to his groin where he in turn took a firm grip. The onlookers had begun to quieten but now they resumed their cacophony. Rob took a deep breath, let out a roar and twisted his body, pushing Thomas over until he found himself underneath with his face against Rob's. He lifted his legs around Rob's waist and strained as if trying to crush him. Rob managed to struggle to his feet and walk backwards a couple of steps, dragging Thomas by the legs. He then twisted round forcing him onto his face and bending his legs back over him.

After a few attempts at wriggling free, he gave up and called out, "All right, you win!" Rob let go and stepped away. Thomas rolled onto his back and Rob gave him a hand up.

They then shook hands and Rob said, "Weel, do ye still think I'm a cooward?"

"No! You're brave and tough. And you're as dirty a fighter as I am."

"Aye, that's true. You're no sae bad for a Sassenach."

"I'm Welsh you fool!"

They both laughed. Lord Seaforth said that he had seldom seen or heard of anyone coming so close to beating Rob Roy in a fight. He wished the Welshmen a safe trip. So did Lord Derwentwater, and Captain Rimmer and his Lancastrians. The other Highlanders said a few things too in their own language, but Billy and Thomas thought it wise to refrain from asking for translations.

Chapter 30

By the time Billy and his companions got back to Mr Rigby's farm, it was too dark to set out in the cart. The farmer apologised for not having a bed to offer but said they were welcome to sleep in his barn. They shared an evening meal of some kind of stew with him and his family, before going to the barn taking some blankets his wife produced. She also provided some ointment for Thomas's back. It was thick, black, greasy stuff, which reminded Billy of something Gareth used on horses when they had been kicked. It did not smell too nice. Megan said, "Take your clothes off, Thomas, and lie face down on this blanket on top of the straw." She rubbed it into his back: the whole length of it. She asked, "Do you want it rubbing anywhere else? You must be hurting in lots of places."

"I know where I'd like rubbing!"

Billy said, "Not with that stuff if it's what I think it is."

Megan rubbed the stuff on several bruises before wiping her hands clean and rubbing his groin. They both enjoyed it. When she had finished, they all lay down together, for warmth and so they could talk. Megan lay in the middle. Thomas fondled her as they talked over the day's events.

Billy said, "Thomas, you really impressed me. I've never heard you use so many words at any one time. Of course, we had nothing to lose. But well done, bach!"

"Thanks, I just got carried away, I was so sick of 'em."

Megan said, "Well, you did well in your fight too. I enjoyed it. I've seen you fight before, but never like that."

"Well, I usually make sure it's fixed."

Megan said, "What are you up to, Thomas? You're getting a bit cheeky for a man who's just had his balls nearly ripped off."

"I'm sore, but I think I'm all right. We'll soon see!"

They soon saw. He was all right. At some stage he fell asleep. Billy was still awake.

Megan said, "You both did well today. I think Bethan would've been impressed too."

Billy replied, "I suppose so. I'm glad you two are happy." He did not sound glad.

She said, "What's the matter? What did I say to upset you? Oh! Are you jealous? You know me. No man is my one and only. I don't think one ever will be. I do like Thomas. I like Allan too. But I still like you. I hope you still like me. Can't we all be friends?"

"Yes. Sorry I was miserable. I just felt jealous. I know you have lots of men, but I'm not usually there at the time."

She pressed against him and put a hand on his face. She kissed him and said, "Let me make it up to you." He let her. She did make it up to him. Then they both fell asleep.

Megan had no idea how long she slept for, but she woke feeling a draught on her left side. The side where Thomas had been. She groped around in the dark and found a man's back on her right. She felt it. She found an arm. Something was wrong. She knew enough about men's anatomy to know that arms do not grow in that position. She felt around a bit more. She was nearly certain that the back belonged to Thomas. She located two arms where they were supposed to be. She suddenly realised that the extra one must belong to Billy. The two men were lying face-to-face and had their arms around each other. Megan had trouble suppressing a laugh. She heard a moan. Thomas rolled onto his back, nearly squashing her. She managed to wriggle enough to free her head and left side. She fumbled around again and found Billy's right arm was still around Thomas and his head was on Thomas's chest. Thomas coughed and half woke himself. He stroked Billy's head with one hand and squeezed an arm with the other. He had managed to find Megan's left arm. Then Billy half woke. They looked into each other's faces. Thomas came fully awake and yelled out, "Get off! Leggo!" Megan could no longer refrain from laughing. She stroked his chest with her left hand and kissed his neck while still laughing. After a minute or so, he realised what was happening and began to laugh too. Billy pulled himself away and called out, "What's going on? What are you doing with me?" Neither Thomas nor Megan could answer for laughing. By the time they could, Billy had worked it out for himself and saw the funny side of it. Thomas rolled over so he was lying on Megan's left again. Most of him, anyway.

Billy said, "Don't either of you tell any of the men about this!" He leaned across Megan so he could look Thomas in the eye. It was not quite pitch dark in there as moonlight was coming in through several gaps in the roof and walls. Even so, they could only just see each other. Billy repeated his request taking hold of Thomas's shoulder.

Thomas said, "How stupid would I 'ave to be?"

Megan said, "They'd never believe it anyway."

Both men were leaning across her. She said, "Have you both got tired of me? Do you want me to get out of the way?"

Billy said, "What do you think?" She did not have to do much thinking. They both demonstrated the answer almost simultaneously.

The next morning they paid Mr Rigby for their board and lodging, such as it was, and set off in the cart towards the Army encampment. As they approached, a soldier appeared from somewhere and challenged them. Billy said who they were and gave the password. The sentry said, "They changed the password yesterday, didn't you know? Where are your uniforms? Have you any papers?"

Billy looked for the General's letter. He must have left it behind with the Jacobite leaders. After some argument, the soldier sent someone to fetch Eddy, who came and persuaded the sentry to let them into the camp. They went straight to the General's tent. The General was very happy. He congratulated all three on their achievement. All the rebel leaders had agreed to surrender. Colonel MacNichol had given Thomas and

Billy most of the credit for persuading them. Billy's commission was now permanent.

The General asked each of them how else they would like to be rewarded. Thomas said a week's leave and a lot of money would be welcome. He also asked to be transferred to Billy's crew. Billy had mixed feelings about it, but did not voice any. The General said, "I can certainly arrange for Gunner Thomas to become part of Lieutenant Rhys's crew. I expect your recent activities have forged something of a bond between you." Billy thought Thomas had probably been involved in forging a few things in his time, but made no comment. Megan thought of the bond all three of them had forged in the night. She asked if she could have Jamie, the horse Billy had borrowed.

The General responded, "I shall buy the animal for you with pleasure, Miss Morgan, and see the money goes to his late owner's widow. Sadly, Gunner Thomas chooses to ask for things that are not entirely within my gift. Not yet! We still have work to do. These rebels need escorting to Lancaster, where they will stand trial for treason. I shall remain there with a small force in case of any rescue attempts. I will do my best to obtain clemency for the rebels, but I cannot guarantee it. Meanwhile, the Duke of Argyll still has a fight on his hands, and I am sending him all the troops I can spare, including the Royal Welch Artillery and the Glamorgan Fusiliers. They will precede those escorting the prisoners, as the need for haste has been impressed upon me in a dispatch from the Duke. Major-General Jones will command the force continuing north, but the artillery will go on ahead of his main force, with a cavalry escort."

They all had visions of another long, hard ride through strange country, but war is war. The General then said to Thomas, "As to money, officially I can pay you only reasonable expenses, although I promise not to scrutinise your claims too closely. However, unofficially I will allow you all to keep whatever you have made from your trading."

When they left the General's tent Billy asked Thomas, "Why did you not ask for a promotion?" He said, "I don't want the responsibility. Any'ow they watch you more when you're a sergeant or even a bombardier. You don't get as much chance to make money."

Billy asked, "How much did we make from the trading?"

Megan told him, as she had been in charge of the money.

They were both impressed. Thomas said, "Let's go somewhere quiet to share it out. Your tent's the best place."

Before doing that, they went to the hospital tent where Perse and Bethan were relieved to see all three of them back safely. The three visitors gave their accounts of their adventure in Preston. Thomas said Billy was being modest in his account of his swordfight with Wee Alex. He said Billy gave luck too much credit and not enough to his courage and skill. Thomas found it hard to remember the details of his fight with Rob Roy, except that he had been aware that it always seemed as if the result could have gone either way. Billy agreed but filled in some of the details. Megan said she admired both of them. They learned that Perse was expecting to be back at his post very soon, but not up to full duties.

When they reached Billy's tent, they found that Allan and Llewellyn were busy elsewhere, so the three trading partners took the opportunity to count the money and put it into three piles. Thomas said, "There's summat I wasn't gonna tell you, but now we've been through so much together, us three like, I gotta be honest with you." They stared at him in amazement. He went on, "I got a few extra bits I was gonna keep, like, but I think we'd better share 'em, isn't it?" He then emptied his pockets of an assortment of coins and pieces of jewellery. Before anyone could ask the obvious question, he answered it.

"I picked these up off some o' them officers and lords what we was with yesterday. They was so busy searching us and questioning us, they never bothered with what I was doing. That Rob Roy'll be mad when 'e finds all this stuff's missing!" he said, pointing to some jewelled brooches and a small jewelled dagger. "Them was pinned to that thing what 'e took off to fight me. I picked it up an' give it to 'im after, but 'e never looked at it. Fool!"

Billy said, "You'll be in trouble if he ever finds you again."

He said, "I might beat 'im next time."

Megan said, "I hope I'm there."

After Thomas left them, Billy said, "I have tried unsuccessfully to banish thoughts of the trouble I'm going to have with him under my command. I don't want him to cheat his comrades or bring my crew into disrepute."

They heard that the surrender had gone ahead and it would soon be time to move. Because of his condition, Perse was ordered to remain with some of the other wounded in Preston. He had been hoping to be well enough to ride when the Artillery moved and was sad to be parted from his crew. The women were supposed to follow with the baggage train, but Bethan was going to stay to help Perse and the other wounded men. Megan said she was not going to wait for the baggage train. She had Jamie. Llewellyn would ride Merlin. Billy would ride Cae again and leave Caledin with Bethan.

When they were alone, Megan told Bethan her version of Billy's duel with Wee Alex and Thomas's fight with Rob Roy. Bethan said, "I think there's something you've left out. How did you spend last night? I can't believe you would miss such an opportunity."

Megan smiled wickedly and said, "And what about you? Who did you spend the night with?"

"I slept in the hospital tent."

"Well, you know I'm riding to Scotland with the boys. You will look after Perse, won't you? I'll take care of Billy and Thomas until you catch up with us."

"Don't wear yourself out. Or them!"

Billy was inspecting the crew when Colonel MacNichol arrived. He said, "Did you meet anyone called Robert Roy MacGregor or a Lord Seaforth when you were in the town? We've received the Enemy's muster rolls and some other papers, and had a roll-call to ensure the surrender was complete but those two weren't there. Of course, the rolls could be wrong, or they could have left before the surrender. That MacGregor character's a bit of a bad lot. Been making trouble for years, well before all this blew up. In fact he's already a wanted man. So the General wants you and your friend Gunner Thomas to think hard. If you could pick them out from among the prisoners, he'd be very grateful. Obviously, I don't suppose every rebel you met gave you his name!"

Billy said, "There were a lot of MacGregors."

"I know. They were the ones who attacked us the other day and they were the worst ones for rejecting the surrender the first time. I've heard that they went around intimidating everyone else if they were thinking of surrendering. I don't think the General will include them in his appeal for clemency!"

Billy said, "Can I think about it and talk to Thomas? We might be able to help each other's memories."

"Certainly, but be quick. We want to get on the road as soon as we can."

He and Megan found Thomas and told them what the Colonel had said. Thomas replied, "I dunno! I don't wanna miss a chance at a reward, but that Rob Roy beat me fair. I think 'e could've slit our throats an' got away with it. If 'e got away, well, good luck to 'im. And that Lord Summat. What's 'e done to us?"

They all agreed to tell the Colonel they could not remember either of them. Megan repeated that she would like to see Thomas and Rob Roy fight again.

Billy said that was most unlikely.

Chapter 31

Bethan helped Perse move into one of the houses the Jacobites had been using. They knew they would be sharing it with another officer and his wife, but Bethan was surprised when she saw Catherine MacNichol. Bethan said, "Is your Iain badly wounded?"

"No, not at all, in fact. Jonesie's put him in charge of administering this place. My father-in-law has convinced him that Iain is good at that sort of thing. I think he's trying to keep him out of harm's way. Pity! I think I'm going to find it a bit boring round here. Well, not if you're here. We can probably liven things up a bit, but we could be stuck here for a long time. The Army's likely to forget about us now. Is your Billy badly wounded?"

"No, he's fine. He's gone off with his regiment. I'm staying to look after Billy's immediate superior, Lieutenant Perseus de Clare. You remember him? I nursed some of the men over in the Netherlands, so I've got experience. Perse was wounded when the Jacobites tried to rush the guns. He'll be all right soon, I hope, but he's not ready for a long ride. And they expect it to be a hard one too."

"Perhaps we can have a bit of fencing practice while we're here."

Bethan said, "Good! But first, let's find out what we've got to do to get any food for ourselves or our men."

"Yes. I expect Iain's so busy making sure all the wounded prisoners are fed, that he'll forget about us."

285

Catherine was right in thinking they were going to stay in Preston for a long time. It was weeks before Iain heard anything. By then, most of the wounded had recovered well, but some died or were left with disabilities, despite the best efforts of the amateur nurses and a couple of local doctors.

Bethan enjoyed her regular fencing practice with Catherine. Iain and Perse watched when they could and there was usually an audience of the walking wounded and a number of townspeople. At first, Catherine dominated these sessions, being more familiar with her own lighter weapon, but gradually Bethan became familiar with the MacKenzie sword, which Billy had left in Perse's care, and found its weight an advantage.

They found they were not welcome among the local people. Once, Perse and Iain had to rescue Bethan and Cathy from a skirmish between camp followers and fishwives, but not before Bethan had dislocated the shoulder of one of their attackers.

Chapter 32

The road north was fairly gentle at first. The Artillery stopped at noon in sight of Lancaster. The castle, where the Jacobites were to be housed, and where their trial was to be held, dominated the landscape. Billy wondered how much clemency there would be. Beyond the castle they could see some hills. It seemed as if they were in for another difficult journey, but Billy wondered if things were not as bad as they looked. Perhaps there was a road through them, or around them, that would not be as steep as he feared. Eddy showed him a map. The direct route would take them over some of the highest places in England and would be very steep at times. Eddy agreed that he could not risk taking the guns over all that. However, the alternative, which they had to adopt, was not very easy either. It involved a diversion along the coast that almost doubled the distance from Lancaster to Carlisle and was also quite steep at times. Billy had heard of the Scottish Highlands but had no idea how mountainous the land in northern England was.

They had some beautiful views of the sea on one side and the hills on the other, but progress was slow. Then it started to rain. Not only did it make life less pleasant, but it also reduced visibility and made the roads treacherous.

After four days they reached Carlisle, where they heard that the Duke of Argyll had defeated the Jacobites at a place called Sheriffmuir, near Stirling, and now controlled most of the Lowlands. He had made Stirling his stronghold from where he intended to advance once he had the reinforcements he was expecting. It was feared that the Enemy controlled most of the country north of that city. The next morning, after they had been going for about an hour Eddy said that, according to the map, they had entered Scotland and were now going through the Lowlands. That night, after a day of struggling up one hill and down the next, time after time, Billy said, "If these are what they call the Lowlands, what must the Highlands be like?"

Eddy said, "Believe me, they are higher and steeper than these little hills. Be ready!"

It took over a week to reach Stirling. When they arrived it was a sunny day, and the town and its castle made a wonderful sight, set among lots more hills. Billy commented on that to Allan and added, "At least we're not going to have to drag the guns over those hills."

He replied, "Didn't I hear Lord Argyll was planning on advancing once we all got here?"

"Oh, no! You could be right. Anyway, we'll get a break because we've got to wait for the infantry to catch up. Not that they're likely to be long. Even they can hardly have been slower than us."

Eddy went to meet the Duke of Argyll. Meanwhile orders were received to station the Artillery on a ridge to the west, just beyond the town. The cavalry were to be just a little behind them. By the time all the guns were set up in suitable places, tents pitched and horses stationed in their lines, Eddy returned and inspected everything. On his order, they fired a few blank charges to make sure the Jacobites knew they were there, just as at Preston.

The Duke generously sent a gift of food, most of which was already cooked. It included venison, as well as beef and mutton. He also sent several casks of wine and whisky. That afternoon Eddy called all his officers together to let them know what the Duke had told him. He only confirmed what everyone had already heard at Carlisle. An infantry officer introduced himself as Colonel John Murray of the Royal Scots Borderers, who were stationed near the Artillery. Billy asked if he could see him sometime. He looked surprised but said he would be happy to see him that evening as long as the Enemy had no objections. He went as soon as he had eaten. Colonel Murray invited him to sit down and said, "Would you care for a wee dram?"

Billy said, "I've never heard of one. What is it?"

"You poor man! It's a drop of whisky."

He was not about to refuse. Murray poured a small amount into each of two small glasses. It was similar to that which the Duke of Argyll had provided but with a distinct flavour.

Billy asked, "Why is it different from the Duke's whisky and from that which I've had elsewhere?"

"There are lots of different ones, just as there are lots of different wines. We make it in what we call a distillery. Each distillery has its own peculiarities. The taste is affected by the water and that in turn by the soil and the rocks it passes over before reaching the distillery. Of course, each distiller claims he has some special secret too. Who knows? A lot of what they sell in England, and Wales I suppose, is blended. So you'll have had something that contains good and, er... not so good, whiskies. I hope you like this one. It's from a distillery on my estate not far from here."

"I do like it. Does that mean your estate is in Enemy hands?"

"I don't know. I hope not. Just north of here almost everyone's a Murray. Some are for King George whilst others are for Prince James. So far, our Chief, the Earl of Athol, has managed to play a canny game. I think he'll wait and join the winning side. It's not like it is with some clans, like the Campbells, who are united behind the Duke of Argyll, or the MacGregors, who are all on the other side. What'll happen if things aren't settled soon, I don't know. But what can I do for you? I don't suppose you just wanted to hear about my family or my whisky."

Billy sipped his whisky and savoured it. Then he said, "I want to ask what you know about the late Lieutenant-Colonel Kenneth MacKenzie, of the Borderers. His widow is related to me and has asked me to find out what led to his death and also how he came to lose all his money. I've spoken to Colonel MacNichol, and he's told me what he knows, but thinks you might be able to help a bit further."

"So you know Major MacNichol? Is he a colonel now? Good for him! Yes, we served together for a while, before he became a staff officer. Is he still on General Jones's staff?"

"No. He's now commanding the Third Battalion of the Glamorgan Fusiliers."

"Oh, good! We'll be seeing him soon then, with any luck. I remember Kenny MacKenzie all right. Mrs MacKenzie too. She's not a woman you'd forget. But I thought her maiden name was Pryce, and you say your name is Rhys? How are you related?"

"Well, you see, Rhys is an old Welsh name and there are lots of ways of spelling it. The English have added their variations to the list." He spelled out a few to illustrate the point: RHYS, REECE, RICE, RHYCE. Then Billy finished his whisky and said, "Now, I need to explain a bit of Welsh, to help you understand the next twist. In Welsh the word 'ap' means 'son of' and is used in a lot of names. So 'Rhys ap Rhys' means 'Rhys the son of Rhys'. Sometimes we say it all at once and it sounds like 'Rhys a Prys' or 'Rhys Prys' and that's how it often gets written, especially by the English. So the Prys or Pryce family are cousins of the Rhys or Rhyce family. It's the same with Probert, Pritchard, Powell and Pugh, for example."

Murray seemed really interested and said, "The English have their own ways of spelling a lot of Scottish names too. Some people have tried to educate them, but it proved a hopeless task." "I'm not surprised. They think their way is the Right Way in everything!"

"Yes, quite. Now I think we'd better change the subject or we'll both end up saying things that make us sound like Jacobites. In truth, I've some sympathy with Prince James, as his father was James the Seventh of Scots and James the Second of England. However, I accept the decision by both parliaments to recognise George of Hanover as our King. Where would we be if every man and his brother thought he could choose his own king? We have to have a system."

"Yes, Sir. I agree. But we were going to change the subject."

"Quite right! Yes, about Kenny MacKenzie. Well, we were captains together: me, him, MacNichol, before we started to get promoted. I'd heard he was killed in a duel, which I found hard to believe. As for the money... well, yes. He spent a lot of his own money on his battalion. Some sort of mix up at the Horse Guards meant they never seemed to get paid. He came to me, because I was the Regiment's Colonel by then. I tried to sort it out. Then we both went to Jonesie and he had a go. We had all written to the Horse Guards and even been there, but had unsatisfactory answers. Then we let Kenny go to London again to get to the bottom of it. I was told it had been sorted out in the end and the Army would repay him. Are you saying that didn't happen?"

"I think he was killed while he was in London before it got sorted out, although they told Mrs MacKenzie that it happened in the Spanish Netherlands."

"I thought he got into a duel on his way back to the Borderers after he'd been to London. Who told you he was killed in London?"

"I've seen his grave and spoken to the vicar who buried him. And another thing: he was not killed in a duel. He was murdered."

"How can you possibly know that?"

"I've seen the bloodstains and powder burns on his coat. He was shot at point blank range."

"Have you told anyone else? This needs taking up at the highest level!"

"I've been very careful who I've told, as I don't know who I can trust. If the Horse Guards have got something to hide, they won't be likely to give me straight answers. Who told you about the alleged duel?" "The officer who we had been dealing with over the money problem, Major Boyle." He sipped his whiskey pensively. He said, "If you're right this is serious. It looks as if there's a connection between Kenny's death and the missing money." "What do you think I should do?"

"Kenny was one of my officers. I need to get to the bottom of this. I think we'd better go to London and demand to see this Major Boyle and ask what he did with the money, and I think we should tell Jonesie about this when he gets here. Obviously we can't do anything until we've dealt with this little problem of the Jacobites!"

Billy thanked him and left. He thought Murray seemed honest and definitely shocked at what Billy had told him. If he was hiding anything, he was doing it very well.

Chapter 33

That afternoon the sun came out and it was surprisingly hot for the time of year. Things were quiet and everyone in the Artillery welcomed a bit of a rest after the exhausting journey of the previous days. A lot of the men had stripped to the waist. Billy was wondering whether to remind them that it was against Army Regulations to be out of uniform except for a good reason, when the Adjutant came along. He said, "Good to see everything's looking tidy and the men are behaving themselves, apart from being improperly dressed. Eddy says not to worry for now, but get them in uniform when it's time to eat. It'll probably turn cold by then anyway."

Billy assured him everything else was all right and he went on his way. Then Billy heard some raised voices and went to investigate. He saw two men, stripped to the waist, fighting and a small group of onlookers. As he approached, he saw that the bigger man was Thomas. He was not surprised. He was, however, horrified when he saw that the other was Llewellyn. He realised that Thomas was a ruffian, but did not think he would hurt a child, especially Bethan's son. The boy was big for his age and strong from all the hard work he had been doing at the inn as a stableboy, but he was no match for a tough soldier. However, Thomas seemed to be using uncharacteristic self-
restraint, as he waited for the boy to get up each time he threw him. Then Allan came up to Billy and said, "Don't worry, Sir, I've separated the pair once and they say it's a

lesson. Your nephew says he wants to learn to fight like Gunner Thomas. He says some of the other lads say he's soft. I can't see any reason to interfere.
He's learning fast by the look of things."

Billy thanked him and agreed to stay out of it. As he drew closer, he could hear some of what they said to each other. Thomas said, "You're still taking too long to get back up! When you're down it's easy for anyone to kick you or jump on you." Then Thomas threw Llewellyn and dropped onto him, pinning him down. They both got up and Thomas said, "Not quick enough yet. Try rolling. It makes it harder for 'em. Lemme show you." They grappled again and Thomas let Llewellyn trip him, then he rolled away just as the boy tried to jump on him, so he missed. Next time Thomas rolled towards the boy, grabbing one of his ankles and pulling him off his feet The third time, Thomas did not roll, but twisted himself so that Llewellyn landed awkwardly on top of him, getting a shoulder in his face and a hip in his stomach.

Llewellyn said, as he sat up, "Ow! That hurt more than a punch or a kick. I won't fall for that again, but I'll try to remember to use it next time I'm down."

Thomas laughed and said, "Wanna try now?" He did. So Thomas threw him and dived onto him. This time the youngster managed to do what the man had done. He was delighted to have managed it and said as they got up, "Wanna try again?"

"Why not?"

Then Thomas threw the lad down again. This time, he dropped onto him more slowly, pinning him

295

down. "That's how to be sure the other feller can't get you by twisting sideways like you've just learned."

"Why is it that whatever I do, you always have another trick that can beat it?"

"Because I've been in a lot more fights than you have. But you're learning fast. You'll be a good fighter soon."

Then a bugle called everyone to his station. It signalled an imminent attack. Everyone rushed about madly. Well, it appeared to be like that, but in fact every soldier knew the drill, and this was definitely methodical rather than mad. Even the camp followers knew how to get out of the way to safety quickly and efficiently. Safety was of course relative. Billy hoped they were not going to be overwhelmed by numbers, or that the Enemy had something clever up his sleeve. Llewellyn followed Thomas, Billy and Allan to their gun and began fetching ammunition as he was ordered. The others checked the gun was loaded and stood by as one man lit a torch, ready to set it to the fuse. For a moment, Billy wondered if it was a false alarm, as he could see no sign of the Jacobites. In fact everything looked as peaceful as it had all day. Then he heard gunfire from somewhere out to his left. He guessed the Enemy must be trying to get round the Army's positions to try to attack the rear.

The Adjutant appeared and said to Billy, "I don't know what they're playing at, but they seem determined to get round the end of our lines. Eddy wants a couple of guns including yours over there to stop them." He indicated the direction of the sound of the muskets. One of the nearer guns fired. Billy picked a suitable spot just beyond the other gun and behind a line of infantry, where he ordered his crew to set up. As he tried to see what they were aiming at, he heard an exchange of musket fire almost directly in front of him.

Eddy came and said, "Well done for getting set up so soon. Get ready, now! The infantry are going to open a gap for the Enemy to come through: straight to our guns!"

The infantry fell back in two directions as Eddy had said. Then a wave of Highlanders charged up a slope towards Billy's position, giving out terrible war cries. Having experienced the incident in Preston, both gun crews were ready for them. As Billy's crew already had a roundshot in the gun, they once again added a bag of grape without unloading. The other gun had not finished reloading when the Enemy came into range but Billy did not need to wait for them. He gave the command and the fuse was lit. The effect was as gory and devastating as it had been at Preston. Just as some of the wounded and some others got to their feet and were joined by another wave of their comrades, the other gun fired. Billy's crew had nearly reloaded when the infantry gave a volley of musket fire from each side, catching the Jacobites in the crossfire. Billy waited for a few seconds to see if another shot was needed. It was. Through the smoke and the carnage, a brave band of Highlanders charged again, in two groups, straight at each of the guns. He ordered his crew to fire again and they did. The Highlanders were almost upon them as they fired, so he could see the faces of the closest ones.

Billy had heard people talk about men going down like corn or grass or skittles. He had heard a battlefield being described as a slaughterhouse. He was sure that all those descriptions were inaccurate. He had cut grass, reaped corn and played skittles. He had even visited a slaughterhouse. Corn does not scream. Grass does not bleed. Skittles do not writhe in agony. A slaughterhouse is, in comparison, orderly and humane. Men fall like men, dead or wounded. Like nothing else. Billy did not know of anyone having nightmares after a day's reaping or an evening of skittles, but he did know how a battle affected him and many others.

He ordered the crew to reload in case there were any more attacks to be repelled. He heard a few more isolated musket shots in both directions but no more volley fire. Then he heard a heavy gun firing from a long way off to the right. The Enemy were attacking in more than one place. Unsuccessfully.

All crews remained at their posts for an hour before Eddy told them to stand down. He said permission had been granted for the Jacobites to send a party to bury their dead. The gunners were to be vigilant in case of any tricks, but otherwise to leave the burial parties to their task. Eddy also said that reinforcements were expected to arrive the next day, and the Enemy had probably seen this as a last chance. Billy hoped he was right, as it suggested they would not be trying again.

Chapter 34

The next day, Major-General Jones arrived at Stirling, as expected, with the reinforcements and the baggage train. They were stationed in various places outside the town to let the Enemy know they were there. The Duke of Argyll hoped that would make them give up what was already a lost cause. Later that day, Eddy took Billy to a meeting with the Duke. Major-General Jones was there with Colonels Murray and MacNichol, as well as a few staff officers. The Duke said, "I'm wondering whether to advance and bring on another battle or to wait and let this thing just fade away. General Jones and Colonel Edwards have told me about you. All your tricks behind the lines. That sort of thing. I'm most impressed. Got a job for you." Billy felt mixed emotions. He was honoured and excited, but apprehensive.

The Duke went on, "I need to know what the Enemy's up to. Don't want to rush right into an ambush, but on the other hand I don't want to sit around here when they're miles away and up to something somewhere else. I've had reports they're planning on attacking Fort William, which we still hold, I hope. Others tell me the Jacobites are going to reinforce Dundee, which they hold, but they think might be attacked by the Navy. You could just go a bit further north and see what you can see."

Eddy added, "If you do go, while you're at it, see where are the best roads for the guns if we're going to be moving them. Take Gunner Thomas with you if you like. Did all right last time. What do you think?"

"Give me time to work out a plan and I'll let you know. Can I have a look at one of your maps?"

"Good idea, but I've not got one of this area."

Colonel Murray said, "I've got one. Since I'm local, perhaps I can give Lieutenant Rhys some advice too. Come to my tent with me after this meeting."

In his tent, Murray gave Billy another wee dram and a large, detailed map of the area, pointing out some of the more interesting features, including places where you had to go on foot, as no horse could manage the terrain. He also showed where he thought the Enemy could be.

Billy said, "I don't know why they chose me for this. I'd have thought there'd be men who know the country that they could have sent. And it'll be obvious to anyone that I'm not Scottish."

"You need to understand the clan system. I doubt whether the Duke could trust everyone in his army. I thinks that's why he's got the Borderers camped out here. They're mostly from the Lowlands and have little affinity with any clans. He's keeping his Highlanders in the castle or the town, where he can keep an eye on them, so there's less chance of desertions or even defections. Apart from his own clan, the Campbells, that is the Argyll Regiment. He wants them near him because he *does* trust them."

"Why not send one of the Campbells to scout the area?"

"They're not very popular around here. A lot of Highlanders hate them even more than they hate the English. If one was found out, there'd be no mercy. At least you'd have a chance. Did Colonel Edwards mention that there's a man with another plan who is a Campbell?

He was in the Argylls once, before he became a staff officer. He hates the Jacobites as much as they hate the Campbells. He'd like a real war, where we'd end up wiping out the MacGregors and other rebel clans. He's not keen on reconciliation, to say the least. I'm glad the Duke's not like that. This morning the fool suggested assassinating the Earl of Mar. Luckily, the
Duke won't allow it."

Billy took a sip of whisky. "Why not? Surely that could save a lot of other people's lives, on both sides?"

"That's what some think. The Duke says he's worried it could do the opposite. You see these
Jacobites aren't a united body like us. I hear you saw that in Preston. Half of them won't take orders from the other half. Well, the Earl of Mar has managed to get the respect and cooperation of nearly all of them. So he can set the strategy. I hope he can decide when to surrender, or at least just go home. What the Duke's afraid of is that without the Earl, there'd be nobody to make such a decision. We could end up with the main rebellion over but lots of little ones in different places. We'd have to keep the Army here for ages, chasing around, getting nowhere. That could make us look like invaders and oppressors. Just what the King and the Government don't want."

He finished his whisky and offered Billy another, which he accepted. Murray was not as mean as the typical Scot, from what Billy had heard.

"So you think my mission will keep him and his friends quiet for a bit?"

301

"I hope so. I do really wish you all the luck you'll need."

Then Billy went to find Thomas. They spent some time trying to think of a plausible story to explain two Welsh civilians in the middle of Scotland. They felt this was a very weak part of the plan. They also wondered how to explain possessing the map, if searched. Suddenly Thomas had one of his brightest ideas. He said, "What about being a couple o' deserters? We could keep our uniforms an' all. We'll just have to think why we'd desert."

"And why we're heading north, instead of back south towards England. And Wales."

"Oh, mmm… errr… I dunno but I can't think of anything better, isn't it?"

They were sitting in Billy's tent and drinking some more whisky as they considered the problems, when Megan came in. They explained the problem to her and she said, "What about taking me? I did all right before, and taking a woman would make you seem more like deserters and less like spies."

"In Preston it worked out all right. But I think this could be even more dangerous," said Billy.

A voice asked, "Why?" It was Llewellyn, who had been listening from behind a pile of boxes. Billy said, "What do you think you're doing? You shouldn't spy on people like that!"

"I'm practising! I want to be able to do what you do."

"I think you need to learn when to do it and when not to."

"Well, what's the answer? Why not take Aunt Megan? And me too! Don't treat me like a child. Do you think I'm too soft to be a soldier like Dada and like you two? I know it's dangerous. I don't mind."

"Don't be ridiculous! Boys are allowed to do certain things in the Army, but they don't go into battle, and nobody ever heard of sending a boy on a dangerous mission behind enemy lines."

Thomas agreed that if taking a woman was stupid enough, taking a boy was insane.

Unexpectedly, Billy said, "Just a minute! If nobody in his right mind would take a child on a mission like this, then if we take him it'll make our story all the more credible. A deserter would take his woman and their child with him, but a spy wouldn't."

Eventually they agreed and Billy went with Eddy to see the Duke again. As soon as they entered the room they could see that he was worried. Colonel Murray and another officer were with him. The Duke said, "Sorry to say there's got to be a change of plan. Things have happened that you need to know about. Just after you left, Captain Dunn came back from Perth." He indicated the strange officer present.

Dunn took his cue and said, "The Earl of Mar is about to go with a small escort to see what's happening at Fort William. He wonders whether it's worth attacking. He's also sending someone to Dundee, to see if they need reinforcements."

Billy wanted to look at the map. He could not remember where these places were. He asked, "Will I need to take longer so as to get more information?"

The Duke replied, "Probably, but there's more. There's a Colonel, Iain Campbell, on Jonesie's staff, who wants to kill all Jacobites. He thinks he should start with the Earl."

"Yes, I know, but I heard you won't allow it. Have you changed your mind?"

"No! But Colonel Campbell and a couple of his pals have gone missing. Private William Campbell, his cousin, and Captain George Graham. They went soon after I told the senior officers and their staff about the Earl's plans. So it looks like they're going to try to kill the Earl without permission."

"What should we do?" asked Eddy.

"I want you, Rhys, to stop the assassination. Arrest Campbell and his friends and bring them back to camp. Prevent them killing the Earl, even if you have to kill Campbell!"

"So is my original mission off?"

"No, I still want to know as much as possible about the Enemy's movements and location. Now, do you know what Colonel Campbell looks like?"

Billy paused before saying, "I saw him at Preston. He wanted to wipe out the town. I don't know if I'd know him again."

Eddy said, "Don't you remember? He was on Jonesie's staff back in the Netherlands. Got Gunner Thomas into trouble a few times. Mind you, Thomas was always getting himself into trouble. Anyway, I'll bet Thomas would recognise him. Graham was usually with him. Thick as thieves they were."

Eddy added that he agreed with Billy's plan, including taking Megan and Llewellyn, as well as Thomas.

The Duke approved and gave Billy written orders to show to any British troops he might encounter, and a letter of authority to arrest Campbell and his friends. He hid them in the lining of his coat.

Billy explained the changed plan to the others. Thomas had plenty to say about Colonel Campbell and he remembered Graham too. Billy concluded the discussion by saying, "So between us all we should be able to find the Colonel and the others, and find out what the Enemy's up to. How easy!" They all laughed, nervously.

Chapter 35

Billy, Megan and Llewellyn rode Cae, Jamie and Merlin, while Thomas rode another artillery horse called Brenin, which means King. They left after dark, having to ride very slowly for fear of potholes and similar hazards. At midnight, they found a quiet clearing in a wood where they tethered the horses and got some sleep.

At dawn, they rode on, trying to make use of trees as cover wherever possible, making for the highest point around so as to get a good view of the country in several directions. They saw no sign of any Jacobites or anyone else. They decided to ride on to the next vantage point. It turned out to be further than it looked. By the time they got anywhere near the top, it was threatening to start raining. They could also see that the cloud around the peak would reduce visibility severely. They started back down the hill. After a while Llewellyn said, "We're not on the same track we came up. I don't remember that fallen tree." The others realised he was right. Of course, the map was of little use, as they did not know where we were. They decided to find somewhere to spend the night and start again in the morning. They saw a lone building on the far side of a valley and wondered if it was a cowshed, a store or a hunting-lodge. Whatever it was, it was better than nothing. It also provided a landmark to aim at. They came to a saddle point. That is a place where the hills go up on two sides and down on two sides, like a saddle. Where they were, was flat. They dismounted and sat down. By then the sun had come out again and they were in a sun-trap.

After a rest, Thomas gave Llewellyn another lesson in fighting. They lost their footing and fell. The ground had a slight slope, and their struggles caused them to roll onto a steeper slope so that they continued rolling ever faster downhill. The others got up and began to walk towards them, taking care not to slip and go the same way. The combatants came to rest about a hundred yards away in a small stream, which ran along the bottom of the slope. Billy called to them to stay there, as he and the others were going down to them.

They led the horses on a track that zigzagged its way down the hill, losing sight of the two fighters where it was wooded. When they got a clear view of them, they had begun wrestling again. Megan said, "Llew really wants to be as good a fighter as Thomas. I'm glad they get on so well." Billy agreed but was worried that the boy would pick up some of Thomas's less desirable attributes, of which there were many. There came a voice calling from beyond them. Then a man appeared holding a musket.

Billy moved closer, remaining out of sight, leaving Megan with all four horses. The man was wearing a plaid like the MacGregors, but with a different tartan. Billy could see the musket was an old-fashioned matchlock type. In other words, you had to light a fuse to fire them, unlike flintlocks, which created a spark when the hammer struck the flint. Matchlocks were slow to load and fire. If the Jacobites were using them, they were even more poorly armed than he had heard. After several attempts at addressing Thomas and Llewellyn in his own language, he tried in a version of

English. "Wha' are ye and what do ye seek here?"

The two wrestlers looked around to see where the voice came from, before staring uncomprehendingly at the man. Thomas answered, "We're lost! Where are we?"

"Are ye Campbells? Or Sassenachs? Ye dinna seem like oor kin."

"We're Welsh and want to get back to Wales."

"Where's that?"

"It's a long way south, ruled by the English."

"Do ye no wear clothes there?"

"We just took them off to practise fighting."

The Highlander had walked towards them while they were speaking and had his back to Billy, who took the opportunity to join the conversation, saying, "It's good to meet you, but put the gun down, please!"

The crofter span round and found a pistol aimed at him. Then he saw Megan with another. Billy added, "We mean no harm. Just let us pass safely and we'll trouble you no more."

Just then, it started to pour with rain. The man said, "Let's no stand here blatherin', let's awa' tae the hoose. We can talk in the dry." They all agreed. Billy called to Megan, and they gave Thomas and Llewellyn their clothes. Not a minute too soon, as they were shivering. They all followed the man up a steep track to the building they had seen earlier. Billy thought he had seen some poor cottages in Wales, but this was the worst he had ever seen. It was no bigger than the shepherd's hut where his brother Owain lived in summer.

A woman opened the door and said something to the man in their own language, to which he replied. She turned and said, "Ye'd best come in. It's no a neet for being ootside. I'd no let King George himsel' stay oot on a neet like this. Och! Ye'd best put the beasts in the back wi' oor garron." She waved a hand, vaguely indicating that they should go round the building. It did not take long. They wondered what a garron was. At the back of the residence there was a lean-to in which was a horse. He was rather like a Welsh Cob, but heavier. In a pen at one end were a few goats. They tethered their horses next to the other one. The man pulled some poor hay down from the roof-space and gave some to each of them.

Billy and his companions followed into the house. The woman said, "Och! Where's oor manners? Sit ye doon." All five sat on a bench against one wall whilst the crofters each sat on a stool. Three small children aged apparently between five and ten sat on the floor along with a shaggy dog. The woman then said, "Noo, do ye ken who we are?" They shook their heads. "Och! Angus, will ye no learn? We're Angus and Morag Stewart. We're crofters here, like Angus's father and his father too. These are oor bairns: Wee Angus, Wee Morag and Iain. Aye, and yon beast's Wee Cali.
That's short for Caledin."

The visitors noted that not all the Stewarts lived like kings. Billy thought Caledin was a horse's name but later remembered that Sir Lancelot named his horse after Caledin of Caledon, King of Caledonia, an old name for

Scotland. They introduced themselves. Angus asked how they came to be there.

Billy said, "We were soldiers in the British Army camped at Stirling, but we've had enough of it. My friends and I are all from Wales and want to get back there."

Angus asked, "Do ye no ken that ye're ganging all wrong? Ye've come north of Stirling when ye want tae gang south."

Billy said, "We're hoping that's what the Army will think and be looking in the wrong places. They won't come north anyway because they think this land is full of Jacobites."

"It's no full of anything, but I see what ye mean. Aye, ye'll be safe up here."

"I hope so. Then we need to go west and get a ship going south."

"We canna help ye there, but the mon ye'd best see is the Laird. Auld Robbie Stewart, in the big hoose over the hill." He waved a hand towards the hill at the back of the cottage.

Morag said, "Noo, ye'r welome tae share our meal, but we've nae much as we were no expecting visitors."

Megan said, "That's all right. We've got some of our own that we can share. A roof over our heads and a warm hearth is all we ask of you tonight." With that, she reached into a saddlebag and pulled out some salt beef and ship's biscuits they had drawn from stores.

Thomas said, "We can offer you a wee dram too." as he produced a small bottle of whisky. The Stewarts were most grateful for all of it. Morag then heated up some goat stew, and they all had a small portion, accompanied by some of the ship's biscuits, followed by a drop of whisky. Nobody asked what the goat had died of. They were so cold and hungry anything would have been welcome, and they were impressed by the generosity of these poor people towards a group of strangers.

The children chatted among themselves for a while, and then Wee Angus, the eldest, addressed Llewellyn in his own language.

His mother said, "Noo, Angus, did ye no hear? They dinna speak Gallic, so we will do oor best in English."

The boy said, "Och, aye. Hoo auld are ye? I'm eleven."

"I'm eleven too. Nearly twelve."

"Ye'r big for eleven. Ye'r nigh as big as me da."

"We're all big in our family. My dad was bigger than these two." He indicated Billy and Thomas with a jerk of his head.

"Is yer da' no here?"

"He's been missing since I was little. He was lost at Malplaquet."

They all looked confused. Billy explained. They expressed sympathy.

Wee Angus spoke again, "Da says ye were fighting wi' this big mon here." "We were just practising. I wouldn't stand a chance against him in a real fight."

"I'll bet my da could beat him, an' I'll bet I could beat you."

His father said, "That's not hoo we speak tae guests."

"Sorry!"

The rain sounded worse than ever. Then it sounded like hailstones. The wind howled. They were all glad of the warmth and shelter. Angus said, "This hoose is in a good place. The hills keep the wind off. It'll be a rough neet over the hill." The visitors wondered what it would be like to be in a less sheltered spot on such a night.

Morag said, "Which of ye shall hae the bed?" There was only one.

Megan said, "You've done enough for us already without giving up your bed. We'll be all right on the floor."

The three men agreed. Morag and Megan argued for a while, then Angus said, "What if the women hae the bed? We men can lie on the floor." So they agreed. There was not much room on the floor. Young Morag and Iain squeezed into the bed with the two women, whilst the two eleven-year-olds joined the three men on the floor. The two lads kept whispering to each other for some time before they fell asleep. Their father managed that feat first, despite the noise of the weather and the hardness of the floor with only a rug under him and a plaid over him.

In the morning, Morag gave everyone a bowl of gruel. It was similar to porridge but without milk. It was in fact quite watery, but it was welcome. Llewellyn and Young Angus kept exchanging glances and pulling faces at each other. The weather had not improved much. Billy said he and his companions were likely to get lost if they went out in it. Angus agreed and said he had to go and check on his cattle, but otherwise it would be pointless to try to do much work in such conditions. He was, however, certain it would blow over during the day. He was right. By noon it was clear. He asked if his guests would mind staying until the next morning. He said he had a job that would be easier with a few extra hands. They said they would be happy to help.

As they were on their way up the hillside, the Laird, Robbie Stewart, arrived to see what damage they had suffered in the storm. When Angus introduced his guests, the Laird said, "You're in luck. An officer came from the Earl of Mar yesterday, to see what the Enemy's up to. Not much, from what I can see, but I think he'd like to meet you, to find out what ye know. He could help you get to a ship, I hope."

"That's all right, but we've had enough of soldiering, whether for King George or for King James. I don't think we know anything he won't know already. The higher ranks don't let us know what they're thinking."

"He'll have tae take ye as he finds ye. Come to my hoose toneet."

With that, the Laird rode away. Billy found it confusing to hear someone talk of the Enemy when he meant the British Army, and to talk of the King when he meant the Pretender. He was not too happy at having to spend the afternoon labouring on a farm in cold, wet weather, but was glad to be able to do something to repay the Stewarts for their kindness.

Angus said that what he wanted was help to unblock a stream. The storm had blown a lot of fallen

313

branches into it and had washed stones and mud down its banks too, so it was not flowing properly. It sounded simple. Billy had a feeling it would not be. The stream turned out to be flowing through some steep, almost inaccessible, places and had many bends in it where debris had built up, so freeing one place merely moved the problem downstream. They had to work in water or mud most of the time. Billy hated it when water came over the tops of his boots. Working with wet stockings as well as wet feet is not enjoyable. He saw the sense of wearing a plaid with bare feet, except that it required having feet that were tough enough to walk on assorted stones and pebbles. He also kept pricking or scratching his hands on thorns and broken twigs. He remembered what he disliked about farming. When they had finished and could see the stream flowing freely again, Billy had to admit to himself that it was satisfying, although that was the sort of satisfaction he could live a long time without.

They all sat down on a drystone wall at the edge of the field. The stones were not exactly dry at the time, but that is what they always call such walls. The two lads were back to making faces at each other. This time they added some gestures too. Llewellyn mimed crushing an object in his hands. Angus mimed wringing out a wet cloth. Then Llewellyn mimed breaking a twig or something. Angus pretended to chew something and spit it out. His father said, "Noo, what's this?" He looked at the two boys who were making ever ruder and more violent gestures at each other. Then he looked at Billy and said, "Would it be wrong of me tae let them get on wi' it? I'm thinking they'll no be content until it's done." Morag agreed. So did Billy and the others.

Angus directed the boys to a patch of muddy ground beside the track. Young Angus removed his plaid just as Rob Roy had done. It was apparently a Highland custom. Lewellyn removed his jacket and shirt. As the other boy was barefoot, Megan told Llewellyn to take his boots off.

The boys eyed each other up and exchanged even more gestures and insults, while circling each other. Morag called out, "Dinna be all day. Get to it!" This prompted her son to try a punch, which failed to connect. Llewellyn laughed. The next one connected. He stopped laughing. There followed a fairly even exchange of punches, mostly to the chest and ribs. Young Angus was stronger than he looked and had quicker reactions than Llewellyn. They closed, exchanged short jabs to the ribs and stomach, and began grappling. The Welsh lad hugged his opponent and lifted him off the ground. He swung him round and let go, sending him flying to land in the mud. Angus got up, and they circled each other again. Then they stepped closer and began another series of jabs. Then Angus grabbed Llewellyn, twisted and tripped him so it was his turn to land in the mud. Angus tried to jump on him, but he rolled away and then back, so he rolled on top of the Scots lad. Angus struggled but found the bigger boy's weight too much. Angus kicked his legs up hitting his opponent in the back several times, but he failed to dislodge him. Angus uttered something in Gaelic. Llewellyn asked if that meant surrender. Morag laughed and said it meant something else. With a huge effort,

Angus contorted his body and tried to hook his feet round the bigger boy's neck. Llewellyn grabbed both ankles and pushed down until the lad's feet were nearly in his face. Angus tried to resist but eventually gave up. His father told him to congratulate the winner, which he did with complete insincerity. Likewise, Llewellyn told him most unconvincingly that he had fought well. Morag ordered them both to go to the stream to get cleaned up, warning them not to start fighting again, and reminding them that it would soon be time for the visitors to go to the 'Big Hoose'.

Chapter 36

Later that afternoon, they rode over to the big house. Billy was amazed at how big it was. He had thought that someone used to a tiny cottage would think an ordinary house was big. This was more like a castle. It had turrets and battlements and comprised four storeys. They were welcomed by the Laird himself, and taken by a servant to two bedrooms on the top floor. The smaller room, which Megan had to herself, was bigger than Angus Stewart's cottage. Both rooms contained fairly old, plain furniture, which had probably been of good quality once. The whole place seemed gloomy, because of the small windows and the limited provision of candles.

They all got washed and tidied up as far as possible. Then the servant returned and led them down to the kitchen. Apart from themselves and an assortment of servants, there was a man wearing tartan breeches.
Billy thought it was familiar, so he asked, "Is that the MacGregor tartan?"

He looked surprised and replied, "Aye, it is. I'm proud to say that I'm Jimmy MacGregor. How do ye come tae ken that?"

"We met a number of your kin recently. At Preston. They were brave men and loyal." He omitted to specify that they were loyal to a usurper and therefore disloyal to the crowned King.

Megan then asked, "Do you not wear a plaid like other Highlanders?"

"Not when I ride a horse. I'm tough, but I'm no that tough, nor that stupid." Everyone laughed.

The meal was then served, so they all concentrated on eating before speaking again. It was good. It was beef and some kind of vegetable. When he had finished eating, Jimmy MacGregor said, "Ye may wonder what I'm doing here. I'm serving an officer on the staff o' the Earl of Mar. Since he's a Sassenach, the Earl said it was best he had a Highlander tae mind him, while he's oot and aboot. I've travelled around the Highlands a lot, and I ken many folk around here. Major Butler will be wanting tae meet ye soon, but he'll be glad for us tae have a talk first. That's what he said. Aye, he wants me tae find oot if it was tae help us or tae help the Sassenachs that ye came."

Billy said to Thomas, in Welsh, "Do you still have the jewellery you took off that fellow in Preston?" Thomas fished in his pockets and produced the brooch.
Billy showed it to Jimmy MacGregor and said, "Can you guess who gave us this and why?"

"It's a MacGregor plaid-pin. It would belong to a leader. Had ye done something for him?"

"Robert Roy MacGregor. He said it would be sure to get us through MacGregor country safely."

"Have ye any proof it was Himself?"

Llewellyn reached to his belt and drew a dagger from a sheath. Billy had noticed it before, assuming it was a bayonet. Even a young powder-monkey was issued with one, not to fight with, but for opening kegs and sacks. This was, however, the MacGregor dagger. He passed it to

Jimmy who said, "This was Rob's ain dirk! He must hae thought a lot of ye."

Billy said, "We were all in serious danger in Preston and we all owe each other a lot. I'm certain he won't forget us any more than we'll forget him."

"Aye, ye're nae ordinary deserters. Oor Robbie wouldna give this tae a cooward or a fool. I'll tell the Major he can talk freely and can heed what ye tell him."

He gave the things back to Billy and went out. A servant soon came and guided the visitors to a big room. The walls were covered with stags heads interspersed with paintings, mainly of depressing views of mountains in the rain. While they waited, Thomas said "I'm sure I've heard of someone called Butler. Was he a major?" Billy said, "I've heard of was the Duke of Ormonde. His name was Butler, but I don't think it'll be him. I remember meeting his nephew, Charles Butler, in London, but it must be a coincidence." Just then, the door opened and in came Robert Stewart, followed by Jimmy MacGregor and Charles Butler.

Charles expressed surprise at seeing Billy and not a little suspicion. Billy explained that Rhodri had asked him to rejoin the British Army and find some useful information, which he should then take to the Earl of Mar. Charles said, "Do you know where Rhodri is now?"

"He is on the Continent. He believes his role in this matter is concluded, and that his remaining in London would serve no purpose. He left me to deal with some of his affairs, before commencing my own role in the service of King James."

"He has been very useful indeed in helping provide funds for our enterprise. I had hoped he would be able to provide yet more. Do you know if that is his intention?"

"I think it is, but he seems to have encountered certain difficulties in that respect. He never told me exactly how he was doing it. It seemed complicated."

"Yes. He was helping Major Boyle transfer funds to us without leaving a trail the Government could follow. Little do they know that the British Army has been funding a substantial part of our enterprise. If you have not brought us any money, what is your purpose in coming here?"

"I had a role to play at Preston. Then I joined the Duke of Argyll's forces to ascertain their strength and pass the information on to the Earl of Mar. I am then to go to Wales to help our cause there."

"You can tell me what you know. We have other sources, of course, but your confirmation would be welcome. I am on the Earl's staff. As you may be aware, my uncle is King James's principal military advisor, but the Scots, particularly the Highlanders, are most reluctant to submit to one whom they consider to be a Sassenach. We are actually an Anglo-Irish family, but that makes little difference. So my uncle uses me to liaise with the Scots. At the moment, the Earl is wavering between reinforcing Dundee and mounting another attack on Fort William. There again, he might keep his forces together until he is ready to make a full attack on Stirling. We have news that the King himself will be joining us soon to lead that attack. We were unlucky at Sheriffmuir, but we won't make the same mistakes again."

"Attacking Stirling would be a big mistake. The Duke now has the reinforcements he was waiting for, including the heavy artillery that was decisive at Preston. Stirling Castle would not be taken without a lot of heavy artillery on our side. We could not besiege it unless we could move half our army south of the Forth, but that would leave both halves at risk of being attacked. I haven't heard anything definite about the Navy being sent to Dundee, but I don't know everything. What do you know about Fort William? Could we get a ship from there to Wales? It would be better than Dundee."

"Thank you. You confirm our other intelligence sources. We were driven back from Fort William a month or so ago. We left just a handful of men near there to stop the Hanoverians pushing out from there into the Highlands, but we'd like to kick them right out. If you can pass as civilians, you might have a chance of getting onto a ship. Obviously, not as deserters, or as Jacobites. I'm going over there with Jimmy to see what the chances are of success. I think you should come along."

When they were alone, Charles asked, "Did Rhodri ever find those letters he was looking for, concerning Lewis Pryce?"

"I don't think so. He was worried about them. I don't see why. Lewis is on our side isn't he?"

"Yes, up to a point. But we're afraid we might take things beyond that point. Then he might just turn his coat, and give a lot of names to the authorities. Anyway, Rhodri said those letters would ensure his discretion, otherwise he'd be condemning himself along with us."

"Do you think he's got the letters back? Or that he knows we haven't got them?"

"I'm not sure. That's why I've had to take other steps to protect myself and my friends."

"Have you got some other letters or something?"

"I've got his daughter. I've written to Lewis, so he knows he's got to keep quiet to ensure she's safe. She's quite a handful. She's lucky I'm so forbearing. You remember her, don't you? She's as bad as that husband of hers was. He and I were friends once. Pity he kept asking too many questions. Now she's at it. Doesn't know when to give up. Some of our friends wanted to shut her up and her father, the way they shut up her husband. I expect Rhodri told you about that? Well, I didn't like that any more than he did. Nor did my uncle. At least Rhodri made a good job of covering it all up."

"Is she here?"

"Not quite, but I have brought her for a little visit to the Highlands. I invited her to visit the ancestral home of the MacKenzies in Glenshiel where my old friend, Willie MacKenzie, the Earl of Seaforth, lives. When we got to Perth, we found things had hotted up, and it wasn't too safe to travel with her. On top of that, the Earl of Mar has had me running around doing little errands like this one. At least she'll have a comfortable place to stay and Perth's a beautiful city, if a little crowded at present."

Billy wanted to go to Perth and rescue Helen, but did not know how, and anyway he had to find Colonel Campbell and prevent an assassination. He thought that the best thing was to go with Charles, although he had no idea what he would do once they got to Fort William. If they got there. He cursed himself for retrieving the letters.

That night Megan joined the others in the big bedroom while they talked over the situation. They agreed with Billy's plan to go with Charles to Fort William and hope to catch up with Colonel Campbell and his companions there, or on the way. Then Megan went to her room, to the disappointment of some.

Billy wished he could stop worrying about Helen. So did the others. Megan thought the woman was probably in less danger than she and her companions were.

Chapter 37

They set off soon after dawn. The route seemed to be an endless succession of climbs and descents. Billy was right in thinking that if the Lowlands were not as low as he had expected, the Highlands must be very high. He had no idea where they were.

Sometime in the afternoon, Billy remarked that he could hear that Charles's horse had a loose shoe. They took it slowly for the rest of the day in case he actually lost the shoe. It was nearly dark when they reached Crieff. Jimmy knew some people there in another "big hoose", which turned out to be not quite as big as the one they had just left. They were received by a servant who led them through to a big hall where they were to wait for his master. The interior of the house had much in common with the other place but was more basic. Soon the owner, Alistair Murray, came to see them. He was suspicious at first, but Jimmy reassured him that Charles and the others were to be trusted.

Charles asked where they would find the local farrier. He was told that, as the next day was the Sabbath, the farrier would not be working. He and his companions were, however, welcome to stay for more than one night. They all agreed that they needed a rest, and they were grateful that they would be resting in a fairly comfortable place. Charles was given a room to himself. The rest were obliged to share a big room with two big beds, and one small one in a little adjoining room. Charles dined with the family, the rest in the kitchen with the servants. The food was plainer and poorer than that which they had enjoyed the previous evening, but it was welcome and they left nothing. After the meal, they went to bed early. They were all tired. Thomas reluctantly shared a bed with Jimmy. For a while the others could hear them talking. They had to make an effort to avoid laughing at them. They had very different accents. They must have found conversation difficult, yet they seemed determined to persevere. Then they laughed. Billy asked what was so funny. Thomas said it was a shame to waste the opportunity: Megan should spend the night with one of them. Jimmy added, "Or maybe two or even all three o' us!" She opened her door and declined the offer. She really wanted some sleep.

As the next day was a Sunday, Jimmy went off to mass in a Catholic church somewhere. Billy was surprised to find Charles was a Protestant, as was his uncle, although his grandfather had been a Catholic. Not all those who supported the Catholic claimant to the throne were themselves Catholics. Thomas wandered off alone somewhere. Billy, Llewellyn and Megan went to a Protestant chapel and sat through a service none of them could understand, since the proceedings were all in Gaelic, but somehow Billy felt they were doing the right thing. He silently confessed his sins, from theft to fornication, and prayed for himself, Megan and Bethan to find a way out the life of deception and immorality they had become accustomed to. He prayed for his father to be free. He also prayed for God to help him find a way of helping Helen, while doing his duty to his country. He had always prayed intermittently, although he had been less and less regular in that habit, but had made more effort since he had met Perse.

They all went back to the Murray's house for some lunch, then went out for a gentle walk around the village, except for Jimmy who said he wanted to visit some other friends while he had the opportunity, and would probably not be joining the others for dinner. Charles said he thought Jimmy was worried about something, but when he had asked him he had just shrugged and said he was fine.

On Monday they took their horses to the farrier. Although only one had a loose shoe, they all had worn their shoes down and needed reshoeing for the long ride ahead. They had a long wait for the farrier to start as he insisted on dealing with his regular clients first.

While they were waiting, they sat on a wall and enjoyed the view. Llewellyn asked Thomas for another lesson in fighting. The rest watched. This time, Thomas concentrated on footwork and speed, landing only light punches on the lad, but letting him see how slow his reactions were. By the end of the session, Llewellyn had improved considerably. He was certainly benefitting from his tuition. Then the lad dared Jimmy to take on Thomas. Jimmy was an experienced fighter, as well as being tough and strong, and, although slightly smaller than Thomas, he beat him twice. Thomas said it was because he had become so used to fighting with the boy that he had got into the habit of not trying too hard. They all expressed scepticism, but secretly thought he was probably right.

Then Jimmy asked if Billy wanted to try. He declined. Jimmy said, "I'm confused. Billy's bigger than me. How can a mon wha's no a fighter get any respect frae Rob Roy?"

Thomas said, "Billy's not so good with 'is fists but there's more'n one kind of fighting."

Megan said, "He doesn't fight for fun, but he can when he has to."

Jimmy apologised and went to see how the farrier was getting on. Slowly. Apparently he took a long lunch and was not breaking the habit just for these outsiders. After a while, Jimmy said, "There's something no reeght!." They all looked puzzled. It was a pleasant day, they had had an adequate meal, and the fighting had been harmless fun. What could be wrong? He enlightened them. "What do ye see? And what hae ye seen everywhere we've been these twa days?"

Billy thought of fields, mountains, trees and clouds. Especially mountains. Sometimes rain. He said, "Nothing to worry me." Charles and the others said the same.

Jimmy said, "Did ye no see all the men in the fields and in the villages? Did ye no see a hoose full o'servants last neet? Canna ye see men here in the streets?" Compared with most places, the Highlands struck them as being rather empty, but Jimmy was more used to the area.

"What's wrong with that?" asked Charles.

"A month or so ago they would hae been empty. All the men were in oor army. We lost a lot after the big fight at Sheriffmuir. I dinna mean just the poor lads killed. I mean the ones that left us every day since."

Charles said, "I'm afraid you're right. We started losing a lot more, when the news got round that Argyll had got heavy guns and reinforcements. I was hoping Billy was going to tell us it wasn't true, but he's confirmed it."

Jimmy said, "Aye! We Highlanders dinna like the big guns. But it's also the time." "What?" said all the rest.

"We're brave and fierce at first in any fight. But we dinna like hanging aboot when naething's going on. The longer we wait the less we like it. If the Earl doesnae get on wi' it soon, he'll be on his ain. There's something else. When I was oot last neet, I saw some auld friends. They say they've heard that the King himself is in Scotland, and he'll be with the Earl and his army soon. I hope folk'll flock back tae the banner when they hear that, but he might hae left it too late."

Charles said, "I hope you're wrong, but I fear you're right. To be fair, Jimmy, these men are not professional soldiers. They've got families and farms and work to think about. They can leave everything and go to war for a time, but after a while they'll start thinking about these other things. I can't blame them. Let's hope the lads we left harassing Fort William are
still at their posts when we get there."

When they went up to their room, Thomas said he was sure it was time Megan got into bed with him."

Jimmy said, "Forget him! I want tae be first. I'll pay if that's yer problem."

Billy wondered for the second time if all the rumours he had heard about the meanness of the Scots were untrue.

"No. I won't take money, but I think I'd like to see you and Thomas fight over me. I was a bit disappointed earlier. You two didn't seem to be trying too hard." Llewellyn said, "Yes! You can beat him, Thomas!"

They left a couple of candles alight, not so much for the benefit of the two combatants as to enable the others to see what happened. Billy and Llewellyn sat on one of the beds. Megan stood. The two fighters began by grappling and testing each other's strength. Thomas managed to push Jimmy backwards onto the empty bed and lay on him, pushing his head over the far edge bending his neck back. After a struggle, Jimmy found himself falling head first off the bed with Thomas still on top of him, taking the bedclothes with them. The others went round to the far side to see what was happening. Thomas continued to slide forwards until he was slightly beyond Jimmy. They rolled off the bed completely, in a tangle. Jimmy grabbed Thomas by the ankles and tried to drag him along the floor but found himself impeded by the bedclothes, which were wrapped around his feet, making him wobble. Thomas took the opportunity to break one foot free and land a heavy kick on his opponent's stomach. Then another. Jimmy rolled back onto the bed to avoid a third, leaving Thomas lying on the floor.

By the time Thomas was on his feet, Jimmy was standing on the other side of the bed. Thomas went round to him. Megan moved out of the way but tried to keep as close as she could. She was excited. The two men were trying harder than they had during the afternoon. She had obviously succeeded in giving them an incentive. They grappled again. This time, Thomas began to push Jimmy towards the bed again but suddenly changed direction and threw him at the other bed making Llewellyn and Billy roll clumsily apart. Jimmy jumped up to get back at Thomas, but he was ready for him, so he got Thomas's shoulder in his face and an elbow in his stomach, sending him back to rejoin the others on the bed. Thomas jumped on top of him, winding him further. Llewellyn rolled aside again. Billy jumped to his feet, colliding with Megan, who was following the fight a bit too closely, but she did not care. Thomas grabbed his opponent, hauling him off the bed before he had fully recovered from the impact of being jumped on. Then he span him round and pushed him forwards onto the other bed, jumping on top of him again. He grabbed both Jimmy's wrists and bent his arms behind his back almost to his neck. Then he shuffled forwards and knelt astride him, saying, "Is that enough? Give up?"

The answer was something that might have been in Gaelic. Or anything. He repeated the question while putting even more pressure on Jimmy's arms.

"Och! All reet! You win!"

Thomas let go and slid off him. Jimmy rolled onto his back rubbing his arms and shoulders. Megan put her arms round Thomas and kissed him on the cheek. When he had recovered enough breath to speak, Jimmy said, "Noo, that's one tae you. I won twice earlier." The others decided to humour him as he was humiliated enough. By this time both men were exhausted. Megan said, "I don't think either of you will be up to it right now. I'll have to find someone else."

Billy and Llewellyn laughed while the two pugilists groaned. Megan said, in an attempt at a Highland accent, "Dinna fash yersel's! I'll get roond to you two later." They all laughed. Thomas was reluctant to share Megan but decided there was no point in arguing. Not when he was out of breath. Megan got into bed between the two exhausted wrestlers, while Billy and Llewellyn got into the other bed. Megan could hear them whispering and laughing. In due course, she kept her word. Both fighters had a good time. So did she.
Billy had to wait for another night.

Chapter 38

Among the camp followers in Preston was Greta, a big Flemish whore, who had a history of fights with Bethan, which tradition looked like being revived on their meeting again, until Perse intervened. Bethan told him their antagonism went back to their time in the Spanish Netherlands. He asked, "How did it start?"

"Greta tried to seduce Henry."

"Would it matter? As long as he did not succumb to her charms?"

"You can't be too careful. Besides, she was so boastful, I couldn't resist taking her on. She beat me well and truly the first time, so I had to try again. I think for both of us it just became a habit after a while. The least thing could set us off."

Perse was bemused, so a few days later, when he saw Greta alone, he asked her about it. She said, "Yes! We had a few fights over Henry. Then we stopped for a time, but after he disappeared, when Bethan became another camp follower like me, we became rivals again. She was one of the few who could give me a good fight."

Perse did not say much, but he was quite shocked. He had not realised that Bethan had been a camp follower. He asked her if it was true. She was evasive at first but finally admitted it. She tried to explain how it had come about, but Perse was appalled. He had thought she was better than that. At one time she had been. Although she was ashamed of herself, when she reflected on her past, she was offended by his reaction.

On their next meeting, Greta wondered why Bethan seemed so aggressive. She asked, "Are you in a bad mood?"

"Yes!"

"You don't have to take it out on me."

"Oh yes, I do!"

"Ouch!"

Their tradition was renewed, but Bethan's relationship with Perse remained a lot cooler after that. She thought it was a good thing that he did not know Billy and she had been a highwayman and a highwaywoman. She kept remembering her uncle and her mother. They would have been as shocked as Perse.

Chapter 39

At Crieff, on the Tuesday morning, on horses that were rested as well as newly shod and well fed, Billy and his companions set off early. They rode through St Fillans, then alongside a big lake. Jimmy insisted it should be called a "loch", and so the others humoured them. Jimmy said it was called Loch Earn. The road was less steep and they managed to get some speed up for most of the morning, but the loch seemed endless. Around noon, Jimmy said they were coming into MacGregor country so everything should be all right. Billy hoped they were not going to meet anyone they had met in Preston, or things would be far from all right. He could not get rid of the memory of the look of hatred in the face of Wee Alex MacGregor. He hoped not to see that again. A little later, Jimmy commented that he had seen fewer men since they had been in that area. He hoped it was because the MacGregors were serving the King loyally. Billy thought it would make little difference if the other clans were deserting.

As the end of the loch came in sight in the distance, Jimmy said, "There's Lochearnhead!" The others thought the name was at least accurate. They saw smoke. Jimmy rode on ahead to investigate. While he was gone, a herd of some thirty or forty cattle came along the road. There were over a dozen men driving them. Some on ponies, most on foot. They turned up a track leading into the hills. Jimmy came back riding

fast. He called out, "Did ye no see them?"

Charles said, "The cattle?"

"The cattle-thieves!"

"Is that what they were?"

"Could ye no tell? Ye could hae stopped them! It's them that set fire tae the village, so the poor villagers had tae choose tae save their homes or their cattle. Noo the fires are under control, some of the people are coming after them. Did ye see where they went?"

Billy said "Up there!" Pointing at the track.

"Come on then!"

Charles said, "This is not our fight. We need to get on."

"These are my people! Some o' these folk hae lost their homes *and* their cattle. That's all they had. Och! Please yersel' but I'm awa' the noo!"

Billy turned Cae in the road. Thomas followed. Megan and Llew followed him. When they reached the place where the cattle-thieves had turned off onto a track, Billy pulled up and called to Thomas, "We'd better leave Megan and Llew here. Things could get a bit rough when we catch up with them."

The three men went on up the track and paused at the top of the ridge. There were plenty of places suitable for an ambush in country like that. It was undulating and intermittently wooded. Then Charles appeared. Megan pointed up the track and watched him ride after the others. Soon the villagers approached: some on ponies, most on foot. They looked fierce. Most had swords. Many carried farm implements. Some had very oldfashioned muskets. They were matchlock weapons. Only a few were carrying tapers or tinderboxes. Megan wondered if they going to have to pass the fire around before using their weapons? Were these the sort of men who made up the Jacobite Army? She thought King

George had little to fear.

Billy and his companions rode slowly down the slope. Shots were fired at them. They dismounted and spread out around a clump of trees where the raiders had taken refuge. The cattle seemed to be unattended, wandering around on the next slope. The firing ceased. Either the thieves had run out of ammunition, or their only source of fire had petered out. Then, over a dozen came from the edge of the wood and rushed at their pursuers, wielding swords. Charles and Jimmy took on some of them with their swords while Billy and Thomas and each fired a pistol. Then they both fired their second pistols. Soon they were in danger of being overwhelmed. They each grabbed a sword that had been dropped and began parrying blows from all round.

Neither of them was a good swordsman, and both found themselves giving ground. They were in danger of becoming surrounded. Billy lost his footing and fell. Someone raised his sword ready to bring it down on him while another prepared to do the same in case he miraculously survived one such blow. Then Megan fired her pistol. Nobody seemed to have noticed her riding close enough to be fairly certain of hitting her target. Billy's immediate attacker bent double and coughed blood from his mouth. His companion made the mistake of looking to see where the shot had come from. Billy did not waste the opportunity. He thrust up at him with his sword from on the ground. The Highlander collapsed with blood gushing from a wound to the groin.

A couple of muskets fired from back up the hill. Some of the villagers had arrived. Nobody knew if they hit anyone, but the rustlers began to run or ride away. Charles shouted for joy and said, "Let's get them!" He ran for his horse. Charles and Jimmy used their swords to cut down the escaping thieves. Billy and Thomas reloaded their pistols before joining the pursuit, but by then no more cattle-thieves were standing. The local people went around killing the wounded and robbing the dead before rounding up the herd. Billy did not like it, but knew it would have been useless to try to persuade the people to show mercy. They were too angry. Some of them came to thank their helpers. Jimmy said they invited them to stay, but the visitors declined, partly because they needed to get on with their journey and partly because they could see the villagers had a lot of clearing up and rebuilding to do.

As they rode along, Jimmy said to Billy, "If I ever dooted yer courage, I was wrong! Ye did fine. Ye can fight when ye have tae, just like yer friends said. I'm glad ye're on oor side and no the other."

Billy asked, "Were they the Enemy?" He wondered if the Campbells or others loyal to King George were making raids on rebel villages.

"Och, no! They're thieves of the MacDonald clan. They probably couldna resist the chance while most of oor men were awa' serving the King."

Chapter 40

The terrain became steeper and more difficult. The area was less populated. It began to rain. Then the rain turned to sleet. Finally, it turned to snow. Jimmy said they were in Glencoe, and he had hoped to reach Glencoe village before nightfall, but it looked unlikely. They passed a few hamlets but he warned them that a lot of people in that area did not like the English, were not at all fond of the MacGregors and really hated the Campbells. He thought they might reach another village where they were a bit more hospitable. Billy was afraid they could have ridden through a village without noticing it as the visibility was so reduced.

Suddenly Jimmy dismounted. He went to the door of a cottage. After a brief conversation with someone in the doorway, he came back and said, "Aye, it'll be all reet, but there's nae hoose here big enough for all o' us. They're asking their neighbours tae tak some o' us too." They waited in the cold and wet a few more minutes. A man came out of the cottage and hurried to another smaller house further up the track only just visible through the falling snow. Then he came back and spoke to Jimmy in Gaelic. Jimmy said, "Aye! It's as I thought. Major Butler had best come wi' me tae this hoose and I'll translate for him. The ones further up speak a bit o' English, so you'll be all reet there." His host said something else in Gaelic, which made Jimmy laugh. Then he said, "Ye'll no mind that some folks roond here say that the far hoose is no quite respectable, will ye?"

Billy, Thomas, Megan and Llewellyn were so cold and wet that respectability was something they could easily have sacrificed. Almost anything was. Their hosts were MacDonalds, as were almost all the families in that valley. The man of the house, Duncan MacDonald, led them to an outbuilding where they put their horses, before taking them into the cottage and inviting them to gather round the fire. Duncan, a stockily built man, introduced his wife, Moira, a tall redhaired beauty. There was an assortment of children and a few dogs who had to wait for their introductions. Moira began warming up some broth over the fire. As the visitors warmed up, they took off their outer garments, and everyone made themselves comfortable on various chairs, stools and benches. Billy told them briefly about their journey and their mission to aid the Jacobites, with whom the MacDonalds were obviously in sympathy.

Billy complimented them on their English, which was by far the best he had heard since arriving in the Highlands. Duncan explained that they had both lived in England at different times, in the households of gentlefolk. For that reason, some of their relatives and neighbours thought they were too anglicised. Moira poured the broth into a bowl for each of them. It was very welcome and quite tasty. Duncan warned them to beware of Hanoverian patrols when they got closer to Fort William. Billy realised that he meant troops serving George of Hanover, whom they did not accept as King. He asked about "our" troops and was told there were hardly any in the area. Charles's fears seemed to have materialised.

Billy said, "It's good of you to put us up. I was afraid we were going to be out in this weather for a long time. We want to be on our way as soon as possible, but I don't know how soon that will be. Will the roads be passable tomorrow if this keeps up?"

Duncan said, "No, but don't worry. I'm pretty sure it won't last. It'll all be gone in a day or two. You'd do better waiting for it to clear than struggling on through snowdrifts."

Billy hoped Charles and Jimmy would be getting the same advice. And heeding it.

The next day it had stopped snowing, but the ground was hidden under a white blanket. They would not have had much chance of staying on the road safely. Jimmy came to say he and Charles had agreed it was best to wait for it to improve. All the local people went out to check on their animals in the fields and to clear snow from certain places. Billy and Llewellyn helped Duncan and his boys. While they were gone, Megan asked Moira, "What was the meaning of the remark about your reputation? Do your neighbours suspect you of having low morals?"

Moira explained, "I went to Glasgow with my first husband, looking for work. When he died, I married an Englishman and we later went to England where we both got work as servants to a country gentleman. When that husband died, I came home and finally married Duncan who had also been away and returned. For a time, I was living in a house by myself with my children. Every time a man came visiting, even my late husband's brother, fingers were pointed. In his case it's understandable. He's

340

fond of the ladies. To hear some folk, you'd think he's had half the women in the Highlands. It's the other half that do all the talking." They laughed. So did some of the children. Others looked puzzled.

Moira went on, "I'm being honest with you because you're bound to hear the rumours, which are worse than the reality, but never mind." Megan thought it unlikely they would hear any of the rumours, not only because they were not planning on socialising around the village, but also because most people there probably did not speak English. Or Welsh.

The others came in when it was beginning to get dark, by which time they had cleared most of the snow. Moira warmed some more stew, to which some of Billy's rations had been added. Just as they were starting to eat it, the dogs barked, only to be silenced by a word from Duncan, so they could all listen for any sound from outside. They heard a horse's hooves and went to investigate.

There was a big man wearing a cape over his plaid leading a pregnant mare. Duncan exclaimed, "Och! Gordon! You gave us a fright. What are you doing here?"

Gordon replied in Gaelic and Duncan said, "We're speaking English today, for the benefit of our guests. Of course, you're welcome to put her in with the others. It'll be a bit of squeeze, but it can't be helped. Then you'd better come in and get warm. You're in luck, we were just sitting down to a good stew." He then explained to his visitors that Gordon had been looking for the mare who had strayed. He had found her near to Duncan's house, and did not want to try to lead her home in the dark.

While the new arrival was bedding down his mare, Duncan explained, "He's Moira's first husband's brother. He lives over there a way." He waved a hand somewhere towards Loch Earn. He went on, "He's a bit rough but we get on all right. He's an old friend of your companion, Jimmy. He's another MacGregor."

Seeing her visitors' surprise, Moira said, "Aye, my Donald was a MacGregor. That's another reason not everybody welcomes us all the time down in the village. MacDonalds and MacGregors don't always get on. We're united at present because we all want to see a Stewart back on the Throne. My two eldest are proud of being MacGregors and that gets them into scraps at times too. They love their Uncle Gordon because he was their father's brother and he's like him in many ways."

Gordon came in and asked, none too politely, who the visitors were. Billy told him what he had told the MacDonalds, including their association with Jimmy. He looked sceptical. He said, "I'm surprised at Jimmy. He's no too fond of Sassenachs."

Duncan said, "These are my guests. Show respect for me, if not for them or Jimmy, while you're under my roof."

Gordon jumped to his feet and half-drew his sword saying to Billy, "Ye can step ootside and let us test yer story if ye like, so we'll no be offending oor host."

Billy said, "I hope that won't be necessary. I don't want my dinner to go cold. Have a look at this and ask yourself if Rob Roy was wrong to trust me." He handed him the bigger brooch.

Gordon looked at it and said, "Perhaps it was Rob who gave ye this, or perhaps someone else. It proves naething."

Duncan said, "It was good enough for Jimmy. Stop looking for trouble."

Llewellyn stood up and said, "Rob gave us something else too, in case we met someone like you."

"Och, aye? What's that?" The boy produced the dagger, apparently from nowhere, and held it to Gordon's chest.

"Is that good enough? Or is it not close enough for you?" He then turned it to show him the designs and jewels on the hilt. The Scotsman tried to take it but was not quick enough. The boy said, "Well? Who gave me that? King George?"

"Aye, well, if Rob thinks that much of ye, I can only think the same, and it is a wee bit cold tae go outside. And here's the stew. That's a braw bonny lad ye've got!"

After they had finished the stew, there was a commotion among the children, who were arguing noisily. Llewellyn had told the others that Thomas was teaching him to fight and had beaten Jimmy at wrestling a couple of nights before. This led to wild boasting among the children as to whether Thomas could beat Duncan or Gordon and whether Llewellyn could beat the biggest of the MacDonald boys, the thirteen-year-old Donald. They were all making bets with money they did not have on the outcome of events that were not even certain to take place.

When order was restored, Moira said, "My Donald's about the same size as Llew, but he's older and stronger. So be careful what you ask for! As for Duncan,

343

he'll not fight unless he needs to, although he can. He's just too easygoing. Wee Iain's like him: a natural peacemaker. I've always been one for settling things the simple way. As for Gordon, he's always ready for a fight."

Megan said, "It's the same with us. Billy only fights if he has to. I've always been the fighter. Thomas is another. I've enjoyed watching him and Jimmy fight, and he's been teaching Llew, who's learning fast."

The children then started arguing again. Duncan said he was happy to see a wrestling match,.

Llewellyn and the other children persuaded Thomas to challenge Gordon to a wrestling match. They had no need to persuade Gordon.

They moved the beds around to form three sides of a square, with a blank wall making the fourth. The fight would be held in the square.

Gordon was bigger than Thomas and looked strong and tough. In fact, Billy would have bet on him, but he wondered if he would be too confident and make mistakes athough he gave the impression of being an experienced fighter. Neither man made any mistakes. Gordon's size and strength were enough for him to pin Thomas down on his front and sit on him after only a brief period of grappling. He then pulled Thomas's head back until he gave in. The children were delighted, especially Donald and his only full sister Isla.

Then the adults gave in to the children's demands to let the two boys fight. Llewellyn soon found that Donald was stronger than him and a good fighter, but some of the tricks Thomas had taught him enabled him to gain an advantage. Donald was shocked to find himself flat on his face with one leg being twisted up his back and Llewellyn's weight pressing down on him. Billy and Duncan had to declare the fight over before either boy would give up. Demands from the other children for a rematch were rejected by all the adults.

Before bed, all the adults swapped stories from the more interesting times in their lives. Duncan and Moira were especially entertaining.

The next day most of the snow had gone before noon, as predicted, so the visitors took their leave of their hosts and set out again. When they were out of the village, Charles said, "The MacDonalds were most generous and hospitable to me. I hope you all found the same. However, it was all an ordeal. It was frustrating having to ask Jimmy to translate all the time. Of course, the food was not the best either." Billy thought of the contrast with the fun he and Megan had had with Duncan and his family. He also suspected that Charles's hostess had not been as good a cook as Moira.

Chapter 41

They rode through mountains again. Jimmy asked a few people about military activity and was always given the same answer. Fort William was securely in the hands of the British Army. Local resistance seemed to be over. They came out of the mountains into more cultivated land where they could see an expanse of water. Jimmy said it was Loch Leven and that they could shorten the journey by several hours if they took the ferry to North Ballachulish. By the time they reached the loch, it was nearly dark and the ferry was not going out again until morning. They saw redcoats in the distance on the other side of the water.

They found an inn. It was greatly inferior to any Billy had seen before. They all ate together. The food was terrible. They could identify neither the meat nor the vegetables. Charles asked, and was given, Gaelic names for everything, which Jimmy found as hard to translate as it was to eat. Billy did not care. He just resolved to avoid eating in that establishment again.

Charles said, "Now, what are we going to do? What if I go alone and claim to be a civilian? I just need a story to say why I'm here."

Billy said, "You could say you're an Anglo-Irish aristocrat trying to return to Ireland after visiting relatives in the Highlands, so you're looking for a ship. It's almost true."

"It might work, and in your uniforms you could present yourselves to the garrison as British soldiers who just got separated from your regiment and got lost in the Highlands. That's almost true too. Then you could 'desert' again to get to Wales after you get to England, or the Lowlands."

Jimmy had been eating his food with more enthusiasm than the rest and had not appeared to be listening. He surprised them by suddenly asking, "Wha' aboot me?"

Charles said, "In those clothes you'd be nothing but a target for the British soldiers. As for any Campbells..."

Billy said, "Jimmy could come with us, if he wasn't wearing MacGregor tartan. Can we not find enough spare clothes between us?"

Thomas said, "Leave it to me. I'll find something." So they left it to him.

They asked the innkeeper for beds for the night. He had just one room for a gentleman. As usual, the rest would have to share. The room was cold, draughty and dark. It felt damp. There was just one big bed in it. The blankets were old, thin, moth-eaten and slightly damp. They were glad they were not staying long. Thomas said he wanted to go out by himself and would join the others later. They said they were not going to wait up for him.

It was far into the night when they were awakened by someone coming into the room. Megan lit a candle, while Billy pointed a pistol towards the door. There stood a stranger. He shouted, "Where's that cheating Sassenach? He was one o' you lot. He's cleaned me oot wi' his tricks. I'm no going tae stand for it!"

They all assured him they did not know what he was talking about and anyway, if he meant Thomas, they did not know where he was. The man stamped across to the bed and waved a sword. Billy asked, "What happened?"

He took off the cape he was wearing. He was left in nothing but a cloth around his middle. He said, "Yer friend played cards wi' me. He had the clothes off ma back as weel as all ma money. He must hae been cheating!"

Billy said, "How do you know he wasn't just lucky?"

He replied unintelligibly. He obviously regarded so much luck as unbelievable. So did Billy, but he was not going to say so. The man waved his sword again.

Megan said, "At least he did not take your sword!"

"Aye, he did! I borrowed this frae a mon wha's too drunk tae use it." Billy and Megan hoped this man was too drunk to use it. His slurred speech encouraged them.

He came closer and said, "Gimme what's mine or I'll cut ye all tae pieces." With that, he raised the sword and fell forwards onto the bed, dropping the weapon. Llewellyn was standing behind him holding a candlestick. Once they had ascertained that the man was still breathing, they wrapped his cape around him and carried him outside. They deposited him in a shed a little way down the road.

When they got back, Thomas was in the room. He laughed when they told him of their encounter with his victim. He insisted that he had not needed to cheat. It was luck and skill. He had won a good plain set of clothes as well as a lot of money.

In the morning, Jimmy dressed in dull brown breeches and a plain cap. The others made him discard everything he had which might identify him as a MacGregor. Thomas had made an arrangement with a whore that she would keep Jimmy's things safe, until either he or Jimmy came back for them. He was sure he could trust her, because he had promised her a fee for her service and had taken a necklace of hers as surety.

They took their horses across the loch on the ferry and rode to Fort William, going straight to the garrison commander. They told him the stories they had prepared. On leaving him, they had to split up. Billy, Thomas and Llewellyn were soldiers, and so had to stay in the barracks. Megan went with Charles and Jimmy to find better accommodation. They all agreed to meet in a tavern that evening.

Billy went to see the commander again. He told him of his real mission, showing him his orders from the Duke of Argyll. The commander told him he had had a visit from Colonel Campbell and a couple of his comrades. They had left two days previously.

When they gathered that evening, Charles said, "It's worse than I thought. Nobody seems to be a Jacobite any more."

Billy said, "I'm not surprised. The soldiers say they've been having it easy for some time. Their patrols never encounter anything."

Charles said, "I don't see how we can win. I need to go back to Perth to report to the Earl, and I need to collect the lovely and infuriating Helen MacKenzie. What about you, Billy?"

"I need to report to the Earl too. So it looks as if we'll be travelling companions again."

Billy wrote a report to the Duke of Argyll, and handed it to the garrison commander. It told the Duke what he had learned about the Enemy's situation, and that he would try to get back to the force at Stirling as soon as possible, after going to Perth in pursuit of Colonel Campbell. He explained this to the commander who assured him he would send it to the Duke, and authorised him to draw supplies from the stores for the journey.

Billy met Charles and the others again and said he had told the commander that he was going to Stirling to rejoin the main force there. They all resigned themselves to another long ride through the mountains in bad weather.

Chapter 42

Billy and his companions rode to North Ballaculish and took the ferry back across the loch. This time they did not stop at the inn, except to recover Jimmy's clothes, but carried on into the mountains. Although it was cold and there were showers of sleet, the sun warmed them intermittently and the way remained passable.

They reached Glencoe just as it was getting dark. Jimmy thought they should make themselves known at the Laird's house before looking for anywhere to stay for the night. The Laird's servants took Charles and Jimmy into another room to see their master. Charles came back later to say the Laird had invited him and Jimmy to stay but, as, he already had other guests, he had to send the rest of the party on their way. Billy said they would ask the family they had stayed with before to take them in again. The Laird's house was much bigger and more luxurious than Duncan's or his neighbours' but Billy had a feeling he would be happier than Charles that night. He had no idea how right he was.

At Duncan's house they were introduced to Flora, Gordon's wife. Moira was just about to serve the evening meal and busied herself to stretch it to feed three more hungry mouths. Billy gave her some of the supplies he had brought, so the family would still have something to eat after the visitors had gone. He asked Flora how Gordon was. She looked puzzled, so Moira explained that she spoke no English. She then answered on her behalf, "Gordon went off again yesterday looking for a cow that had strayed at the same time as the mare and hasn't been seen since. Flora came here after trying her nearer neighbours. She's really worried because the cow came home by herself last night. The thing is, the English have declared the MacGregors to be outlaws. They offer a bounty on them. They say they were the worst of the rebels at Preston and are still making the most trouble."

Billy could see they had a point. He said, "Surely he'll be safe anywhere round here? I thought Highlanders didn't care too much for what the British Government said. Don't they stick together, even rival clans?"

Duncan answered, "That's been true ever since we joined together for our cause, but our hope is rapidly fading. With that fades a lot of our unity. There's plenty round here would like to collect a golden guinea more than they'd like to help a clansman of a rival clan. The Laird's a typical case. I'm afraid he might be the one who's got Gordon. Tomorrow I'll go and see. Perhaps I can offer to pay for him. I'd have to outbid the English, but I expect Gordon'll repay me when he can. He's got his faults, but ingratitude's not one of them."

A horrible thought then struck Billy. Was that the reason the Laird had let Jimmy stay in his house? Was Gordon one of the 'other guests' they were told of? Did the Laird hope for a reward for an English, or Anglo-Irish, Jacobite officer? Had he not wanted the rest of them, because he perceived them to be of no value to him?

He shared his fears with the others. Flora strained to listen, and Duncan translated for her, while Moira served the meal.

It was something unique to the Highlands. It was a skin filled with minced meat and vegetables. A cross between a sausage and a pie. They called it "haggis". The Welsh visitors enjoyed it.

They spent most of the evening talking over the situation, trying to develop a plan. It occurred to Billy that he could abandon Charles and Jimmy to their fate and head on to Perth as quickly as possible. However, he felt a strange sense of loyalty to these two travelling companions despite being on opposite sides.

Duncan said, "I think I should go alone in the morning to the Laird. The servants might tell me what's going on."

Billy said, "Please do. I think I'll be ready to pay the Laird a visit as soon as I know what's what. I'll wait just out of sight from the village. I noticed a few side valleys leading off the main one."

"Hadn't we better gather as many friends as we can, if we're going to rescue them?"

"No! I don't intend to fight the Laird and his men. I've got a more subtle plan in mind. I would like to borrow a sword, but I hope I won't need to use it. I don't suppose you've got one that's not a Highland sword? The basket handle is so distinctive. I want to look every inch a British officer."

He could hardly believe his luck. Moira had a sword which her first husband had acquired: a straight cavalry sword with a Tudor rose carved on the pommel. Not the least Scottish. Billy borrowed the scabbard and belt too.

In the morning, Billy waited for over an hour after Duncan had set out for the Laird's house. The he and Thomas left Megan and Llewellyn at the MacDonald's cottage. Just before Glencoe village they turned up a track beside a stream coming from a small valley joining the main one, where Duncan was waiting. He said their fears were confirmed: Charles, Jimmy and Gordon were being held as prisoners pending being taken to Fort William where the Laird hoped to collect his reward.

Billy rode up to the front door and demanded to see the Laird. He refused to discuss anything with anyone else, saying the Laird would not thank him for divulging such matters to his servants, no matter how trusted. After some argument, they gave in and showed him in, along with Thomas. The Laird received them in his private room. He introduced himself as Donald MacDonald. Billy showed him the letter he had from the Duke of Argyll authorising him to conduct operations as he saw fit and requiring other British officers to cooperate with him. He hid the page about arresting Colonel Campbell.

Billy said, "I believe you have been clever enough to capture one of the most cunning and dangerous Jacobite officers who is going by the name Charles Butler. He is wanted as a spy. I have had several close encounters with him, but so far he has always escaped. I shall be delighted to have him in my custody at last. If it turns out that it really is him, you will be rewarded, and I am to take him to Edinburgh to be questioned."

The Laird's face lit up when he heard "rewarded" and he said, "I'll show him to ye the noo. Do ye ken that

I've also got a pair o' MacGregors? There'll be a reward for them too, I doobt!" Billy agreed. With that, the Laird summoned his servants to bring the prisoners. Billy hoped they would not greet him and his companions as old friends. He need not have worried. Charles just stared incredulously. Jimmy looked dazed. It was Gordon who became the centre of attention. He cursed and threatened in Gaelic. Then he was kind enough to provide a translation. Helen could not have outdone him for vitriol.

The Laird asked, "Have ye met before?"

Billy was hoping to avoid admitting that, but Thomas came to the rescue, saying, "Yes, Sir! We arrested this fellow not long ago. We didn't know he was a MacGregor. I just thought he was a drunken brawler. We won't be letting him go so soon this time."
He smiled malevolently at Gordon to add credibility.

The Laird said, "I see there's nae but the twa o' you. Will ye need some o' my men tae help guard these dangerous ootlaws?"

Billy replied, "Thank you for your generosity, Sir, but I can assure you they will be making a very big mistake if they try any tricks. I almost hope they will. Of course, we will soon be joining the rest of my troop further up the valley." He drew one of his pistols and walked around the room twirling it, stopping from time to time to point it at each of them. "What do you think, Thomas? Can we manage this little band?"

"Yes Sir! I'd love to teach them a lesson, before we hand them over, especially this one!"

Thomas smiled again at Gordon, who snarled back at him. The prisoners' hands were already tied behind their backs, but Thomas made a point of untying and retying the knots. He was not gentle.

They began marching them to the front door. Billy asked for someone to bring their horses. One of the servants remarked that Gordon was on foot. Billy said he had better keep up with the rest, or he would suffer. He also asked for their weapons and personal effects. The Laird said he thought he was entitled to them. They compromised. He could keep their money and valuables, but their weapons had to be forfeit to the Crown. They had almost reached the door when the Laird exclaimed, "Och! Have ye no forgotten something?" He made a gesture of a man counting money.

Billy said, "Don't worry! Can I use your paper and pen?" Donald MacDonald seemed surprised. Billy added, "I do not carry large sums in gold when patrolling the Highlands, but the King's credit is good anywhere. Of course, you could accompany us to Edinburgh and be paid in gold coin by the authorities there."

"Och, no! I'm sure King George's paper is good anywhere."

Billy wrote him a promissory note similar to some he had handled in Rhodri's office. Billy asked for a long rope and for the prisoners' horses to be made ready. He looped the rope around the necks of all the prisoners and held onto one end while Thomas held the other. They led them out and, with the help of some of the servants, got two of them mounted. They arranged the horses in a line and tied them one behind another.

Billy rode ahead, holding the rope, with Charles's horse tethered to his. Jimmy rode behind him. Lastly came Gordon on foot with Thomas riding behind him, urging him to keep up. This clearly gave Thomas pleasure.

About a mile along the road they rounded a bend and then came to the valley where Duncan was waiting. He was riding one of his Highland ponies, or 'garrons' as he called them, and leading another for Gordon to ride. They untied the prisoners and gave them back their weapons. Charles burst out laughing. Jimmy was still confused. When he realised what Billy had done, he was more amazed than amused. He said again that he was glad Billy was on "our" side. Gordon was still angry. The others tried to explain that everything had been an act, the purpose of which had been to rescue him and the others, but he was still smarting from the humiliation. He said he was not sure whether to accept the offer of a ride since he was wearing his plaid, not breeches, but he did decide to mount when he saw that Duncan had put a pad of rags on top of the saddle. He swore to get even with Thomas, who still found it amusing.

Back at Duncan's house, the women were relieved and astonished to get Gordon and the others back so soon and to learn that nobody was going to be coming looking for them, at least not for a long time. Gordon's mood had begun to lighten somewhat on the way, until he began to feel the effects of riding a horse in a plaid. Then an argument broke out among the children. Llewellyn and some of the others had been highly amused to hear how Gordon had really believed he was being taken away by

Hanoverians and had had to march quickly to keep up with the horses, whilst Donald and Isla had defended their uncle.

Gordon said to Thomas, "Noo I ken ye were helping me, but ye didna have tae enjoy it."

"You made it such fun, by getting so angry. I loved it."

"Do ye no remember who won oor wee fight not sae long ago?"

"Yes! That made me enjoy it more."

"Do ye ken what I'd enjoy?" There was a long pause. The children giggled and whispered together. Gordon enlightened anyone who had not guessed, saying, "I'd enjoy another fight with you."

Flora said something in Gaelic. This produced a renewed chorus of arguing from the children. Moira translated, "She says she thinks her Gordon's being ungrateful, but she wants to see these two fight. She's sorry she missed the last one. She also says Thomas is asking for it, the way he keeps laughing. I agree."

They faced each other on a wet patch of grass where the snow had just melted. They stripped as before. Flora kissed her husband and whispered something to him. Then she turned to Thomas and said something. Moira translated again. "This'll wipe that grin off your face!"

Megan kissed Thomas and said aloud, "It's time to get your own back. Teach him a lesson in humility."

Thomas kept antagonising Gordon with facial expressions and gestures as well as a few more verbal insults. Gordon growled. Thomas kept moving around and out of the reach of his opponent, who exercised a great deal of discipline to refrain from rushing at him. Gordon kept looking focussed on Thomas, making several feints in order to unsettle him. When he did make his move, it was fast. He grabbed Thomas with one hand and swung him round landing several punches on him with his other hand. Thomas seemed to stumble, then came back at Gordon with great ferocity, butting him in the face and punching him in the stomach. He then pushed, pulled and tripped him all at once, so he fell heavily with Thomas on top. He tried to butt Thomas, but his face was just out of reach. Gordon then heaved himself upwards and sideways, tipping Thomas off him and trying to roll on top of him. Thomas, however, anticipated that and rolled out of the way before rolling back again to get on top of him and hold him face down. He pulled Gordon's head back, while pressing a knee into his back and twisting one arm up between his shoulder blades. Gordon groaned, growled and uttered something in Gaelic. It sounded defiant.

Moira confirmed this by calling out, "He says you'll have to try harder than that!"

Flora called out something else in Gaelic. Despite his discomfort, Gordon laughed. Moira called to Thomas, "She says you underestimate Gordon's strength. She should know!"

Megan called out, "Don't listen to them, Thomas, keep it up!"

The children all called out encouragement: some for Gordon, others for Thomas. Thomas seemed to take Megan's advice, which strangely coincided with

Gordon's. He tried harder, pulling the big man's head back further, twisting his arm higher up his back and pressing his knee harder into him. Gordon let out an unintelligible sound. The onlookers renewed their chorus, which, by then, was as unintelligible as he was.
Thomas gasped and said something to Gordon, whose next utterance sounded like, "Aye."

Thomas got up. Gordon rolled onto his back and lay there for a minute to get his breath. Then he got up. His already limited command of English seemed to desert him completely. He made several attempts at speech in that language, before reverting to Gaelic. Duncan interpreted. "He congratulates you, and thanks you for getting him out of the Laird's grasp."

Chapter 43

Back in Preston, Cathy MacNichol went with Bethan to the fishmarket. Since the end of the fighting, fishermen had been bringing their catches. A large fish hit Bethan in the face, apparently out of nowhere. Discovering the source of its propulsion proved easier than it might have been, since a loud laugh drew everyone's attention to the unmistakeable figure of Hatty Sutton, the biggest of the group from which Bethan and Cathy had previously been rescued, standing behind a fish stall. The other fishwives gave voice to their amusement and to their admiration for the accuracy of the throw.

Bethan asked, "Are you practising for some local sporting event?"

"You lot are not welcome. My shoulder still 'urts, even though I've 'ad to pay good money to a wise woman to set it right, you bitch!"

"You asked for it. Stop complaining!"

The big woman picked up another fish, but Bethan was ready for it. She ducked and began to run as Hatty, and some of her friends, came charging towards her and her companion. Cathy turned up an alley out of sight. Bethan was surprised, when Hatty overtook her in a sudden burst of speed. She was gasping for breath by the time she reached the entrance to the alley, but continued to lumber forwards. A scream came from the alley. Everyone froze, apart from Bethan who rushed onwards. As she rounded the corner into the alley, she saw Hatty lying on the ground with Cathy standing just beyond her.

Then she saw blood coming from underneath her. Bethan managed to turn her over onto her side and saw a knife sticking out of her stomach.

Half a dozen fishwives clustered around in what little space there was. Bethan eased the knife out and tried to stem the flow of blood with cloths torn from Hatty's skirt and her own.

Someone shouted at Cathy, "What have you done? Did you stab her?"

Someone else said, "No! Look. It's Hatty's own knife. Her fish-gutting one. It was in her belt as usual, and she must've tripped and fallen on it."

Another asked Cathy, "Well? Did you see?"

"No! She was behind me. I only turned round when I heard her scream. She was probably going to use that thing on me."

"Never! She'd have given you a thumping, but that's all. She never uses her knife on anyone."

"She doesn't need to. She's dangerous enough without one!"

Bethan and some of the others lifted Hatty onto a handcart and took her to a house which was still being used as a hospital by the Army. Despite the best efforts of a local doctor, the woman died that night. Bethan was worried. She explained to Perse, "A lot of the fishwives are angry at Cathy. They blame her, wrongly, for Hatty's death. In a way the woman brought it upon herself, but it was an accident."

"I'll talk to Iain. He'll make sure she's kept safe. Perhaps you can help. Make sure she doesn't go into the town again. Is there something else?"

"It's the way Cathy's reacted. I know she didn't know Hatty and didn't have any reason to like her. She says she thought the woman was going to try to kill her, although I believe the others, that she was only meaning to hurt her. Still, Cathy doesn't seem bothered by it. It's as if she doesn't care about what happened to Hatty."

"Yes, it is a bit odd, I suppose. However, we don't all show our feelings in the same way. As you say, from her point of view, it could seem that Hatty only got what she asked for."

All this time Perse and Bethan had been finding it frustrating that they had had no news of Billy or the Scottish campaign generally. Similarly, Iain was anxious for news about his father. Such communications as he had received had contained very little information. He was not sure whether this was due to a deliberate, if excessive, policy of secrecy, or mere poor communications. Both explanations seemed equally likely. The next message Iain received contained orders to take all the soldiers and prisoners who were fit, to travel to London, apart from the Welsh who were to travel to Cardiff under Perse's command.

Some of the soldiers held a party on their last night in Preston. Bethan and the camp followers went. It was quite wild. Accounts of the party afterwards were exaggerated, especially those rendered by people who had been too drunk to notice what was going on. Perse heard a story about a supposed competition between Bethan and

Greta to see how many men each of them could satisfy. When he asked Bethan about it, she was so offended that she refused to answer. When he asked Greta, she found it amusing and boasted that she had won. Both women told Cathy the truth: that it had not happened. However, even she could not mend the rift between Perse and Bethan.

Chapter 44

December 1715

Two days after leaving the MacDonalds, Billy and his companions arrived at Perth, and were soon at the house Charles had been renting. As soon as they entered the hall, a woman burst in, followed by two others. It was Helen. She did not seem to notice Billy or Megan at first. She was as angry as they had ever seen her. She berated Charles, saying, "So now you have condescended to come back! Is this how you treat a lady? You bring me here on the pretence of showing me the ancestral home of the MacKenzies, only to abandon me in this miserable place, where I am held as a prisoner. I haven't seen a MacKenzie since I've been here. I don't think there are any in Perth!"

Charles said, "You do me a disservice, Madam, I will take you to the seat of the MacKenzies, when it is safe to do so. We are in a state of war, and it is not safe to travel far. Indeed that is why I am not permitting you to leave this house unescorted. May I remind you that I have been away on the King's urgent business, but have been looking forward to returning to this, my humble Scottish residence, to see you. Now, may I present my other guests, Lieutenant William Rhys, Gunner Thomas Thomas, Mr James MacGregor, Miss Megan Morgan and young Mr Llewellyn Tudor."

On recognising Billy and Megan, Helen nearly exploded. "You add insult to injury. How dare you bring such creatures under the same roof as me! Let me warn

365

you that this man is not all that he seems: he is an expert at deception and dissemblance, one of the most disreputable individuals it has been my lot to encounter. Do you not recall that in London he used a different name and persona? As for that woman, I am appalled that you should permit her into your circle. She is his doxy, a common whore! Are there no indignities you will refrain from inflicting upon me?"

Charles kept amazingly calm and replied, "I am indeed aware that Mr Rhys is a man of many parts. For that I am truly grateful. As for this lady, she has conducted herself with admirable fortitude throughout our recent adventures and deserves all our gratitude for numerous reasons, as you shall soon hear, I do not doubt."

"I do not wish to hear any such things. How you insult me! A man of many parts? I wish he were! If there was any justice he would have been hanged drawn and quartered long ago, and his many parts displayed for all to see. And I know a whore when I see one. Do not take me for a fool!"

Before anyone could respond, a servant interrupted. The Earl of Mar had been informed of the group's arrival, so now he required Charles to accompany him to the Earl's headquarters. Charles ordered a servant to fetch his carriage and took Jimmy and Billy with him, as soon as they had washed and made themselves relatively presentable, on the short journey through the city to the mansion serving as the Jacobite headquarters. Charles even lent each of them a clean shirt.

The Earl was pleased to see Charles, was cordial in greeting Jimmy, but was curious as to who Billy was.

The others took some trouble to reassure him and tell him of his association with Rhodri and with Rob Roy. This seemed to satisfy the Earl, who then asked Charles for his report. After hearing Charles's assessment of the situation, he asked Jimmy what he thought. He said, "Aye, My Lord. I agree with every word. The Major and I hae talked it over and I canna say anything for yer comfort. Fort William remains securely in the hands of oor enemies. There is little resistance. The Hanoverians are winning."

The Earl then looked at Billy and asked what he had to tell him. He told him of the strength of the Duke of Argyll's force and confirmed what Charles had said. The Earl looked sad and said, "I have to say that nothing you have said surprises me, but I had so hoped you would have found things to be different. I thank you for your candour, gentlemen, and for your observant and shrewd assessment of all you have seen. I am not looking forward to my meeting with the King. Aye! He should be here tomorrow or the next day. I do not think he has come all this way just to be told his cause is lost. He is bound to ask whether we have served him as well as we should. He is bound to blame us for our lack of success. I have to say that, as I look back, I think there were moments at Sheriffmuir when we might have won, had I taken advantage of certain opportunities I think I had. Yet what use is there in all this? We are in the position we are in and no other. I am not going to advise His Majesty to throw away the lives of my countrymen needlessly, which it would be, would it not, if we were to attack Stirling or Fort William?"

They all agreed. They could see how bitterly

Jimmy in particular regretted having to say so. Although they were enemies, Billy felt sorry for him. For Charles and the Earl it was sad too, but for Jimmy it was more personal.

The Earl said to Billy, "Do you think the Hanoverians will attack us?"

"I can't be sure, but I don't think so. I think the Duke of Argyll is a patient man and probably believes that time is on his side, which I think it is. His men will stay where they are for as long as necessary. They're professionals. In fact most of them have nowhere to go, unlike the Highlanders, who have their farms and families to go back to."

"Aye! I expect you're right. Let's hope so. I'll wait for the King before doing anything. Will you three dine with me tonight?" They all said they would be honoured. Billy did not ask about his other companions. For a general or an earl to invite a mere lieutenant to dine with him was generous. It would be too much to expect him to extend it to a gunner, let alone aa powder- monkey or a camp follower. He was surprised at
Jimmy's being included, but he was a leader among the MacGregors and the Earl obviously knew him.

On their return to Charles's house, they found that Helen had stormed off and shut herself in her room. Charles went to see her and succeeded in persuading her to join him at the Earl's table that evening. He then assured the others that they would be well catered for by his own cook while he was out.

When Helen had left them, Charles said,

"Helen's moods are unpredictable. She can be as hostile as anything, but a minute later she can be charming. I know it's partly because she hopes to find out what happened to her husband and won't take 'don't know' for an answer, but I think it's not just that. I find her attractive in either mood. I don't know whether I'd like her for a wife. She's got a lot of good qualities, but she could be trouble. Perhaps she'd be better as a mistress."

Billy said, "They say mistresses can be trouble too." Charles laughed and signalled his agreement.

Billy looked serious and asked, "Do you have any idea what did happen to her husband? You implied he was murdered because he was asking awkward questions, but do you know who decided to kill him, or have him killed? She thinks Rhodri was involved and so, in her mind, I must have been too, but I had nothing to do with it, I can assure you."

"Well, I know Rhodri was horrified about the murder, but he took charge of cleaning up the mess. Whether he knew exactly what happened, I don't know."

"What about Major Boyle?"

"He was certainly worried about Kenny's inquisitiveness, but he's too much of a pen pusher to commit murder. He would never do anything without clear instructions. He wouldn't have used his initiative. I'm afraid there are plenty of other candidates."

Helen took ages to get ready for the dinner. The result was impressive, to say the least. All evening she was most attentive to Charles and behaved herself remarkably well.

Billy was frustrated that he could never be alone with her, so that he could tell her what he was really doing there and find out what she could tell him. He also wanted to agree a plan for getting her back to safety.

Jimmy had taken Thomas and Llewellyn out to meet some friends of his. When Megan went to her room, she found a note from Charles inviting her to join him in his room. Apparently, Helen had not been receptive to his considerable charms. That was her misfortune. Megan was happy to accept the invitation.

The next day, while Charles went to another meeting with the Earl, Billy went out into the garden. It was a sorry sight, as it was December. Helen came out to join him. Billy said, "Do you want rescuing? Are you here because you want to be, or are you really a sort of prisoner, as you said?"

"Why should I tell you? I don't know who you are, or whose side you're on!"

"It's quite simple. I'm Billy Rhys, an officer in the British Army. I'm here under cover as a deserter.
Charles thinks I'm working for Rhodri on the side of the Jacobites. While I'm at it, I've been trying to find out who killed your husband, but so far I only know who didn't. Well, I think I know. Neither Charles, nor Rhodri."

"So what are you going to do now?"

"I want to get back to the Army, but there's something I need to do first. When I go, I want to take you with me. Will you cooperate?"

"Did Charles tell you why he brought me here?"

"He wants to make sure your father doesn't tell the authorities who's involved in this rebellion. That's also why they originally took the letters. They know that Rhodri hasn't got them any more, so they needed you as a hostage."

"So I'm stuck here because I made you find the letters? It's all my fault?"

"You could put it like that, I suppose, but you couldn't have known Charles would kidnap you when he heard the letters were missing, could you?" "Thanks! You're quite sweet for a highwayman. You hide your good side so well, I often forget it's there." She held his hand and squeezed it, smiling. He was reminded that she could be quite sweet too, at times.

Before he could respond, a servant came running out of the house shouting that the King was just about to enter the city. They rushed to join the others, and the rest of the city, to cheer him. Thomas said he could see Colonel Campbell at some distance, but they were unable to get near to him due to the crowd.

When things eventually quietened down, they returned to the house. There was a message saying they were all invited by the Earl of Mar to a ball being held the following evening, to welcome King James.

Chapter 45

That night Billy was in bed when he heard screams. He jumped up, threw some clothes on and stepped out onto the landing where he found some of the servants had also come to investigate the noise. There was a crash, like some china breaking, followed by a laugh. It sounded like Charles. Next came a dull thud and Charles's voice called out, "Ouch! That hurt!"

Helen's voice replied, "Good! Hope this does too!" Another thud. A sort of yelp came from Charles. Then a series of crashes and thuds.

Billy said, "I don't know what to do. How violent is it going to get?"

One of the servants replied, "It sounds like she's giving as good as she's getting."

The screaming started again. Billy said, "I can never tell what she wants. Perhaps we had better leave them to it." He still sounded uncertain. They heard the heaviest thud so far. Charles groaned. Helen laughed.

Billy supposed Helen must have landed on top that time. They heard a swishing sound followed by more scream, through which they could just detect the sound of laughter. Charles was laughing. There also came a woman's laugh. The door opened and Helen came out, looking dishevelled and angry. Charles appeared in the doorway, followed by Megan.

Helen snarled at Billy, "What are you doing there? Hoping for a spectacle? Leave me alone!" She went back to her own room holding her head high, trying to look dignified. Megan was smiling. Charles looked angry. They all went back to bed. Billy was no longer kept awake by sounds of violence.

In the morning they were having breakfast before the two antagonists came down. Thomas said, "Who were making all that din last night? We could 'ear screams. What were you all up to?"

Billy said, "It was Helen. She had a fight with Charles in his room. I was a bit worried. It wasn't just screams. There all sorts of noises. It sounded terrible!"

Megan came in while he was speaking and said, "I went into Charles's room again, but this time Helen came in soon after, and she started calling us both all sorts of names. I just laughed, but Charles took it badly. He lost his temper when she wouldn't stop, and they got into a fight. She kept throwing things until he held her down and gave her a few slaps on the bottom. Then I saw his riding whip and handed it to him. To my satisfaction, he gave her a real thrashing. Then he let her go, as you saw. I helped him recover from his ordeal."

Billy said, "How could you enjoy that? I heard you laugh and I saw how you looked when you came to the door with Charles."

"I'm used to violence at the Mermaid. Some people seem to like it. The gentry are the worst: men and women. I think Helen's like that."

The objects of the discussion appeared. Helen had a bruise on her face, which was visible only because her hair was brushed back on the right-hand side. On the left, it fell forwards like a curtain. Charles had fresh teethmarks and scratches on his face too. The others

373

wondered what marks were hidden by their clothes and hair. To the surprise of the others, far from being sullen or hostile, the couple seemed quite friendly, chatting pleasantly with each other as they had breakfast.

When he had finished eating, Charles got up and announced, "I've got to go now. I've a meeting with the Earl and King James. I don't know how long I'll be." Helen stood up and kissed him as he left the room. After that the others spent a lot of time speculating as to the next move the Pretender would make. To attack Stirling, or reinforce Dundee? Try to recruit more men? In other words, try to persuade men who had deserted to go back to the Jacobite Army. From lunchtime onwards, the focus was on the ball. Everyone rushed about sorting out what to wear. Some even washed.

When he got the chance, Billy asked Helen, "I heard you and Charles making a lot of noise last night. I thought of trying to rescue you, but I wasn't sure if you'd want me to."

She spoke with none of her usual hostility. In fact she sounded as if she appreciated his concern, despite his inaction. "He invited me to his room, but when I got there I found your whore had beaten me to it. I was annoyed and called them both what they are, and things did get a bit rough. I threw a few ornaments at him. When he lost his temper he used a horsewhip. It really hurt. I didn't mind. I can take it. I could always have run off. He did stop when I asked him. I'll deal with her sometime."

Billy pretended to understand, but he did not. She was a most confusing woman. She left him to begin the next phase of her preparation for the ball. He had ample time for his simpler attempts at improving his appearance.

If it was possible for Helen to look even better than she had done the previous evening, she managed it. Megan had bought a dress in the town. She was hardly going to compete with Helen, but she looked attractive. When they got there they found the place was full of women dressed to kill. A lot of the men seemed to be trying just as hard to impress. Billy had only his British Army uniform. So did Thomas and Llewellyn. Jimmy surprised them by appearing in a different version of Highland Dress. It looked as if he had cut his plaid in two. He wore a skirt-like garment that he said should be called a kilt and a cape made of the same tartan material over one shoulder. He had also acquired a clean shirt, woollen knee-high stockings and highly polished shoes.

When at the ball, Billy and his companions kept looking out for Colonel Campbell and his associates. Several times they thought they saw them but were not certain. Billy wondered about trying to warn the Earl, but knew that that would mean admitting he and his companions were spies. He was not sure they would be believed. He thought it strange that, as far as he was aware, nobody had made any attempt on the Earl's life, although the Campbell contingent must have been in Perth for a few days already. Perhaps the Colonel had some other plan. Billy wanted to find him and confront him if possible, so they could all escape alive.

Apart from that, the evening went well for a long time until someone said, "What in God's name are you three doing here? Have you changed sides, or are you spying again?" They turned and found themselves facing William MacKenzie, Earl of Seaforth. Several Highlanders, mostly MacKenzies, gathered around.

Billy said, "I am delighted to see you are here, My Lord. I trust you had a pleasant journey from Preston. I came here in the company of Major Butler with information for the Earl of Mar. Please ask them if I am welcome or not." Thomas hurried to fetch Charles and Jimmy.

Several swords were drawn, but Lord Seaforth ordered them to be sheathed, saying, "This man's not so stupid as to try to fight us all. I see you've not got your MacKenzie sword tonight?"

Charles arrived and said, "You must be mistaken, My Lord. This man has been of enormous help to me and to our cause. Besides, I knew him in London. He was an assistant to Rhodri Jones, who was one of the Members of Parliament working for our success."

Jimmy said, "Och, aye! This mon's a friend o' mine and o' Rob Roy himself."

Lord Seaforth said, "Really! Perhaps we should call upon Mr MacGregor to vouch for him." With that, several Highlanders rushed off as if expecting to find Rob Roy in the room. They were not disappointed. He was sitting in a small group around the Pretender. They brought the famous outlaw to join the discussion. He looked at Billy and at Thomas in recognition and in astonishment. Lord Seaforth said, "I'm sure you remember these men, as I do. Please confirm that they are Hanoverians."

"Aye! That they are."

Jimmy was astonished. When he regained his power of speech, he said, "Noo Rob, ye canna mean that. They showed me the things ye gave them yersel' as tokens of yer friendship. Show them, Billy!" Billy knew it would not have the effect Jimmy expected, but he presented the jewels and the dagger to Rob Roy.

He laughed and said, "Ye've got a cheek! Have ye been using these things ye stole from me as tokens of my friendship?" "Err...Yes!"

Jimmy looked as if the world had just turned upside down. Rob laughed and said, "I've got tae hand it to ye. Ye're as big a pair o' tricksters as I am. Och! Did ye no miss that letter from General Wills? I had it. Aye, and it was guy useful at times. It got me past a few English patrols. I suppose we're even the noo."

Most people laughed, but a stern voice silenced them. It belonged to the Earl of Mar, who said, "That's enough! These people are Hanoverian spies, like vipers in our bosom. And they fooled us all, so that even I was beguiled into trusting them. I am grateful to you, Lord Seaforth, for unmasking them. Take them away somewhere safe. We'll decide what to do with them tomorrow."

Billy seized what looked like being his last opportunity and said, "Lord Seaforth, will you do me one favour? Please ensure this lady gets back home safely." He pointed to Helen. "She's being held here as a hostage because some people are afraid that her father,
Lewis Pryce, the Member of Parliament for Cardiganshire, might betray them, and because she's

trying to find out who murdered her husband, Kenny MacKenzie."

There were gasps and murmurs. Lord Seaforth said to Helen, "Why would you think any here would be involved in murdering a MacKenzie?"

Billy answered for her, "Because he found out that Major Boyle was paying British Government money to your cause." There were more gasps and murmurs, some quite hostile.

Then another voice joined the discussion. "Who says Lewis Pryce would betray me? Who thinks we need to resort to kidnapping to keep his loyalty?" It was Prince James Edward Francis Stewart, otherwise known as the Pretender, or in certain circles as King James the Third. He added, "Lewis Pryce is a good man. He was a friend of my father, and has helped me in various ways. He advised against this enterprise, and I am beginning to think he was right. He will not betray his friends. Madam, I offer you my personal protection. You may remain with me and travel with me wherever I go, if you wish, or else I will ensure you are restored safely to your father."

Helen looked dazed. She was speechless, probably for the first time in her life. Charles opened his mouth but no sound came out, so he closed it.

The Pretender continued, "I assure you all that I do not order or condone murder. I will use all my authority to bring your husband's killer to justice, and when I take my throne I will ensure all my subjects have justice, whichever side they were on."

Lord Seaforth said, "Well said, Sire! We all look forward to that day. Right now, do you wish to give your judgement on these spies? Before you do, although I am the one who discovered them, I wish to ask for mercy for them. I remember what they did in Preston. They saved us from a pointless massacre. I now hear that Charles Butler and Jimmy MacGregor speak well of them for their more recent actions. I would ask you to spare them, Sire. Do you agree, Robbie?" He did.

Helen curtsied beautifully to the Prince and kissed his hand. Before standing up again, she said, "I pray you have mercy on these men. You heard how concerned they were for my welfare, and for justice for my late husband, despite their own predicament."

The Pretender replied, "I hear what you all say. I respect the judgement of Lord Seaforth, and I know that Rob Roy does not usually show tenderness to his enemies or mine, so these people must be exceptional. I order them to be kept under lock and key until the bigger issue is resolved. Then they are to be released unharmed, whichever way it goes. I require their incarceration only to prevent their giving our enemies news of our progress. Search them and disarm them now. They can be given back what's theirs when you let them go."

They searched them all, roughly and thoroughly. They took their weapons, coins and items of jewellery.

Then Billy and Thomas had a quick conversation in Welsh before Thomas said to Rob Roy, "I'm sorry we can't finish that fight we had!"

Rob replied, "But we did! You lost. Do ye no remember? Or do ye think it wasna fair?"

"Aye, it were a fair fight, like, but at the finish you were lucky, isn't it?"

Megan called out, "He's right too! You were losing until the last minute!"

Rob looked stunned. He said to the men who were trying to push the prisoners towards the door,

"Hold on, lads. Let us settle it the noo! Can ye no spare a few minutes?" There were several voices from the crowd demanding to see them fight.

Lord Seaforth said, "I saw it and Rob won. I don't know why you would challenge him again, but I won't deny you the privilege. Let them fight again!" Nobody seemed to object, so the Highlanders let go of Thomas and he stood in front of Rob. They stripped as before and began circling and testing each other with jabs and feints. Then they tried a few kicks. After a few that only just connected, Thomas landed one in Rob's groin. He laughed and danced from side to side as his opponent grimaced and took some deep breaths. After they exchanged a few more punches, somewhat heavier than before, Rob swung a heavy kick at Thomas, which caught him on the thigh, but Thomas was ready for it and caught the foot in one hand, pulling it sharply upwards. Rob hopped for a few moments, before falling onto his back. Thomas grabbed an ankle, pulling the leg out at full stretch. Then he dragged Rob along by the foot, suddenly changing direction and making his opponent roll onto his front. Then he bent the leg back until it nearly touched Rob's shoulder-blades. Rob gasped and writhed. Thomas knelt on Rob's back to hold him down while increasing the pressure on his leg and so through to his back, calling out in an attempt at a Scottish accent, "Are we even the noo?" Rob's reply was a sort of roar. Then he made an enormous effort to push himself up and struck out at Thomas with a fist. It did not do him much harm, but he did let go of the foot.

Rob sprang to his feet and there followed a fast and furious exchange of kicks and punches, starting at a safe distance apart and working closer until they were grappling again. They made several attempts at throwing or tripping each other, until they fell in a tangle with Rob more or less on top. This time Thomas kneed Rob in the groin, to which he retaliated by grabbing

Thomas's testicles.

There then began an episode of rolling around untidily, after which Thomas found himself lying flat on his face with Rob pressing on his back. He tried to push up and twist several times. Rob managed to hold on and force him back down each time and laughed. He also appeared to whisper something into Thomas's ear. Finally however, Thomas managed to roll over, pushing his opponent over too, so that Rob was lying on his back with Thomas lying face-up on top of him. Rob pushed his knees up into Thomas's back. At first it did not seem to worry him much, but then Rob managed to hook one leg round one of Thomas's and pulled it back under him, bending him like a bow. After a few unsuccessful attempts at breaking free, Thomas called out with surprising clarity, "All right! You've won again, you...!"

The last word was in Welsh and was not complimentary. Rob let go and they both got up. They shook hands, and Rob said to the crowd in Gaelic and then in English, "This Welshman's good! I dinna ken when anyone gave me so good a fight for years."

The next thing they knew, the Hanoverians were thrown into a room in the basement and locked in.

Chapter 46

It did not look as if the room was usually used as a cell. It contained piles of boxes and sacks. On examining them, they found them to be empty. As they heard heavy footsteps going away along the corridor, Billy sat down and relaxed on a pile of sacks. The rest looked at him disapprovingly.

Thomas asked, "Are you all right? You don't look as if you realise how much trouble we're in! I'm not sure I trust them to let us go unharmed when they've lost, or even if they win. Why are you looking so cheerful?"

Billy smiled. Megan and Llewellyn looked puzzled.

Thomas spoke again, trying to take off Rob Roy, but still letting his Anglo-Welsh accent come through, "When we were fighting, Rob says to me once, 'Toneeght'll be the best time to get awa', when they'll all be busy and drunk and there'll be a reeght lot o' noise. They'll likely no miss ye until weell into tomorrow.' So we'd better get on with trying to break out, but I can't see 'ow."

Billy replied, "He's right. You remember when I said in Welsh that we needed a fight because it would be a good distraction? Well, it was."

Thomas replied, "I know! I thought you was gonna try summat while I was fighting but you didn't." The others expressed agreement.

Billy explained, "While you and Rob were busy stroking each other's balls, and everyone else was watching with such interest, I reclaimed some of the things they'd taken off us. The only one who noticed was Jimmy. He handed me back the things we stole from Rob before. I had to leave most of our weapons and gold coins because they'd miss those soonest, but I've got my lock-picking tools. I also managed to get back my ammunition pouch. They thought it was empty because it's got a false bottom, which is just a smaller pouch sewn inside it."

Megan said "Well, that'll be a fat lot of use, when we haven't got a gun between us." Billy smiled and drew a long pistol out of a boot.

The others gasped. "How?" they all asked.

Llewellyn said, "I remember when they searched us they made us take our boots off. I had to help you because yours got a bit stuck."

"Yes! I slid the pistol out and up my sleeve while we were struggling with the boot. Then I slid it back when we'd finished."

The boy said, "I didn't notice. That was clever!"

Billy said, "Well, I did time it carefully. You know when they searched you, Megan, some of them seemed to be enjoying it, and you teased them a bit? That's when I did it."

Thomas said, "You really are as crafty as me."

They heard heavy footsteps outside. A door opened somewhere nearby. Voices. They could hear them clearly even from inside their cell.

"Good. The things are all here, like Jock said."
"Let's go!"

"Hold on! Let's make sure we all know what we're to do. Graham. What are you doing?"

"Getting as close to the dais as I can. I'm to stay quiet until you've made your move. Then I start shooting to distract them all. Unless you fail. Then I'm to shoot the man myself."

"Good! Willie?"

"I'm tae wait by the door with these twa muskets. If ye both fail, I'm tae shoot the mon wi one o' these. I'll stand on a chair or a table, so I'll be shooting above their heads."

"Good! Jamie?"

"I'll just stand ootside the door wi' this, and make sure naebody comes in."

"Good. And I'll get as close as I can and go up on the dais, when he gets up to make his speech. I'll say I've got a present for him from his loyal kinsmen, the Stewarts. Then I'll show him this. When I'm close enough I'll stab him with it. After he's dead we all run for our lives. BUT NOT BEFORE! All right?"

"Aye, Sir!"

"Of course."

"Yes, Sir!"

"Och, aye!"

There came the sound of footsteps going away. Billy said, "That must have been Colonel Campbell and his crew. They really are going to do it. But it's not quite what we thought. The Earl's not a Stewart. They mean to kill the Pretender. That's why they've waited until tonight."

Thomas said, "I'll bet the Colonel's the one giving the orders. I think Willie, with the muskets, was Private William Campbell, one of his family and his personal servant. He'll do anything for the Colonel. I dunno about them other two."

Billy said, "I'm thinking Graham will be Lieutenant George Graham, the other staff officer. Murray say he hates the Jacobites as much as Campbell does. A good shot with a pistol too. Jamie must be someone who's joined them since they left camp. The Duke said there were just the three of them.

Llewellyn said, "Lieutenant Graham? I remember him. Always sounded as if he was the most important man in the Army."

Billy added, "I expect Jamie will be a local man. One who knows this house. We must stop them. When we get into the ballroom we'll have to be quick, before we get arrested again. We'd better spread out so we can each take one of them. I'll try to get as near as I can to the Prince, so I can get between him and the Colonel."

Thomas interrupted, "No! I'll recognise him and I'm a better fighter. You try to take one of the others."

Billy said, "All right! I'll take the one at the door with the muskets. Llew, since you'll recognise Lieutenant Graham, you'd better find him and make sure he misses when he shoots." "Don't worry. He'll miss!"

Billy said, "Thanks. Now, how do we get past the one outside, with whatever weapon he's got?"

Megan said, "Leave him to me! I know how to distract a man!"

Billy used his lock-picking tools to get the door open. They went along the corridor, trying to make as little noise as possible. They were all tense as they climbed the stone stairs, expecting to be heard and knowing there was nowhere to hide. Once at the top they walked on carpets and kept near doorways, until they came to the corner of the little hall leading to the ballroom. Megan went first. The others kept out of sight. They crowded just around the corner, listening keenly. Thomas remembered to look behind them in case anyone came.

They heard Jamie challenge Megan. "Noone's allowed in here the noo!"

"Why not?"

"I've got my orders."

"Well, can I stay here with you? I'm sure we both need a little company."

"Aye. All reet. Dinna make any trouble."

"I won't give you any trouble. Not a big, strong man like you, with a big sword like that." Silence.

"You must be strong to be able to fight with that. It looks so heavy. I probably couldn't lift it."

Billy whispered, "What's she doing? She's wasting time."

Thomas said, "She knows what she's doing. Wait and see."

Megan said, "Oh, can I feel that sword? It is heavy, but it's beautiful. Oh, yes." More silence. "Don't move! Don't make a sound!"

Billy and the others went round the corner and found the man pinned against the wall with his sword at his throat. They gagged and bound him and went into the ballroom, except for Megan who stayed to guard her prisoner. They did not go in together, and they did not hurry. There was nothing to draw anyone's attention. Billy stayed near the door. Thomas made his way in stages to the edge of the stage, wondering why they called it a dais. Llewelyn wandered around casually. Then he turned back, made his way to where he had spotted Lieutenant Graham and stood right behind him.

The Pretender got up onto the stage, accompanied by the Earl of Mar, Lord Seaforth and a couple of other important-looking men. The Earl stepped forward first and made a speech welcoming the Prince. It sounded as if the rest of Britain was about to welcome him as King with no opposition. Everyone applauded. Then the Earl stepped back and the Prince moved forwards. Colonel Campbell climbed onto the stage. The Prince looked surprised but not alarmed. Thomas jumped up and grabbed the Colonel. Several others grabbed Thomas.

He said, "This man's a Campbell, come to kill the King! Arrest him! Search him!" Campbell stood calmly while a few of the Pretender's entourage searched him. He had nothing suspicious on him apart from a fine jewelled dagger that he had been holding in its highly decorated sheath.

Thomas said, "There, you fools. He had that dagger to kill King James."

Campbell replied, "I'm a Stewart, as you can see from my tartan. And this dagger is a present for him from a lot of loyal kinsmen."

Lord Seaforth said, "Aye, and this man is one of the Hanoverians we arrested earlier."

The Earl of Mar agreed, saying, "Take him away and see he's locked up properly this time. I'm indebted to you again, MacKenzie. Will you do me one more favour? Go with them and ensure they lock him in. And check where the rest of his company are. I hope they're not going to make any more disturbances this evening."

A shot echoed around the room and a lump of plaster fell from the ceiling. A fight broke out near the dais. Lieutenant Graham dropped a pistol and struggled to draw another, but Llewellyn managed to prevent him. They were separated by several onlookers. Graham said, "I just stopped this boy shooting the King. He managed to fire his gun, but I knocked his hand. Is he with that other one?" Llewellyn tried to say that it was he who had knocked the assassin's arm, not vice versa, but to no avail.

A louder shot sounded and a mirror behind the dais shattered. Willie fell from a table, pushed by Billy. They struggled to take possession of the second musket, which had been hanging from a strap over Willie's shoulder. Several people tried to restrain them both. Billy tried to draw the pistol in his boot, but could not reach it for bodies piling up on top of him. They overpowered Billy, as well as Willie. The crowd then manhandled both of them up to the Pretender. The two muskets were placed on the dais. The Earl said, "I should have guessed you'd be involved. How many more of you are there? Was there not a woman in your company?"

"Yes, she's outside that door, keeping an eye on one of the conspirators. A big fellow called Jamie, I believe. He's gagged and bound."

"Conspirators? You are the conspirators! I think we have all worked that out by now. It's no use trying to put the blame onto the people who stopped you."

Billy said, "I suppose I can see how it looks, but please let me show you my orders. They come from the Duke of Argyll. He does not want you to be killed."

"I don't see how your orders can help you now. You've been caught. That's an end to it!"

By then, Charles had joined the rapidly growing group on the little stage. He said, "Please, My Lord. I would like to know who this man really is, and what he was up to. It can't hurt to read the orders."

The Pretender said, "I agree. Let's see them."

Billy extracted some papers from the lining of his coat and handed them to the Pretender. The Earl and Charles read over his shoulder. There was silence.

Colonel Campbell suddenly made a run for the door. Several people went after him. Billy and his companions felt frustrated at not being able to move, as they were surrounded. A loud thud was heard from just outside the door, followed by a hearty curse and a female laugh. The pursuers dragged the Colonel back into the room, followed by a smiling Megan. Billy realised he should have known that she would not let him down.

As soon as quiet was re-established, the Pretender said in a loud voice, "My Lords, Ladies and Gentlemen, I have to inform you, that my life has just been saved by a group of men and a woman serving our enemies. They were acting under orders from our countryman, the Duke of Argyll. The plot to kill either the Earl of Mar, or myself, was hatched and nearly carried out by a group of Hanoverians acting contrary to the Duke's express orders. Thanks to these unlikely allies of ours, the conspirators are now in our custody. You may now continue enjoying yourselves. I will be rejoining you in a few minutes."

They took Billy and his companions to another room, where the Pretender sat at a desk and wrote a letter. He sealed it with his official seal, to which the Earl appended his. He handed it to Billy. It gave him and his comrades safe conduct back to the British Army. In it, he also expressed his gratitude. The Earl added verbally, "Please also convey my gratitude to the Duke of Argyll. I knew him to be an honourable man, but he has exceeded my expectations."

After reading it and thanking them, Billy asked, "What is to become of Colonel Campbell and his conspirators?"

The Pretender answered, "They will remain in custody here until we have time to try them. I know there are some who would have them killed right now, but I do not intend to be a tyrant. When I take my rightful throne, I will rule according to the Law. I am starting now." He then returned to the ballroom.

Before leaving the mansion, Billy and his companions shook hands and exchanged a few words with Rob Roy and Lord Seaforth. Charles took them back to his house for the rest of the night. He was unusually quiet, trying to make sense of everything. The others spent a lot of time talking before going to sleep.

Chapter 47

The next morning, there were fond farewells all round. Helen kissed Billy and whispered that she was safe. She hoped to see him again soon, so they could get back to investigating her husband's death. Charles said he had never known anyone who could deceive him so successfully so often, and be his enemy and his friend at the same time. Jimmy told Thomas he was proud to have fought and beaten, at least sometimes, the man who had almost beaten Rob Roy. He also said he had learned a few new tricks from him

Finally, Charles and Jimmy searched Thomas for any property he had stolen from them. They said they did not care about anything he had stolen from anyone else. They found very little, just a few silver spoons and a gold ring. Thomas laughed and said, "Win some, lose some!"

Then Billy and his companions set out for Stirling. After a few minutes, Thomas asked Llewellyn if he still had all the things they had stolen from Charles and Jimmy. The boy assured him they were safe.

They reached their destination soon after noon. As soon as they entered the camp, Billy was ordered to report to the Duke. When he got there, he found Eddy, Jonesie, and Colonels Murray and MacNichol sitting around the big table, as well as a few of the Duke's staff officers. The Duke told him he had been anxious at the length of his absence, but had been reassured, only a few days previously, when his dispatches from Fort William had arrived. Billy then reported verbally on his mission. He ended by showing the letter from the Pretender, giving him safe passage, and he passed on the Earl's final remarks. This all took some time, and Billy had been glad of a few "wee drams" provided by the Duke for all those present.

The Duke asked, "What do you think will happen now?"

"I really don't know, Sir. I don't think they'll attack us. If we wait a bit longer, they might give up. The Pretender seems like a proud man, and probably won't surrender. I think he'll just let things go quiet. Unless he can recruit a lot more men, he'll know he can't win. I don't think he'll be able to recruit many at this time of year. I think he left everything too late."

"I hope you're right. Well, you have been before. I'll wait a little longer, as you suggest. I don't want to waste lives. Well done!"

Billy, Megan and Llewellyn had plenty of opportunity to worry and speculate about Bethan's and Perse's welfare, because, after their return to camp, there was no action and little activity. They spent Christmas in the camp. The Duke of Argyll did his best to make it something of a festival, although many Scots were in the habit of making it a quieter, more sombre time than was common among the English and Welsh, and he wanted to respect everyone's feelings.

Each day that went by without contact with the Enemy encouraged everyone to believe that Billy's assessment of the situation was correct. It was, however, not until late January that news reached them that the Pretender had abandoned his campaign and left Scotland. He had in fact gone to Spain. Billy wondered whether Charles had gone with the Prince and, if so, whether he had taken Helen. He also wondered whether the Highlanders would now remain peaceful.

Megan surprised herself by spending most nights with Billy. She had enjoyed her times with the others. She thought about all the men she had known at the Mermaid. Why was Billy better than any of them? He was not, she realised. It was something else. It was a good job he was her second cousin, not a first cousin. People said you should not marry your first cousin. Marry? That would be the day! She had better make the most of their time in this camp. When they were back in Cardiff she would have to go back to her profession. She could not see any future with Billy. A highwayman with no better prospects. What was she hoping for? A miracle? She knew what her brother David would have said. He did not understand. But neither did she.

When the Army was at last ordered to strike camp, Billy for one was looking forward to seeing Wales again. Never again would he complain about the steepness of the hills, the state of the roads, or even the poverty of the people. He had seen the Highlands. He wondered whether the willingness of the clans to rebel had had more to do with their overall condition than with any views on the Succession, or even on religion. He found it hard to feel any hostility towards any of the people he had met: neither the crofters, nor the Earl of Mar, nor Rob Roy, nor even the Pretender himself. There were plenty of people he would rather hate, and they all professed loyalty to King George.

The journey back to Cardiff was uneventful. As soon as they were dismissed, Billy, Llewellyn and Megan went Megan to the Coach and Horses to greet his aunt and uncle and to ask after Bethan. They learned that she had been there about a week earlier, but had since gone to Rhodri's house. Billy knew he had better not stay too long at the inn for fear of arrest, so he and Llewellyn went next to Rhodri's house. Megan went with them to see Bethan before returning to the Mermaid to resume her former life.

Olwen welcomed them and said she hoped Billy would go with her to London, as she was desperate for money. He was quite happy to do so, as he wanted to continue his investigation into Kenny MacKenzie's death. Olwen said they would stay at Rhodri's London house. This would give him an opportunity to look for Helen and to confront Major Boyle as well as drawing the money they were owed from Rhodri's bank. They agreed Bethan would go with them, as there would be little for her to do in the Cardiff house.

The next day, Billy drove Bethan to Maindy and asked for Major-General Jones but was told he had duties elsewhere. They were just about to leave when a familiar voice hailed them. It was Perse. He was wearing a typical red coat rather than the black of the Artillery. He said that was because he was now a staff officer, one of Jonesie's. Billy told him why they wanted the Major-General, and he said that in his absence he could accompany them to London to investigate the embezzlement of Army money and the murder of an officer. Billy and Bethan were delighted to have his company as well as the additional authority for their investigation. Perse went to the acting Commanding Officer of the garrison, who was Colonel MacNichol, to get his authorisation for the trip. He wished them luck and issued Perse with a letter authorising him to handle the matter. Billy asked Perse if he had a coach, as they wanted to take Rhodri's housekeeper to London. He said he had, fortunately, as such a long ride would put a strain on his wounds, which were not fully healed. They added Jamie and Caledin to the team of four coach horses. Perse was as polite and charming as ever but somewhat subdued, partly due to the difficult relations with Bethan, and also because his wounds still caused him some discomfort.

Chapter 48

February 1716

When they reached London, they found Rhodri's house closed. All the servants had left. There was no coach in the coachhouse, only the chaise. Olwen immediately began opening shutters and curtains, while Bethan lit fires in several rooms. They then took stock of what provisions were in the pantry and the larder. It did not take long as there was so little. Similarly, there was fuel for a few days only. Perse said he would take them all out to dinner somewhere that night, and the women could stock up the next morning.

Billy said he wanted to go to Lewis Pryce's house to get news of Helen, so he set off almost immediately. He was relieved to find both Lewis and Helen at home. Lewis invited him in and offered him a glass of port, which he gladly accepted.

Lewis said, "I am glad you are safe. I have heard a lot about your adventures in Scotland. I am grateful to you for your efforts at protecting my daughter."

Helen said, "Would you believe the cheek of that Charles Butler? He had the audacity to ask me to marry him. Yes! It was after you and your friends had departed. He reminded me he was a Duke's nephew and heir to estates in England as well as Ireland. He also claimed that his family were all close to the King, as he called him, and would come into favour when he returned to reclaim his throne. This, after having got me to Scotland by deception and holding me prisoner. His behaviour was extraordinary. He had even shared his bed with your whore, while I was under the same roof! You are not the only man who thinks he can get away with treating me in a shameful and most offensive way!"

Billy smiled at that thought but did not reply. Lewis also looked amused. He commented, "Did you know that Parliament has stripped Ormonde of his titles and possessions? So Charles will be heir to nothing unless Prince James is in a position to reward him more generously than I imagine."

Helen said, "Strangely, that wild Highlander, Jimmy MacGregor and his friend Rob Roy spoke well of you and your companions despite everything. That redhaired whore of yours made quite an impression too, I noticed."

Again he refrained from retaliating but merely asked, "What did you say to Charles's proposal?"

"I was so amazed and offended that I replied in the most intemperate terms. I said I would not marry him if he were the last man on Earth, even if he were to inherit a kingdom, let alone a dukedom! I must confess, however, that after he had again apologised and explained his behaviour, I responded in a more conciliatory way. I left him thinking I was considering his offer. He does have a most persuasive and charming manner, and is of course extremely handsome.
Unfortunately, I am only too aware that I am not the only woman to hold that opinion."

Billy thought a marriage between those two would be interesting. He almost wished them upon one another.

He said, "Apart from satisfying myself that you are safe, I came here to return something belonging to you." He handed her the MacKenzie sword.

Lewis said, "I am grateful to you not only for trying to help Helen but also for returning the letters. It has been alleged that I was involved in the recent uprising, and I cannot disprove the allegation, but equally nobody can prove anything. Fortunately, there remains a certain respect for truth and justice in this country. I shall resign my seat in Parliament, but I will be allowed to live peacefully on my estates in Wales. I might have to give up this house, as I will probably be unwelcome in London Society. Many of my friends have been arrested and others have fled. Only a few are staying here and defying anyone to prove anything against them."

Billy said, "I am sorry to hear that. Perhaps things will settle down in time. After all, the rebellion has failed. There is no longer a danger. You were right in saying that foreign help would be needed, and since the Peace it is unlikely to be forthcoming."

"I hope you are right. Time will tell."

"I must be going soon. I have promised to dine with some companions in Town. I will start making enquiries into Kenny's death in the next day or so. I intend to go to the Horse Guards and confront Major Boyle."

Helen surprised him by saying, "While you are in London, perhaps we could go to the theatre again."

"Can we go tomorrow night?"

She agreed. Billy then took his leave and joined the others for dinner.

Over dinner, Bethan said she hoped Billy would also take her to the theatre while they were in London. Perse offered to take Bethan, to her surprise and delight. Olwen said she was not interested in the theatre and was happy to stay in the house and look after Llewellyn. Billy was pleased, but doubted that the lad needed looking after.

The next day Billy, Olwen and Bethan went to the bank. They had to wait for what seemed like hours but eventually were taken to a big office and met someone who obviously thought he was important. However, he was also helpful and paid each of them all the money owed. He had already paid the London servants, but retained sufficient funds for Olwen and Billy to draw on should Mr Jones remain abroad much longer. Billy thought Rhodri would remain abroad a lot longer.

There was just time for Olwen and Bethan to go to various markets and stock up with provisions before everywhere closed for the day. Billy was relieved when Olwen said she would cook for them while in London, and Bethan would deal with various other household chores.

After the theatre, they went to an inn and enjoyed the food and wine while they talked. Suddenly they found themselves being addressed. "Mr Rhys, Mrs Tudor, Mrs MacKenzie! Good evening to you all. And to your companions. How pleasant a surprise this is." To their astonishment, it was Charles. Billy introduced him to Perse and Olwen. Billy said, "Are you not in danger of being recognised in this city?"

"Not really. Hardly anyone knows of my involvement in certain recent events. I hope I can count on your discretion, considering how leniently my comrades-in-arms treated you?"

"I doubt that my word alone would matter, but I agree that it is best to put our differences behind us. Am I to believe that you are able to forgive me for deceiving you as to my part in those events?"

"You are. I confess that at one time I was resentful of being taken in by you, but, on reflection, I can see that you were being true to your conscience and, of course, I am grateful that you saved the life of King James. I have also been able to recall the things we shared which brought us together."

He turned to Helen and said, "My dear Mrs MacKenzie, I am so pleased to meet you again. I was intending to seek you out while in London as, quite apart from enjoying your company, I believe there are things we must discuss, such as the opportunity to complete our itinerary of the Highlands, including the ancient seat of the MacKenzies, now that peace has returned to that region."

Helen said, "I do not wish to leave London, until I have discovered my husband's killer. Perhaps after that I will be able to accompany you again to Scotland."

Billy was surprised at his audacity, as much as at her mild response. He said, "I hope to be able to make some progress in my investigation into that crime in the next few days. So you may both obtain what you wish for."

The next morning Billy, Perse and Helen went to the Army Headquarters. After being passed around, they eventually got to seeing Major Boyle. Billy showed him the letter from Rhodri authorising him to deal with his various affairs in his absence.

He said, "One thing I am not satisfied about concerns the payments you have made to Rhodri's bank. I think there is at least one missing. Can you show me what payments you have made?"

Boyle seemed somewhat disgruntled but not surprised. It was obvious that he had been making such payments. He showed them some files on which were records of payments to various regiments for their men's pay and regimental expenses. He pointed out the payments to the Fifth Battalion of the Royal Scots Borderers, from the creation of the battalion to the end of the War. Billy asked, "How many of those actually went to the Borderers?"

"Only the first, which was far too little. That was a genuine mistake."

"What payments did you make to Colonel MacKenzie, when he began to enquire?"

"None. See these entries here? They all say they were paid to him. Of course, they were not. They too were paid to Rhodri Jones."

Perse asked, "Would not a closer examination of the records reveal this?"

"Quite possibly. But nobody has noticed. Don't worry. If they do, I can shuffle money between accounts as long as necessary to make it look as if I've found an error and corrected it."

Billy thought he had got all the information needed to confirm his suspicions, but still lacked evidence. What came next was a real shock. Perse asked, "What did you tell Colonel MacKenzie when he came here?"

"Well, the first time I said it had been paid, so the error must be his, or his bank's. When he came the second time, with Messrs. Murray and MacNichol, I had to say it was a mistake, and I was going to correct it. That's why there are all those entries purporting to be payments to Mr MacKenzie. Of course the actual bank drafts all say Mr Jones, but nobody ever looks at those."

He kindly showed them copies of the bank drafts on the files. Perse made notes of the dates and amounts. Boyle went on, "Of course, I got worried when he wouldn't give up and threatened to go to the General, so I had to tell Mr Jones. Mr Rhodri Jones I mean. I also told Mr Butler, who was acting on behalf of his uncle, who was away on the Continent. They were both most annoyed when Mr MacKenzie was killed.

Although it solved one problem for us, they could see it was likely to cause others. Nobody ever told me who arranged the killing. Perhaps the man really did get himself into a duel over something else."

They thanked him and left. They went to the bank again. They asked to check the payments into the account from the Army. The banker was surprised but had no objection. The amounts and dates all agreed at first, but each of the last six months' entries showed a lesser amount. The banker checked some more of his records and said he could do nothing but confirm that the amounts shown were correct. He had no idea why they had reduced from the earlier ones. They thanked him and went back to the Horse Guards, where they made another appointment for the following day. Billy wondered if Boyle had been tricking Rhodri as well as Kenny, but thought it unlikely. It appeared that Rhodri had not queried the reductions in the payments.

That evening they all dined at Rhodri's house. Bethan decided to take it as a challenge and competed in a good-humoured way. She had brought one of her best dresses with her and it had survived the journey quite well. She thought she looked good in it. So did Perse and Charles.

Charles announced that he had to leave soon, as his uncle had asked him to deal with some of his business in Ireland and added, "I hope to be back soon. Then I will need to speak to Helen about a matter of considerable importance to us both. Until then, I wish you success in seeking the truth about your late husband." He then surprised everyone by leaving, although it was still early.

The next day they had to wait a long time before they could see Major Boyle again.

Billy asked about the discrepancies between the Army's records and the bank's.

He said, "Did Rhodri not explain? Or did he think I could pay MacNichol from my own money? We discussed what to do about him and agreed to buy him off. I had to reduce the payments to Rhodri to do so."

"At what stage did Mr MacNichol get involved?"

"Immediately after he had accompanied his father, when he came with Colonels MacKenzie and Murray. He was the only one to realise what was happening. Colonels MacNichol and Murray went away satisfied that I was correcting an administrative error, but

MacKenzie didn't seem happy. That is why he came back again. I was most anxious about it, but soon after that, he got himself killed in a duel, so all I had to worry about was keeping Captain MacNichol quiet."

"Is he not on our side?"

"I think he's on his own side. Of course, I have heard he has a demanding wife to satisfy. That's probably why he needs the money so much. I'm pretty sure he'll behave as long as we keep paying him. Surely Rhodri knew all that?"

"Perhaps he just had not explained it to me as clearly as you have. Thank you."

They went back to the house where they sat down to talk things over. Billy said to Helen, "I know you started off thinking Rhodri was at the back of Kenny's murder, but I just can't see it. The more I got to know him, the less like a murderer he seemed. The same goes for Charles."

Perse said, "If you really don't think Charles or Rhodri could have murdered Kenny, do you think it could have been Iain MacNichol? He always struck me as a decent sort of fellow, but you can't be sure about people, can you?"

Billy said, "I don't know. I also don't see how we can find out. He certainly had a motive, but so did all the Jacobites. How can we ever prove it, even if we think we know?"

Helen said, "I suppose we could go to him and see what he says!"

Perse replied, "He's hardly going to admit it. Of course, his father knows what we've come here for. I'm surprised he hasn't tried to make sure we don't find out too much."

Billy said, "If it is Iain MacNichol, his father might not know."

Perse broke the ensuing silence, asking, "Did you ever go to the place where he was killed?"

Billy said, "No. I don't know where it was."

Bethan said, "What about that vicar? The one who buried him. Do you think he'd know?"

Billy said, "I don't think so, but it's possible. It couldn't do any harm to pay him another visit, I suppose."

They all went to the church. The vicar remembered Billy, Bethan and Helen. They introduced Perse as a former comrade-in-arms of Kenny, who wanted to see his grave and also the place where he died. The vicar led them to the grave and waited for them to pay their respects before saying, "As to the place where it happened. I remember your friend Mr Jones saying it was in St. James's Park, between Whitehall and the Mall. I can't say exactly whereabouts, but I think it was near the old Palace of Whitehall, which is now in such a sorry state of disrepair, since the two fires of 1691 and 1698."

The group of investigators thanked the vicar and went to the park, where they wandered aimlessly, as if expecting evidence to jump up at them. Perse said, "I don't know why I thought this would help. It's not as if any witnesses would still be here."

As they looked around, Bethan found herself gazing at a line of rather nice houses looking onto the park from Whitehall, close to the derelict palace. She said, "They'll still be here if they live here." So they began knocking on doors. Some did not open. Some were opened by servants who were unable or unwilling to talk in the absence of their employers. They tried four or five houses before they had any luck. A servant was just in the process of making excuses when, a gentleman appeared behind him asking what the callers wanted. He looked at Helen and was obviously impressed by her beauty. She responded by using all her charm to get his cooperation. He said his name was Alphonse ffrench, in spite of which he seemed typically English. He invited them in and had a servant fetch some tea. He led his guests into a big room with windows overlooking the park.

Helen said, "I have been told that my husband was killed in a duel in the park about three years ago, but am unable to discover any details of the others involved, or the cause of the quarrel. Perhaps if you or anyone in this house saw anything, it might lead me to the person I need to speak to. I feel I cannot rest until I have the facts. I hope you do not think me foolish?"

He did not. He asked for the date of the duel. Billy offered the date when the body had been taken to the church. Mr ffrench called all the servants and asked if any of them could help. One of the youngest maids remembered it.

"It was at dawn and I was the first up in the 'ouse, lighting fires and lamps and such. I couldn't 'elp seeing a group of men out there. Some was in uniform, but a couple wasn't. And there was a couple of women with 'em too. I could see they was preparing for a duel. They made a big thing of loading their pistols and of pacing out the distance between 'em. The first to fire must've missed, 'cos the other one just stood there. Well, then this other one took 'is shot, but the gun didn't fire proper. A big flame came out of the gun and there wasn't much of a bang."

Helen challenged the girl, "So was that all? Nobody was shot?"

"Oh no, Madam! That weren't the end of it. They all got together, as if they was talking. Probably trying to decide what to do. Anyway, they reloads the guns, but one of 'em starts to walk away and drops 'is gun. I reckon he'd 'ad enough. Then one of the women snatches up the gun and runs after 'im. She grabs 'is sleeve, so he turns round, and bang! The feller never 'ad a chance, she was that close. Then the others all seems to go into a panic. Some of 'em cleared off right quick, but a bloke in civvies seemed to take over, ordering the rest of 'em about, until they carried the dead one away." Perse asked, "Could you describe this woman?"

"Well, she was a real lady. Well dressed. Fair hair."

Perse asked, "Was that all?"

"I think so. I did tell Cook, but she says to mind my own business. I 'ope I've not done anything wrong, 'ave I?"

Perse assured her that she had done the right thing by telling him. Her master seemed quite shocked.

The visitors thanked them both and went back to Rhodri's house. Bethan poured each of them a glass of brandy. They all needed it. Perse asked what Rhodri's wife looked like. Billy said she was not very tall, only about Bethan's height, and seemed too sweet to be a killer.

A thought had been trying to occur to him ever since he had heard the story. Now it materialised. He said, "Catherine MacNichol fits the description."

Bethan said, "Yes! She's got an aggressive side to her. Remember our first swordfight? She enjoyed it too. Then there was the way she reacted to the death of that fishwife in Preston. She's a funny one."

Perse said, "She's tall and fair, and she is a bit strange, but I hadn't thought of her as a murderess. I don't know. Even if we're right, we've no proof. That servant girl couldn't say for sure who it was."

Bethan refilled everyone's glass, and they all talked at great length to no benefit.

Finally, Perse said, "I think we should tell Jonesie everything we know and ask his advice, but I've no idea how to find him at present."

Billy added, "I would go to Colonel Murray, but he's in Edinburgh."

Perse surprised them by saying, "Well, I could ask Captain MacNichol about the money. I'd be acting within my authority for that. Then we can give Jonesie a bit more to work with. I suggest we say nothing about the murder, until we've got more evidence."

They had one more evening in London and decided to make the most of it, going to the theatre. That evening Helen was particularly pleasant to everyone. Bethan was worried that Billy would become too attracted to her if she kept that up, but comforted herself by considering how unlikely that was.

Chapter 49

They had a good journey back to Cardiff, spending one night at an inn near Swindon, where Bethan shared a bed with Helen. This reminded them both of the time they had shared her bed at the Coach and Horses and led to a good deal of giggling and whispering.

At Chepstow, the servant, Meredith, recognised Billy and Bethan and told them that Captain and Mrs MacNichol were visiting friends at St Fagans.

Helen said, "I know who the friends are. Let's go there. I can't stand waiting."

Billy was worried that Richard Jenkins would recognise him as "Captain Gareth Evans" whom he knew from the Mermaid. Everyone said he had better stick to his Billy Rhys persona. They agreed that Perse would take the lead in interviewing the MacNichols in his official capacity to investigate the misappropriation of funds. They hoped to gain enough information from that to enable them to solve the murder.

Richard Jenkins welcomed Helen, who introduced the others as friends of hers, and went on to say that Perse had some official business with the MacNichols. This resulted in a large gathering around a dining room table. Perse showed Iain his letter of authority signed by Colonel MacNichol. Billy thought this ironic. Perse went on to tell them about the information he had gained from Major Boyle about the embezzlement of funds and the payments made to secure Captain MacNichol's silence. From their reactions, it was obvious that this all came as news to the

Jenkins family but not to either of the MacNichols, who both reacted by questioning whether Major Boyle's word would stand up in court, rather than claiming ignorance of the whole thing. Perse said the documentation he had seen proved a fraud had taken place and that certain payments had been made to Iain MacNichol as well as to Rhodri Jones. It was also clear that no payments had been made to reimburse Kenny MacKenzie.

Both Richard Jenkins and his father were totally confused and could not see how Perse could have known all this. Iain looked aghast. He apparently felt he had been found out. He began to say something but was silenced by his wife, who was keeping her head and trying not to give Perse more information than he already had. He went on to ask about Kenny MacKenzie's investigations. Iain denied having had anything to do with Kenny's death. Since Perse had made no such allegation, this was the kind of denial which served only to admit that which was being denied. Cathy looked daggers at her husband, but this time was too late to prevent the damage. Perse realised he was winning and pushed his luck. He asked whose idea the duel had been. Iain said it was Kenny's. Helen made a derisive noise. Perse asked who had shot Kenny. There was a deafening silence. Richard Jenkins Senior said, "Surely you can't know, can you, Iain? I mean, you didn't see it, did you?"

The silence intensified. Perse said, "I have found someone who saw it. Do you want to own up, Cathy?"

There were gasps from the Jenkins family. Iain closed his eyes and put his head in his hands. Cathy said, "I don't believe you! You're trying to trick me!" Helen finally could no longer keep her promise to stay silent. "You don't deny it, do you? You aren't even surprised. It was you, wasn't it?"

Perse was not sure if his authority extended to arresting a civilian. He said, "I must ask that you and your husband remain in this house until I fetch a magistrate. Lieutenant Rhys will remain until I return." He stood up, preparing to go.

Cathy had another suggestion for resolving the matter. "Would you like another duel, Helen? Both our husbands were pathetic. Neither wanted to fight. Not really. After the first two shots resulted in nothing, neither had the guts to carry on. Both said 'honour was satisfied', which it wasn't. If your husband had won, we were in deep trouble. He was going to go higher up and make a fuss. If mine had won, we'd have got away with it. A draw was no use. So I had to finish what they'd started. Even then, Rhodri Jones was the only one man enough to take charge. Iain just stood there. Considering how efficient he is at managing Chepstow Castle and how good he was as a staff officer, it was ridiculous how useless he was when it was personal. I was afraid you'd be as persistent as your Kenny.
Anyway, now you know."

"Yes! Now I know that you killed my Kenny. Of course I accept your challenge. Don't expect any mercy from me!"

"I don't! I'll enjoy it, as I enjoyed killing that fat fishwife. Yes! I knew she had a knife. So I tripped her as she came round the corner. It went better than I had hoped. She fell right on her own blade and killed herself.

So neat." Everyone looked amazed, especially Iain. Cathy looked at Helen and said, "It's got to be to the death, of course. I don't want to go on trial and end up being hanged. I want to win or lose."

"I agree. It's all or nothing!"

They agreed a time and place: the next morning on Cardiff's Heath. Billy and Bethan were to be Helen's seconds. Cathy's were her husband and the young Richard Jenkins. Richard Jenkins Senior was to be the referee and would bring his own doctor. Billy, Bethan and Perse tried to talk Helen out of it. She was dismissive.

Once it started, it was apparent that both protagonists were experienced swordswomen, and, whilst neither wanted to make any mistakes, both were alert for any opportunities. They both moved swiftly and gracefully. After several minutes, Helen managed to trick her opponent with a feint, causing her to open her guard sufficiently to receive a cut to the right shoulder. The referee insisted on a pause while the doctor examined it. His conclusion was, unsurprisingly, that Catherine was fit to continue. Although this minor wound was an irritation to Catherine, and an encouragement to Helen, neither woman showed any sign of changing her style or tactics. They were both too experienced and wily to let themselves be unduly influenced by it.

After another minute or two they found themselves face to face with their swords meeting at the hilt. Helen pushed Catherine back, then jumped backwards and to one side so that her opponent stumbled forwards, temporarily off balance. With a quick lunge

Helen managed to cut Catherine on the thigh, through her dress. Another brief medical examination ensued. The doctor was prepared to agree it did not need bandaging. Catherine tucked the hem of her dress into her belt to leave the cut exposed rather than having the distraction of it's being irritated by the material when she moved.

They both continued to fight cautiously until Catherine seemed to slip and step back to recover herself. She took her eyes off her opponent for the first time and looked down. Helen saw an opportunity and lunged. Catherine had set a trap and it had worked. She span out of the way of the sword and made a quick riposte. Her sword found its mark in Helen's side. It went in deep. The doctor examined her. She was losing blood rapidly and was in pain. He cut away part of her dress and examined the wound. He advised her to sit down. She nearly fainted. She lay down. The doctor said she was obviously not fit to carry on.

Mr Jenkins said, "It seems that Catherine is the winner. Do you concede, Helen? Do you accept that honour is satisfied, Catherine?"

Both women said "No!"

Catherine said, "Then get up and let's finish this! Or will you swear to forget your stupid allegations?"

Helen squirmed.

The referee said, "I am sorry to say that if you do not continue, you will have to concede the duel and therefore accept that your honour is satisfied. That would mean abandoning your accusation." Helen managed to shake her head. Billy and Bethan murmured. Iain looked relieved.

Perse asked, "What if someone substitutes for Helen?" He and Billy both offered.

Mr Jenkins said, "I know you can substitute before a duel starts, but I have never heard of doing it at this stage."

Bethan surprised them, saying, "I think we should keep it to the women. I will be Helen's substitute!" Even as she said it, she wondered what was the matter with herself.

Helen murmured, "Are you mad? You can't fight with a sword!"

Catherine said, "Yes, she can. She's beaten me once before. Let her try to do it again. I'd love to have another chance."

Helen whispered to Bethan, "I always knew you and I would get into a fight sometime, but I never dreamt we'd both be on the same side." At that, she handed over her sword and whispered, "Good luck, brave girl!"

It was too late for Bethan to change her mind. She began much as Helen had: cautiously.

Billy whispered to Perse, "If she kills Bethan, I'll shoot her, just as she shot Kenny. Let them hang me. It'll be worth it!"

Bethan knew that Catherine was the better swordswoman. She remembered John's advice. He had said to her and Billy, "Some people treat fencing as a gentleman's game. Or a lady's. They think it should be graceful. Artistic even. Well, I don't. In my experience, it's a matter of fighting for your life. You do what you have to. I often strike an enemy with my left fist or a foot or the pommel of my sword. I want to stay alive." Bethan was going to stay alive if she could. She took no chances. She was alert for any tricks. She knew she was stronger than Catherine and hoped she could make strength count. Perhaps, on the other hand, she would see an opportunity and do something clever. She could be clever sometimes. She went back to dodge a feint and slipped. She dropped onto one knee. She parried a cut and slashed at Catherine's feet, making her jump back.

Bethan sprang up and forwards with all the force she could manage. Their swords met. She kept moving upwards and forwards pushing Catherine back. Catherine made the mistake of trying to counterattack at that moment. Bethan's knuckle-guard came up into her face while the blade parried the intended blow from her sword. Catherine went limp and fell flat on her back, dropping her sword. Bethan stood over her, touching her chest with the tip of her sword.

As Catherine lay there, several thoughts flashed through Bethan's mind. Had she won? What if she was declared the winner, because her opponent was unconscious? Would Catherine stand trial or get away with murder? Would all this have been for nothing?

Mr Jenkins called to her to stand back and put up her sword. She thought of Kenny MacKenzie. She thought of Hatty Sutton. She pretended not to hear. She plunged her sword through the murderer's chest. She convulsed for a few moments before lying still. Deathly still. The doctor pronounced her dead. The referee said,

"Did you not hear me? I ordered you to stand back and put up your sword. Catherine was unconscious. You cannot continue under such circumstances!"

Perse said, "She was conscious. I saw her hand move as if to grab her sword."

Bethan was dumbfounded. So was everyone else. Mr Jenkins said, "Well, if you're sure. Then that's it." And it was.

Historical Notes

The Eighteenth Century was a time when materialism and immorality competed with piety for people's hearts and minds and I have tried to give a realistic impression of that time.

The Jacobite Rebellion of 1715 was much as described in this book. The lack of support both at home and abroad made its failure almost inevitable regardless of any decisions made by the leaders. I have no reason to believe Army money was embezzled to fund the Rebellion, but who knows?

The Battle of Preston did involve Highlanders as well as rebels from various parts of the North of England. Their lack of a unified command led to a two stage surrender. Clandestine operations may well have taken place, there and in Scotland, but remain unknown.

The Jacobites named in the book are almost all taken from lists of those accused of being involved, rightly or wrongly. Rhodri Jones is fictitious.

Lewis Pryce was the Member of Parliament for Cardiganshire. His involvement in the Rebellion was never proven and no action was taken against him, but he resigned his seat in Parliament. I have put a lot of words into his mouth. His children are fictitious.

James Butler, Second Duke of Ormonde, was suspected of being one of the leaders of the rebellion and left the country for Spain to avoid confronting his accusers. He was deprived of his lands and titles by the authorities. His nephew, Charles, is fictitious.

Rob Roy MacGregor was involved in the Rebellion, but whether in Preston or elsewhere is uncertain.

The MacGregors were excluded from the amnesty given to other rebels afterwards.

Artillery did play a vital part at Preston and in Scotland. However, no artillery regiment was formed until 1716. There was no separate Welsh one.

Other regiments are all fictitious except the Argylls.

The Spanish Netherlands was the name for the country now called Belgium.

Penrhys does exist but is no longer farmland.

Castell Coch did fall into disrepair in the late Seventeenth Century. It was rebuilt completely in the late Eighteenth and early Nineteenth Centuries by the Earls of Bute.

Chepstow Castle likewise fell into disrepair but has been restored rather than rebuilt.

St Fagans Castle is in good repair and the Welsh National Folk Museum now covers a large, mainly outdoor, area adjacent to it. Both are worth a visit.

William Congreve wrote several Restoration Comedies in reign of Charles II. His work has had many revivals.

Peter Monamy was a portrait painter prior to becoming famous for paintings of ships.

What Next?

So we know who killed Kenny MacKenzie and she has paid the price, but Billy and Bethan still have a lot to do.

- They need to raise more money to get their father out of gaol.
- They need avoid the long arm of the Law.
- Bethan needs to find the truth about her Henry.
- On top of these things, they are just about to learn a lot about the slave trade.
- Their Christian upbringing and the realities of the Eighteenth Century are still in conflict. □ Then there are the Jacobites.

Follow their next adventures in 'The King's Justice' soon to be published. Chapter 1 is on the next few pages.

Highwaypersons

Book II

The King's Justice

Chapter 1

March 1716

The big coach drawn by six big carthorses made good progress through the southern English countryside. The roads were in better condition than most of those in Wales and the borders. The land was also less hilly. Billy Rhys thought of the irony that he and his sister, Bethan, should be travelling in the coach they had once held up and robbed. That had been the beginning of their life of crime, over two years before.

The coach's owner, Lewis Pryce, was not with them. He was keeping to his estates in Cardiganshire, having been forced to resign his seat in Parliament, as a result of allegations that he had been connected with the Jacobite rebellion which had only been over for a couple of months. Billy Rhys had played a vital part in its defeat.

Lewis Pryce's daughter, Helen MacKenzie, was in the coach. She was on her way to London to try to recover some of her late husband's fortune, embezzled by an officer administering Army funds. She was aware of Billy's secret life as a highwayman, but she had always had mixed feelings towards him and those feelings were mutual. She had mixed feelings for Bethan too. She had only recently

discovered that she was his sister and not his mistress. She had al〵
liked her, although they had often come close to blows, but it
Bethan who had killed the woman who had murdered Helen's husl
Kenny.

They had spent the first night of their journey at an ir
Gloucester, and the second in Swindon in the house of a doctor
had been friends with Lewis Pryce for years. He looked after thei
with great civility and generosity. Not for the first time, Helen
Bethan had been obliged to share a bed. Helen had asked, "Do
think the Army will have any more information about your Henry

"Well, you know I went to see General Jones just before w
Cardiff? Well, he says they might have more information about ;
of his fellow prisoners-of-war. If I can find any of them, that n
lead me to Henry. The General gave me a lot of letters he wrote ;
ago from prison in Amiens. I just want to know what's happen
him."

"Yes. I miss my Kenny, but at least I know, thanks to you
Billy, what happened to him. I can't imagine how I'd feel if he's
gone missing and I didn't know any more than that."

"Billy says it happened to lots of people, especially afte
battles like the one at Malplaquet where my Henry disappeared."

As they got into bed, Helen said, "We do have more in con
than a lot of people think."

"Let's not get too sentimental. I might yet give you a good
you can be so annoying. Billy's too soft."

"Just you try!"

Before they said any more, they went to sleep.

The coach now passed through some particularly bea〵
countryside. Bethan, asked, "What is this place? It is quite u
anything I can remember."

Helen replied, "It is called the Vale of the White Horse. I always enjoy passing through it."

Helen's younger brother, James, commented, "I suppose this is nice country, but Jane and I prefer life in London. We find the country rather tiresome, don't we?"

James's wife, Jane, looked at each of the others in turn before saying, "I do agree, but, of course, one's enjoyment of anywhere depends somewhat on one's company. I am sure I shall continue to enjoy this journey, Gareth and Perse are such interesting companions. But London always excites me." Billy used the alias Gareth Evans when he played the role of a gentleman. He hoped James would not see through his disguise. They had never got on well.

Jane had flirted with Billy and the other man in the coach, Perseus de Clare, Billy's friend and former comrade-in-arms, for most of the journey. Bethan had retaliated by flirting with James.

Olwen Davies was the oldest passenger, being nearly forty. She was the housekeeper and mistress of Rhodri Jones, the Member of Parliament for Cardiff and a friend of Lewis Pryce. She was going to London to draw some money from her employer's bank, as he had authorised, due to his extended absence abroad. It was beginning to occur to her that he was involved with the Jacobites. Billy and Bethan knew how much but saw no reason to worry Olwen.

They came upon a large farm cart called a hay wain, the sort that are often pulled by oxen. This one was hardly moving and Billy could not imagine any other animal being so slow. James became impatient and leaned out of the door to call to Iwan, the coachman, asking him if he could find a way to pass the wain. He apologised but said the road was too narrow and had ditches on both sides. After a few more minutes they had covered less than a hundred yards and James called to him again asking him to think of something. Iwan spoke to Evans, Helen's manservant, who was sitting on the dickie seat

at the rear, to jump down and run ahead to ask if the ox-driver c
pull off the road to let the coach pass. As he began to run past the v
he disappeared from view, as there was a slight bend in the road.

The wain came to a halt. The man did not return. Nobody
appeared either. Iwan spoke to Bethan's twelve-year-old
Llewellyn, who was sitting beside him, to go and find out what
going on. He jumped down and soon vanished from sight too.
waiting continued. Finally, four men came around the wain.
looked like farm labourers. The coachman called to them, aski
they could help them pass the wain. One of them, a short, stout f
of about thirty, said, "We think you can 'elp us."

"I'm sure we will if we can, but we must get on with
journey soon."

"Come down!" said the man, in a rather aggressive
Suddenly Billy felt anxious. Up to then he had regarded this inc
as merely tiresome. Now it began to feel sinister.

James opened the door and called out to the man, "Please
what you want and let us see if we are able to help, but be brief."

"I want you to get out of that coach and hand over your mor
he said, producing a blunderbuss from under his coat. The other
had cudgels and knives.

By then one of the men had come to the door. He reache
grabbed James's leg and pulled him roughly to the ground. The
man opened the other door and called to the rest to get out. Billy c
tell that he was not going to be open to discussing the idea. The
as instructed. They all turned out their pockets. The robbers took
money and valuables. Then one of them got into the coach and bro
out their coats and small items of luggage. Going through Billy's
one of them found his purse, while his companion found his two Fr
pistols in the small case with his writing things. They ordered Iw

424

throw down his weapons and then climb down. One of them began to search Bethan. He made the most of it.

Billy was worried that they were not wearing masks. They were not afraid of being identified. He was also worried that Llewellyn and Evans had not reappeared. The first man appeared to be their principal spokesman, although he spoke with as thick a local accent as the others. He said, "There's not much money between the lot of you. Ye'll need more on a long journey. Your sort allus 'as money. Where is it?"

Perse replied, "I do not carry much money these days, because I have a lot deposited in a bank in London, where I can draw it out when I need it."

"Dunno what ye mean! Keep money in a bank like that'n?" He pointed to a bank separating two fields. Billy would have laughed, if things had not looked so serious. One of the others started hitting Perse and threatened him with his cudgel. "Now! Where is it? Where've ye 'idden it? Or 'ave we gotta take this coach apart?"

Iwan said, "You have all my money. Now, please tell me what's happened to the others!"

"If ye want see 'em again ye'd best tell us where yer money is."

The coachman looked terrified and said, "Master! Please let them have what they want. I beg you! Think of Evans and young Llewellyn!"

James said, "I would but I cannot. They have got all the money I had with me. What he said about the bank was true of me too."

The man resumed beating James. Perse begged him to stop. He turned and hit Perse hard in the face with his cudgel, saying, "Stop yer whining, all of ye! Tell us where yer money is." He then hit him again. He fell down clutching his head. The man started kicking him.

Billy said, "There may be some more money in my coat. It has many pockets. Let me have a look."

They had already searched it, but not as thoroughly as they might have. The talkative one threw the coat at Billy and said, "There'd best be loads of it! What we've got 'ere ain't much." He began rummaging through the coat pockets, producing a guinea, which he threw towards one of them. He fumbled for it, dropped it and looked down to where it had fallen. Billy fired a pistol into his belly. He always had one in his coat. He also always had one in his boot. He drew it and shot the man holding the blunderbuss while he was staring at him in disbelief. He got him in the chest. He fell and lay silent. The remaining two men ran for their lives. Billy grabbed the large pistol that Iwan had thrown down earlier and ran off after them.

Bethan retrieved the two French pistols and ran after him. He ran past the wain to where the man and the boy were tied up. They were both bleeding from wounds to the head and they looked terrified. The men stood by them and waved their cudgels. One shouted, "Don't come near me! I'll kill these two!" They both stopped running. There were three horses tethered nearby. Their escape plan, presumably.

Billy aimed the pistol and said, "Give it up! You can't escape!" Evans begged him to let the men go. He hesitated. They started to mount two of the horses, holding the reins of the other. Billy pulled the trigger.

The lads screamed, "No!" The gun misfired making a pathetic sound and producing a flame rather than an explosion. The men rode off taking the third horse with them. By then Bethan had realised that the French pistols were not loaded. She and her brother struggled to untie the captives.

Evans seemed unable to speak coherently, but Llewellyn said, "It was awful! As soon as I got near, Evans tried to call out to warn me and they laid into him. Then they laid into me. Then they tied us up. My head hurts but I think he's hurt worse." Bethan felt their wounds. She realised that Evans's shoulder was smashed, making his

426

right arm useless, and a big lump was swelling up on his forehead. Llewellyn did not seem so badly hurt. Bethan said they needed to get Evans to a doctor as soon as possible.

Helen and Iwan arrived and said Perse was in a similar condition to Evans, but James had suffered injuries to his body rather than his head. Bethan said that Llewellyn was not badly harmed but frightened. Then Iwan asked if they would help him to turn the coach round so he could take them all back to the doctor in Swindon.

They made stretchers out of planks they removed from the wain and carried Evans back to the coach, laying him on the floor after laying Perse on one of the seats. James sat on the opposite seat with a tearful Jane trying to comfort him. Bethan got in and continued trying to treat their wounds. She had experience of that sort of thing.

Billy untied his grey horse Caledin from the back of the coach and helped back the coach to a place where there was no ditch so the coachman could drive it onto a field to turn it round. Then Billy asked him to stop for a minute. He was surprised but cooperated. Billy pulled his saddle and bridle off the rack below the driver's seat. Then he began to saddle Caledin.

James leaned out of the door and asked, "Whatever do you think you are doing?"

"I'm going after the ones who think they've got away. They're going to pay for what they've done!" He was fond of Perse and knew Helen and her father were fond of Evans.

Helen said, "But it's been too long. You'll never catch them now!"

"That's what they probably think."

"You're mad!" cried James as the coach moved away. Billy wished he had not had to give the men such a good start, but on the other hand, he thought, complacency had been the downfall of better men than them. There had been times when he had successfully followed cold trails before, in the Spanish Netherlands.

All this time, the man Billy had wounded had been begging them to help him. They tried to ignore him. Billy was so angry that he had to restrain himself from hurting him further, and also feared that he could not afford to waste any more time. However, he remembered that in the War they had always tried to look after wounded prisoners. He felt torn, but called out to stop the coach and wait while he and Llewellyn lifted the man into the coach.

Meanwhile Bethan reloaded all Billy's pistols before he remounted. He rode past the hay wain and on down the road at a brisk trot. He did not go any faster as he was looking out for signs of his quarry. They might have turned off somewhere. With three horses, they were likely to have left some tracks. He stopped several times to study tracks but they all looked too old.

Even at the time, he recognised the irony of a highwayman hunting down men many would regard as fellow criminals. He did not so regard them. Neither he nor his mentor, John, would have hurt people unnecessarily. They would certainly have avoided injuring heads if possible. These men seemed not only ruthless, but positively bloodthirsty. Billy had known soldiers who said they got like that, but usually only in the heat of battle, not in cold blood. Poor Evans was a kind, gentle man who had probably never had a chance. Billy thought he would probably never recover from his injuries.

He wished he had been on Merlin, because, although he was smaller than Caledin, he was faster, especially over a long distance, and he did not know how long this hunt was going to be. He saw an isolated barn and, although he could not see any tracks, he thought it worth checking. He dismounted and led Caledin around the barn listening for any sound. Nothing.

He was reluctant to try to open the big double doors, as it would have demanded a lot of effort and concentration, making him vulnerable to anyone hiding inside. Suddenly he realised that he was ignoring a small side door right in front of him. He began to open it cautiously, holding a cocked pistol in his right hand, leaving Caledin to graze. The barn was, of course, dark inside. Billy peered into it and slid through the half-open door, immediately jumping to the right so as to avoid staying in the light any longer than he had to. He stood still and listened. Nothing.

Then he heard something. Hoofbeats approaching. He went out and stood next to Caledin who had turned his head in the direction of the sound. He ducked and peered under the horse's neck, hoping to use its body to screen him from view. He could not see anything. The hoofbeats had stopped. He crept forwards and looked in the direction they had been coming from. He saw a loose horse grazing near Caledin. It was saddled. Billy expected to see whoever had recently dismounted, but nobody was in sight. He heard a voice behind him.

"Drop the pistol and turn round. Slowly. I've got a gun pointing at you!"

Made in the USA
Charleston, SC
19 September 2016